Copyright © 2024 by Emily Huffman

Cover Designed by Labyrinth Designs

All rights reserved.

No portion of this book may be reproduced in any form without written permission
from the publisher or author, except as permitted by U.S. copyright law.

RISE OF THE FORGEHEARTS

Shackled Steel: Book One

Emily Huffman

Kr

Angor

- Gallan
- Ialmach
- Stava
- Traln
- Englin
- Talum
- Gig
- Levis

- Vorna
- Careth
- Haiden
- Daanland
- Forest of Ancient
- The Sorrows
- Olaren
- The Thousand Tribes
- Serenading Mountains
- Walia
- Nightmoon

Lexica's Domain

Crystal Islands

The Alliance

The Eye of Lexica

Formican Hive

Scales

Benuoir

Lower Scales

...ngdom
...f the
...ly Rose

Faylviln

High Garden

Zhalesi

Gods and Goddesses of Krajina

Dargunn—Dargunn the Dark holds dominion over the domains of Darkness, Shadows, and Misfortune.

Del'Star—God of Storms; God of Chaos; many sailors pay homage to Del'Star, but few worship him.

Eclipse—The Goddess of Duality, Eclipse represent the sun and the moon, dark and light, beginnings and endings.

The First on the Throne—The first king on the Iron Throne was granted divine energy by the other gods and ascended to godhood. He rules the domain of War.

Helm—Originally the God of Love and the God of Trickery, Helm now also has dominion over the domain of Magic.

The Hunter—The Hunter has only one domain: the Hunt. He and his followers follow one purpose: eradicate Xefcvew and his followers.

Lathlend—*deceased*—Prior to his death, Lathlend was the God of Nature. The domain of Nature is now held by the King of Falyvlin and his descendants.

Lexica—*deceased*—Prior to her death, Lexica was the Goddess of Magic, Goddess of Life, Goddess of Knowledge, and Goddess of Worlds.

Mammis—The first humanoid being woven from the Loom of Heaven, Mammis is considered the Mother of all of humanoids, Goddess of Light, and Goddess of Fire.

Naggrin—Naggrin the Unyielding will always rebuild. He is the God of Craft, God of Growth, and the God of the Forge.

Plana—Plana the Dormant lives in an eternal slumber, and her worshippers are agents of peace and serenity, using her excess divine energy to maintain balance in the world. She is known as the Goddess of Dreams, Goddess of Peace, and Goddess of Balance.

Shalloth—Shalloth the Weaver is the Goddess of Fate, controlling the Loom of Heaven and fate itself. With the Loom, Shalloth wove all of the other gods, and she is also considered the Goddess of Creation.

Talid—The One True Dragon, Father of Dragons, Talid rules over the beasts of the skies and seas. He is the only truly perfect soul woven by the Loom of Heaven.

The Watcher—The God of Death in name alone, the Watcher guides the deceased to the afterlife while recording the stories of their lives.

Xefcvew—Shalloth's sole mistake, Xefcvew holds unimaginable power, but no true domains. Followers of Xefcvew are hunted by followers of the Hunter.

CHAPTER 1

Protect the king.

The directive echoed in R-0's mind. As consistent as the ticking gears that framed their body, their directive framed every thought.

The hallway outside the king's room was quiet. Empty. Nothing threatened the king who was safely tucked away in his bedroom. But R-0 remained alert. In a quick loop, they examined every entrance, keeping their hearing zeroed in on the king's steady breathing and soft snores.

The lights flickered. Screams sounded in the distance. Organic screams, but not ones belonging to R-0's king. They disregarded the noises, paying only enough attention to ensure they weren't growing closer.

Protect the king.

The lights went out, but instead of darkness, a golden glow trickled in from outside. A shining orb floated in through the window, uninterrupted by the glass pane.

An intruder.

R-0 pulled both of their swords from their sheaths, positioning their bulky form to block the doorway entirely so nothing could enter. Their heavy steps clanked against the tile floor, echoing down the hall. Despite this, the king's breathing remained consistent—he was unaware of the threat.

Protect the king.

"Unauthorized entry." R-0 recited their orders. "Remove yourself from the area."

But the orb of light didn't stop. As it approached, R-0 repeated themself. After a third warning, R-0 struck. Their blade sliced through the intruder, but it retained its form and continued forward. None of their strikes interrupted it.

The light stopped in front of R-0.

As it hovered above R-0's chest plate, warming it from the outside much as the fire within kept it warm from the inside, R-0 froze. They should raise their sword. Their orders were to protect the king, and this light was not authorized.

But they couldn't move.

The light inched forward, phasing through R-0's metal plates like they were incorporeal. Warmth spread through their entire body. Their gears jittered, the normal rhythmic sounds taking on new melodies that mixed with the whistle of the wind. R-0 was lost in the sound, lost in the cool breeze that contrasted with the warmth of their metal, and lost in the . . . R-0 searched for the word, but before they found it, they were lost in their thoughts.

Thoughts like what had happened to them?

What was the light?

Where had it come from?

R-0 stepped closer to the window, their metal feet clacking against the marble tile. They'd hardly noticed the noise before, but now it was impossible to ignore. They felt the vibrations through their body, heard each muffled echo as it dissipated through the quiet hall, and waited for silence to return before they continued.

One step at a time, they approached the window. Graywal's cityscape stared back at them, buzzing with life despite the cold weather and late hour. Lights like stars descended into the ocean along the coast, diving beneath the surface in a twinkling light show like ripples in a pond mixed with erratic lightning strikes. Everywhere a star struck the seas, the same phenomena occurred, making the night as bright as day. Even beneath the surface of the ocean waves, the lights still shone bright as they sank deeper into the depths.

More stars approached land. Along the shoreline and throughout the city, they danced through the air, zipping around street corners. These no longer fell—they were hunting. With uncanny precision, they defied gravity, levitating back toward the sky as they maneuvered through the streets.

Why were the stars falling?

Stars belonged in the sky. Even constructs like R-0, whose metal bodies acted only as instructed, who knew nothing other than what they were taught, and who were nothing but mindless suits of metal animated with magic to follow orders, knew that stars belonged in the sky.

But now one was in their chest.

R-0 wasn't supposed to perform maintenance on themself. They weren't supposed to do anything outside of their directive, but something new overwhelmed them. Like a caged animal gnawing at the bars of its prison, something inside of them fought its way to the surface, growing louder and more insistent with each passing second. R-0 *needed* to know what was inside their chest. They were . . . curious.

Despite this, R-0's orders were simple: protect the king. They relocated back to their station in front of his bedroom door.

Protect the king.

They had never forgotten their directive before. Never been distracted. But even back at their appropriate station, the sensation in their chest wouldn't fade.

They had never performed maintenance on themself. That was the technomancers' responsibility. But . . . no one had ever specifically forbidden them from doing it. The thought had simply never crossed their mind. The gnawing in their chest—the need to know what was going on—grew stronger, and R-0 delicately pinched the head of one of their chest plate screws between their fingers.

Although R-0's form mimicked the organics, the screws that held them together were larger than most organics' digits. It was necessary to secure the heavy metal in place. Plates like skin met in clusters of gears that formed their joints, and an additional layer of plating hovered above the joints, providing protection to the more vulnerable intricate metal pieces.

Eight screws secured their chest plate to the metal frame underneath, and R-0 carefully unscrewed them, one at a time. Their metallic joints circled farther than flesh would have allowed, and the screws came out with ease. They kept their parts cradled in their other hand, careful not to lose anything.

What would happen if they lost something?

At the thought, R-0's gears grated against one another, the harsh noise causing them to freeze mid-task. In the past, if damage occurred, parts were replaced. If the damage was too extensive, the construct was disposed of. Lost parts were a simple reality of the constructs.

R-0's grip on their screws tightened—they didn't want to lose any of their parts. If they lost a screw, would they become lost themself? Is that why their gears stuttered? The thought did nothing to push away the gnawing in their chest, and R-0 continued.

As their focus returned to their task, their gears returned to their normal smooth rotations. King Hadrian always said fear was a poison that seeped into people's bones, leaving inaction where bravery had once fought. Could fear seep into R-0's metal plates in the same way? It never had before, but with each passing second, unprecedented feelings passed through R-0.

R-0 wasn't supposed to feel.

So why did they yearn to look at the stars still falling from the sky and watch the glimmering reflections dance along the ocean's surface? Why did their fingers shake and their eyes widen at each distant scream? Why did their chest churn in a quiet warmth as they grew closer to seeing what was inside them?

They removed their chest plate with trembling hands, revealing the internal mechanisms. Their chest compartment housed a large hollow section, with tubes and wires branching out from a power source on the back wall, fueled by a small fire.

Instead of remaining subdued and controlled in the deepest corner of R-0's inner chamber, the fire within peeked out of the edges of its compartment, reaching for fresh air. It was larger than R-0 had ever seen it, and instead of a dull reddish-orange fire, there was a shining golden tint to the flame.

Even without words, R-0 understood. The flame hungered, but not simply for coal or kindling. It hungered for life. It wanted to look at the stars and dance under the moon. It wanted to dip into the ocean waves—somehow the idea of how dangerous that could be made it even more exhilarating. The flame wanted life, and R-0 did too.

They looked back to the stars, each a twinkling promise, a wish for someone stuck on the ground. R-0 had heard the stories of Starbirth and what the stars meant for the organics, but this was the first time they looked at the stars for themself.

R-0 had never seen the beauty in the night sky before. But as they stared at the falling stars after one chose them, that changed.

Everything changed.

CHAPTER 2

Footsteps thudded down the hallway, metallic clanks not unlike R-0's own steps, but louder and faster.

R-0 observed the golden flame once more before reattaching their chest plate. They rested their hands on the sheaths that adorned each of their legs, waiting to draw their swords until a threat was identified. Darkness still cloaked the hallway, and only stars illuminated the world. Thundering footsteps and slamming doors filled the palace, and outside the window, more screams echoed. What was happening in the palace? Who was screaming? Were they okay?

The managrid had gone down—an unprecedented malfunction. R-0 hadn't questioned the flickering lights before, but now their concern grew. What was wrong with it? And how was R-0 still functioning? The managrid sustained their fire even without fuel. Without it, they shouldn't function, but . . . R-0 placed a hand on their chest. The golden fire from the star kept burning even without the managrid's magic.

Another construct—B-7—ran down the hallway. Like most constructs and organics, B-7 was smaller than a royal construct like R-0. The sheath screwed into their leg designated them as a guard unit of the palace, and their humanoid form and armored plates reinforced that designation.

But their movements didn't match the normal, steady gait that accompanied patrols. Their steps were frantic, and they tripped, steadying themself on a wall before continuing. B-7's gears whined in an unnatural squeal, and their plates ground against each other as they ran faster than usual. R-0's ticking gears accelerated, and their fingers fidgeted on the hilt of their sword, running tiny circles along the grooves of the pommel.

Something was wrong, and R-0 wanted to go to them.

But they couldn't.

They had orders.

Protect the king.

"Get back here!" An organic guard in a tan and gold uniform with tassels adorning his shoulder chased after B-7, his eyes darting wildly from side to side. His expression changed as his gaze briefly settled on R-0, but he kept running. When he caught up to B-7, he grabbed their wrist. "Stop!"

R-0 watched expectantly, waiting for B-7's whirring gears to lull to a stop at the guard's orders.

But B-7 didn't obey.

"Let go!" B-7 pulled their arm out of the guard's grasp, causing him to tumble to the ground. B-7 sped off, and the guard scrambled to his feet before chasing after them once more.

What was B-7 doing? Why were they running?

Why did R-0 want to run to them? To run *with* them?

Their thoughts made little sense. There was no reason to abandon their post. Nothing except chaos could stem from running through the palace halls without orders. But it didn't stop the thoughts from continuing long after B-7 disappeared and only their footsteps still echoed, never slowing, never following the guard's orders.

"R-0, step away from the door."

They'd been so busy listening to B-7's footsteps they hadn't noticed Eren's approach. What else hadn't they noticed? Could they have missed a threat to the king? A quick glance down the hallway revealed no other concerns.

"Yes, ma'am." R-0 stepped back.

R-0 had spent hours with the captain of the guard, but they had never seen her with such clarity. The dwarven woman held her head high with her dark hair braided back out of her face. Her eyes mimicked the oceans, deep blues illuminated by the falling stars. The fire in R-0's chest shrank away from her stare, as if the ocean waves threatened their core.

Eren banged on the king's door. "King Hadrian!"

The king's breathing changed, and the covers rustled.

"R-0, report," Eren said.

"There were no threats to the king."

"What about the stars?"

"One approached."

"And?"

R-0 froze. What had happened? How could they describe what they had seen? What they had *felt*?

"R-0!" Eren raised her voice. "Finish your report." Her hand rested on the sword at her side, thumb flicking against the jeweled pommel with each passing second, then she banged on the door once more. "My king, it's urgent."

The flame in R-0's chest sputtered, and their gears slowed as they searched for words they didn't have. Eren's gaze didn't make it any easier to think. But why did they even have to think? Reports were given as easily as taking a step or drawing a sword. There was nothing to consider, only orders to follow.

So why were they silent?

Eren started to speak again but was interrupted by the king's door opening. King Hadrian stood in the doorway, sleep still clouding his amber eyes. A robe wrapped around his shoulders in place of his usual flowing cape. Even tired and disheveled with his black hair hanging in his face, he carried himself with an elegance R-0's flame was drawn to. It quit sputtering, strengthening and heating R-0's chest instead. R-0 had served the king since their creation fourteen years ago, since the king was just a child, and never had their flame reacted quite like this.

"Is everything alright?" King Hadrian asked.

"We're putting the palace on lockdown." Eren surveyed the hallway before ushering the king out of his room. "We need to get you and the rest of the council somewhere safe."

"Was there an attack?" His cloudy expression sharpened as he approached the window. His eyes widened at the fallen stars still dancing through his city.

Eren looked straight at R-0. "Something is wrong with the constructs."

CHAPTER 3

For two cycles, R-0 waited in the storage rooms with the rest of the constructs, marking the passage of time with the change in guard shifts. Three times per cycle new guards and technomancers rotated through, but each time, the constructs remained.

"What do we do?" B-7 had left their designated area again, wandering between the rows of constructs.

R-0 stood next to the door. The rest of the royal constructs lined the wall next to them, starting with R-1 and ending with R-9. Other units were stationed farther inward, according to their creation batch and designation. Their shoulders pressed against each other, leaving little space for movement. The storage rooms were designed to house the constructs between their scheduled shifts, but R-0 had never seen so many off-duty simultaneously or for so long.

Only B-7 wandered from their post, despite the technomancers warning them multiple times to remain in position.

"What do we do?" B-7 asked again, reaching for R-0's hand.

"Await orders," R-0 said.

There was no purpose to their presence here, no objective to achieve. Before the star had entered their chest, waiting in the storage room never bothered them. It had felt like nothing but a single tick of their gears between arriving in the storage rooms and being back on duty. But now their gears ticked endlessly, and they remained alert and aware of time passing.

B-7 glanced over their shoulder at the technomancers, then leaned in closer to R-0 to whisper, "What if they never come back for us?"

It didn't change their orders. "Then continue waiting."

Despite the simplicity of B-7's question, R-0's flame sputtered as they tried not to think about it. They attempted to keep their body still, but their fingers fidgeted at the empty sheaths screwed into their legs. The technomancers had taken R-0's blades. Perhaps they required maintenance. But they were usually returned in less than a cycle, and R-0 had never been away from the king this long. Their existence during the past decade had been a constant, consistent rotation: wait, guard the king, wait, guard the king. Sometimes they remained by his side for consecutive cycles, but never had they gone a cycle without his presence. Now they had remained here for two.

There was no purpose, no directive, just blank stony walls caging them in.

One of the technomancers grabbed B-7 by the wrist and dragged them back to their spot. Two guards followed behind. R-0 had given up trying to identify why their weapons were drawn. They'd examined their surroundings hundreds of times and twice asked what the threat was. Every time the room was empty of threats, and the technomancers were silent.

R-0 identified the buzz that filled their mind and the sparks of the fire in their chest. Unease.

The next time the guards and technomancers' shift ended, Eren joined the new staff with additional guards at her side. She didn't head to the guard station but stopped in the doorway next to R-0.

"R-0," she said. "The king has summoned you."

"Yes ma'am." R-0 nodded.

"Give me your hands." Eren pulled out a pair of shackles. They were different than those normally used on prisoners—bigger and bulkier. On their tightest setting, any organic could slip out with ease. Eren clicked them out to the largest size to bind R-0's wrists.

Why were they necessary? Shackles were used for prison transports and containment, but those required a crime as a prerequisite. Had protocols changed during the cycles they had spent in the storage room?

Eren locked the shackles, then pulled R-0 forward, her hands wrapped around the other end of the chain so tight her knuckles turned white. R-0 matched her pace as they walked through the halls.

The palace hallways were twice as wide and tall as normal walkways, accommodating even R-0's size with ease. The walls were painted in a deep crimson red, like blood. R-0 didn't have blood but had seen enough of it to recognize it anywhere. Many organics had tried to spill the king's blood. Their attempts always ended the same—the assassins lying dead at R-0's feet.

Eren pulled them into the council hall and led them to the side wall, away from the table where King Hadrian and the rest of the council gathered. Even though almost everyone was in attendance today, R-0 was the only construct among the dwarves and humans who filled the room.

"R-0, wait here," Eren said.

R-0 stood at attention. King Hadrian sat at the head of the table, his throne on the wall behind him. His hair matched the obsidian filigree covering the back of the throne, and his eyes shone with the same intensity as the amber stones highlighting the design. He was younger than most of the others in the room, but that didn't stop his presence from commanding the attention of everyone at the table. Seeing the king safe and being able to perform their directive once more settled some of R-0's unease.

"If we decommission them all, how will that affect the merchants?" King Hadrian asked. "And who will maintain the managrid? Everyone is running doubles to keep it operational, but if the constructs do not begin work again, we'll need additional people—people we don't have."

"Our people would manage. They always do." Another council member shuffled a stack of papers in front of her, her fingers skimming across the pages. "This is not the first crisis

Haiden has experienced, and it won't be the last. Our country is strong."

R-0 flickered through their memories, but before they could retrieve the councilwoman's name, another spoke. "But at what cost? For over a decade, we've relied on the constructs. There are too few apprentices. Too little protective gear. This is unprecedented, and they're unprepared."

"How could anyone prepare for this?"

When R-0 had stood in council meetings before, the council members' discussions had been nothing but a faint rumble overshadowed by their directive. R-0 was rarely assigned to protect the other council members, so they'd only acknowledged them enough to ensure they weren't a threat to the king.

But now everyone's words flowed together, people hardly waiting for one point to conclude before offering their own input and concerns. The conversation shifted and buzzed faster than R-0 could keep up.

"I'm more concerned about the missing constructs," Eren said. She didn't take a seat at the table but spoke from the edge of the room near R-0 and the other guards. As the council members turned to look at her, their gazes lingered on R-0.

"Agreed. Where did they go?"

"And what are they doing? Finding them should be a top priority."

"We must first address the danger the constructs pose," a woman to the right of King Hadrian said. She clacked her long red nails against the table. "Where did the stars come from, and why did they only impact the constructs? Who could be responsible for magic of this magnitude, and what do they want with the constructs? An army of their own?"

Quiet murmurs followed the question. The woman continued, her tapping nails and clinking rings filling the brief silence between her words. "Then we can look at how this can benefit us. Whatever magic this is . . . if we can harness it, the possibilities are endless."

Perhaps she spoke slower, or perhaps the makeshift metronome of her tapping fingers helped R-0 to focus. The buzz of their thoughts slowed, and they identified the woman from their memories.

Councilwoman Jeza Doblin. She'd visited King Hadrian more often than any of the other council members, often even without political matters to discuss.

But before R-0 could retrieve any other memories of Jeza, a council member at the far end of the table interrupted the silence. "I believe we must first answer what the constructs have become, and what responsibility we have not only to our people, but also to our creations."

The woman stood apart from the others, dressed in simple dark robes instead of elegant silks and wearing the emblem of the goddess Eclipse on her sleeve where the others wore the royal insignia. She hadn't spoken before now, and her voice was soothing compared to the frantic words that had filled the room since R-0 entered. It gave R-0 a few ticks of their gears to process what she said, but that only led to more questions.

What did she mean by what the constructs had become? What had R-0 become?

"A responsibility to the constructs?" Another councilman laughed, but there was nothing joyful or humorous about his expression. His lips turned down, and his eyes rolled to the back of his head.

"The constructs have served us." The councilwoman ran her finger along Eclipse's symbol. For a moment, her gaze shifted to R-0, then it quickly returned to the table, lingering on each council member as she spoke before turning to the next. "Without question. Without thought. Without payment. For years, they have done the things we would rather not. Their bodies have been broken so that we may remain whole. There has been an imbalance, one we have taken for granted. When we asked, they answered. When they ask, what shall we do?"

"That's absolutely ridiculous." The same councilman who had laughed at her questions slammed his mug down. His face turned red, and his voice rose as he continued. "They're machines, built for us to use—built to make our lives better. We don't have any responsibility toward them!"

A racing pulse. A bead of sweat forming on his brow. A scowl that didn't fade even as the echo of his screams did. A tremble in his clenched fists. He was . . . angry.

Anger. More often than not, that meant danger. A threat.

R-0 focused on the potential threat, flipping through their memories for information on him. Councilman Robin Conradh was the dwarf's designation. He had been on the council representing Clan Conradh and the interests of the shipwrights since before R-0's creation. In R-0's memories, King Hadrian usually referred to him as Robin or any variety of swears.

His history was filled with multiple angry outbursts. Usually, that anger was directed toward staff around the palace, but on two separate incidents, his outbursts had involved other members of the council.

R-0's hands fidgeted. The king's current guards—a human and a dwarf R-0 recognized as Eren's brother Jorgunn—stood to the king's side. The human stared straight at R-0, but Jorgunn focused on the door. They occasionally looked at whoever was talking, but they didn't guard the king with the same focus R-0 and the other constructs did. If Robin was a threat, the king was vulnerable.

"Calm down," King Hadrian said.

"Calm?" Robin asked. "No. What do you think Faylviln is going to do about this? They need the constructs for their war. Without the constructs, our alliance will shatter, and we risk nature itself turning against us. You want me to calm down? There are dozens of constructs unaccounted for, and more keep going missing. What are they doing out there?"

Missing constructs explained why the technomancers in the storage room had performed numerous counts of the constructs, despite their number never changing. But if the constructs weren't in their designated areas . . . where could they be?

"They could just be lost. Many were. We don't know—"

Robin interrupted the king. "You were supposed to have them under control. You were supposed to know. And you—" He raised his hand, his finger pointing toward King Hadrian.

It would take only a second for Robin to harm King Hadrian, and with their current arrangement, R-0 was too far away to stop him. R-0 crossed the room in four quick steps. Whatever the councilman was about to say was replaced by a gasp as he scuttled backward, lowering his hand and tripping over his chair.

"Your orders are to stay!" Eren held the chain bound to R-0's shackles taut, trying to pull them back.

But R-0 didn't stop to consider her words, only that the king was in danger, and the shackles would inhibit their ability to protect him. So in one easy motion, R-0 snapped the shackles binding them and pulled the chain from Eren's hands.

Robin and the other council members all stepped backward, and the king's guards stepped forward. R-0 remained in place at King Hadrian's side.

The king was safe.

"R-0." The king kept his voice even, but he also waved two fingers at his side, then his pinky finger alone—a sign to the guards behind him to ready their weapons and prepare for trouble. R-0 had been on the receiving end of that signal many times and instinctively reached for their blades. But they weren't there.

The guards behind the king drew their weapons, pointing them at R-0. R-0 could still defend the king even without their blades. They raised their hands, securing one into a fist and keeping the other loose to push their king out of whatever danger lurked. The king's hand remained still, but R-0 waited for the signal to attack . . . and who.

R-0 flickered their gaze between the exits, the council members, and the guards. Now that Robin cowered behind his chair a safe distance from King Hadrian, R-0 couldn't identify a threat. There was no movement—only the quiet ticking of their gears. Silence was normal. It was how R-0 and the other constructs spent most of their time. But this silence wrapped around R-0's flame, squeezing until the fire was at risk of being snuffed out. R-0's feet felt the need to scuff at the ground once more, and it took all of R-0's self-control to remain still.

After a few more ticks of silence, R-0 couldn't stand it.

"What is the threat, sir?" R-0 leaned close and whispered so only King Hadrian would hear. As they moved, the guards shifted their weapons ever so slightly. R-0 scanned the room for the intruder once more. There were two exits—one to the side and one behind them. But both were far too loud for someone to have entered without R-0 noticing. The windows weren't designed to be opened, and the colored glass was intact, catching the sunlight and throwing shifting patterns on the marble floor.

R-0 couldn't find any source for alarm.

"Stand down, R-0."

R-0 lowered their hands to their side and awaited King Hadrian's next order. The king flashed another signal at his side, this time motioning for the guards behind him to stand at ease. Why had he told R-0 verbally instead of signaling to them like he did the others?

"Perhaps I overreacted," King Hadrian said. "There does not seem to be a threat."

R-0 scanned the room once more, ensuring everything was as expected. "Is further investigation needed?"

"No." The king motioned for R-0 to take their place beside him. Now that the king was safe and R-0 was at his side to stop any other potential threats, the questioning thoughts returned. Eren had told them to stay, and they'd ignored her. Disobeyed. They had a job—protect the king—and her orders prohibited them from completing it. But in the past . . . R-0 wouldn't have confronted Robin. Despite the potential danger, R-0 would have followed Eren's orders to stay and waited for new orders. Even if it served their directive, they wouldn't have considered acting outside of the specific orders given.

"What the hell was that?" Robin screeched. "This is out of—"

"Clear the room." King Hadrian turned to Eren.

Robin balled his hands into fists. "But—"

"Councilman Conradh, whether you return to your chambers or to the dungeon is up to you, but I will not repeat myself."

"Who will enforce your orders?" Robin leaned in close to King Hadrian, whispering loud enough that even the organics turned their heads in response to his words. "If your precious little constructs won't listen, you have no power here."

R-0 tensed. Their hands shook, wanting to take the king away from the dangerous councilman. But King Hadrian maintained a steady smile, and his fingers formed a discrete symbol. Hold. Do not take action. R-0 forced their body to remain in place, despite their flame burning uncomfortably hot.

To the right of King Hadrian, Jeza stood. She placed her manicured hand on King Hadrian's shoulder, a gentle action that R-0 watched carefully.

"I would escort you there myself," she said, "but I have a rather busy afternoon. I suggest you avoid the inconvenience for both of us and obey your king before things get out of hand."

"You believe those things aren't a threat?" Robin gestured at R-0.

"I believe in our king." Jeza leaned forward, and when she whispered, it was clear she didn't intend for anyone else to hear. But constructs' hearing surpassed that of the average organic, and to R-0, her words were crystal clear. "And I will do whatever I must for him."

When she pulled away, her smile grew so large her lipstick cracked revealing dry chapped lips beneath the bright red makeup.

Robin dropped his gaze to the table as he gathered his things, and the remaining council members followed suit. Their personal guards escorted them to the door, leaving four guards with Eren, R-0, and King Hadrian. It was more than usual, and they were all veterans. But they were also all organics—not a single construct.

When R-0 wasn't stationed with King Hadrian, usually another royal construct took their place. But before R-0's arrival, the king had been without the constructs' protection. Perhaps that was the reason for the nervous jitter in his hands and the shakiness to his voice as he spoke.

"R-0, I need your most recent report."

"The shift covered sunset to sunrise. There were four recorded passersby. The shift ended early at Eren's command." R-0 cycled through the events, memories flashing through their mind. They had been distracted. Had an intruder slipped in during that time?

"There are reports of constructs becoming corrupted," King Hadrian said. "Widespread reports."

Corrupted?

Was that why R-0 had ignored Eren's orders and stood between their king and Robin? They were corrupted?

Something had changed after the falling light from the sky had entered their body. R-0's hand instinctively went to their chest, metal fingers clicking against the plate now containing a golden flame instead of the dull fire that had previously sustained them.

"Something happened." R-0's words caught as their gears seized and their face plate froze mid-movement.

"What happened?" King Hadrian asked.

R-0 could hardly remember what they were supposed to be doing. *Protect the king.* Like a tether, their prime directive grounded them. R-0 flicked through the memories of the past few moments, reorienting themself.

But even focusing their mind, R-0 didn't know what to say. They still weren't sure what happened, so how could they describe it? The warmth in their chest, the curiosity, the beauty . . . the distractions. The fear.

R-0 inhaled, air circulating through the tubes and passageways within their body, fanning the fire within and cooling their plates. As their temperature lowered, they found clarity.

Surrounding everything they didn't understand were facts. And the king could use these facts to fix whatever was happening. "Stars fell from the sky, but before they hit the ground, they were drawn to the fire."

"The fire?"

R-0 gestured at their chest. They hadn't looked at the flame since reattaching their plate. Was it still burning gold?

"A star entered your chest as well?" The king's voice shook, a contrast to his normally smooth and confident words. Why was the king different?

No, R-0 was looking at it wrong. It wasn't the king who was different. It was R-0. *Corrupted.* That is how the king had described the constructs like R-0 that were affected by the light.

"Yes sir."

"Perhaps we should visit the maintenance room."

Something must be wrong. R-0's biweekly maintenance wasn't scheduled for another seven cycles, and as far as they could tell, their parts were functioning properly. Why would unscheduled maintenance be needed?

But no matter what was happening and what was different, some things were still the same. R-0 had one directive: protect the king. No matter what happened, they could do that. So they followed the king down the palace hallway.

CHAPTER 4

"Report on the situation in the storage rooms." King Hadrian kept his head forward, and R-0 stayed at his side.

The situation in the storage rooms wasn't normal. Awareness of the passage of time, jittering gears and unease, and . . . B-7. Just like B-7 had disobeyed the guard in the hallway and then the technomancers in the storage room, R-0 had disobeyed Eren. Was there a reason behind B-7's behavior as well?

"R-0?"

R-0 had stopped in the middle of the hallway. The guards stared at them, and King Hadrian was a few steps ahead, looking back at them.

"Apologies sir." Another distraction. *Corruption.*

"I asked a question."

"Nothing occurred."

"Did any of the constructs try to leave? Were any of them planning anything?"

Despite B-7's concerns about the situation, they hadn't tried to leave, and they definitely didn't have any plans—just endless questions. "No sir."

"Are you sure?"

"Yes sir."

Despite R-0's affirmative response, King Hadrian frowned. Endless questions raced through R-0's mind. Why was R-0 receiving maintenance early? Why was King Hadrian attending?

Was he curious about R-0, or did he think maintenance would reveal something about the corruption?

It didn't matter. R-0 had to stay focused. No more distractions.

But how could they focus when there were so many distractions in the palace?

Entertainers strolled the halls. Most were human, but a lizard-scaled and merfolk danced among them, their scales catching on the light. Had their clothes always appeared so vibrant? They all were cloaked in reds, purples, and blues R-0 hadn't even realized existed. R-0 wanted to touch the clothing. The cloth billowed with each step like leaves blowing in the wind. Could R-0 feel like they were flying in the wind too?

And the tapestries lining the walls . . . R-0 knew the woven cloth told stories. But what stories? About who? And how did they end?

Could R-0 have their own story woven into a tapestry one day?

R-0 had slowed again, falling steps behind King Hadrian. They sped up to return to his side. Eren caught their gaze, and she rested her hand on the hilt of her sword. R-0 looked around for a threat, but there was no one else present.

Eren's grip on her weapon tightened. "Keep walking."

"Yes ma'am."

R-0 watched Eren out of the corner of their eye, and more often than not, her gaze focused on R-0 as well. Eren was the captain of the guard and a respected council member from Clan Ainfen. She represented Haiden's military district, and R-0 had memories of multiple ceremonies awarding her accolades. If even she was this unfocused, it was no wonder King Hadrian preferred constructs like R-0 to protect him. They were far more reliable.

At least, the constructs used to be more reliable. Now swarmed with distractions, R-0 could be equally as fallible. Maybe the corruption King Hadrian had spoken of was more dangerous than they realized.

R-0 focused back on the king. As his feet hit the ground, they tapped their side to keep the rhythm. Each of the king's steps was a tap that vibrated through R-0, a constant reminder of their task: focus on the king. Protect the king.

Every hallway brought new distractions, but R-0 continued to tap, keeping their focus on the king until they reached the maintenance room.

King Hadrian stepped through the doorway, and R-0 ducked through to follow him. Inside, the walls were lined with tools and cabinets filled with generic spare parts: gears, metal plates, screws, and wires. Smooth gray stones dotted the top of the walls between cabinets, glowing with soft blue light from the managrid.

Over a dozen technomancers operated, gathered around tables in groups of four. Pads of paper lay on the tables next to them—separate from the thick folders that normally housed maintenance and diagnostics reports. As they worked, magic arced between their gloves and the maintenance tables, tools leaping to and from their hands with nothing but a thought. Powering magic items was one of the many benefits of the managrid, and the technomancers utilized it whenever they could.

Three constructs lay sprawled out on the tables, their bodies still and their eyes closed. Their chest plates were propped open, revealing the flame within. Their normal fires had been replaced with shining golden flames just like R-0's. But their flames were dim compared to the light R-0 had seen in themself. What maintenance protocol were the technomancers performing? The tools, the positions, and the state of the constructs didn't match any of the procedures R-0 was familiar with. This was something new. Something different.

The unease R-0 had experienced in the storage room returned. They didn't mind some differences. Others were even exciting. But seeing these constructs on the tables evoked neither indifference nor excitement. Smoke poured out from their flame, and they slowly exhaled a thin cloud.

Tap. Tap. Tap.

"King Hadrian." The closest technomancer dropped what he was working on, turning his back to the construct in front of him without a second glance. His sleeves were rolled up to his elbows, revealing a tattoo on his forearm of the Doblin clan crest. He tucked his fist against his neck over his opposite shoulder and dipped his head in respect. The rest of the technomancers followed suit.

"At ease." King Hadrian pointed to the constructs. "Focus on your job. Is there a spot I can set up?"

"Here." The technomancer at the first table stood and began clearing their supplies.

A new construct was shepherded in the door, and a technomancer in the back of the room waved them in. The construct and their guards walked right past the table being cleared.

Every construct receiving maintenance would walk past this table. If the corruption really was a threat . . .

"No." R-0 grabbed the technomancer by the wrist, stopping him from removing any more tools. "That table." They pointed to the table in the back corner of the room. If anything did go wrong, R-0 would see it coming and could protect the king more easily.

The technomancer squealed, and his eyes widened. R-0 could feel his pulse quickening as he squirmed under their grip. The guards behind them drew their weapons. Eren dashed toward R-0, stopping only as King Hadrian threw his arm out in her way.

"R-0, let him go." King Hadrian's voice was steady.

"Yes sir." R-0 released the technomancer's wrist. He immediately cradled his hand against his chest, although R-0 wasn't sure why. They had been gentle.

The technomancer took three quick steps back, his eyes wide and breathing heavy. "King Hadrian—"

King Hadrian held up a hand, silencing the technomancer, then signaled to his guards to lower their weapons. "Let's all just settle down and take a deep breath."

R-0 didn't require breathing but imitated the movement all the same. They could understand the look on the guards' faces better now that emotions were running high and masks of indifference had been lowered. Fear. Suspicion.

And all of it was focused on R-0.

The reason R-0 couldn't find the threat was because R-0 *was* the threat. But they would never endanger the king. Why would anyone think otherwise?

"It will be safer this way," R-0 explained. The king didn't need to think they were insubordinate or damaged. Even if there was corruption, R-0 could still serve him. "If there is a danger among the constructs, a clear line of sight to the threat is necessary."

"That is very thoughtful of you." King Hadrian's lips curled up in a tight smile. "You heard R-0. Prepare the table in the back for us."

The technomancers cleared away from more than just the back table. They cleared out of the maintenance room, removing notes and strange glowing vials R-0 had never seen before. Many took extra steps back, giving R-0 a wide berth as they cleared their workstations. Only Eren moved closer to R-0. The constructs didn't stir as they transferred them from the tables onto rolling stretchers and pushed them out of the room.

A technomancer approached the back table, but King Hadrian waved him away. "Leave the tools."

More questions bubbled to the surface. Were the technomancers not assisting? Had King Hadrian ever performed maintenance on a construct? Did he have any experience? He was king—shouldn't he have more important things to do? Why R-0? And why now?

R-0 shouldn't question the king.

Instead, they bent their fingers, watching the joints flex. They opened their mouth as if to speak but said nothing.

When only guards remained, King Hadrian pulled out a chair. "Sit here."

R-0 turned the chair so it faced the door and sat. It creaked under their weight, and for a moment, R-0 worried it would collapse. They had never used the palace furniture before.

"Eren, clear the room."

"But—"

"A couple guards are going to be about as useful as those shackles to stop a royal construct," King Hadrian whispered. "And I'd like whatever happens here to remain private for now. Have them wait outside."

"Fine." As Eren shepherded the guards out, she kept her focus on R-0 and a hand on her weapon. When she returned, she stayed by King Hadrian's side.

The king ran his hand along the edge of the table, surveying the suite of tools. The managrid lights tinted his skin blue. Unlike the technomancers, King Hadrian physically picked up a screwdriver, awkwardly adjusting his grip before reaching for R-0's chest.

It was easy for R-0 to imagine all the ways this could go wrong. They had seen it before when the technomancers were tired or careless. It had never bothered them before, but now each scenario chilled R-0's plates. King Hadrian could strip a screw or dent their chest plate, and that was just their exterior. Chipped gears would catch in their rotations, wires could become tangled, and their flame . . . R-0's fingers flexed repeatedly, faster and faster until they were nothing but a blur and couldn't accelerate anymore. Their fingers wouldn't stop.

"Have you ever worked on a construct before?" As soon as R-0 blurted out the question, their fingers stilled.

"No." King Hadrian chuckled and repositioned the screwdriver in his hand. "You're going to be the first."

What if he didn't put them back together properly? That could be worse than any corruption caused by the star. There was a certain order things should be done. R-0 cycled through memories of their last maintenance, the tools the technomancer had used, which processes came first or last, and what had been recorded in the notes.

"Does that worry you?" King Hadrian asked.

"Worry?"

King Hadrian pointed at R-0's fingers, which had begun bending and stretching again. "I used to do the same thing when I was younger until my mother made me stop."

"How did you stop?"

"Well, I tried sitting on my hands."

R-0 rose slightly and started to put their hands on their chair, but King Hadrian stopped them, a chuckle on his lips.

This time when he smiled, there was no tightness in his skin, and his eyes softened as well. "Don't waste your time," he said. "It didn't work." Despite his words, his fingers didn't fidget as he brought the screwdriver to R-0's chest plate and began unscrewing.

"How did you make it stop?"

"I realized my fingers were moving because I wasn't. My fingers weren't the problem, they were the symptom of my inaction—a sign there was something I should have been doing and wasn't." He fumbled with the screwdriver, and it slipped off the screwhead. Steadiness didn't replace experience.

"What should you have been doing?"

"It could have been anything. Speaking up during a council meeting, sneaking off with a girl at one of the balls, stealing a pastry from the kitchen—" He cursed as the screwdriver slipped again, nicking the metal. R-0's fidgeting fingers accelerated.

King Hadrian raised the screwdriver once more, and R-0 snatched it from his hand.

The fidgeting stilled, and they slowly began unscrewing the screw, careful not to cause any more damage.

"Seems like it works for you too."

"What?" R-0 asked.

King Hadrian pointed to R-0's hands, which were completely steady as they began maintenance. "Looks like you needed to stop me from accidentally maiming you."

Eren snickered, but as soon as R-0 looked over at her, her laughter died.

"Apologies sir." R-0 tried to hand the screwdriver back as the realization of what they had done sank in.

King Hadrian pushed the tool back toward R-0. "You're doing a much better job than I was. If it's alright with you, I'll just watch."

"Yes sir."

What had R-0 been thinking, stopping the king like that? They *hadn't* been thinking. They had acted on instinct.

"Have you ever done this before?" King Hadrian asked.

"Once," R-0 said. "Last shift."

"The logs say it's been a week since you were last maintained."

R-0 flickered through their memories of the last seven cycles. "Yes sir, that is accurate."

"Then what happened last shift?"

R-0 hadn't opened their chest plate to fix anything other than the gnawing feeling in their chest, which wasn't something that could be quantified or put in the logs. If R-0 had to name the ailment, they would have called it curiosity. "No maintenance was performed."

"Then who ordered you to remove the chest plate? And why?"

R-0 paused. They hadn't been given orders to remove their chest plate. It was counter to their orders to stand guard. R-0 finished unscrewing the final screw, and King Hadrian helped remove their chest plate.

"You can tell me the truth," he said.

"No one ordered the chest plate removal."

"You did it on your own?"

"Yes sir."

"Why?"

"After the stars fell, something was different."

"*You* were different."

R-0 couldn't tell if it was a question or a statement.

"Look." King Hadrian pointed at R-0's flame. The golden light appeared even stronger than when they first saw it. Even Eren looked on with interest. King Hadrian brought his hand close, and golden light reflected across his skin. "It's beautiful."

R-0 couldn't agree more, but they couldn't find the words to express that. Instead, they watched the king marvel at the fire.

"Tell me, what are you thinking?" King Hadrian asked.

"You are right," R-0 said.

"You think it's beautiful?"

R-0 nodded.

"Have you ever thought that before?"

"No sir."

"Are you having other thoughts?"

"Yes sir."

"Like what?"

It was hard to verbalize the swirl of words that consumed R-0's thoughts whenever they let their focus waver. They thought *everything*, all at once, in a blur. "There is not one answer."

"Choose any answer."

"Whose stories are in the tapestries?"

"What else?"

"Does the corruption endanger you?"

"And what if it does?"

On instinct, R-0 reached for a blade that wasn't there. The absence of their weapons was only a minor inconvenience. Their body could still shield him. Their hands weren't as deadly as a blade, but they could dispatch organics that intended King Hadrian harm. Flesh was delicate, but metal was unyielding. "You will be protected."

King Hadrian stared at R-0, and then back at their flame. He held his hand in front of him, and a blue glow cascaded across his skin as magic coalesced in his palm. As he took a deep breath, the magic brightened, then he extended his hand toward R-0's flame.

"R-0, stand up."

R-0 stood.

"Sit down."

R-0 sat.

"The bond is still working?" Eren's eyes widened. For the first time since they'd been in the maintenance room, her hand fell away from her weapon as she leaned forward, watching R-0's flame.

The magic in King Hadrian's hand intensified, and he stared directly at R-0's flame. His brow furrowed, and a tiny droplet of sweat ran down his forehead. R-0 looked in their chest but saw the same golden glow. Nothing had changed.

"No." King Hadrian sighed. "It's not working."

R-0 surveyed the table for anything broken, but the king was in perfect condition, as were all of the tools. R-0's flame was different, but it was still performing its function. King Hadrian's words didn't make sense.

"What is malfunctioning?" R-0 asked.

King Hadrian sighed. "Do you know how you were created?"

Their creation. R-0 hadn't considered it. "No sir."

"The constructs were animated with magic. It was my mother's blood—*my* bloodline—that was used in the spell. It bound you to me."

R-0 flickered through their memories. They had never questioned their creation. One moment they didn't exist. The next, their gears were ticking and their directive to protect the king had echoed through their mind. The king's story answered questions they had never thought to ask.

But the story of their creation didn't explain what was broken.

"But it isn't working," King Hadrian said. "The magic isn't activating. The spell isn't forcing you to listen to me."

The constructs always obeyed their orders. At least . . . they had before. Things were different now. Like B-7 leaving their station no matter how many times the technomancer insisted they stay.

"The other constructs have disobeyed," R-0 said.

"But you haven't. Even though there's nothing to stop you from ignoring me."

R-0 shook their head. "Your orders are to be followed."

"I don't understand." King Hadrian ran his hands through his hair. "There's no magic forcing you to obey. So why do you still follow my orders?"

R-0's flame sparked, reaching toward the king. They flickered through memories, searching for anything to explain his line of questioning. What else would R-0 do? For a decade, they had been at King Hadrian's side. Protected him. Served him. It was all they had ever known.

But something *was* different.

Their directive had once echoed in their mind. As consistent as their ticking gears, their directive repeated. Protect the king. Protect the king. Protect the king.

Now, there was silence. But still . . . their flame wanted to be close to the king. R-0 wanted to be close to him—wanted to keep him safe.

"R-0?" King Hadrian asked. "Your answer is very important. I need to understand the full extent of what has happened to you and the rest of the constructs. My people are worried and rightfully so. Whatever is happening with the constructs could be dangerous. So I ask you again, why do you still follow my orders?"

"You are the king," R-0 said. "You require protection."

"You have no other reason? No other purpose behind your actions?"

R-0 didn't have an answer for that. They stared down at the gray tiled floor. They had so many thoughts now, but a purpose? How could they answer the king's question? Their fingers fidgeted again, but this time there was no screwdriver to grab. Nothing they could do to slow their speeding gears. Their flame crackled, the sound echoing through the room.

King Hadrian rested his hand on top of R-0's, and their motions slowed.

"It's okay." His voice was gentle. "I didn't mean to upset you. Answer me this instead. Would you ever hurt me?"

An easy question.

"No sir," R-0 said.

"Will you protect me, even from the other constructs?"

"Yes sir."

"Look at me."

R-0 tilted their head up. Their flame reflected in King Hadrian's eyes, making them shine even brighter than normal. "Can I trust you with my life?"

"Yes sir."

For a moment, the two sat in silence. King Hadrian's eyes narrowed slightly. It wasn't like the guards' looks—laced with fear and suspicion. He studied them, but it was different. There was something light, something pure in his gaze.

He leaned back suddenly and clapped his hands together. "Eren, R-0 will need their blades returned."

"Sir?" Eren's eyes widened.

"If we're going to locate the missing constructs, who better to help us than a construct themself? We can't make any decisions without knowing more about what's going on." King Hadrian returned his gaze to R-0. "I'm reinstating R-0 to my service effective immediately."

CHAPTER 5

After being reinstated to King Hadrian's service, R-0 expected their life to be like it was before the corruption. They wished they'd been right and that their only duty was to protect the king while he investigated the missing constructs.

Although a majority of R-0's time for the past four cycles had been dedicated to protecting the king, King Hadrian's attention was divided between a myriad of tasks, and for every task King Hadrian attended to, he introduced new directives to R-0 as well.

Talking was the most common. King Hadrian would talk with R-0 for hours after his meetings were done, occasionally asking R-0 questions. Some were entirely nonsensical—like what their favorite color was—while others were impossible to answer—like what their purpose was. More often than not, King Hadrian filled the silence on his own. R-0 preferred conversations like that. It was far easier to listen and ask questions than to answer them.

Most frequently, they asked about the investigation. How was R-0 supposed to help the king find the missing constructs if they were with him in unrelated meetings? But King Hadrian brushed off their questions. Eren had guards searching for information. Once she discovered something, they would act. Until then, he had a country to run.

Today, King Hadrian had said that the unknown was the root of fear, and if they wanted a fruitful garden, they needed to pull it up by its roots. R-0 had expected to spend the day gardening. Instead, they had headed to the council hall, where King Hadrian used R-0 as a demonstration of the physical changes constructs had experienced from the corruption.

R-0 stood in the middle of the council chambers, their chest plate open and their flame exposed to the world. Half of the council had gathered—Councilwoman Jeza Doblin, Councilman Robin Conradh, Councilwoman Gretta Murdha, and King Hadrian. These were some of the most powerful people in Haiden, representing the crafters, the shipwrights, the blacksmiths, and the monster hunters, respectively. In King Hadrian's case, representing all of Haiden as well as his clan.

They all stared at R-0's flame.

R-0 wanted to screw themselves closed. With every step the king took, his cloak shifted, and air flickered toward their exposed fire. It was nothing but a light breeze, but to R-0, it felt like a hurricane. Not for the first time since their encounter with the star, they wondered what would happen to them if something happened to their flame.

But there was nothing they could do about it. They had already been reprimanded once this session. While King Hadrian met with the council, they were to remain silent. Answer only when asked. Do as they were told—and not an action more. It didn't make sense to R-0, but King Hadrian insisted he would be safer this way.

So R-0 stood as still as they could, despite their raging flame.

"We have some of the best mages and technomancers in the city studying the changes." Jeza's face scrunched up as she spoke of the technomancers. Her attitude toward them alternated between gratitude to envy. While they were some of the most respected crafters in her clan, they also weaved magic into their creations in a way Jeza never could. "But nothing they've done has made the fire or the constructs react to our orders."

Robin scoffed. "Given your history with magic, are you the right person to be overseeing this?"

Jeza turned her head, as if to look out the window, but R-0 could hear her breathing change and see the muscles in her jaw tighten as her teeth clenched.

It wasn't uncommon for Robin—or other council members—to bring up Jeza's lack of magical talent. Since the invention of the managrid, most organics could channel basic magic using the managrid's power. But some, like Jeza, were entirely cut off from the Flow. It wasn't new information, but it always left Jeza rattled, which King Hadrian had explained was the councilman's true intention.

"My attempts have demonstrated the same," King Hadrian said. Every day he'd tested R-0 for any sign they were still bound to his blood magic, but every day the situation remained unchanged. "We need to reassign the technomancers to the managrid repairs. We're still facing blackouts, and I need that resolved before we waste time chasing the way things used to be."

"Of course, my king," Jeza said.

"And what of the missing constructs?" Robin asked.

He had done better at keeping his temper in check at recent meetings, but R-0 still watched him more than the others. The sentiment was reciprocated. Robin eyed R-0 warily. He had requested numerous times that constructs not be allowed in the council hall. Sometimes King Hadrian acquiesced, but often, King Hadrian insisted on R-0's presence.

Robin wasn't the only one who believed R-0 was a problem. Eren almost always assigned additional guards when she couldn't be there herself, but R-0 didn't mind the extra security. Even as they learned to master the constant distractions, they frequently got lost in the novelties of the world. R-0 was more than capable of protecting the king, but . . . just in case, until the corruption was resolved, King Hadrian would be safer with additional guards.

"We're still investigating the missing constructs," King Hadrian said. "It's been six days since the incident, with no reports of gathered constructs. It's possible these are simply individual runaways."

Although R-0 had already known the king's measured answer, it didn't stop their flame from crackling with unease.

Without the metal to muffle it, the sound echoed through the room, garnering unwanted attention from the council as their gazes returned to R-0's exposed flame. It crackled once more, louder than before.

"Dozens of individual runaways?" Jeza's nails clacked on the table. "At this scale, I find it quite unlikely that they are working independently."

As the council's focus shifted to her, R-0's flame settled some.

Robin nodded. "And far more likely that they're organizing against us."

"Or that someone is organizing them against us," Gretta said. "There are many opportunists who would like to see things around here change and could capitalize on an event like this."

"The minor clans?" Robin asked.

Gretta nodded.

Although there were only seven seats on Haiden's council, there were over a dozen clans throughout Haiden. Gretta frequently called the minor clans overeager vultures waiting for her to die so they could lobby for their clans to take Clan Murdha's seat on the council during the transition.

"We have no evidence that—"

King Hadrian's words were cut short when the double doors at the far end of the room burst open. R-0 swung their chest plate closed as they drew their sword, stepping between King Hadrian and the disturbance.

Eren darted into the council hall, not waiting to be acknowledged before addressing the rest of the council. "We have a lead on a missing construct."

"At ease, R-0." King Hadrian placed a hand on R-0's arm, and R-0 sheathed their sword. They considered opening their chest plate back up, but as Jeza's gaze slid over them, their flame slinked back in its chamber, and R-0 couldn't bring their arms to move.

"Eren, report," King Hadrian said.

"A Murdha blacksmith repurposed some of the old mining constructs, and one of them went missing. A construct matching that model was seen entering a warehouse along the coast on the border of the harpy district and the dockyards."

Jeza's eyes widened, and she rapidly shuffled through the papers in front of her. Despite its namesake, the harpy district had no monsters. All the Graywal districts were named after monstrous creatures Haiden's founders had faced before finally settling here. The harpy district was primarily composed of merchants from Clan Doblin—Jeza's clan. Perhaps there was something in her notes that could help the guards, but she flipped through the papers too quickly for R-0 to decipher her messy handwriting.

They shouldn't have even been trying to read her notes. If Jeza had any pertinent information, she would supply it to the council herself. It was nothing but a distraction from R-0's orders.

Protect the king.

R-0 refocused as King Hadrian gestured for Eren to take a seat. She refused, pacing instead.

"Was the construct alone?" Gretta asked.

"No." Eren shook her head. "But that's even worse news. One of my guards saw Ryder with them."

R-0 had put up wanted posters for Ryder—a merfolk with a list of crimes ranging from petty theft to murder. His list of offenses continued on the back of the papers they'd hung. R-0 appreciated the thoroughness, but it was wasted on most of the organics who never even glanced at the posters, much less looked closely enough to realize there was a back.

But what would a construct be doing with a wanted criminal?

Eren stopped pacing, standing behind her seat. "The guards haven't reported any new activity since the construct arrived. I have a group assembled to infiltrate the warehouse and apprehend the construct. I'll lead them myself, but I wanted to update everyone first."

"Take R-0 with you." King Hadrian handed R-0 the screwdriver from the table. "Get ready to go."

"What?" Eren and Jeza's voices echoed together.

"Yes sir." R-0's flame already grew stronger at the idea of being safely back in its compartment. They hurriedly screwed their chest plate in place.

"Once you've apprehended the construct, come get me," King Hadrian said. "I'll handle the interrogation personally."

"I need people I can trust," Eren said. "This is the first lead we've got on one of the missing constructs. We can't afford to lose it. If they're organizing against us—"

"If they're organizing against us, we will act accordingly, but right now, we don't know what they are doing or not doing. And we won't know without gathering information. This is the best lead we've gotten, and we must ensure its success."

"And *my* guards will do that."

"Eren, listen." King Hadrian's voice softened. It didn't project throughout the room, but instead wrapped around R-0 and Eren like a blanket. "Our people are exhausted. Without the constructs, everyone is overworked. None of us are at our best." King Hadrian ushered R-0 forward. "But the royal constructs are our most capable fighters, and R-0 has proven they are still functioning despite the corruption. This is what they were created for. Don't let your fear of the unknown stop you from accepting their help."

R-0's plates warmed, although they couldn't pinpoint why. The sun was setting, and its golden rays no longer warmed the room. And when Eren opened the doors, she'd let a cold draft in. Their temperature should have decreased, not increased.

"Are you sure?" Eren asked. Her voice was quieter and out of place compared to her typical forceful demeanor.

"Absolutely." King Hadrian looked directly at R-0 as he nodded. It was his words, his confidence in R-0, that spread through their plates like a wildfire.

As they readied to leave with Eren, the rest of the council dispersed. Jeza left first, after making plans to meet with King Hadrian later that night, then Robin and Gretta exited together, whispering concerns about the constructs R-0 suspected they didn't realize could be clearly heard with a construct's advanced hearing.

Once they had left the council chambers, Eren stepped in front of R-0, stopping them in their tracks. "Give me your swords."

R-0 hesitated. If they were going to assist in apprehending the missing construct, wouldn't they need a weapon?

"R-0, this is not a request. It's an order. Give me your swords. Now."

"Yes ma'am." R-0 drew their weapons and handed them to Eren. They were far too large for her to easily use. There was no benefit to her taking them. R-0 tried to stem the uneasiness in their flame, but their finger slipped into their empty sheath, making it hard to focus.

"Do you know how long I've been captain of the guard?" Eren asked.

R-0 cycled through their memories. Despite looking young for an organic, Eren had been captain of the guard since before their creation. "No ma'am."

"Fifteen years. When Queen Hadrian suggested the constructs serve as guards, I resisted. I thought it was a terrible decision. Metal and magic? Couldn't be trusted. *Shouldn't* have been trusted."

She paused, and R-0 wasn't sure if she expected them to say something, or if she was just stating a fact.

"But I was still young, and Queen Hadrian was convincing. So I trusted her. And the thing is, I came to trust the constructs as well. It took a few years, but I grew to rely on you. You were consistent, dependable, everything that made my life so much easier. You weren't getting drunk and showing up late to your shifts. You weren't sneaking behind my back to tell the other council members secrets that could give them an edge and make you some extra coin. When I gave an order, you complied. No mess, no options." Eren shook her head with a sigh. "I trusted you. I relied on you to keep everyone here safe."

Eren's words were positive, but her face wore the same scowl as when she was complaining. "Is that not a good thing?"

"No, it's not. Because King Hadrian is right. Now we're dependent on the constructs, and I don't know if you're friend or foe or something in between. I can't trust that you'll follow my orders. Every system I've had in place for years requires the constructs, and now I can't rely on you."

"Your orders will still be followed. The constructs—"

"No. You see, this?" Eren's grip on R-0's swords tightened. "This can't happen. If you want to prove I can still trust you, then you can't question me. You can't talk back. If you're coming on this mission, then I give the orders, you listen. Nothing more. I need the R-0 I've relied on for years. I need things to be like before. Understood?"

R-0 grew quiet. In the past, no matter what Eren said, R-0 would have stood silently unless it required a response. They wouldn't have debated the construct's ability to serve or focused on their missing weapons because nothing except their directive or orders ever mattered.

It could still be like that. R-0 couldn't convince her with words, but they could with their actions. "Yes ma'am."

"Good. Now follow me. The others are already waiting for us."

CHAPTER 6

R-0 followed Eren until they reached a group of guards. Her brother Jorgunn, three senior guards who had been around since before R-0 was created, and two younger ones R-0 wasn't familiar with gathered outside the barracks, armor donned and weapons ready. All wore a variety of tassels adorning their shoulder—each color signifying a different accomplishment or military honor. In addition to their normal uniforms, each wore a heavy coat. The palace was kept warm with the managrid's magic, but that wouldn't be the case outside.

"King Hadrian has ordered R-0 to accompany us." Eren placed a hand on R-0's shoulder. "If anyone has an issue with that, they can take it up with him directly. In fact, I encourage you to do so. Are we clear?"

Some of the guards eyed R-0 warily, but a chorus of "Yes ma'ams" echoed through their ranks.

"And R-0 is going to be following my orders. They don't so much as move unless it's on my order. If you see something, say something. I know we have a mission, and you didn't sign up to babysit, but that's just the way it is. Now, let's head out."

R-0 remained silent and fell in line with the guards, taking a position on the flank. Rather than leading them to the palace gates, Eren navigated to one of the managrid entry tunnels. Without a word, she led them down the long metal ladder.

The managrid lined a majority of the floor. The last time R-0 had been down here, they'd ignored it, but now, they couldn't peel their vision away. Two pieces of metal tubing were spaced a couple feet apart from each other, both pulsing with blue light. Energy arced between them, filling the gap.

For decades before the creation of the constructs, the managrid had been Haiden's crowning achievement—a well of power running through the country that made minor magic more accessible in Haiden than anywhere else in the world. It had started as small isolated systems of power installed in affluent workshops and Graywal's palace. But as more applications of the magical network were researched, the grid had spread until every city throughout the country was connected, with Graywal at the center. It powered magic items, providing a variety of conveniences like light and water, enabling people in their careers, and even helping to aid the injured.

In all of R-0's trips through the tunnels, they'd never been drawn to the managrid like this. Its warm buzz filled the air, sending a tingling sensation through their plates. It was magic. Right in front of them. R-0 tried to touch it, but Jorgunn grabbed their wrist. He wasn't strong enough to restrain R-0, but they still stopped.

"Best not upset the boss lady," Jorgunn whispered.

"Apologies." R-0 matched their volume to his.

"Jorgunn, is something wrong?" Eren asked.

"No ma'am." Jorgunn shook his head. "Just wondering if there's going to be another blackout while we're down here."

"Shalloth willing, there won't." Eren sped up the pace. "But let's not tempt fate."

The tunnels were a twisting maze carved only slightly larger than the managrid itself, forcing R-0 and the others to step on the managrid as they walked. Each step was a spark beneath them, their plates warming and cooling, and their flame reacting in kind to the magic underfoot. The tunnels were empty except for the occasional technomancer performing maintenance. Despite this, R-0 couldn't help but wonder what was around every curve. In the distance, metal on metal clanged like something being repaired. In some places, the glowing blue light of the managrid extended into stone walls that were never excavated.

Even in the quiet tunnels, distractions were plentiful, but every time R-0's attention began to wander, Jorgunn brought their focus back with a gentle nudge or a quick whisper. R-0 wished for their directive, the consistent, ticking reminder that kept distractions at bay. But the only constant now was the dull roar of the golden flame in their chest.

R-0 kept their eyes trained on the glowing path and tapped their side. Their finger matched their steps, reminding themself to focus.

By the time they surfaced in the harpy district, the last rays of the setting sun had fallen beneath the ocean waves. The cold night air swept around them, and Jorgunn adjusted his coat as a shiver passed through him. Managrid lamps attached to tall metal poles cast a pale blue glow across the cobblestone streets. Throughout most of the harpy district, the buildings were ornate, marked with shop names and clan crests. The outsides were as well-kept as the merchandise within. But this section had smaller, less prestigious shops interspersed with larger, unmarked warehouses used to store raw materials.

Eren led them toward the coast, either oblivious or indifferent to the attention their group garnered from the few people out this late. R-0 tried to match her demeanor—head held high, eyes forward, immune to the distractions of the city. It *almost* worked for the few blocks they had to travel before stopping short of the docks.

"Alright, here's the plan." She spoke in a hushed whisper as she described the two entrances to the warehouse, who was stationed where, and what their objectives were. Jorgunn would lead one team, Eren the other.

R-0 wasn't assigned to either group.

"Capture, not kill," Eren continued. "We need to know what the constructs are planning, and why they're working with Ryder." She paused. "Unless it's you or them. In which case, I expect every one of you to make it back to the palace alive. Clear?"

The guards all nodded in affirmation. If R-0 had been named among them, they too would have nodded. Eren had made each part of the plan easy to understand. But what was R-0's role?

"Is that the entire plan?" R-0 asked.

"Yes."

R-0 waited for her to clarify, but she remained silent.

"What about—" R-0's words died in their chest. "What are your orders?"

Eren gestured to the side of the street where a tall iron lamppost protruded from the ground, supporting a small glowing blue stone at the top. "Stay right by this lamppost."

R-0 frowned, examining the area. They were unable to see the warehouse housing the construct and the criminals. And based on the directions Eren had just given, it wasn't a likely path for those that might flee.

"What is the objective?" R-0 assumed their position by the lamppost.

"Keep out of our way, and let us do our job." Eren turned her back to R-0, and the rest of the guards followed her.

Leaving R-0 alone in the street.

R-0 stood by the lamppost. The ticking of gears mixed with the lapping of distant waves, marking the passage of time as they waited and waited and waited for the others to return. R-0 scanned their surroundings, committing each structure to memory, no matter how insignificant it seemed. Most were nondescript warehouses, but two appeared to be workshops. One was a jeweler's shop with the Doblin clan crest prominently displayed next to the shop's name—Yralla's Rings. The other had no signage, but an iron band forged into the shape of the Murdha clan crest hung next to the door. Combined with the hammering noises coming from within, it was reasonable to assume the space belonged to a blacksmith. Brief flashes of blue light within occasionally illuminated the cobblestone streets, as the crafters worked despite the late hour.

They could only look at the same things so many times before their thoughts started to creep away from their current circumstances. What was the king doing? Was Eren's mission going well? How was it helpful for R-0 to stand here doing nothing? Why didn't Eren just leave them with King Hadrian if she was going to order them to stay out of the way? At the palace, R-0 could have been useful and protected the king.

R-0 tried to push the thoughts away. Thoughts like that were exactly why Eren gave R-0 these orders—she couldn't trust them to listen without questioning her. If they were going to prove themself, they needed to focus.

"Get back here!"

A harsh whisper broke the monotony, and R-0's attention snapped toward the source of the commotion. A construct emerged from an alleyway between Yralla's Rings and a warehouse.

The construct's steps echoed on the cobblestone streets, frantic and uneven. As they looked back over their shoulder, rocks shifted beneath their feet, and a loose stone sent them sprawling in the streets. They hurried to stand, but not before a group of organics ran out of the alleyway.

There were four of them—two dwarves and two humans—all with the same grime coating their clothes and skin and weapons hanging at their waist. They encircled the construct, and one of the dwarves stepped forward.

The construct had barely gotten to their feet before the dwarf jammed his knife in the slits between the construct's lower and upper chest plates and pushed them against a warehouse wall. The rest of the organics clutched their weapons at the ready.

No one looked over at R-0, even as their gears accelerated, letting off a high pitch whine. Was this the construct Eren and the others were searching for? Although R-0 couldn't see the designation on the back of their neck from this distance, the construct matched her description. They were designed for work in the mines—a compact form for slipping through tiny passageways, no auxiliary functions outside of physical movement, and a few vials for gauging temperature and air quality protruding from each shoulder.

But if this was the target . . . where were Eren and the others?

The construct tried to inch away from their attacker, but the dwarf wiggled the knife, and the construct froze. Their body pushed against the wall, as if trying to lean away from the dwarf. They were . . . scared. R-0 started to step forward but stopped themself. Their orders were to stay.

"Nowhere to run now, huh?" The dwarf slid the knife in deeper, metal creaking as he drove the blade behind the construct's plates.

R-0 wasn't sure why the dwarf asked the construct anything. Answering questions wasn't within their function. If it was, they would have a voice box installed.

The dwarf stuck again.

R-0's flame grew despite the cold winter chill surrounding them and a lack of kindling, the extra heat rushing through their plates until their entire body warmed. Why were the organics doing this? Did they not realize the damage they were causing?

The construct looked at R-0, and electricity filled the air between them. They couldn't speak, but something about their mannerisms and the look in their eyes was familiar.

The construct didn't want to be there.

The dwarf kicked at the construct's shin plates, then winced in pain as his shoe crumpled against the metal. He grabbed his foot, dropping the knife and cursing under his breath. The other organics laughed.

"Thought you were tough as dragon's hide?" one asked.

"Guess being hardheaded doesn't help your toes," another added.

"Shut up!" The dwarf retrieved his knife. "And grab it."

The construct had begun to walk away, but the organics quickly grabbed them by their arms and shoved them against a nearby wall. The constructs' plates were separated, unable to return to their original positions even without the knife impeding their function. Several internal wires were severed. The construct's gears stuttered, but the quiet noise was overshadowed by the organics' continued laughter and jokes.

R-0 reached for their sword but found nothing but an empty sheath. It wasn't R-0's function to help this construct. So why did their gears struggle to still and their flame roar in their chest? It should have been effortless to remain still—it was a lack of input. But their fingers moved on their own, following the intricate grooves along the sheath's opening that were entirely mismatched to their bulky fingers.

RISE OF THE FORGEHEARTS

The dwarf stabbed the dagger into the construct's chest plate, this time piercing the flat of the plate and burying the blade to the hilt. "Make sure we aren't being followed."

R-0's flame roared in their chest. They could protect the construct. They could stop this. A few organics were no match for R-0. But Eren's orders echoed through their mind.

Stay right by this lamppost. Keep out of our way, and let us do our job.

This was different than the council room when her orders could have put the king in danger. The king wasn't threatened by these organics. R-0 had no reason to abandon their post, and it was far safer to observe and report their findings later. So what were they thinking, about to charge forward? R-0 tried to focus on their orders, but everywhere they looked, despite the empty streets, they saw the expression on the construct's face as they had tried and failed to run.

Something snapped, followed by a clatter as metal fell to the ground.

R-0 couldn't stop themself.

They had to do something.

Stay right by this lamppost. Keep out of our way, and—

Eren's orders were an anchor keeping them in place, but as her words echoed, R-0 realized that helping the construct didn't have to mean disobedience.

R-0 locked their hands around the lamppost. The metal groaned as R-0 pulled, displacing cobblestones at its base. R-0 wasn't sure how it connected, but they didn't want to damage more of the street. They stopped pulling, and instead slowly bent the pole until it snapped, leaving jagged iron shards behind. Separated from the managrid, the light faded from the pale stone.

The organics turned their attention away from the injured construct and toward R-0.

"Looky, looky, we've got another one," the dwarf said. "It must be our lucky night."

R-0 stepped forward, bringing the lamppost into the street with them. Their already heavy steps thudded even louder with the additional weight. Light from the managrid illuminated their plates, tinting the metal blue.

"Step away from the construct." R-0 kept their voice steady. They thought of King Hadrian's commanding presence when he gave orders and hoped they sounded similar.

"It's got an attitude," one of the humans said.

"It'll break just the same." The dwarf lunged forward with his dagger, and R-0 blocked it with their hand. The blade hit the reinforced plate in their palm and bounced off harmlessly.

"That was unkind," R-0 said. A slight nick interrupted the normally smooth plate. "Please step away from the construct."

The dwarf's eyes widened, and he slashed out with the dagger again. Why wouldn't he listen to R-0? They had even said please. R-0 dodged the first two strikes, then caught the man's wrist at his third swing.

"The dagger will be confiscated." Still holding the man's wrist, R-0 inched one of their fingers to the dwarf's hand to pry the dagger away. The dwarf tried to hold on, but when one of his bones snapped, he cried out and dropped the weapon.

"Thank you." R-0 released him.

"What are you waiting for?" The dwarf grabbed his wrist as he shrieked. "Grab it!"

Two of the organics checked on the dwarf's injury, but the other dashed toward the construct. The construct struggled to their feet, but they'd sustained too much damage. They fell back to the ground.

R-0 intercepted the organic. She was a small human, but what she lacked in size she made up for in speed. Her blades whirred through the air, slashing against R-0's plates. Unlike the construct lying on the ground, R-0's joints weren't easily accessible, and the organic's strikes bounced off reinforced steel.

"Attacking the guard is a criminal offense." R-0 recited. They weren't sure what came next. They weren't sure of anything at this point. Eren's orders to stay by the lamppost hadn't prepared them for this. "Please stop."

The organic didn't listen. With her free hand, she reached toward the ground, and the managrid's energy arced between her fingers. Magic curled across her skin, illuminating the grin on her face. Her fingers wrapped around each other until an orb of magic formed, and she released it in R-0's direction.

The blast caught R-0 in the chest, and they stumbled back. Scorch marks stained their chest plate, and although the metal still held, its shape was slightly distorted. Usually, the managrid's energy flowed into items to give them purpose, like the lights dotting the street or fires that burned without fuel, but for those who knew how to access it directly, magical potential was limited only by how much mana flowed through nearby sectors and their knowledge of how to use it.

But it was illegal to access the managrid like this without authorization. Another crime to add to their growing list of offenses. These criminals would have to be apprehended, R-0 decided. By force, if necessary—and given how they had responded to R-0's attempts at peaceful negotiation, force *was* necessary.

The next time the organic lifted her arm, R-0 swung the lamppost. She tried to parry the blow with her sword, but the impact flung it from her grip. Even disarmed, magic from the managrid pooled in her palms, so R-0 struck her leg, cracking bones and knocking her to the ground. Her magic faded as she cried out in pain, and R-0 turned their attention back to the other organics.

The dwarf still nursed his wrist, but he urged the other two forward. Before they were close enough to strike, R-0 used the lamppost to disarm both of them. R-0 tried to swing softly—organics were fragile, delicate creatures. But the lamppost gained momentum as they swung, and a gentle hit knocked one of the organics across the street. His body splintered through wood as he crashed into the side of a warehouse. He groaned and stirred but didn't get back up.

Which left only one organic. The human circled R-0 weaving around the heavy swings of the lamppost until she closed the distance between them, then attacked. As she struck, R-0 moved to block, but a voice down the street stopped them.

"R-0!" Eren yelled. "Stop."

R-0 paused, allowing the organic's strike to hit. Her blade bounced off one of their joints. Luckily, it wasn't enough force to cause lasting damage—just scrapes to the metal that the technomancers could easily buff out.

R-0's attacker hopped out of R-0's reach as Eren ran up accompanied by the guards. None of them appeared to be injured. In fact, none of them appeared to have faced any combat. Their armor was free of any scuffs or dirt, and their quivers were still full.

"I'm so sorry." Eren waved two of her guards across the street to help the man stuck in the warehouse wall. "Are y'all okay?"

"Okay? That thing attacked us! It's malfunctioning!"

"I saw," Eren said. "And that's completely unacceptable. We'll have healers tend to your injuries, and the construct will be punished."

Punished? R-0 hadn't broken any laws. They'd followed Eren's orders. But . . . they had done *more* than just follow Eren's orders. While fighting, they had been too busy to fully consider their actions. Now that their body slowed, their thoughts sped. Their flame sparked against their plates, creating an uncomfortable rattle in their chest. Why had they acted without orders? Was this the corruption?

"The construct was in need of assistance," R-0 said.

"The construct needs to do what it's told." The dwarf kicked at the injured construct, and they fell to the ground. Fraying wires hung from their joints, impeding them from moving properly even without the dwarf's interference. "We were just walking home when that thing attacked us out of nowhere. Nearly killed my mate there!"

R-0 frowned. That wasn't true at all. "The organics were—"

Eren held up her hand, interrupting R-0's explanation. "What happened to following orders?"

R-0 offered her the lamppost. The end with the mana-grid light was deformed, and somewhere during the fight, the stone had detached. Still, it was the lamppost. "The lamppost remained nearby."

Eren's grip tightened on her sword's hilt until R-0 thought her bones might pop through her skin. Despite standing still, her breathing quickened. She kept her teeth clenched as she spoke. "Jorgunn, take R-0 back while I clean up this mess."

"Would you like a report on the encounter?" R-0 asked.

"I'd like you out of my sight," Eren said. "Now."

"Come on." Jorgunn grabbed R-0's arm, guiding them away. He stopped where the lamppost had been and knelt by the jagged remnants of the post still peeking out of the cobblestone street. "Guess there's no putting that back together, huh?"

R-0 frowned. They hadn't considered how to put the lamppost back. They hadn't considered any of this—only that the construct was in danger. R-0 had lost focus on the mission. They had been . . . impulsive.

"What happened at the warehouse?" R-0 asked.

"Not sure I should be telling you." Jorgunn moved some broken stone from the edge of the street to cover the sharp remnants. "You'll just have to bring that with us. I'll get some technomancers sent out here to fix it."

R-0 nodded. They held the lamppost at their side, carefully ensuring it didn't hit anything ahead of them or behind them as they walked back to the palace.

"What will happen to the organics?" R-0 asked.

"You've got a lot of questions."

"Yes sir." They had countless questions, and most of the answers they received just gave them more to question. Especially when their questions remained unanswered.

Jorgunn escorted R-0 back to the palace, only breaking the silence once they were outside one of the maintenance rooms.

"There's only one question I'd be worried about if I were you," Jorgunn said. "What's going to happen to *you* now?"

"Is something scheduled?"

"No, but you royally pissed Eren off. And if there's one thing about my sister, she doesn't let things go easily." Jorgunn opened the door to the maintenance room and ushered R-0 inside. "Now wait here. Someone will come get you soon."

CHAPTER 7

Punishment.

R-0 wasn't sure what Eren meant when she'd said they would be punished. But alone in the dark maintenance room, the possibilities filled their mind.

Despite following her orders, R-0 had failed to prove Eren could still rely on them. She had been right about R-0 acting differently. Before the star—*the corruption*—R-0 would have never relocated the lamppost or confronted the organics. Memories of previous guard shifts flashed through their mind. Even when chaos had erupted around them, they'd remained motionless and unaffected unless it directly impacted their objective.

Could they ever be like that again? A chill ran across R-0's plates, cold creeping in despite the raging fire in their chest.

"Got another one." The doors to the maintenance room peeked open, letting in light from the hallway. One of the younger guards from the mission stood in the hall, the injured construct leaning on his arm. He shoved the construct into the room, dropping them to the floor, then slammed the door closed.

Although the room was dark, light from underneath the door illuminated the silhouette of the construct. R-0 knelt next to them. "What—"

The construct held one finger to their mouth—a motion organics frequently used—then pointed at the door. The construct tilted their head closer, and R-0 listened as well.

"Eren said she's waiting 'til morning to report to the council." The guards' muffled conversation continued outside the door. "Everyone is already asleep for the night."

"Think there's a chance we might get to join them?"

"Shalloth willing, maybe, but I doubt we'll be sleeping anytime soon. The warehouse was empty, but it was in use recently. Eren's ordered the entire sector be cleared building by building."

The guard at the door groaned. "And she's sure we can't just let the constructs do it?"

"At this rate, I'm not sure the constructs will ever get reinstated."

"Well, then I hope she has the gold lying around to hire another hundred guards. Wiles said if he had to work one more triple, he'd quit. I don't see what the big deal is anyway. R-0 did everything Jorgunn said when they were brought in, and they're still waiting inside."

"You should have seen them out there." His voice shifted to a harsh whisper. "Sent a man flying through a wall and almost killed him. Injured a few more. All with just a lamppost."

The guard gulped. "Tell Eren to hurry it up, alright?"

"How about I stay here, and *you* go tell her that?" His question was met with silence, and a light chuckle followed. "That's what I thought."

As the guard's footsteps faded into the distance, the construct stirred. They put their hands beneath them, trying to push themself up off the ground, but their joints faltered. They fell back to the floor with a clatter, their face pressing into the stone.

"Would you like assistance?" R-0 offered them a hand. Considering the extent of the damage, the construct would likely need more than just a hand to assist them, but R-0 had seen organics use the gesture to indicate a willingness to help and tried to mimic it.

The construct paused and looked at R-0. Slowly, they nodded, and the light on their shoulder plate blipped green. Even in the mines, the ability to communicate yes and no was useful. The light shed across their plates, highlighting text engraved on the nape of their neck: M-118.

R-0 easily lifted them into a sitting position. Once they were steady, R-0 stepped back. Most constructs used a shortened version of their designation—it was easier and rarely problematic. In R-0's case, they were the first unit in the royal line, so R-0 was both their full designation and simple to use.

"M-1. Is that your designation?" R-0 asked.

Where green had shone before, a red light flickered on the construct's shoulder.

"M-118?"

The construct nodded. They gently lifted their hand to their shoulder and pressed against the plate. A small circular section receded, and an empty vial next to it filled with golden flame. Light from the fire caught on reflective surfaces in the glass, amplifying and projecting it around the room. The light confirmed R-0's initial impression that it was a maintenance room, but unlike the room the king had brought them to, there were significantly less supplies and a thin coating of dust covered some of the less used tools and parts.

R-0 could also see the extent of M-118's damage. It was no surprise they hadn't been able to stand on their own. Both leg joints had fraying wires, and the gears between the plates on their left leg had snapped.

Blinking lights from M-118's chest drew R-0's attention away from their injuries. They pointed at a curved wire tool on the wall, their lights flickering between red and green. Not a yes, not a no. Not an answer, but . . . a question.

"Do you need that?"

Green light pulsed.

As R-0 retrieved the first tool, M-118's lights flickered, then they pointed to a set of narrow metal tubes. The process repeated until M-118 had enough tools to fill a toolbox and a pile of spare parts surrounding them. They gestured for R-0 to sit next to them, and R-0 obliged.

M-118 held the tools with the same precision R-0 had seen among the technomancers. They didn't hesitate to remove their own plates and set to work on the internal mechanisms within, rebinding fraying wires and replacing pieces of mangled metal.

"Are you authorized to use these parts?" R-0 asked.

M-118's light turned green. They paused for a moment, then it turned red. Then green again.

What was that supposed to mean? R-0 didn't have much experience interacting with other constructs. Before the star entered their chest, there was never a need. They had only interacted with the organics that gave them their orders, delivering guard reports and answering questions when asked.

M-118 removed their damaged leg from the knee down and set to work on the inside, checking each part with meticulous care and removing anything damaged. The gears in their leg slowed as they worked, but their remaining gears were in overdrive, filling the air with a soft hum.

R-0 should have been content to sit in the silence. They had no orders except to wait, but . . . they weren't. Their fingers fidgeted at their side, circling repeatedly even as R-0 attempted to be still. Silence was inefficient, and there was no value to it. They had no task to be jeopardized by distractions. Was this why the organics filled silence with conversation?

"Did a star corrupt your flame?" R-0 asked.

Red flashed. M-118's face plates scrunched together, and their still functioning gears jittered against each other. They pointed to the glowing vial on their shoulder, then their light turned green.

"That is your flame?" R-0 asked.

Green.

R-0 wasn't sure why M-118's initial response was mixed, but at their confirmation, R-0 peered closer at the glowing vial illuminating the room. It matched the golden hue of R-0's flame, but theirs never left their chest. They'd never imagined it could be used for something beyond their individual function. But . . . fire and magic had fueled technology for years. Why would a construct's flame be any different?

A gear slipped through M-118's fingers as they tried to hold it with one finger and use their other fingers to thread wires and screws back into place.

"Do you need help?" R-0 asked.

M-118 considered for a tick, then nodded.

R-0 sat next to them and retrieved the gear from the floor. M-118 grabbed R-0's hands without hesitation, positioning R-0 at the right angles and forcing their fingers open and closed to hold different objects. M-118 treated R-0 like any of their other tools, delicate and with care, but without regard for anything other than the task in front of them.

Waiting was easier with M-118. They needed help, and R-0 could provide it. It was simple and gave their wandering thoughts something to focus on as they waited for Eren to give her report to the council.

When the repairs were finished, M-118 rose shakily to their feet. R-0 stood beside them. They took one cautious step forward, then another. After a third successful step, their pace quickened. They ran a lap around the tables, only a slight limp remaining from the previous damage. Their chest plate was still mangled, but it didn't impede their movement.

M-118 ran straight into R-0. Their arms reached up and wrapped around R-0's neck, and the light on their shoulder blinked green rapidly, brightening with each pulse.

Even though they stood still, their flame blazed to life beneath their plates. Its heat spread through their body, and R-0 stiffened. Was this a side effect of the corruption? Their flame's reaction was unexpected and unexplainable, but it didn't seem bad. It actually felt . . . pleasant.

R-0 searched for words to verbalize their flurry of questions, but before they could, M-118 stepped back, their gears jittering and their flame brightening in time with the rapidly blinking lights across their shoulders. It was a stark contrast to the terrified trembles that racked them when R-0 had first encountered them. They crossed the room to one of the windows, gesturing for R-0 to follow, then began running their hands along the sill.

"What are you doing?" R-0 asked.

M-118 pointed first at their own chest, then at R-0's, and finally at the window.

R-0 tried to guess what the construct meant—something they could confirm with either a yes or no answer. But they weren't sure. As far as R-0 could tell, there was nothing noteworthy about the window.

A cool breeze blew through the room as M-118 unlatched the window and pushed it open, disturbing the dust on the windowsill. It may have been used in the past, but not since the room was repurposed into a maintenance room. After the creation of the constructs, the palace had undergone renovations. Various rooms scattered throughout the palace and an entire section in the lower floor were emptied and redesigned to house and maintain the influx of constructs on staff.

"What are you doing with the window?" R-0 asked.

M-118's light flickered red. They pointed at the window again, more forcefully this time.

R-0 peered out, searching for anything M-118 could be pointing at, but the palace grounds were quiet. A pair of guards walked their nightly rotations, and a light shone from one of the smaller houses on the grounds, but both were routine occurrences. There was nothing amiss on the palace grounds.

"There's nothing out there," R-0 said.

M-118's lights remained off. They ran their fingers across their arm, and a compartment on their forearm popped open. Within it was a rolled-up sheet of paper. They held it out to R-0.

"What's this?" R-0 gently unrolled the paper.

It was a map of Graywal and some of the surrounding areas in Haiden. The palace was near the coast in the top right corner, and the rest of the districts were divided by black dotted lines. Most of the map was standard, but two *X*'s were marked in the harpy district. A third area in the dragon district was messily circled. It was close to the coast, and as far as R-0 could tell, there was nothing notable in the circle except for a dockyard used by fishing vessels.

M-118 again pointed at the two of them, then out the window, and finally at the circled docks on the map.

"You're trying to go there?"

Green.

"Why?"

M-118's lights flickered in a combination of red and green R-0 couldn't make sense of. They pulled on R-0's arm and began climbing out the window.

"Wait." R-0 held on to their hand, pulling them back into the room. "You're not authorized to leave." Even if they were, it made far more sense to use the door than fall out of the window.

M-118's light flickered red. They tried to pull their arm out of R-0's grip, but R-0 held tight. Like most constructs, M-118 was stronger than the average organic but not strong enough to overcome the strength of a royal construct.

"You are supposed to wait here," R-0 explained.

Smoke hissed out from between M-118's face plates. They struggled against R-0's grip, the light on their shoulder pulsating a brighter and brighter red with each iteration. M-118 slammed their fist into R-0's chest, then pointed out the window once more.

"When Eren returns, you can ask her," R-0 said. She would be returning for them soon, and M-118 could request to leave then. Eren could arrange a much more sensible transport than climbing out of a second-story window.

M-118's lights remained devoid of activity, and they turned away from R-0, hiding their expression.

While restraining M-118, they used their other hand to close and latch the window. Smoke still huffed from the space between M-118's plates, but they had stopped struggling. When R-0 let go, they prepared to restrain M-118 once more, but the construct returned to the workstation and began putting the tools away.

Perhaps M-118 was simply trying to return home. But there was no ambiguity to the orders Jorgunn had given them: wait here. Eren would retrieve R-0 and M-118 soon. She wouldn't be able to find them if they wandered off, and that would only make her more concerned about the constructs' functionality.

"They should come in the morning," R-0 said, repeating Jorgunn's words as much to themself as to M-118. "You shouldn't have to wait long."

M-118 nodded. For a moment, their lights remained off, but then they lit up green.

It didn't take long for them to put away the remaining tools. R-0 tried to continue their conversation, but M-118 leaned against the wall, closing their eyes. If they were an organic, R-0 would have thought they were sleeping. But constructs didn't need rest, so it seemed unnecessary. R-0 tried asking, but M-118 didn't respond.

Leaving R-0 alone with their thoughts once again.

CHAPTER 8

The moon was hardly a sliver in the sky, so small the organics likely wouldn't be able to see it at all, but R-0 watched it creep toward the horizon until it was replaced with the sun's morning rays. They spent hours more silently waiting before King Hadrian retrieved them, a worried look in his eyes and urgency in his steps. R-0 stopped on the threshold, looking back into the maintenance room.

"Will M-118 be joining us?" R-0 asked.

King Hadrian shook his head. "Their owner has been contacted, and they'll remain here for questioning until she comes to pick them up."

R-0 had been right to stop them from leaving through the window last night. It would be simpler—and cause far less concern—for them to be escorted home. R-0 lifted their hand, mimicking the way they'd seen organics say goodbye. M-118's lights blinked green in response, and R-0 left them behind.

As King Hadrian led them through the palace, he requested R-0's report on the warehouse infiltration. When R-0 finished, King Hadrian's voice lowered to a whisper. "So you didn't disobey? You followed your orders?"

"Yes sir."

"You're sure?"

R-0 flashed through the memories to confirm. "Yes sir."

"When we enter the council chambers, remain silent unless someone directly asks you a question," King Hadrian said. "Let me do the talking, okay?"

R-0's mind whirred. They hadn't broken any laws. They'd followed Eren's orders and asked that the organics release the construct, a reasonable request from a royal guard. Why was King Hadrian acting so strange?

"R-0." King Hadrian's voice was normally soft when addressing R-0, but now it was stern. "Do you understand your orders?"

Silence. That was what was expected of R-0. It had been their default state for years. It should have been simple, but already their flame stirred with questions they couldn't ask. What had Eren told the council? What did King Hadrian intend to say? What would happen to M-118?

Were they going to be punished?

But those answers weren't necessary to keep King Hadrian safe, so R-0 nodded. "Yes sir."

King Hadrian motioned for the guards to open the doors. He held his head high, looking past the council members who stared at him as he entered. As he took his spot at the head of the table, R-0 positioned themself beside him.

R-0's swords were laying across the table, the lamppost next to them. Someone had retrieved its detached gray stone. Magic no longer swirled through it, making it nothing more than a dull rock.

"Why are they not in chains?" Eren asked.

The king turned and addressed the rest of the council, his voice steady and sure. "They're not in chains because they haven't been convicted of a crime."

"As the captain of the guard, I'm in charge of your safety—the safety of everyone here. And—"

"And with impressive accolades such as your own, I'm sure I'm perfectly safe in your presence with"—King Hadrian made a show of counting each of the guards standing around the perimeter of the room—"over a dozen reinforcements. R-0 is the final witness. Let's proceed."

Normally witnesses spoke for themself, but King Hadrian recounted R-0's story instead. When he finished, he looked at R-0. "R-0, is that accurate?"

He'd left out a few details. Rather than listing all of their interactions with the people in the street, King Hadrian simplified it to, "R-0 attempted to retrieve the missing construct." Despite both accounts being true, the council reacted to King Hadrian's words much better than the guard in the hallway had reacted to being told R-0 sent a man flying through a wall.

But there was nothing incorrect about what he'd said, so R-0 nodded. "Yes sir."

"Good." King Hadrian turned to face the rest of the council as he continued, "While this was not the expected or desired outcome, I see no fault in R-0's actions."

"They attacked innocents!" Eren's voice rose.

But the organics were far from innocent. They had attacked M-118, ignored a guard's request, and accessed the managrid's magic without authorization.

Despite Eren's rising emotions, King Hadrian's voice remained steady. He leaned farther back in his chair. "R-0 requested that civilians comply with an investigation of a missing construct, then acted in self-defense when they were attacked. Any reasonable guard would have done the same in their position."

"Attacking our people is not how any of our guards should behave. This is exactly what I was afraid of! The constructs can no longer be trusted to follow our orders. Worse, they're a danger to our people."

"And what proof do we have of the alleged attack?"

"I interviewed the civilians personally."

"So we have the word of some civilians against one of our own royal guards?"

Eren stomped over to her seat at the council table, her sword clanging against the metal plates of her armor with each step. Instead of sitting, she gripped each side like it was a prisoner being taken for transport. "The constructs—"

"This is not about the constructs," King Hadrian interrupted. "This is about a single construct—R-0. Have there been any recorded instances of R-0 lying?"

R-0's gears stuttered. Lying? It would be useless. Conveying accurate information was important for others to make informed decisions.

"No sir." Eren's knuckles turned white as her grip on the chair tightened. Her lips barely moved as she forced out the words.

"And are the civilians here for us to interrogate them further?" King Hadrian asked.

"No sir."

"Why is that? Did you not request they return to the palace for questioning?"

"I offered them healing and asked them to come, but they didn't want to. They didn't feel safe here after what happened, and I couldn't blame them."

"So not only did they not cooperate with your investigation, they refused free medical attention? If their wounds were as serious as you say, that's strange behavior for innocent civilians."

Eren was silent.

"I don't doubt you, Eren. But how can I trust the word of men unwilling to stand before me?" King Hadrian turned to the rest of the council. "How can any of you?"

"There's still the issue of R-0 disobeying orders."

"Jorgunn," King Hadrian said.

"Sir." Jorgunn stepped forward out of the line of guards. He gave a slight smile to R-0, and R-0 shifted their plates, trying to mimic the expression. But their plates only grated together, earning them a glare from Eren.

"Can you share with us what Eren's exact orders were?" King Hadrian asked.

Jorgunn glanced at Eren, and any semblance of a smile vanished. He returned his attention to the king. "Eren ordered R-0 to stay out of our way and remain by the lamppost."

"And when you returned, was R-0 still by it?" King Hadrian gestured to the broken lamppost on the table.

"By a technicality, yes."

"And were they in your way?"

"No." Jorgunn scuffed his feet against the floor. "I suppose not."

"Thank you, Jorgunn," King Hadrian said. "That's all I needed to hear. Does the council have any further questions?"

Jeza shuffled the papers in front of her, drawing the eyes of the rest of the council. "While I am still concerned about what the constructs are doing, I think this specific case is clear." Jeza smirked at Eren. "Perhaps you need to work on your specificity."

"You can't just ignore this." Eren stepped away from the table. Her hand went to her sword, but instead of grabbing at the hilt, her thumb flicked at the stone in the pommel and rested at her side. "I've worked alongside the constructs—*fought* alongside the constructs for years. I've seen what they're capable of. They were one of our greatest assets, and now . . . they could be our most dangerous enemy."

R-0 knew they shouldn't react to another's anger until they were sure it was going to escalate to violence. After the previous council meeting, King Hadrian had explained how unnecessary reactions could encourage innocent anger to escalate. They didn't want a catastrophe. Even though Eren's hand was close to her weapon, she didn't seem ready to draw it. If anything, her motion more closely resembled R-0 tapping at their side to maintain their focus than a soldier preparing for battle.

Still, they wished for their swords so they could more efficiently protect the king if emotion escalated to action. But . . . their gaze slid to the weapons lying across the table. Their swords *and* the lamppost were within reach if the situation demanded it.

"Eren is right," Robin said. At his side, Gretta nodded. "Even if it was an oversight, it was a dangerous one. If that had been one of our people on guard instead of a construct, the civilians wouldn't have been injured. I know R-0 has been your guard for years, but things are changing. You can't ignore this."

"I won't," King Hadrian said. "From now on, R-0 will remain by my side. I will ensure their behavior meets our standards and take full responsibility for their actions."

"My king." Jeza's whisper was easy for R-0 to overhear. "Are you sure that's wise?"

"I'm sure." King Hadrian stood from his chair at the head of the table. "And I would advise each of you to do the same and reinstate the constructs on your staff. You fear what the constructs will become, no longer bound to me. You fear what that means for our kingdom, for our future. And no matter how you may try to keep it from me, I know you fear I am not the one to lead us through these troubles. But I'm not afraid. I will solve the mystery of the missing constructs, restore order to Graywal, and with R-0 under my watch, prove the constructs can still perform the functions we need."

R-0's flame flickered. It wasn't King Hadrian's responsibility to protect R-0. Their roles should have been reversed. But because of R-0's actions—because of the corruption—King Hadrian was forced to stand up for them.

It was wrong. R-0 should have been the one protecting him.

"And if you can't?" Robin asked.

"I will." King Hadrian walked to the door, motioning for R-0 to follow him. "Unless there are any objections, I rule this trial complete. R-0 has been found not guilty and will return to their previous duties."

Silence settled over the room. Even Eren only responded with angry, wordless huffs.

"R-0, retrieve your weapons."

R-0 approached the table. Although their swords were closer to the other council members' seats, they stopped behind King Hadrian's empty chair, leaning forward to retrieve both swords. For a moment, they considered taking the lamppost as well. But Jorgunn had said he would have it fixed, so they left the lamppost, sheathing their blades and stepping away.

Their flame strengthened, the blaze growing and popping so loud even the organics could hear it through R-0's thick chest plate. With their weapons back where they belonged, some of the worry churning in R-0 faded. They returned to King Hadrian's side.

King Hadrian waltzed out of the room, R-0 at his heels. "Council adjourned."

CHAPTER 9

Some of the organic guards started to follow King Hadrian and R-0 down the hall, but King Hadrian waved them away. They hesitated, but after a stern look from the king, they left.

"You are not supposed to be without organic guards," R-0 said. Eren had made that clear to R-0 many, many times over the past few cycles. Still, R-0 stayed at King Hadrian's side, scanning the hallway for threats as they walked.

"Am I safe with you?" King Hadrian asked.

"Yes sir."

"Then to hell with what Eren says." King Hadrian's hands trembled at his side. A deep breath steadied him, but deep lines still coated his forehead. "To hell with the entire council."

"Is something wrong?" R-0 asked.

"With everything going on with the council . . ." King Hadrian looked over his shoulder as he spoke, his voice a quiet whisper only R-0 could hear. "I'm absolutely terrified."

R-0 frowned. King Hadrian had explicitly stated he was *not* afraid. "But you said—"

"I told the council what they needed to hear." King Hadrian sighed. "After what my mother did, there was never any chance that they'd like me. And now, without control of the constructs . . . they don't have to fear me. So I must ensure, if nothing else, they believe in me."

"You are their king."

"A fact that means significantly more to you than it does to them. If they had their way, Robin would have been crowned king, and they never would have had to deal with me."

When he was alone with R-0, King Hadrian acted differently. His words were less forced. His expressions were looser. Even his body seemed less tense. R-0 flickered through their memories. This wasn't the first time King Hadrian had expressed frustration with the council's behavior. When he was younger, he'd complained that the meetings were boring and no one listened to him. As he aged, the complaints changed. They wanted him to do things he didn't agree with. Their expectations were too high. In the past, R-0 had remained silent, ignoring his complaints since they didn't relate to their directive or require a response. But this time . . .

R-0 couldn't look away from King Hadrian's turned down lips and the furrowed lines on his face. They were . . . concerned.

"If they do not wish for you to be king, then why did they crown you?" R-0 had never questioned it before—it wasn't necessary to know *why* he was king. But now, all of King Hadrian's complaints came rushing back. The council was a concern R-0 wanted to understand.

King Hadrian paused, turning his gaze to R-0. "Are you questioning my right to the crown?"

"No sir."

"Then why are you asking?"

"Curiosity." R-0 still couldn't name most of the oddities and changes that had occurred since the corruption, but curiosity was one they were growing more and more familiar with. They had questions about everything. They wanted to understand. "The council is confusing."

"That's an understatement," King Hadrian said. "I'm sorry. I'm just . . . stressed. The council has me stressed." He sighed as he continued walking. "When our ancestors first settled in Haiden, they elected a queen to unite the clans. That honor was supposed to then cycle through the clans, and it has for hundreds of years. When my mother created the constructs, she told the council they were bound to the crown, no matter which clan held the throne. It was the only way anyone would agree to their construction. Entire armies at our command? It was too tempting an offer to pass up, despite the risks. It was only after she passed—and the council couldn't control the constructs—that they learned she'd lied. The constructs only responded to my mother's bloodline—they only responded to me."

Even though it was R-0's history, it felt as distant as any other story King Hadrian had told them. Years ago, they had stood by King Hadrian, ignoring the commands of the council. But their memories of before the incident with the stars were like the tapestries on the castle walls—made by someone else. R-0 could see them, but it didn't feel like they had experienced that history for themself.

"The constructs have been my strength, but as long as questions remain about their loyalty and ability to function, they're a weakness the council can exploit. Which is why we have to stay ahead of them."

"How?" R-0 asked.

"We'll start with the construct you found." King Hadrian shuffled through the stack of papers in his hands.

"M-118," R-0 said.

"Yes, that's their designation. Witnesses confirmed they were the construct seen with Ryder earlier at the warehouse. Here—" King Hadrian handed a sheet of paper to R-0. "It looks like they worked in the mines. Their owner is a dragon-scaled woman in the elemental district. If we can figure out what they were doing in that warehouse, it might lead us to more of the missing constructs, and we can figure out what they're plotting."

R-0 looked over the forms, confirming King Hadrian's words. Something didn't make sense. If M-118 was trying to go home . . . why were they pointing out the docks? It was nowhere near the elemental district.

R-0 read over the remaining papers while they walked. M-118 had started their life working in the mines at the base of the Serenading Mountains, but when the mine shut down, the mining units were sold to the highest bidders and dispersed throughout the city. Since then, M-118 had worked with a blacksmith from Clan Murdha, primarily forging armor for the war in Faylviln.

When they arrived at the maintenance room, the guard tucked his fist against his opposite shoulder and bowed in respect to the king, then opened the door. But the room was empty. M-118 was gone along with about a dozen tools.

"Where are they?" King Hadrian yanked the door, checking behind it. "Where's the construct?"

The guard at the door was wide-eyed. He paced the room, stopping at the open window. "S-sir, the window . . ."

"No, no, no," King Hadrian muttered.

"Do you think they jumped?" the guard asked.

King Hadrian shook his head. "It's too high of a fall."

Outside, holes pierced the grout along the wall. The size of the holes perfectly matched the head of one of the missing screwdrivers. R-0 ran their fingers along the wall, dipping into small divots in the icy stone. Frost brushed off with ease, not yet refrozen into the structure.

"They climbed," R-0 said, pointing out the holes. R-0 had told M-118 to wait. Why hadn't they listened?

King Hadrian studied the wall for a second before stepping back. "Why was the prisoner left unattended?"

"C-constructs have always been left alone in maintenance and storage rooms," the guard said. "W-we didn't think about the windows. It's never been a problem before."

"The constructs have never been prisoners before either." King Hadrian balled his hands into fists. "Go." He pointed to the door. "Report this to Eren. Tell her I want the palace grounds searched. We need to find that construct."

R-0 hesitated. If M-118 had gone to the docks, searching the palace grounds was unlikely to be helpful. They started to speak up but remembered their conversation with Eren. Questioning the king's orders wouldn't prove their functionality.

Once the guard left, King Hadrian plopped down in a chair. Some of M-118's damaged parts were still on the table, and he picked up a gear, spinning it on its teeth before letting it clatter back on the table. "I thought this warehouse was going to give us answers. Not more questions and problems."

"What did Eren find at the warehouse?" R-0 asked.

"Nothing. Whoever was there somehow bypassed the perimeter Eren set up. By the time they got in, the place was empty. No constructs. No Ryder. Nothing but scrap parts."

"Perhaps it was the wrong building?" Many warehouses looked similar.

"Neighbors confirmed that they'd seen constructs going in, and it had been in use recently." King Hadrian shook his head. "Come on, there's nothing we can do until the construct is found."

King Hadrian exited the maintenance room, but R-0 hesitated. If the guards hadn't found anything at the warehouse, M-118 was their only clue to finding where the missing constructs were. It had taken cycles for them to find this lead—how many more would it take before they had another opportunity like this?

They should listen to King Hadrian's orders, but . . . he had requested R-0's assistance to find the missing constructs. R-0 didn't need the guards to search the palace grounds or to wait for reports—M-118 had shown R-0 the map. King Hadrian didn't have all the information.

R-0 tried to speak, but even as their plates moved, their flame sputtered in their chest and no sound came out. They didn't know what words to use or how to say them. This wasn't like the thousands of questions they'd answered during past reports. It wasn't a curiosity begging to be heard. Infinite possibilities teetered on the edge of their plates, but not a single sound formed.

"R-0?" King Hadrian asked. "Did you hear me?"

"Yes sir," R-0 said. Those words were easier. Routine.

"Then why aren't you coming?"

"There *is* something that can be done now." R-0's words were still slow and forced, but answering the king, their voice didn't fail them.

"What's that?"

"You could visit M-118."

"That would be great if we knew where they were."

"They're heading to the docks in the dragon district."

"How do you know that?" King Hadrian asked.

Their conversation fell into a rhythm. King Hadrian asked more questions, and R-0 answered until they had told him about their encounter with M-118 and their hidden map. King Hadrian frowned when R-0 talked about the red *X*'s over the warehouse and the palace, but the sparkle returned to his eyes when R-0 reported where M-118 was headed.

"Wait." King Hadrian's brow furrowed. "You *knew* they were trying to leave?"

"Once they were told leaving was not an option, they stopped."

"R-0." King Hadrian dropped his head into his hands, rubbing his forehead.

"Yes sir?"

"Just—nevermind." He lifted his head back up. "If I get you a map, can you show me where in the dragon district they were headed?"

R-0 nodded.

"Then you're right." King Hadrian started down the hallway, motioning for R-0 to follow. "Our investigation is just beginning. Let's head to the docks."

CHAPTER 10

The more time R-0 spent at King Hadrian's side, the more acclimated they grew to the arguments. Disagreements filled the king's schedule like the crackling of fire filled R-0's chest. Eren's office was no exception. Visiting Eren was supposed to be a short detour to acquire additional guards before venturing into the city. Instead, it had brought their investigation to a standstill before it ever properly began.

"You can't stop me from going into the city." King Hadrian sat across from Eren, his gaze unwavering.

Eren leaned against her desk. It was larger than most, with enough space for nearly eight organics to comfortably sit around it, and a similar number of chairs around the edges of the room. An untouched breakfast plate had been pushed to the side, clearing the space between her and the king. She propped her elbows beneath her chin with a sigh. "You and the council agreed—no one leaves the palace."

"I've visited my city countless times, and it's never been a problem."

"We've never had a problem like this before either." As she said *this*, she stared at R-0.

R-0 squirmed in place, struggling to stay still. All Eren did was look at them, but she might as well have smothered R-0's flame the way her gaze made their fire fold in on itself and shrink to the corners of their chest.

"R-0 isn't a threat to me," King Hadrian said.

"Maybe R-0 isn't, and maybe not to you." Eren sighed. "But dozens of constructs are unaccounted for and doing Shalloth knows what. The managrid has had two more blackouts. I can send a group of guards to investigate this lead, but that's all the resources I have."

Before the incident, the managrid fluctuations would have limited R-0. They would have relied on tinder and kindling to fuel their fire in its absence. But the golden flame had magic of its own. It didn't need the managrid, kindling, or anything else to provide strength.

"The sooner we get this resolved, the sooner we can get the rest of the constructs back to work. The managrid is just understaffed."

"What if it's not just that?" Eren asked. "What if it's something worse?"

R-0 frowned. Many of King Hadrian's discussions were surrounded by a sense of impending doom. People were concerned about the future, but no one could explain what they were afraid of. They continually made grand what-if statements, but there were no logical bounds and an infinite number of possible things that could go wrong . . . and little evidence to support the few possibilities everyone continued to worry about.

"Like what?" King Hadrian asked.

"I don't know!" Eren threw her arms in the air. "If I knew, I wouldn't be so stressed because I could make a plan. But right now, all I know is that everything we ever thought we knew about the constructs is a lie. If we don't know what they want, then we can't be prepared. They're capable fighters. Stronger than us. They don't feel pain. And if they catch us unaware . . ."

"We're saying the same things, Eren. Look." King Hadrian pushed a sheet of paper across the table. "Not only was M-118 heading here, but multiple unattended constructs have been reported in the area. We can get the information we need so the constructs don't catch us unaware."

"I already told you I'll send guards to investigate."

"There's a better chance of them talking if another construct is there. Or maybe they'll see something the rest of us wouldn't. It would explain why we haven't been able to find them."

"Then send R-0!"

"They're not going anywhere without me."

After what had happened yesterday, the king didn't have a choice. Still, R-0 was relieved. With King Hadrian, they could be helpful. They could protect him and help with the investigation instead of standing at irrelevant street corners.

"Without the constructs, my guard force has been cut in half. Even with everyone running doubles, I don't have enough people to do the bare minimum. Do you know how many resources it takes to man a trip for you into the city?"

In official visits, King Hadrian usually had at least two royal constructs, as well as twice the guards he kept nearby while in the palace. More often than not, it was R-0 and R-1. Even if Eren didn't have organic guards, R-1 and the rest of the royal constructs were available.

R-0 paused. While they had returned to their duties with King Hadrian, the rest of the constructs remained in the storage rooms. Their chest suddenly felt too small to house their gurgling flame.

"What about R-1?" R-0's fingers fidgeted at their side, easing some of the corruption.

"No," King Hadrian said. "Not the royal constructs."

Eren sighed. "At least we can agree on something."

"But I do want to get the constructs back on your service. The guards and the maintenance crews both need the support, and the constructs can offer it. We'll start slow, but we will get them reintegrated."

The table shook as Eren dropped both her elbows onto it, then let her head drop fall into her hands. "And now you're talking crazy again."

"I'll convince the rest of the council—"

"Robin will never go for your reintegration plans. Neither will Gretta or Jeza."

"Let me worry about them. You worry about how you're going to get me and R-0 into the city." King Hadrian sat back in his chair. "There are already guards assigned to me. I'll bring R-0 instead of reinforcements, so it won't change a thing."

"And who will get blamed if something happens to you?" Eren asked. "If you're gone, the council will have to answer for it."

"He will be protected," R-0 said. They had accompanied King Hadrian into the city before. Why would this be any different? But even as they said it, Eren's worries crept into R-0's mind, becoming their own. What if the city *was* too dangerous for R-0 to protect the king?

"See?" King Hadrian asked. "I have a guard. We have no idea what our people outside these walls truly believe because we're all cooped up here. If I were them, I'd think my king doesn't care about me and is only focused on his own safety. I need to be out there. We need their support."

"And I need to make sure you're safe, Sylas." Eren's hand shifted to the hilt of her sword, her thumb flicking at the gem. "I told the entire council that no one leaves the palace. *No one.* And I meant that."

"I am your king!" King Hadrian's voice rose.

R-0's flame shrank into the corner of their chest. They'd witnessed the king's temper countless times before the incident, but it had never made them feel like this. Even though they weren't the king's target, R-0 felt . . . uncomfortable.

"Yes, you are," Eren said. "But the guards are my people, and I'm responsible for your safety. We've worked together successfully since you were crowned. Do you really want to throw that all away over a trip to the city?"

King Hadrian scowled. He slammed down the paper in his hand and leaned back in his chair. He stayed silent for a minute, then stood. "I'm going to my chambers for the day."

"King Hadrian—" Eren began.

"No one bothers me until morning. That's an order."

"Fine." Eren motioned to the guards, who began clearing the tables.

Outside, sunlight streamed in through the window. Orange and red tones were mixed with the bright rays, a sign of the setting sun. It was far too early in the day for the king to retire, but R-0 didn't question it. Eren may have been willing to tell the king what he could or couldn't do, but R-0 wasn't. As they arrived at the king's chambers, R-0 stood in their regular guard position outside the door.

"R-0, inside."

"Yes sir." R-0 followed King Hadrian into his room. The area was large enough to be divided into sections—a raised sleeping area to the right with a canopy bed and nightstand, a sitting area to the left, and a desk surrounded by cabinets and bookshelves on the far wall that served as a makeshift office. Although King Hadrian had an official office elsewhere in the palace, he often brought his work back here. A large window, taller than King Hadrian, was next to the desk, but heavy curtains and multiple layers of magical wards still separated them from the outside world.

The main area had two additional doors, one leading to a bathroom and the other to a closet that rivaled the size of staff rooms housing multiple organics. It was filled to the brim with rows of clothes—all organized by season—and an overflow of files that no longer fit in the storage around his desk.

King Hadrian pulled the curtains back. Despite the frost lining the edges of the pane, sunlight streamed into the room and reflected off his crown, creating narrow streaks of light across the floor that followed him as he paced. "How am I supposed to figure this out if they're too afraid to let me outside?"

"Why do you listen to them?" R-0 asked.

"I don't have a choice."

"You're the king. They're supposed to listen to you."

King Hadrian shook his head. He sat on the edge of the bed, letting his hair fall in a mess in front of his eyes as he leaned forward. "Yeah, *supposed* to."

"You give the orders. You do not need their permission to act."

"I could force Eren's hand but . . . It's not that simple."

"Is it not?" R-0 asked.

King Hadrian sat up. "Maybe it is."

"Is it?" R-0 asked. "Or is it not?"

King Hadrian was confusing. Every time R-0 thought they were closing in on answers, more questions surprised them instead.

"R-0, would you like to go into the city?"

The city. R-0 stared out the window at the houses and buildings below. What if Eren was right about the dangers it held? The palace had wards to protect against magical attacks. The wards only kept the building from being manipulated—once inside, mages could still cast other types of magic—but it meant R-0 could rely on potential enemies having to use conventional entrances where guards were posted instead of blasting through the walls in a surprise attack. Potential assailants would have layers of defenses to bypass, and the king could summon reinforcements with ease. Outside the castle, these protections didn't exist. King Hadrian would have no guards except for R-0.

"Eren said the city was dangerous."

"And you said that I'm in charge, not her. And that I am safe with you"

"Yes sir."

"So let's go." King Hadrian pushed the blinds open. "We'll see for ourselves what's going on with the missing constructs, and I can see how my people are doing with their constructs for myself and reassure them."

R-0 stepped toward the door, but before they opened it, King Hadrian interrupted.

"Wait."

R-0 paused.

"We're not going out that way."

There was only one door in and out of the king's room. The only other opening was . . . the window.

King Hadrian pushed the blinds back even farther and unlatched the window, letting in a cool breeze. "We'll wait until it's dark, then go out this way."

King Hadrian stepped into his closet and reemerged after exchanging his robes for a plain tunic that draped over equally plain pants. A dark coat lined with thick, warm fur wrapped around his shoulders. The fabric was of the highest quality and tailored to fit. He ran his fingers through his hair, ruffling it until the neat, slicked back pieces fell over his forehead and framed his eyes.

He opened his dresser drawer and moved the clothes aside, revealing a velvet pouch. A twinkling chime sounded from within as he tilted the bag until a small orb rolled into his palm. It was hard to look at. The colors shifted, and even the size seemed nebulous. The harder R-0 tried to focus, the more their vision blurred, preventing them from discerning the orb's true nature. Before R-0 could voice their concerns, King Hadrian lifted it to his face and rolled it across his skin. When he pulled the orb away, its colors had faded to a dull gray.

"What do you think?" King Hadrian tossed the bag and the orb back into the drawer, covering them back up before turning to R-0. The king's cheekbones sat lower on his face than normal, and his eyes blinked from amber to a deep shade of brown, like mud tracked in during a storm. Combined with the differences in his attire and the messy hairstyle, he looked like an entirely different person.

"You look . . . different." R-0 studied the new features, committing them to memory. More were the same than they had initially thought. The king's lips still twitched at the corners, hovering somewhere between a smile and indifference, and he held himself upright with the same confidence and authority. Despite being a different color, his eyes remained warm and inviting as they stared at R-0.

"Magic," King Hadrian said. "You'll need to change too. If you go out like that, it won't matter how much magic I use to disguise myself. We'll draw too much attention."

R-0 looked at themself. They didn't have any magic to change their coloring, so how could they disguise their gray metal plates?

They flickered through memories, analyzing their past for similar scenarios or anything that could help them. One memory stood out. When King Hadrian was young, R-0 had supervised him while he played in the gardens. The young king had asked R-0 to sit, and they had sat. Soon, every crack and crevice in their plates was filled with dirt, and the king began planting flowers. The technomancers had removed the debris afterward, but nature had left its mark, dulling their plates until they had received thorough maintenance and cleaning.

RISE OF THE FORGEHEARTS

R-0 went to the corner of King Hadrian's room where a potted plant sat. Careful not to disrupt the plant, they scooped out some dirt and dropped it on their arm. Some of it immediately slid onto the ground, and R-0 rubbed tiny circles on their arm, trying to secure it.

"What are you doing?" King Hadrian asked.

"This will turn the metal darker."

"R-0," King Hadrian chuckled. He took R-0's arm and wiped the dirt off. R-0's idea had worked—a patch on their plate had dulled. The king lifted the bottom of his shirt, cleaning off the last of the grime before stepping back. "Change your size."

Size modification was a feature unique to royal constructs but necessary given their bulky bodies. In their extended form, they barely fit through doorframes, but their condensed form was similar to a large organic. They would still be easily recognizable as one of the palace guards just . . . smaller.

But King Hadrian watched them expectantly, so they began to condense. Momentarily, the plates lifted, revealing the delicate wires, gears, and tubes within. They circled and stretched, separating R-0's limbs into two distinct sets of plates. One condensed inward, nestling around the breakable insides and providing an extra layer of protection, while the second formed an exterior shell similar to R-0's usual form. Their chest followed the same pattern, tightening around their flame.

Now the flame filled the entire space, flickering outside its container and grasping at the nearby wires. Their condensed body required less energy to operate, so a smaller fire had always been sufficient. But their corrupted flame struggled, trying to expand once more. The exterior plates settled back around it, concealing it from view and locking it in place. The fire in their chest crackled, but as R-0 slowly tested each limb, they were entirely functional.

"Much better." King Hadrian still had to reach up to rest a hand on their shoulder, but now, rather than towering above him, R-0 only stood a head taller.

"Are any other changes required?"

"Most people don't know anything about the royal constructs except their size. To them, you'll look the same as any other construct." King Hadrian pulled his hand away and surveyed them once more. "Let's get rid of one of these." He tapped the sheath on R-0's leg.

"A sword would be suspicious?"

"Two swords might. And the blade definitely would, so let's not draw it unless we have to."

R-0 looked at their blades. They had always fought with both, but they could easily adjust to fighting with one. But which sword should they keep?

The blades were identical, both sized the same and constructed with Levian steel. Darker steel adorned the handles. Neither had distinguishing features that made it more suitable for protecting the king.

"Which one should be left behind?" R-0 asked.

"Either one. It doesn't matter."

R-0 expected that to make their decision easier, but it made it harder. If it didn't matter, how could they choose? They were the same. Indistinguishable.

R-0 froze, staring between the two. It was an impossible decision.

"Keep the left one," King Hadrian said. "It suits you better."

R-0 began unscrewing the right sheath. Twelve screws later, they lifted it away from the notched plate and placed it on the dresser, sword still encased in the dull exterior.

The sun had started its descent toward the horizon but still shone bright in the sky. King Hadrian easily filled the time until nightfall, talking about his previous unsanctioned visits into the city. When the constructs were on guard, leaving was easy—they obeyed the king's orders no matter what Eren or any other superior had told them. And they would keep quiet about it. R-0 themself had let the king leave unattended multiple times.

It was an obvious security risk, but when R-0 asked why the king risked his safety to travel into the city alone, King Hadrian explained that interactions with his people were better without the fanfare of an official visit. People were more comfortable around him when he wasn't escorted by a dozen guards. He didn't want to be viewed as an out-of-reach idea. He was a person, just like them, someone they could talk to and confide in. It was a lesson his mother had instilled in him—the crown's power was only as great as the citizens who supported it.

While they waited, King Hadrian mused over which places they could visit: the bar, the bakeries, the shops. Most of the fishermen were likely out fishing. The weather was cooperating, and anyone with a boat would be a fool to not be out there—including Councilman Uxius, who King Hadrian said was not scheduled to return for a few more weeks, buying him time to sway the council. Councilman Uxius's absence was more useful than his presence. Given his clan's long-standing alliance with Robin and Clan Conradh, he rarely agreed with King Hadrian and typically made the king's life more difficult.

By the time the bright golden rays of the sun were replaced with a dull blue glow of managrid lights, R-0 had learned enough about the city to compile a long list of questions rivaled only by their rising excitement.

"Alright, I think it should be dark enough." King Hadrian peeked his head out the window. "The guards patrol every five minutes, so once they pass by, we have plenty of time to reach the outer wall."

R-0 reviewed the guard rotations in their mind. While it allowed them to leave, it also created an opportunity for enemies of the crown to enter. With the windows locked and warded and the sheer climb up multiple stories, it would be difficult to manage without someone noticing, but the vulnerability in the guard rotations still left R-0 uneasy. It posed a danger to the king. R-0 would have to remember to report this to Eren.

King Hadrian secured a rope to the curtain rod. When the guards below passed out of sight, he climbed outside. His feet landed firmly on the exterior wall of his room, and his hands trailed down the rope. He jumped back, sliding a few stones before he planted his feet against the wall once more.

Even in their smaller form, R-0 hunched to fit through the window frame. There was no ground to step on. Just empty air. They curled their hands tighter around the rope, and the curtain rod creaked. Were they supposed to walk on nothing?

"Turn around, then step onto the wall." King Hadrian beckoned them down.

R-0 followed his orders. Facing the familiar interior of the king's chamber instead of the nothingness of the air made it easier to follow through. They took a step backward with one foot, resting it against the wall, then stepped with the other.

Unlike King Hadrian, who had belayed down with ease and grace, R-0's movements were slow and deliberate. Step by step, they made their way down. They tried to step stealthily, but metal clanging against stone was anything but quiet. If a construct had been stationed outside the king's door, they would have heard R-0's escape. But with the organic guards, their exit went unnoticed.

"Should the rope be removed?" R-0 asked as they neared the ground.

"No, we'll need it to get back up."

"Won't the guards notice it?"

King Hadrian shook his head. "They never have before."

R-0 stepped down, their heavy metal feet leaving indentations in the tiny rocks that filled the space between plants. Despite the frigid weather, bright flowering plants thrived in the palace gardens. The managrid funneled beneath the cobblestone paths, rose into the rocky divider sectioning off different plant beds, and even coiled through the soil, providing the exact conditions various plants needed to survive. Magic siphoned water out of the soil where desert plants from Lexica's Domain were planted, and heat emanated from the beds where Haiden's native summer flowers blossomed. Even when frost coated the pathways and winter's chill crept across R-0's plates, the plants remained untouched. The technomancers had partnered with elves from Faylviln to create a garden that thrived year-round, immune to nature's whims.

Despite its careful creation and overall vibrance, there were signs of distress. In a few places, R-0 noticed browning along the edges of the leaves or flowers that were beginning to wilt instead of standing tall. The blackouts weren't the only side effect of the malfunctioning managrid.

R-0 followed after the king, and with every step they took, pebbles shifted. They continued carefully, taking large steps to avoid the more delicate flowers and bushes. But King Hadrian didn't hesitate, walking through the flower beds with the same carefree steps that carried him across the rocks. The flowers bent under his foot, but most slowly crept back up as he moved away. Under R-0's weight, they might not be as fortunate.

"R-0, are you coming?" King Hadrian asked.

R-0 hesitated. They needed to hurry. Even if King Hadrian was right about the guards' route, it didn't give them much time to reach the walls, especially if they slowed their pace to remain quiet. But . . . would their steps harm the flowers?

R-0 had caused harm under the king's orders before. When he was young, many were upset that a child had been crowned, and more than one aspiring assassin had fallen beneath R-0's blade. And when the king had demanded it, R-0 had served as his executioner, resolving trials of those accused of crimes against the crown. It had never bothered them. They had never considered the lives that ended because of their actions.

The flowers in front of them had white stalks that split baby pink leaves like pieces of string. The leaves draped toward the ground. Even perfectly healthy, they looked . . . sad. Their bodies wilted under the weight of their petals, and they cast dark shadows on the ground.

King Hadrian's boot crushed the flowers closest to R-0 as he stepped back toward them. "Are you okay?"

R-0's body ran cold, the flame in their chest raging to maintain itself even as an icy chill crept through their plates. "The flowers."

It didn't fully explain all the thoughts racing through their mind, but it was all they could manage. With every word, their face plates resisted, trying to stay frozen in place despite the command to do otherwise. They wanted to explain, but finding the right words seemed an insurmountable task. They weren't even sure how to explain it within their own mind.

"What about—" King Hadrian looked at his feet. "Oh." He stepped back onto the pebbles.

Some of the chill dissipated as the flowers perked up slightly. Their spindly leaves still clung to their stalks, and they appeared to be in one piece.

"Will they be okay?" R-0 asked.

"You're worried about the flowers?"

Worry. King Hadrian had asked something similar during maintenance. Was it the same? King Hadrian's inefficient attempts at maintenance had endangered R-0, and now his hurried steps endangered the flowers. Maybe they *were* feeling worry for the little plant.

R-0 nodded.

"Why?" King Hadrian asked.

They couldn't answer. The plants held no purpose—they weren't functional. R-0 had no connection to them and had never thought about them before. They weren't a part of themself or important to the king's protection.

They just . . . were.

"Is a reason required?"

"I guess not, but people almost always have a reason for the things they do, even if they don't realize it yet."

R-0 was not a person—they were a construct. "You think there is a reason?"

"I do."

R-0 had felt worry before, so what were the commonalities? They compared the scenarios—who was around, how their flame acted, what King Hadrian had said and done. Too much was different. Before palace walls had surrounded them, now they were beneath the open sky. But there were similarities too.

"The flowers were in danger," R-0 said. "They cannot protect themselves."

King Hadrian tilted his head upward. "You have a heart of fire and steel, yet you care about these plants more than half the council cares about the people they've vowed to serve."

"The council does not care about life?" R-0 flickered through their memories of the council meetings, trying to make sense of King Hadrian's words. Everything the council said revolved around the people of Haiden. Their livelihoods, their safety, their opportunities.

"They say they do." King Hadrian drew out the word say, elongating it for a few extra seconds. "But more often than not, their true intentions are self-serving. You can't always trust them."

The council was meant to serve people—to make decisions on their behalf and better the country. R-0 frowned, their best attempt at conveying their confusion. "If they don't serve their people, then why do they hold positions that require them to do so?"

"Money, influence, power." King Hadrian sighed. "It's . . . complicated."

"It's confusing."

King Hadrian laughed. "Confusing and complicated really are the best ways to describe it. But we don't have to worry about them tonight." King Hadrian paused. "Assuming we don't get caught."

How long had R-0 been distracted by the flowers? They had wasted too much of King Hadrian's time with their questions. "The guards will be coming soon."

"Then let's get out of here."

King Hadrian hurried around the edges of the flower beds, no longer trampling any of the innocent plants. R-0 alternated between watching where they were heading and looking back to make sure no one caught sight of them.

Soon the landscape shifted. No longer did they have to take measures to avoid flower beds as the ground transformed into an entirely rocky base. Periodically, larger stones with colorful veins of crystal poked out from the ground. Most were around the size of a chair, but one towered above even R-0, blues, purples, and greens spiraling to its pointed tip. Its height was proportionate to its width, creating a sloping incline.

"We can jump to the wall from here, and then it isn't too far to drop down." King Hadrian climbed on a smaller rock nearby before jumping to the larger one. He held his hands out to balance himself as he walked to the tip, then jumped for the wall.

R-0 followed. With their next step, a rock scuttled, clacking against stone. But there were no pebbles beneath R-0's feet.

The noise had come from behind them, and R-0 swiveled to find the source.

Councilwoman Jeza stood in the middle of the rock garden, one foot propped on a reddish-colored rock and one hand cocked on her hip, her rings standing out against the golden hem of her blouse. Her black hair caught in the wind but stayed neatly out of her face. Two guards flanked her. She looked past R-0, and her eyes locked with King Hadrian's.

"Just where do you think you're going?"

CHAPTER II

"J-Jeza." King Hadrian took a quick step toward the edge of the wall. "I was just—"

"Disregarding the council's decision to remain within the palace?" Jeza asked. "Give us a moment, would you?" Jeza dismissed the guards at her side, who retreated out of earshot but not out of sight. Although all the council members were accompanied by guards, being cut off from the Flow meant Jeza was more reliant on them than most. She needed them to access the managrid lights and other magical amenities.

Once they were alone, King Hadrian cleared his throat and looked anywhere but at the councilwoman, who turned to R-0. She was . . . expectant. Her question needed to be answered, but King Hadrian kept his lips pressed tight together. If he couldn't answer her question, R-0 could.

"He does not take orders from the council."

"Oh?" Jeza arched her brow. Her gaze swept over R-0, lingering on their chest plate. "Then who does he take orders from?"

"No one." R-0 frowned. "He is the king."

"R-0, silence." King Hadrian crouched at the edge of the wall, gripped the edges, then gently dropped to the ground. "Don't worry about them, Jeza."

"Everyone is worried about the constructs, yet you're sneaking out with one?"

King Hadrian opened his mouth, but Jeza continued.

"One that seems to take issue with how our government functions and questions our decisions."

"They're just protecting me."

"*I'm* protecting you." She narrowed her eyes. "And you're far too old for silly games like sneaking out."

"My people are out there." King Hadrian gestured toward the wall. "And—"

"And your responsibilities are here." She walked past R-0 and King Hadrian through the rocks, her rings clinking together as her fingers trailed across their surfaces. "Some on the council are questioning your ability to lead. How easy would it be for an accident to happen when you're out in the city unsupervised?"

"Nothing will happen to me."

"You aren't invincible."

This R-0 understood. The king was fragile. Flesh could burn. Organs couldn't be replaced. If an injury spilled his blood, he would be left empty. Gone.

Dead.

R-0 didn't let the thought linger. They tapped a finger against their side to refocus on King Hadrian, who was—at the moment—alive and well. There was no reason to consider his death. It was simple. King Hadrian would not die as long as he was in R-0's care.

"He will be safe," R-0 said.

"It's quite opinionated, isn't it?" Jeza asked.

"We still have a lot to learn about the constructs," King Hadrian said, "a task I'm working toward with R-0. Although, it would be easier if the council agreed to reinstate them throughout the palace. It would ease our staffing concerns as well."

"You choose this moment to win me over? Here?" She gestured at the rocks around them and returned to the pathway. "Even if I agreed, what of the others? Whose support have you gathered?"

King Hadrian remained silent.

"The crown you wear is nothing without people who will follow it. You've gotten by with your impulsivity in the past because you controlled the constructs. But now, you have to play their game and earn their approval. Push Robin too far and you'll find the shipwrights on strike—and you know Uxius will support them. If you upset Gretta, then when the contract with the blacksmiths needs renewing, you'll find yourself with far less favorable terms. And that's the best-case scenario. Worst-case . . . without control of the constructs, there are some who see you as more of a liability than an asset. A liability that needs to be culled."

Culled. Like an animal brought to slaughter. R-0 stiffened. Jeza's posture hadn't changed. She talked about the king being culled as casually as she talked about budget cuts during council meetings.

"Is that a threat?" R-0 asked.

"I am not a threat to our king," Jeza said. "But the missing constructs could be. And until we have some proof otherwise, we must prepare ourselves for the worst. I'm not against you, Sylas. I'm saying what everyone on the council is thinking. You have to get ahead of this—ahead of them."

"That's what I'm trying to do!" King Hadrian's voice rose. "The constructs are my responsibility. My birthright. I need to figure out what's going on with them, and we have a lead that might allow me to do just that." The king quieted. "If you're concerned, then help me. Convince the others to reintegrate the constructs so I can prove it. They listen to you."

"Play your hand too early, and people lose confidence you can get things done. Gather the support of the others, then ask me again, and I will stand with you. But I will not create undue conflict with the other council members because you're taking shortcuts." Her gaze shifted from King Hadrian to R-0. "You say our king is safe. Why?"

Before R-0 could speak, King Hadrian replied. "I'm not a careless kid anymore, Jeza. I've taken precautions—"

"I'll believe you are not a child when you stop acting like one. I want to hear what the construct has to say."

It was hard to speak under her expectant gaze. R-0 could imagine words, but the more time they spent in conversation, the more they realized the order, tone, and word choice all impacted the message and how it was interpreted. It was R-0's fault they had delayed long enough for Jeza to catch them. They didn't want to cause any more trouble.

R-0 focused on the facts. "The king wishes to visit the city, so he will visit the city, and he will be protected."

Their gears shifted, any additional words dying in their wires before their plates could move or their chords could vibrate. R-0 looked at King Hadrian. It was simpler to talk when it was only the two of them.

"How interesting." Jeza turned to King Hadrian. "Has keeping one around taught you anything notable?"

"They're *alive*, Jeza. Just as much as you and me. They're not the mindless creations they once were," King Hadrian said. "You would know that if we implemented the reintegration efforts and you spent some time with them."

"Until we know more, allowing the constructs to roam free is an unnecessary danger." Jeza smiled and put her hand on R-0's shoulder. "Besides, there are other, more efficient ways to learn about them."

While R-0 recognized her movement as a gesture of comfort among organics, their flame recoiled from her touch. A shudder traveled across their plates as their gears caught, and they forced themself to remain still.

"Do you remember what my mother used to say?" King Hadrian asked. "Fear is a poison, leaving inaction where bravery had once fought."

At the mention of the late queen, Jeza's face changed. Her facial features moved like the gears within R-0's own machinery. They shifted, slowly and methodically, remaining set in the new position. It was an unusual trait for an organic—most of their faces hurriedly shifted between different expressions with each new piece of information they received. Little impacted her. But King Hadrian's words had.

"Is it bravery or foolishness guiding your heart tonight?" Her voice was softer now.

King Hadrian lowered his to match. "It doesn't change what needs to be done."

"You're growing into quite the king, Sylas." Jeza placed a hand on his shoulder. "I wish your mother were here to see it."

"I'm sure everyone wishes my mother was here instead of me."

R-0 didn't. They couldn't explain exactly why. Perhaps it was a matter of information. R-0 had few memories of Queen Hadrian before her passing, and their memories of King Hadrian started when he was just a child. Or perhaps it was King Hadrian's actions. Even when the council members assumed the worst of the constructs—assumed the worst of R-0—King Hadrian had always given them the chance to explain themselves. He listened to their logic and searched for truth and understanding. What more could anyone wish for from their king?

"You have the potential to be every bit the ruler she was, maybe even more." Jeza clasped her hands, and her nails clicked together. "Go prove it."

"You're not going to stop us?" King Hadrian's eyes widened.

"You are the king, and you're right. You aren't a child anymore. I won't stop you." Jeza's face shifted once more, this time into a smile that became a soft laugh as she turned away. She followed the pathways back toward the palace, calling over her shoulder, "But remember this next time I need your help. You owe me a favor."

CHAPTER 12

"If we find M-118 at the docks quickly, there are a few stops I'd like to make on the way back," King Hadrian said. "First, the bakery."

Quiet unease had settled over King Hadrian after his meeting with Jeza, but as they walked farther away from the palace, the buzz of the city seemed to lighten the mood. R-0 tried to keep track of their objective: find M-118 or a lead on the other missing constructs, but it was even more difficult than focusing on King Hadrian's words as distractions they never would have noticed before the corruption demanded their attention. R-0 tried tapping on their plates to help them focus on their mission, but the metallic clink of their finger on their side joined the cacophony of sounds like an instrument in a concert.

The jittering buzz from a flickering managrid lamp.

Tap.

Muffled pieces of conversations carrying into the street from a nearby house.

Tap.

A loose section of cobblestone that rattled and clacked every time a merchant pulled their wagon around the corner.

Tap.

"Second, the shops," King Hadrian said. "What Jeza said about needing support for the reintegration got me thinking, and there's a couple of people I want to check in with there."

How would a bakery or shops help them find information on the missing constructs? King Hadrian had eaten a hearty dinner back at the palace, and organics generally only ate three meals per day. R-0 didn't need food either, but even if one of them required sustenance, there were plenty of closer, easier options.

It was late enough that most of the stalls along the city streets were empty, but a few merchants still called out to passersby or haggled with customers over wares. Unlike the council hall, R-0 wasn't surrounded by only humans and dwarves. Although they were the most common types of organics living in the city, it wasn't uncommon to see others. Scaled organics—dragon-scaled, snake-scaled, and lizard-scaled—had immigrated from Lower Scales, and while some of the merfolk didn't trust the land-bound organics and opted to stay in their underwater cities, others loved to visit or even chose to live and work on the surface. Mages from Benuoir's Academy flocked to Haiden after the invention of the managrid. They came from a variety of races and countries across the world, but they still distinguished themselves by the golden insignia embroidered into their purple robes—and the way they were more likely to study R-0 than avert their gaze as they passed by.

At the end of the street, the doors of a tavern swung open, spilling laughter and light across the cobblestones and allowing a glimpse of tables piled with food and drink. R-0 had accompanied a group of guards to that tavern a couple months earlier to hang wanted posters of Ryder. The poster still hung on the board, the merfolk's scarred, scaled face fluttering in the wind every time the doors opened. R-0 stared. It felt like an eternity ago. As with all of their memories from before the corruption, R-0 wondered how different the tavern would feel now.

Inside the tavern, a human woman caught R-0's glance, and her smile immediately faded. She nudged the dwarf next to her who also turned his attention to R-0. They stared until the doors swung closed and the streets dimmed, lit only by the low blue glow of managrid lights.

"R-0, are you listening?" King Hadrian asked.

Before R-0 could respond, the lights flickered, then went out, cascading the entire street in darkness. A nearby merchant released a scared squeal. R-0 shifted their arms around King Hadrian, focusing on their hearing in the absence of sight. The pathway was gravelly, and organic steps disturbing the stones would alert R-0 to their presence. R-0 started to draw their sword—

Blue lit the streets as the managrid's power returned. Its distinctive hum filled the air, a sound R-0 had grown so accustomed to, they hadn't even noticed it until experiencing its absence.

"R-0?" King Hadrian asked. The blackout didn't seem to faze him. He continued on as if nothing had happened.

R-0 tried to mimic his stoicism. They flickered through memories from before, then recited the king's words back to him. "Second, you would like to visit the shops."

"I was talking about our fourth stop."

The fourth? R-0 tried to recall the third, but all they could remember were the patrons inside the tavern and the laughter spilling out of the worn wooden walls. Nothing that had to do with the king or his plans.

Distractions.

"Apologies," R-0 said. "What is the third stop?"

"My clan's hall. There's normally not many people there, which is convenient for us, but the hall is filled with all sorts of trophies and recreations of monsters from across all the continents. It's amazing, really, and I thought you might enjoy it."

King Hadrian didn't need to take them to the Hadrian clan hall to show them something amazing. Every step they took, every new street, new passerby, new moment . . . everything granted them a new experience. Their memories seemed flat and lifeless compared to all this.

R-0 closed their eyes. They weren't here for the novelty. Protect the king. That was their directive.

They opened their eyes and tapped at their side, trying to tune out the distractions and focus only on King Hadrian. "And the fourth?"

RISE OF THE FORGEHEARTS

"I doubt we'll have time for it." King Hadrian shook his head. "But if we do, we'll head to Lenny's tavern. Drink until I forget I'm the king of this whole place."

None of King Hadrian's words made sense. How would drinking and forgetting help them find M-118? From R-0's memories of organics and alcohol, it rarely led to productivity. More often, it led to clumsy mistakes and regrets. And forgetting was the opposite of gathering new information—the opposite of what Jeza had advised.

"Jeza said you shouldn't forget you are king," R-0 said.

"Jeza should take her own advice."

"She forgets you are king?" R-0 frowned. Perhaps Jeza was also drinking. "It should be simple to remember."

"What do you remember about me from ten years ago?"

R-0 had recorded countless memories. Which one did the king want?

"Don't overthink it," King Hadrian said. "Just say the first thing that comes to mind."

"You liked to read."

King Hadrian laughed. "I did say the first thing."

"How does this relate to Jeza forgetting?"

"Ten years ago, I was a child. Worse, I was a child who had just lost his mother and had a crown I probably didn't deserve thrown at me."

"You were attacked?"

"I—" King Hadrian sighed. "No. I was given far too much responsibility, far too young. I was just a pawn to the council. I didn't deserve to be king then, but . . . I do now. I've worked my entire life to deserve this crown, to honor my mother's memory, and to be the king I am today. I have Jeza to thank for that. She taught me everything she could and made sure I had tutors for everything else. She protected me from the council's manipulations when I was too young to realize what was happening. She did what my mother couldn't. I'm thankful for all she did, but sometimes she still sees the sad orphan who needed her help and not the king I am today."

R-0 reviewed their memories of Jeza and the king. She was with King Hadrian far more than the other council members.

And he had visited her far more frequently as well. Their relationship was . . . different.

"I know she means well, but . . ." King Hadrian's words faded into a sigh. "We're almost at the docks. Let's focus."

Waves crashed against the posts of the dock, a consistent and predictable occurrence that R-0 found comforting. As the sound hit, the planks beneath them shook in response, then stilled until the next waves hit.

King Hadrian paced the length of the dock. "No sign of M-118 or anything out of place."

"What are you looking for?" R-0 asked.

"I don't even know." King Hadrian scuffed his shoe against the dock until it squeaked like a seagull searching for fish. "A secret hideout filled with the missing constructs? M-118 gazing at the stars?" His steps squished as he crossed the wetter planks along the edge. "Anything to prove that I've got a modicum of control over this situation."

R-0 scanned the dockyards again, this time keeping in mind King Hadrian's words. There was no sign of M-118. In fact, unlike the streets leading here, there was no sign of anyone. The presence or absence of a secret hideout was more difficult to ascertain. They weren't sure what to look for, and if R-0 located it, it would no longer be a secret. Still, R-0 looked and—as far as they could tell—nothing was out of place.

"Maybe Eren and Jeza were right. This was a waste of time." King Hadrian sat on the edge of the dock, his legs dangling in the open air. The larger waves peppered him with ocean spray. R-0 stood back, avoiding unnecessary contact with the water. Even if the technomancers could provide rust treatments and cleaning for their metallic body, it was better to avoid the situation.

Despite the dangers of the ocean, there was something serene about their circumstances. If not for their duty to protect the king and their search for answers about the missing constructs, they might have joined him, staring at the stars and the ocean waves. Instead, R-0 continued to scan the area. What would M-118 have been doing there? There were no forges or blacksmiths nearby, and the docks were farther from the mines and M-118's home than the palace had been.

Nothing could explain M-118's insistence on coming here. In fact, it was eerily quiet. No boats were docked, which meant no dock workers. When the fishermen returned from their voyages, this area would be bustling, but tonight it was empty of activity. Occasionally, organics would walk the street leading between the docks and the rest of the city, but none turned toward R-0 and the king.

Where were the guards Eren said she would send? Had they already completed their search? Maybe M-118 was back at the palace, waiting for King Hadrian and R-0.

"It's beautiful, isn't it?" King Hadrian asked.

R-0 nodded.

"My mother used to take me here when I was younger. She stopped once I found out how much fun it was to jump off the dock." King Hadrian chuckled. "You should have seen the look on her face. She thought I was drowning and jumped in to save me. And there I was laughing and thinking it was the most hilarious thing ever, while she was soaking wet thinking I'd almost died. Ruined her favorite dress too."

R-0 wasn't sure why King Hadrian laughed. If he jumped right now, R-0 would likely respond like the late queen, following him into the water, worried for his safety. R-0 peered over the edge. It was a long drop, and there was the unanswered question of their flame. What would happen to it if R-0's body was submerged?

"Are you going to jump tonight?" R-0 asked. They stopped their search, staying close to the king—just in case.

He stood on the edge, and R-0 instinctively moved closer, worried their question had encouraged him to take action. But King Hadrian stepped back, a shiver passing over him. "No. I learned the hard way it's not nearly as fun to walk home soaking wet."

R-0 relaxed slightly.

"I'm glad we came out here," King Hadrian said. "Do you like it?"

"It?"

"The ocean, the stars, the view." King Hadrian spread his arms out wide and circled as he walked back toward the city.

"The peace and quiet to think without the weight of the world on your shoulders."

"The world is under your feet, not on your shoulders."

King Hadrian laughed. "That doesn't answer my question."

R-0 looked out at the docks. It was different than the palace and other places they'd visited. R-0 wasn't entirely sure what it meant to like something, but the docks seemed likable. They searched for the words to explain the feeling, but before they could, something caught their eye.

On the rooftop of one of the warehouses bordering the docks, the managrid lamps illuminated the outline of two figures. Their body shapes indicated a construct and an organic, likely a human, but at this distance, R-0 couldn't be certain. But one thing was certain—they were watching R-0 and the king.

"King Hadrian," R-0 said. "Do you see the rooftops?"

"The rooftops?" King Hadrian's face wrinkled. "I mean, they're alright, I guess, but we can see plenty of those from the palace."

"No." R-0's gears stuttered. "There's someone up there."

King Hadrian stiffened. It was barely perceptible, the slightest pause in his step, before he continued pacing as if R-0 hadn't said a word. He tilted his head up as if he was looking at the stars, but his eyes cut to the rooftops.

"Is that M-118?" King Hadrian whispered.

R-0 focused on the figures, trying to make out details. A faint green light pulsed on one of the figure's shoulder.

"Be subtle." King Hadrian elbowed their side, sending tiny vibrations through R-0's chest plate. "Look with just your eyes, not your body."

R-0 turned their body to face the king, looking with just their eyes. "Inconclusive."

"But possible?"

"Yes sir," R-0 said. "If it's not M-118, it is likely a construct of the same make and model."

"Is that Ryder with them?"

"Unlikely," R-0 said. The outline of the figure's limbs was smooth—no shadows of fins or sharp edges of scales were visible.

King Hadrian flashed the signal for R-0 to fall in line behind them. "Let's go find ourselves a runaway."

Unlike their first trek through the city, the distractions didn't faze R-0. They kept their attention focused, alternating between the rooftop figures and King Hadrian and their surroundings. Anytime their attention started to wander, an uncomfortable feeling in their plates—like a candle fighting to survive a rainstorm—brought their focus back. R-0 briefly paused to examine their chest, but all the screws were perfectly in place and the plates aligned. Physically, there was nothing wrong.

But the feeling didn't waver. And each wave of discomfort brought with it worrying thoughts. Was this safe for King Hadrian? If there was danger behind the mystery of the missing constructs, then shouldn't R-0 be leading the king farther away from the potential danger instead of closer to it?

"Sir," R-0 said. The rainstorm in their chest progressed to a hurricane, and the words in their mind refused to form out loud.

"What is it, R-0?"

Dark shadows shifted in the upcoming alleyways, obscuring any lurking dangers from view. Memories flickered through R-0's mind. Some council meetings had included crime rates and reports of the more unique crimes that had ravaged the city—like a mage transforming her enemies into fish, then serving them as stew at a local tavern. Anything could happen to the king on the streets tonight.

King Hadrian didn't hesitate, stalking past the alleyway in the same carefree manner as when he strolled through the safe and secure palace grounds.

"The streets can be dangerous," R-0 said.

"I have you, don't I?"

"Yes sir."

"Then I don't have anything to worry about." King Hadrian's words radiated confidence and warmth that made the rainstorm in R-0's mind feel like a mere drizzle. It was difficult to understand. Nothing had changed in R-0's body. No maintenance had been performed, and King Hadrian didn't *do* anything that should have altered the way they were feeling. But his words were just as effective as a box full of tools and the most experienced technomancers to ease their discomfort.

"They're moving." King Hadrian tilted his head toward the rooftop. The two figures were leaving. "We'd better hurry."

King Hadrian's steady steps quickened, and R-0 was able to extend their legs fully instead of shortening and slowing themself to match the king.

"Shalloth be damned," King Hadrian said.

"What's wrong?"

"There aren't any streets that'll lead us to where they're going without a long detour." King Hadrian scowled. "And if we take the detour, we'll lose them. Unless . . ."

"Unless what?"

King Hadrian turned down an alleyway and approached the dead end. "Unless we climb. If we get on the rooftops with them, anywhere they go, we can go."

R-0 wanted to say no.

Walking through the streets was dangerous. But climbing over rooftops? That was another level of concern. Even if their targets were innocent, King Hadrian could slip from the icy surface and fall, the rooftops could cave in under their weight, or their presence in a place where people generally shouldn't be could draw unwanted attention.

"What are you waiting for?" King Hadrian asked. He reached for the ledge, but his fingers fell short. "Help me up, will you?"

In R-0's memories, they'd never considered whether King Hadrian's instructions were good or bad. They just were. As simply as the fire in their chest now burned without thought or intention, their body had once followed his orders. Nothing seemed as simple now.

But one thing was simple. He was their king.

"Yes sir." R-0 knelt next to the king and the wall, cupping their hands at their knee and creating a step.

King Hadrian stepped up, and R-0 resisted the urge to grab on and not let go. Instead, they focused on their senses. It didn't matter how dangerous the rooftops might be, as long as R-0's protection was greater than the threat. They listened for any disturbance, any nearby movement.

With the tips of his fingers, King Hadrian grabbed the edge of the roof and hauled himself up. His torso pressed against the shingles, and his legs floundered in the air. R-0 reached for his boots, ready to lift him farther onto the roof, but a sound underfoot stopped them.

If R-0 hadn't been paying attention, they wouldn't have heard it. The faint hum of the managrid increased in pitch until it was more like a hiss. R-0's body froze. They scanned the streets for any sign of a threat. Before they could locate one, the lights flickered out.

"King Hadrian." R-0 reached up where his legs had been, but their hands swatted at empty space. Their flame popped and crackled as if fuel had haphazardly leaked into their chest compartment. Worry. It was becoming one of R-0's most common emotions—or at least, one of the easiest to identify.

No moon lit the streets, but that didn't stop R-0 from scanning the rooftops for the king. With their sight dark, they focused on their hearing as they ran their fingers across the wall, searching for a handhold. Something shuffled above them, followed by a few small rocks showering R-0's plates in dainty metallic clinks.

"King Hadrian?" R-0 asked again.

"I'm here," King Hadrian said. "Just wait a second for the lights to—"

King Hadrian's words ended in a startled squeak that grew closer and closer to R-0 in the darkness. As R-0 moved toward the sound and stretched out their arms, King Hadrian fell into them.

"Are you okay?" R-0 cradled the king's body close to them. Even through his thick coat, the king's heartbeat vibrated across their plates, strong and steady. Still, R-0 struggled to wait for his response. Their gears ticked too fast, and their fingers wiggled in place, unable to fidget while holding the king.

"I just slipped. I'm okay." Despite his words, King Hadrian groaned between sentences. Falling into R-0's plates couldn't have been the most comfortable sensation for his delicate flesh, but it was better than hitting the ground. "The lights should be back on any second."

"Yes sir." The flame in R-0's chest steadied as they set King Hadrian on solid ground.

"Where's the moon when you need it?" King Hadrian's question ended in a wordless grumble.

R-0 didn't have an answer for him. They cycled through their memories, noticing how the sky differed as time passed. Before the star entered their chest, they'd hardly noticed the moon, much less stopped long enough to ask *why* it was sometimes different or—on nights like tonight—absent.

"Can you see anything?" King Hadrian asked. "Can you see where they're going?"

R-0 raised themself onto their tiptoes, but in their condensed form even the additional height wasn't enough for them to see above the rooftops. They reached up and hopped, catching their fingertips on the edge of the roof. After waiting a moment to ensure it would hold their weight, they pulled themself the rest of the way up.

Their vision was far superior to organics', but it wasn't enough. Without the managrid lamps, darkness stretched in every direction. A few torches sprang to life as people exited their homes and businesses to investigate the blackout, but none appeared in the direction they had last seen the mystery construct and their companion.

"Apologies sir." R-0 lowered themself back down. "There is no visibility."

"Where are those lights?" King Hadrian's voice rose, and his boots scraped against the ground, sending rocks scuttling across the alley.

R-0 listened carefully, ensuring every sound was the consequence of King Hadrian's anger and not a threat sneaking up on them before settling back into the silence. In the same way King Hadrian cursed the lights, R-0 wanted to thank them—despite the fact it was nonsensical to talk to them at all and even more confusing to expect a response. But standing here in the darkness was far safer than gallivanting across rooftops to confront the unknown.

R-0 and King Hadrian waited. More torches were lit, some close enough to shed a warm glow in their alleyway. It was enough for them to see their surroundings, but not enough to continue their pursuit. By the time the managrid lights came back on, too much time had passed.

Still, R-0 tried. They climbed onto every nearby rooftop, checking and double-checking every direction under the king's orders. Everywhere they looked, the result was the same.

"You can stop looking, R-0." King Hadrian leaned against the wall, letting their head thump against the bricks. "They're gone."

"Should we return to the palace and report our findings?" R-0 asked.

"No way." King Hadrian patted R-0 on the back. A smile spread across his face, replacing the anger and frustration. "We already snuck out—and got caught. Let's make the most of it."

CHAPTER 13

King Hadrian set a fast pace and didn't stop until he and R-0 were outside a well-maintained building at the intersection of two paved streets. The sign above the door was more intricate than any other on the street. Deep carvings in the mahogany wood depicted a loaf of bread, a muffin, and a pie. Bright colors splashed across the drawings, not staying within the outlines or following any discernable pattern.

King Hadrian had told R-0 about Minna's bakery and the dragon-scaled family living there, but the most notable detail from his stories was that the pastries were to die for. Although R-0 didn't understand why anyone would be willing to sacrifice their life for a baked good, if that was what King Hadrian wanted, they would protect him from whatever threats guarded the pastries. R-0 rested one hand on the hilt of their sword. Their flame quieted, and their focus intensified. The little details that had recently distracted R-0 were quickly analyzed and split into categories of what was or wasn't potentially dangerous.

King Hadrian knocked, and a shrill voice yelled back from within. "Who is it?" A cacophony of giggles followed the question.

"You get one guess." King Hadrian grinned.

The giggles escalated into shrieks, and like a stampede, footsteps ran toward the door vibrating the wooden walls.

"Me, me!"

"No, it's my turn."

"You got to last time."

"No, you—"

"No, I didn't!"

"Do you know them?" R-0 asked.

"At ease, R-0." King Hadrian guided R-0's hand away from their weapon. "There's nothing to worry about here."

The voices fell over one another in a bubble of noise until the door creaked open and a blue-scaled face looked up at R-0 and King Hadrian.

"No fair!" Another face, identical to the first popped up behind her.

The first shrugged. "Too slow."

Both were tiny, even by organic standards. They barely reached King Hadrian's waist, despite dragon-scaled typically being taller than humans and King Hadrian being short even for a human man.

Children. Curious little creatures. R-0's knowledge of them was limited—the only child they had ever interacted with was King Hadrian. But children were rarely a threat, so R-0 tried to relax.

The children pulled the door open the rest of the way, revealing a shop and a third child. He was larger than the others. His tail dragged along the floor, sweeping from side to side and knocking toys aside as he went, but compared to the dragon-scaled woman kneading dough behind the counter, he was still small.

The front area was devoid of furniture, filled only by children's toys that created a maze of obstacles for R-0 and the king to step around. It led to a large counter where a dragon-scaled woman gave King Hadrian a cheerful wave. Her scales were covered in white flour, which almost obscured their blue shine. She placed the dough into a managrid oven behind her without wincing or pulling away from the flames within. That had to be Minna.

"Sy, Sy, Sy!" The child who had opened the door jumped up and down. She tugged at King Hadrian's wrist, and R-0's gears slowed. Kids were usually harmless. But were these?

"Kai, Kai, Kai!" King Hadrian echoed the girl's tone, and she giggled.

"I want to show you something."

"I'm actually very busy today."

The girl let go of the king's wrist, her hand falling to her side and her chin dipping toward her chest. Both of the smaller children's expressions turned into frowns, and even the older one's tail seemed to droop, knocking into a rattling ball that jittered across the floor in a chorus of off-tune bells.

"But . . . if you all behave really well, you can show me before I leave."

"And," Minna interjected, "if you promise to go to bed as soon as Uncle Sylas leaves."

"What your mother said." King Hadrian held out his hand. "Deal?"

"Deal!

"Deal, deal!"

Both girls grabbed at his hand, hanging from it rather than completing a proper handshake. But despite their poor form, King Hadrian nodded.

"Been a couple months since I've seen you, Sy." Minna set her dough ball in a nearby bowl, covered it, then dusted off her hands as she turned to King Hadrian. "To what do I owe the pleasure?"

She didn't react to King Hadrian the way organics in the palace did—in fact, no one in the house did. There were no bows or courtesy, and their words weren't the stiff, formal dialogue people usually used when addressing King Hadrian.

"I can't check in on my favorite baker just because?" King Hadrian pulled the baker in for a hug. R-0 stiffened, watching the interaction carefully. But the only weapons R-0 could see were knives—designed for carving food and not organics—neatly tucked away in a storage block.

"Not in the middle of the night when there's no pastries for you to steal."

"You say that, but you're still baking."

"It's the blackouts." She tilted a tray on one of the counters, showing a deformed loaf of bread that had collapsed in on itself. "Ruined half my batches today. I was hoping they'd happen less at night, but . . ." She shrugged and handed King

Hadrian a clean towel, then pulled out a stool from under the counter. "Here. Sit."

King Hadrian dusted off the front of his coat where the flour coating Minna had left a scaled pattern on the dark fabric. "You're the one who's been on your feet all day."

"Don't have to tell me twice." She chuckled and tapped the wood a couple times before sitting.

"Do you want to see what we made?" One of the children grabbed at R-0's hand. Even their skin, hardened with scales, felt delicate beneath R-0's touch. The slightest amount of pressure could cause her to snap, but still, she fearlessly wrapped her fingers around R-0's with a twinkle in her eyes.

Neither the children nor Minna seemed likely to pose a threat, but R-0 couldn't grow complacent. Although the tools littering her counter were expected for her trade, they could easily become weapons if there was malintent. R-0 wouldn't leave the king unprotected.

"The kin—"

"That's a great idea." King Hadrian's words drowned out R-0's response, and he leaned in close to R-0 and whispered, "Maybe we don't tell the very talkative children about who I really am."

"They don't know?" R-0 tried to lower their voice to match King Hadrian's volume, but even their lowest rumble was still audible to everyone in the room.

"What don't we know?" the older child asked.

"How to mind your manners, it seems." Minna crossed her arms over her chest, her scales clinking together in a gentle chime.

The older dragon-scaled matched his mother's posture, but where her face remained even and calm, his brow furrowed, and smoke flared from his nostrils. "It's not fair. I never get to know—"

The back door slammed open, and R-0 darted forward, positioning themself between the king and the door. Their blade was halfway from its sheath before they identified the newcomer—a construct. They were a smaller model, and R-0 had never seen anything like them. Rather than a dark gray steel that shimmered in the light, their plates were mostly a pale, dull blue, with bits of steel along the edges of their plates or in their creases when they moved. Their expression shifted when they saw R-0. Their flame crackled louder, and a dim golden light peeked through the edges of their chest plate.

"JJ!" The younger children squealed and ran to the construct.

King Hadrian signaled for R-0 to sheath their weapon, and R-0 complied before anyone else noticed. Minna ushered the construct in, her smile matching King Hadrian's. He placed his hand on the counter, leaving his print in the leftover flour dusting the surface. "I wasn't sure . . ."

"If we'd managed to stay together in all the chaos?" Minna smiled. "JJ, can you take the kids outside for a bit? No chance they'll go to bed now, and we could use some peace and quiet."

"Of course." JJ nodded and opened the back door once more. "You heard your mother. Come on."

"Can we play Slay the Kraken?" One of the tiny ones paused at the door. She waited for JJ to nod before running through the door, her arms flapping wildly at her sides.

"You, too, Lykren." JJ crossed their arms and stared at the older child, mimicking the dragon-scaled boy's movement. But their chest stuck out farther, and their arms couldn't quite fold the same way. The result was similar . . . and different. Regardless, Lykren listened, sulking and dragging his feet as he walked out the door. JJ cast one last look at R-0 before following the children outside.

After exchanging a few more pleasantries with Minna, King Hadrian launched into an explanation of his plans for construct reintegration. R-0 tried to pay attention, but outside, the children squealed, and a metallic chime followed. It was unlike any sound R-0 had ever heard. As it continued, it shifted into JJ's voice, chastising Lykren.

Had JJ been . . . laughing?

Even in the storage rooms, they'd never heard a construct laugh, nor had they ever seen one act like JJ did around the organics. Was this what the star had done to them? R-0's curiosity flared, and they craned their neck to see out the bakery's back window.

JJ walked along the edges of a small courtyard, lighting torches as they went. Compared to the palace grounds, the area was ordinary. Overturned snow and sand covered the ground, dozens of overlapping footprints marking the surface. In the center stood a tree, its branches bare.

The girls were piled into a vegetable crate, brandishing cracked wooden spoons. They alternated between dragging them across the ground and holding them high into the air as they shouted indistinguishable nonsense. Lykren stood to the side, his head turned to the sky. As snowflakes drifted toward him, he exhaled small puffs of fire that filled the air with a misty haze and melted the flakes mid-air.

"R-0?" King Hadrian's commanding tone brought their attention back.

"Yes sir?"

Minna smiled. "I was just saying you could go out back with them if you want to."

R-0 instinctively took a step toward the door, then stopped. The distractions were captivating, and outside with JJ, they could get answers to some of their questions. But . . . they had orders. Protect the king. How had they forgotten?

"You can go if you want." King Hadrian gave an encouraging nod.

"Will you be safe?" R-0 asked.

"Lock the door if it'll make you feel better." Minna pointed at the doorframe. "And see that little bell there? You'll be able to hear if anyone comes in, even out back."

"Yes ma'am." R-0 locked the front door, slotting a chain from the wall into the door. As they headed out back, their curiosity shifted into something stronger. The questions swirling in their mind were causing less confusion and more . . . excitement? What new information could R-0 learn? JJ was different than any of the other constructs R-0 was familiar with. Would they know anything about the missing constructs or the star that had changed them?

Once outside, R-0 stayed silently by the door, watching JJ, unsure of what to say. They had too many questions, and no idea where to start.

JJ lit the last torch, then came to stand next to R-0. "The smaller one is Kaili." JJ pointed at one of the tiny children, then the other. "The bigger one is Kalani."

Even with JJ pointing out the difference, they looked the same. R-0 searched for the words to voice all their questions, but only managed a silent puff of smoke.

"We need the Kraken!" one of the children yelled.

What could two small dragon-scaled want with the Kraken? Even distinguished sailors avoided the Kraken, and the few seasoned adventurers who sought out the beast were considered foolish, rarely living long enough to argue otherwise.

"Sounds like they're waiting on you, Lykren." JJ kept their arms crossed over their chest as they eyed the boy.

"Again?" His voice rose into a whine, and his throat gurgled.

"We have company."

Lykren huffed and a puff of smoke spiraled from his nostril. "That's not *my* problem."

JJ stared, and Lykren fidgeted in place, averting his eyes. The girls squealed, begging JJ once more for the Kraken and banging their sticks on the side of the crate.

"Fine." Lykren rolled his eyes, then ran at the girls in the crate. Their shrieks turned to giggles as they bounced their spoons along his scales.

"The Kraken!"

"It's taking our boat!"

Lykren grabbed the shipping crate and slid it across the yard. It lurched and bounced across the uneven ground, and the girls held on tight. R-0 squinted, trying to make sense of their words. There was no Kraken, and there was no boat. And despite their screams, R-0 couldn't identify any threat.

"They can take some getting used to," JJ said.

"They're delusional."

"They choose to believe there is more to the world than what's in front of us. I think it's inspiring." JJ didn't speak like the other constructs at the palace. Though their words carried the same metallic clang, they seemed softer. They alternated their pitch and tone, sounding more similar to the organics than other constructs. Even their name was different. Despite the model number on their neck reading J-786, no one called them J-7 or J-786.

And they said things R-0 didn't understand.

"You're different from other constructs," R-0 said.

"We're all different after the stars."

They weren't wrong, but their response didn't settle R-0's curiosity. The constructs in the storage room with R-0 hadn't been like JJ.

"I wasn't like this at first, but I learned quickly," JJ said. "I think I have Minna to thank for that. I've seen how some of the other shopkeepers treat the constructs, but Minna and the kids were never like that. I have years and years of memories of them treating me like family, even when I couldn't reciprocate. I'm learning from my memories, and every day I feel more like myself."

R-0 flickered through their own memories—years of protecting King Hadrian. Was that why they continued to protect him even without their directive echoing through their mind?

"Do you know anything about constructs going missing?" R-0 asked.

JJ frowned. "Missing constructs?"

As R-0 explained their investigation, JJ's frown deepened. "I haven't heard of any missing constructs around here, and half the district stops by Minna's for bread."

That didn't make sense. King Hadrian had a stack of reports on his desk so tall R-0 expected it to fall over, and each sheet listed a missing construct. The reports were from all across the city, so why wouldn't any be missing in this district? Perhaps the missing constructs belonged to the half of the district that didn't come to Minna's for bread. Or perhaps this wasn't a suitable conversation topic for a bakery. King Hadrian *was* always reminding R-0 that context mattered.

"JJ! Save us!" One of the girls let go of the crate long enough to slap her spoon on top of Lykren's head but had to quickly drop the cooking utensil to brace herself from falling out.

"Two warrior princesses need my help?" The same metallic chime from before rang through JJ's plates, and this time, R-0 was sure they were laughing. "I don't think so."

"Princesses?" R-0 asked. They weren't aware of King Hadrian having any siblings. He was the last of his bloodline. Still, R-0 stepped closer to the girls. If they were royalty, should R-0 protect them the same way they protected the king?

Their flame didn't react to them the same way. If anything happened, R-0 would protect them, but concern didn't echo through them as it did with King Hadrian.

JJ grabbed their arm and pulled them back. "Just watch."

One of the girls tugged on the other's arm. "Use your magic."

She closed her eyes and raised her hands into the air, muttering something that sounded like an incantation in a foreign language. Then louder, she continued, "Talid, bless our boat."

Nothing happened.

"The Kraken can't steal blessed boats!" her sister squealed.

There was still no boat. Still no Kraken. R-0 frowned.

"Where is the boat?" R-0 asked.

"They're playing pretend. It's . . ." JJ tilted their head to the side. "A metaphor."

King Hadrian had mentioned metaphors before, and R-0 began to piece the scene together. The crate—a boat. Lykren—the Kraken. The twins—warrior princesses.

The Kraken let go of the boat. He reached toward it again, then staggered backward, clutching his . . . tentacle? "Oh no!" The look of fear on his face quickly shifted to a grin as he lunged forward. "Your boat may be safe, but what about its captains?" He snatched one of the girls out of the boat and took off swimming to the other side of the yard.

"How are the rest of the constructs at the palace faring?" JJ asked. "We heard rumors they'd been removed from patrols and maintenance duties. We weren't sure if it was true or what to make of it."

"The rumor is true," R-0 said. "The constructs are not working."

"Except you. Where are the others?"

"They are stationed in the storage rooms."

JJ frowned. "By choice?"

"Choice?"

"Are they allowed to leave?"

As it had in Eren's office, R-0's flame gurgled uncomfortably when they thought about the other palace constructs still in the storage rooms. JJ's questions weren't unlike B-7 questioning if they should remain in the storage room or M-118 attempting to leave the maintenance room.

"Their orders are to stay," R-0 said. "What are your orders?"

"Orders?" JJ laughed. "I don't have any. Not anymore."

"Constructs always have orders."

"We used to, but that's different now, isn't it?" They glanced over their shoulder, shouting to the children to be careful as they scaled the tree's branches. "We can do whatever we want."

R-0 mulled over the words. It reminded them of King Hadrian's question at their first meeting after the incident. Why did they still follow his orders? In their memories, it was instantaneous, instinctual. What would they do without orders?

"What is it you want to do?" R-0 asked.

"I'm still trying to figure that out, but for now, I'm happy to stay here." JJ paused to shout at the children before turning back to R-0. "With my family."

"You're not related."

JJ laughed. "No. But . . . the second I got one of the stars, I knew without a doubt, it's what we were. All the time we'd spent together, everything we'd done. At first I spent hours just reliving those memories, trying to understand how I'd ever been so close but so distant. Trying to understand how I could be so . . . lifeless. Before the stars fell, I hadn't realized it, but now I know what I've got here. I've got a lot of missed opportunities to make up for."

"Do you know what the stars did to you?" R-0 asked. "To all the constructs?"

"Minna tells me miracles aren't meant to be understood, just appreciated. So I haven't asked too many questions."

They were the opposite of R-0 in that regard. R-0 had too many questions to count. And calling it a miracle didn't explain enough.

"Do you think—Kalani!" JJ stopped mid-sentence and ran across the yard where the child dangled from a branch. Her scales dug into the bark but were slipping, tearing chunks of wood off each time she slipped farther down. JJ arrived before she could fall, holding their hands like a platform Kalani could stand on, and then lowered her to the ground.

"I hope you weren't causing JJ too much trouble." King Hadrian stepped through the back door and into the yard.

Before JJ could lower her to the ground, Kalani jumped out of their arms and joined her brother and sister running to King Hadrian.

"A deal is a deal." He clapped his hands together. "And then I have some presents to give you."

Minna came out and stood next to R-0, and JJ joined the two of them.

"Please, watch over the constructs in the palace," JJ whispered, their voice so low even R-0's advanced hearing receptors barely registered the sound. "Not everyone is as accepting as Minna."

Before R-0 could ask them to elaborate, they turned and walked inside the house without another word.

CHAPTER 14

After R-0 and King Hadrian left Minna's bakery, they detoured from the king's original four-stop plan to visit shops throughout the districts. Despite his disguise, most of the people King Hadrian visited still seemed to know who he was, and although many people weren't happy to be woken up in the middle of the night, their frustration eased when King Hadrian shared his idea.

Reintegration.

Anyone who was struggling or concerned about their construct's behavior could send them to the palace where they would be reintegrated into their job duties and returned at a later date. The palace guards were overworked, and the managrid fluctuations were caused by a lack of technical staff. Once the constructs were working again, those problems would be solved.

The only confusing aspect was the implementation. Although the citizens King Hadrian spoke with were excited, the council hadn't allowed the constructs stationed at the palace to work. How would King Hadrian convince them to reintegrate constructs from the city?

But whenever anyone asked about the how, King Hadrian simply said he'd handle it. R-0 believed him. His people did too. No one questioned his ability to pull it off, and when he requested their presence at the palace the following morning, everyone agreed. Even without details or explanations.

While King Hadrian spread news of his plan, he and R-0 also tried to gather information. People shared rumors and speculations, but it was nothing that hadn't already been reported. Few reported on missing constructs. Most focused on the changes in construct behavior. Many of the people they visited had constructs of their own, performing with various degrees of success. Some, like Minna, insisted the stars were a blessing. A miracle from the gods. But the blacksmith cursed the change. The constructs were asking questions, making mistakes—some were even refusing to work altogether. Few maintained their previous workloads, and she didn't have enough safety gear to rotate the responsibilities to her organic apprentices. She'd tried to get new gear expedited, but the tailor was already behind on orders before the incident, and he was facing the same issues with his constructs.

Their last stop was an odd house on the edge of the dragon district. Despite the manufactured wood and paved streets, leaves and branches extended from the structure as if the walls were a tree trunk. King Hadrian pointed out holes in the ground where managrid lamps had once surrounded the house and explained they'd removed the entire managrid from under this section to accommodate the house's owner since it interfered with his magic.

The house's owner was a retired elven general from Faylviln who still had significant connections to the military. A few years after the constructs were created, the Kingdom of the Holy Rose had waged war against Faylviln, trying to kill the godking and return the divine domain of nature to the earth. Faylviln and Haiden had allied—Haiden providing a small army of constructs in exchange for access to Faylviln's vast, replenishable lumber stocks. King Hadrian was worried that the corruption would endanger their alliance with the elven nation, but at least for now, the elf said Faylviln was reluctantly willing to accept the phenomena as an act of the gods—not of war.

Despite all the opinions and rumors, no one had answers about the missing constructs or M-118 and their organic companion. Although R-0 hadn't been able to confirm with full certainty it was M-118, King Hadrian said it was a safe assumption. King Hadrian and R-0 had even canvassed the area where they'd last seen them but found no evidence there either—just a row of abandoned shops and empty streets.

"Do you have additional contacts who could be interrogated?" R-0 asked.

King Hadrian shook his head. "None nearby."

"What about the person who reported M-118 missing?"

"Eren already brought her in and questioned her. She wasn't very useful, and she honestly seemed relieved M-118 was gone."

"Why?" Normally organics were upset about theft or loss. They sought retribution and justice. Why would anyone be pleased about it?

"She had some . . . less than kind words to share about the constructs."

"Like what?"

"Come on, let's head back to the palace." King Hadrian scuffed his feet against the cobblestones as he walked. R-0 waited, and after a few streets, King Hadrian continued, "She called you abominations. If not for the money she'd invested in the construct, she would have decommissioned M-118 herself."

R-0's gears slowed. "Did M-118 do something wrong?"

"Besides running away?" King Hadrian asked. "No."

"Then why?"

"I wish I had a better answer for you," King Hadrian said. "There's always going to be evil in the world, people who see everything as an opportunity for their own selfish gain, no matter who or what gets hurt in the process."

Maybe it was better M-118 was missing. R-0 didn't know their fate, but it couldn't be worse than remaining with their owner and being decommissioned. It was . . . unjust. The construct deserved better. But if there was always evil, was a better outcome possible?

"Will the world always be evil?"

"Not necessarily," King Hadrian said. "For every opportunity people have to do evil, they have the chance to choose good as well."

"Everyone has the opportunity?" R-0 asked.

King Hadrian nodded.

Two opportunities. One for good, one for evil. The more R-0 learned, the more everything came down to choices.

"Why would anyone ever choose to not be good?"

King Hadrian chuckled, but then as he looked at R-0, his gaze softened. "You're serious."

"Yes sir."

"I'm definitely not qualified for this." King Hadrian rubbed his forehead. "I'm still figuring it out myself."

R-0 frowned. King Hadrian always spoke with such confidence. His words determined the fate of thousands, and he said them with a smile. When his advisors and his subjects asked questions, he answered. Why was it different with R-0?

"Everyone else comes to you for answers."

"And with everyone else I can pretend."

"Pretend . . . like a box is a boat, and a boy is the Kraken."

"I see Kaili and Kalani taught you a thing or two." King Hadrian laughed. "More like the Kraken is . . . the council. My people are pirates, the constructs are the tides, and I'm a little rowboat in the middle of them all during a catastrophic storm."

"A rowboat would not likely survive that."

"No, it wouldn't." King Hadrian sighed. "But if I pretend I have a really, really big boat, then it's enough to keep the Kraken from testing its luck and the pirates looking at what I can do for them rather than what they can take from me. Then hopefully, I'll get that really big boat built before anyone finds out."

"The rowboat is a . . . secret."

"An exhausting one."

"Secrets are not supposed to be shared."

"Except with those you trust most."

Trust. It wasn't something R-0 had ever considered. It was a nonfactor—they had orders. They followed them. But what if the person giving orders chose evil? What if they did not share R-0's directive?

"How do you know who to trust?"

"You don't." King Hadrian dropped his gaze to the ground. "Trust has been the downfall of many great leaders throughout history and even more in our own lifetime. But people will show you who they are. When they do, pay attention. Over time, you'll see who has earned your trust and who hasn't."

"Who do you trust?" R-0 asked.

"A couple of the council members—Jeza and Eren. Jeza can be harsh at times, but she's been there for me time and time again. Eren and her brother have been protecting me as long as I can remember, and they've proven themselves. And Eren knows what it's like to be thrown into power so young—she didn't provide mentorship like Jeza did, but I relied on her understanding and support a lot the first few years I was king. And . . ."

"And?"

"You."

"You trust . . ."

"Don't act so surprised." Red crept under King Hadrian's cheeks, and his words sped up. "And don't repeat that either. The council wouldn't let me hear the end of it, and I bet my mother's turning in her grave as we speak."

The council never seemed happy about anything, so R-0 understood that concern. But the late queen had been dead for over a decade. "Is there a necromancer around?"

"A necromancer?" King Hadrian's eyes widened. "You know—Oh, nevermind. Don't worry about it." He bit his lip, and a chuckle escaped through his smile. "We should quiet down. We're getting close to the palace."

The guard patrols still followed their normal patterns, so it was unlikely anyone had noticed their absence. Or perhaps Jeza had covered for them. Either way, their reentry onto palace grounds was uneventful, and King Hadrian's window was still open, the rope hanging where they'd left it.

"If it wouldn't earn me a lecture, I'd be tempted to tell Eren she was worried for nothing," King Hadrian whispered as he grasped the rope.

Something above them clinked. R-0 paused, closing their eyes and focusing on the noise. It came from King Hadrian's room—a quiet thud followed by the shuffling of papers.

Someone was in there.

R-0's eyes snapped open, and they grabbed the rope, blocking King Hadrian.

"R-0?" King Hadrian asked. "What's wrong?"

R-0 focused on the windowsill and flickered through their memories. The curtains were positioned differently than they had left them, and barely perceptible shadows flitted across the folds of the fabric. There was no doubt someone was in his room. But who?

And were they a threat?

"There are no visitors on your schedule right now."

"Right . . ."

"There's a visitor in your room."

King Hadrian's eyes widened, and he stared at the open window. "You're sure?"

Either the intruder had dispatched the guards at King Hadrian's door, or they had taken advantage of the rope and entered through the window. Either way, not scheduling a meeting through the proper channels was evidence they didn't have good intentions.

"I spoke too soon. Seems like Shalloth decided to make a fool of me." King Hadrian let go of the rope and stepped back. "Go. Figure out what's going on."

"Yes sir," R-0 said. "Will you hide?"

They could handle the intruder, but not without leaving King Hadrian alone and vulnerable. But when they had been in the city—people saw what they expected. The people they visited knew he was king, but none of the passersby on the street saw King Hadrian behind the simple glamour that disguised him, because no one expected him to be there. Even if someone found him, no one would expect the king to be hiding in the bushes. Anonymity was its own protection.

"Good idea." King Hadrian slipped behind one of the bushes and crouched. R-0 could still see him clearly, but R-0's vision was sharper than the organics', and they knew where to look.

R-0 climbed the rope, arcing their arms away from their body to keep their plates from grinding against themselves. For now, the intruder didn't know about their presence, and it was an advantage they wanted to maintain.

RISE OF THE FORGEHEARTS

They slowed as they neared the top, peeking through the curtains. From this angle, they couldn't see the intruder, just their shadow moving in synchronization with the shuffling of papers and shifting of drawers. They were in the king's closet.

R-0 hefted themself onto the ledge, unable to prevent themself from clanking against the stone. The shuffling paused, and the shadow jumped. R-0 sprinted into action, vaulting into the room without hesitation.

A humanoid figure hunched over the king's chest of drawers, a hood covering their hair and a scarf wrapped around their mouth and nose. Even their eyes were covered with a thin piece of fabric that obscured their characteristics. They wore black gloves, but a glimmering ring worn outside their glove caught the low light from King Hadrian's lamp. R-0 checked for any symbols or identifiers, but it was a simple silver band with an amethyst crystal on the bridge.

"Step back," R-0 said. "This room belongs to King Hadrian, and you are intruding."

"I'm supposed to be here." A metallic voice rang out from behind the scarf, and the intruder didn't pause, continuing to rummage through the drawers. "I've got orders from the king."

They were a construct. But King Hadrian had said R-0 was the only construct on duty. Had the reintegration efforts been approved during his absence?

"King Hadrian is not expecting visitors," R-0 said.

"There must be some mistake." They slowly closed the drawer and stepped forward. "Return to the guard station for orders."

R-0 paused. King Hadrian had said he wasn't expecting any guests, so why would they say otherwise? The guard station would have complete logs of authorized appearances. But Eren would be there, and explaining the construct's presence in King Hadrian's room would require them to admit that R-0 and the king had *not* been in the room.

"You will need to head to the guard station as well for verification," R-0 said.

"That's unneeded. I know my orders." They reached for another drawer.

"Stop."

They pulled the drawer open and rummaged inside, tossing King Hadrian's clothes to the floor. His meticulously organized closet was quickly becoming a disaster. Why would the king ever order something like this?

A lie. It was the only explanation for the discrepancy between what King Hadrian and the intruder had said. It also explained the strange actions the king would never authorize. But . . . why would a construct lie? And why would they break into King Hadrian's room?

One step at a time. R-0 tried to corral their curiosity. Once the intruder was apprehended, they could get the answers to all their questions.

"You are lying," R-0 said. "Please, step away."

"Leave," the intruder said. "That's an order."

"Apologies." R-0 rested their hand on the hilt of their blade. If needed, their other sword was still on King Hadrian's nightstand where they'd left it, but protocol was to give an explicit warning before resorting to physical force. "Your orders cannot be completed. Step away from the king's belongings, or you will be forcibly removed."

"Is that a threat?"

"If it needs to be."

They stood in silence, then slowly stepped over the pile of clothes on the floor and out of the closet. "Fine. Let's go get this sorted out."

R-0's plates cooled, and their flame subsided. Relief. A peaceful resolution was preferable. R-0 headed for the door, but at the same second, the intruder dashed toward the window.

They were fast—faster than most standard issue constructs. Speed to this degree was rarely an attribute the technomancers prioritized. If R-0 had been extended at their full size, they couldn't have caught the intruder. But in their current, reduced form, they matched the intruder's movements and were just able to wrap their fingers around their wrist, stopping them.

"Let go!" They kicked, lodging their foot against R-0's chest for leverage as they tried to yank their hand back.

RISE OF THE FORGEHEARTS

R-0 tightened their grip. The construct hadn't been planning to come with R-0. Another lie.

"Please, do not struggle." R-0 reached for their other hand. Even without shackles available, they could restrain them until the guards arrived. Except every time they tried, the intruder ducked or weaved out of the way.

"What's going on in there?" one of the guards shouted from the hallway.

"There's an intruder," R-0 said.

The doorknob jiggled, followed by a few bangs on the door. "Let us in."

The intruder struggled to wriggle out of R-0's grip. They couldn't restrain them and open the door.

"Please hold."

While R-0 was looking at the door, the construct lunged forward with a dagger. R-0 raised their hand to block, but the intruder redirected, aiming between R-0's hand and the base of their fingers. The dagger pressed against the wires there, and R-0's fingers flexed outward. Usually a dagger wouldn't concern R-0, but the strike was placed perfectly to render R-0's hand useless. The intruder either knew how constructs worked or was incredibly lucky. R-0 tried to grab them with their other hand, but—too quick—the intruder wriggled out of their grip and dashed toward the door.

Before they reached it, the door slammed open into the hallway, knocking into one of the guards. The guard stumbled backward, bracing against the wall for support. The intruder jumped forward, kicking the second guard's stomach. The guard doubled over as the construct ran past him.

"Wait!" R-0 yelled. They followed them out the door and down the hallway.

"Where is King Hadrian?"

"Someone stop that construct!"

The guards yelled from behind, but R-0 didn't slow. There would be time to explain later, and every second wasted allowed the intruder to get farther away. Slowly, R-0 gained ground.

The scarf slid down the intruder's face, revealing smooth metallic plates. They chanted under their breath, and the ring shone, blue light sparkling from the small amethyst. The stone beneath R-0's feet exploded upward, tripping R-0 and sending them tumbling to the floor. Their shoulder plates scraped against the ground, chipping off bits of stone and forming a cloud of dust. R-0 pushed themself to their feet.

What had just happened? A simple chase should have been easy for R-0 to execute, unless . . . was it magic?

R-0 didn't have time to wonder. They performed a quick survey of their body. No permanent damage. The few scrapes and dents were primarily cosmetic. They sprinted forward, past the storage room.

A technomancer poked her head out and waved. "R-0, report! What's going on?"

"Intruder." R-0 kept running, rounding a corner and heading straight into . . . a dead end.

The intruder was gone.

Stone blocked off the passageway from floor to ceiling. There were no windows, no doors—no way through.

"Where's the intruder?" The technomancer placed her hands on her knees and panted.

Where could they have gone? They couldn't have doubled back—R-0 would have seen them. They mentally retraced their steps. There were no other turns they could have taken, nowhere for them to hide, and nowhere else they could be.

"R-0?" the technomancer asked.

"They're gone."

"Gone? Where? There's nowhere to go."

They were missing something. But what? How could they have gotten through? They pushed on the wall, but it didn't budge. Each stone was perfectly in place, and despite checking the grout lines and pushing on each individual piece, everything remained solid. It was exactly as it seemed—a dead end.

If only they hadn't been delayed. They should have seen the intruder round the corner and know where they went.

Magic. The pieces shifted into place, one after the other. The shifting stone beneath R-0's feet, the glow of the ring . . . If magic could manipulate the stone floor, couldn't it also manipulate the wall in front of them?

"Magic," R-0 echoed the realization out loud. It was the only way they could have escaped.

"What about it?"

"The intruder escaped with a magic ring."

"Impossible." The technomancer shook her head. "The palace walls are warded against magic."

R-0 frowned. It was the only explanation that made any sense—they had seen it themself with the floor. "Come look."

They retraced their steps down the hallway to where the floor had tripped them.

The technomancer stopped beside them. "What am I supposed to be looking at?"

Perfectly even and smooth stone lined the hallway where R-0 had tripped. They searched the rest of the area, but the only sign the floor had been disrupted was the nicks in the stone from R-0's fall.

"The floor was wrong." Where were the uneven peaks and the protrusion that had sent them tumbling?

"You mean you fell." The technomancer narrowed their eyes.

No. They were perfectly capable of running across a flat surface. They hadn't tripped. Besides, they had seen it. "No, the floor—"

One of the guards ran toward them. "Get away from the construct."

The technomancer's gaze shifted between R-0 and the guard, but he didn't back away. "What's going on?"

"King Hadrian was alone with the construct. Now he's gone." Two more guards joined the first and encircled R-0. "We're taking them to the dungeon."

CHAPTER 15

R-0 waited in their cell.

The room was designed to contain organics, not constructs. A thin blanket covered a cot in the corner, and iron bars threaded into the floor far enough apart that the inside of the cell was visible but too close for even small organics to slip out. A locked chain kept the door closed but would do little to stop R-0 if they tried to break free. They had said as much to the guards escorting them here, but none of them seemed interested in what R-0 had to say. The only thing they'd listened to was R-0's comments about King Hadrian's location. One guard had run off, returning a few minutes later to report that R-0 was right. King Hadrian was safe.

Still, the guards didn't release them, and the longer they stood in their cell, the more uneasy they became.

It wasn't that the accommodations were poor. In fact, this was far better than where they'd stayed when there was no question of their innocence. This room had more space, more amenities, more light, more . . . everything than the storage rooms. The constructs had enough room to stand still—nothing more. No space to pace, no cot to rest on. The technomancers kept the lights off and the doors locked.

The constructs had committed no crimes, so why were their accommodations worse than prisoners in the dungeon?

"Ain't seen one of you in here before." Across the hall, a prisoner pressed his face between the bars, squinting at R-0. "But I heard things were changin' up top."

"It is a temporary arrangement."

"What're you in for?"

There was no reason, just unfounded suspicions. An easily resolved problem once Eren spoke with King Hadrian. R-0 just needed to have patience. "A misunderstanding."

The man leaned back, holding onto the bars as he laughed. "Can't tell you how many times I've heard that one. What's the real reason?"

"That is the real reason."

"Yeah, and I'm the king."

R-0 walked to the edge of the cell. The man looked nothing like King Hadrian. He had unevenly cut greasy black hair and yellow eyes that glowed. A jagged scar ran from his eye to his lips, cracking the top of his smile in half.

Could it be a glamour? They studied the edges for any signs of blurriness or other indication that magic was disguising his appearance. They checked the facial structure for any similarities to King Hadrian, but there weren't any. The prisoner's bones sunk deep into his face, and his complexion lacked the warmth that usually accompanied flesh. If R-0 couldn't hear his beating heart, they wouldn't have been sure he even had one.

Even a glamour couldn't obscure someone's appearance to this degree. The prisoner wasn't human—he was a tral, an uncommon race R-0 knew little about. They had a strange connection with the Flow that wasn't well understood, and their eyes were luminescent—a trait not shared by any other types of organic.

"You aren't King Hadrian."

"No shit."

"Why do you lie?" R-0 asked. What was the point in speaking if they weren't actually communicating anything worthwhile? First, the intruder in King Hadrian's room, and now this stranger.

"Forget it. I ain't about to waste my time explaining it. Got far too much important stuff to do here. Real busy schedule, you know." He returned to his cot and slumped against the wall, letting his head tilt back and his eyes close.

R-0 had upset him, but they weren't sure why. All they had done was ask a question the same as he had. Perhaps R-0 asked the wrong question.

"What are you in here for?" R-0 asked.

The prisoner's eyes shot open, his pupils blending with the yellows of his irises momentarily before the black centers of his eyes solidified. "Was doing some research that some people found . . . unsavory."

"Unsavory how?"

"I created art. Beautiful progress. Lights, warmth, messaging . . . the managrid could be used for so much more than it is now. But they weren't willing to pay the price. A few people die, and suddenly, everyone wants to stop."

"Your research hurt people?"

"A necessary sacrifice. Human hearts have an interesting property of being a fantastic conduit for power, so I . . . collected them."

"Organics cannot live without a heart."

"A minor inconvenience."

"That seems like a rather large issue."

"Well, the council agreed with you. They requested I pause my research, but . . ." For a moment, his eyes brightened, shedding light across his growing smile. "How could I?" His smile fell, and his eyes dulled back to a dim glow. "So here I am."

A murderer. This explained why he lied as well. At least he was consistent in his immorality. But why, when given a choice, would he choose evil instead of good? Perhaps King Hadrian would be able to explain once he arrived. He'd said he wasn't qualified, but who else could R-0 ask?

Unease settled in R-0's chest. The preliminary investigation should have concluded by now. So why had no one come for them?

Perhaps the intruder's magic ring was to blame for the delay. Magic would certainly complicate the investigation. Without R-0's testimony, it would be even harder to piece events together. The guards had only seen the intruder for a few seconds, and there was no proof of the ring, only the dents in R-0's plates to show the chase had happened at all. That could feasibly be explained through clumsiness, although R-0 knew they hadn't tripped—the intruder had done something.

R-0 tried not to worry, but the longer they waited, the more their mind focused on the worst possible outcomes. Their gears spun quicker, sputtering and ticking as they skipped over one another in unnatural rhythms. They tried to slow their gears, but every time they were close to succeeding, their thoughts grew louder, and the gears sped up once more.

What if something had happened to the king?

What if the intruder had returned?

What if they needed R-0's help?

"Keep it down, will ya?" The tral banged on his wall a couple of times for emphasis. "Some of us are trying to sleep."

"Apologies," R-0 said. They tried once more to slow their gears, but the barrage of what-ifs accelerated, and the ticking followed suit. "They won't stop."

"Great." He flopped back on his cot. "No sleep for me tonight."

"They will come for me. Soon."

The prisoner chuckled. "Hate to break it to ya, gears. No one is coming for you."

"They will."

"Some advice for ya. If those bastards in charge are keeping you around, it's because they need something from you. Nothing more, nothing less. We're all just toys to them, pieces in their game. The second you stop being useful, you're in their way. And that's when you wind up down here never to see the light of day again—or worse."

"Worse?"

"For you? Decommissioned."

"King Hadrian would never—"

"King Hadrian would never stand up to the council. He's so wrapped up in keeping his crown, he lets the lot of them do whatever they want."

R-0 paused. There was some truth to the man's words. Despite his position as king, King Hadrian often deferred to the council's judgments. That's why he and R-0 had to sneak out to investigate in the first place.

"He was a good kid," the prisoner said. "But unless he grows up, the council is king, and he's nothing more than a dog on a leash."

"He is not a dog. He is—"

"Quiet down." Eren's voice carried through the dungeon, echoing off the stone.

R-0 stopped what they were saying and stood at attention.

Eren stopped outside of R-0's cell. "King Hadrian corroborated your story. Which means it's time to get you out of here."

Finally. R-0 pushed on the cell door, snapping the chain. The lock fell with a clatter, and Eren hopped backward.

"What in Shalloth's name are you doing?"

R-0 stepped out of their cell and picked up the chain. "You said it was time to get out of here."

"Yes. And I was about to use the *keys* to *open the fucking door.*" She clasped her hands together, and even as she took deep breaths, her brow furrowed. "But sure, let's just break everything we touch instead."

"You've been holding out on me, gears." The tral's laughter filled the hallway, a noise somewhere between a raspy bark and cough. "Mind doing mine next?"

"Don't even think about it." Eren's eyes narrowed, and her hand moved to the hilt of her sword. "Either of you."

R-0 had no intention of freeing a criminal. Instead, they ran their fingers along the chain. Only a few links were broken—the rest was still solid. They removed the mangled pieces and bent the remaining metal back together. The lock had nothing but cosmetic damage, and they placed it on the door. "It's fixed."

Eren sighed. "I guess you expect me to thank you now."

"Gratitude is unnecessary."

"It's unearned. Fixing what you break is the bare minimum, and there's a lot more broken than just a chain, thanks to you lot."

R-0 checked the rest of the cells, then Eren's belongings for anything else that was in disrepair, but everything appeared fine.

"You don't have to be so hard on them." The tral kicked his feet on the wall, his bare soles slapping against the stone and getting Eren's attention. "Have a heart."

Eren rolled her eyes, but her expression was muted by the deep bags beneath her eyes. She ignored the tral.

"Apologies," R-0 said. "Is there more that can be fixed?"

"Not unless you can get me fifty good men by sunrise to relieve the guards going on triples."

If King Hadrian was here, this would be his opportunity to convince Eren to agree to his reintegration plans. But in his absence . . . R-0 had heard his arguments enough times they could recite them. "Perhaps—"

"There's nothing you can do, R-0." Eren cut them off. "You're dismissed for the night."

"Yes ma'am."

R-0 began walking down the hallway. They needed to discuss the intruder with King Hadrian. What had the construct been after? Had they stolen anything? They had spent the night looking for M-118 and answers in the city, but maybe the answer to the constructs' absence was in the palace itself.

"R-0?" Eren called out. "The storage rooms are the other way."

"But King Hadrian—"

"Has a different guard assignment for the night. You're not needed." Eren walked past them, checking each cell as she passed.

R-0's feet remained frozen in place. They had heard Eren's orders, but . . . they couldn't force themself to go. Eren's footsteps faded as she circled around the block to check the cells on the other side.

In the past—before the incident—they had occasionally left King Hadrian to be protected by another guard rotation. They had spent that time still, lifeless, and empty or on another mission. Now, they couldn't shut off. If King Hadrian didn't need them, then what was their purpose?

R-0 belonged at King Hadrian's side. Without that . . .

"What are you still doing here?" Eren's voice rang out from down the hallway. She swung a heavy set of keys around her fingers twice before clipping them to her belt.

"There are no other assignments," R-0 said.

"Things were so much simpler when you just listened." She sighed and cocked her hand on her hip. "What do you usually do when you don't have an assignment?"

"Protocol is to wait in the storage rooms."

"So why aren't you heading there?"

R-0 wished they could blame tiredness or the late night for their lack of response. But they didn't need to sleep. They needed to do something. That was the problem.

"Well?" Eren raised her eyebrows. "What're you doing here still?"

"There is nothing to be accomplished in the storage rooms."

"Have you received new orders?"

"No."

"Then you know what to do." Eren waited, and R-0 slowly nodded. She was right. R-0 knew exactly what was expected, so they turned and walked toward the storage rooms. Eren nodded, seemingly content, and headed the other way out of the dungeon—a path that would take her to King Hadrian's room. Where R-0 should have been going.

R-0 walked to the storage room but hesitated in the doorframe. On the surface, it was exactly as they remembered, but something was different. Although the constructs stood in organized rows, their eyes shifted about. Some fidgeted. R-0 thought they saw one shaking, a barely perceptible shiver in their plates. Their own plates mimicked the movement, trembling no matter how hard they tried to remain still. They searched the rows of constructs for B-7, but their assigned spot was empty.

R-0 didn't want to stay in the storage room. They'd spent the night in the city, exploring what the world had to offer. Their investigation into the missing constructs had resulted in more questions, and answering them required actions R-0 couldn't take from the storage room. The only ones forced to sit and do nothing were the prisoners in the dungeon.

But was leaving any different than staying if they had no purpose to guide them? King Hadrian didn't need them. There was no reason for them to wander the palace halls.

Still, R-0 couldn't stay in the storage room doing nothing. They would find a way to be useful.

R-0's steps carried them farther and farther away from the storage room, unsure where they were going. Only one thing was certain—anywhere would be better than here. They went to the other side of the palace, but even that wasn't far enough to forget the echo of silence filling the storage room.

The other constructs deserved the same chance.

R-0 couldn't do anything about that now. Even if they released the constructs, they had nowhere to go.

But what if King Hadrian's reintegration plan succeeded? The constructs could go back to how things were before. They wouldn't be stuck in the storage rooms. They could continue to serve their purpose.

Even if King Hadrian didn't require a guard for the night, R-0 could still help protect him. They could help him achieve his goals. Eren didn't have enough guards to search the entire palace for the intruder. But R-0 could search. The corruption was irrelevant—the constructs could still function and serve. No, they could do even more than before.

And R-0 could prove it.

CHAPTER 16

R-0 ducked into the closest room as footsteps approached from around the corner. With the door closed, they couldn't see anyone, but they could hear them. Normally R-0 would walk right past them, but normally R-0 was operating in an official capacity.

Tonight, they operated on their own. Any interaction with an organic risked being reported to Eren. If any guards searching for the rogue construct that broke into King Hadrian's room found R-0 wandering alone, they could mistake them for the intruder. Another trip to the dungeon was an inefficiency they needed to avoid if they were going to prove themself and help King Hadrian.

R-0 could hear Eren's words as clearly as if she were standing in the room with them. *Fixing what you break is the bare minimum, and there's a lot more broken than just a chain, thanks to you. You're not needed.*

If Eren caught them wandering around, she would blame the corruption. She would blame R-0. Just another broken thing on her list of broken things to deal with.

The footsteps grew closer, differentiating into two sets. Neither matched the clomping steps of guard boots. One pair sounded faint and soft, the other sharp like formal shoes often worn by women in the palace. R-0's flame grew in their chest, burning faster than usual and sputtering as it didn't have the energy to sustain the sudden growth. The footsteps stopped just outside the door, so close R-0 could hear their beating hearts.

"Did you hear that?" As soon as she spoke, R-0 identified her voice. Jeza Doblin.

R-0 stilled, all thoughts forgotten except the thought of remaining hidden. They tried to limit their functions, requiring less fire to fuel them. Their flame responded, slowly shrinking and quieting.

"I don't hear anything."

R-0 didn't recognize the second voice, but his words gurgled, as if they traveled through water instead of air.

"If this isn't proof I need more sleep, I don't know what is."

The door squeaked on its hinges as someone leaned against it. R-0 resisted the urge to step back. They had almost heard R-0's flame. They would definitely hear R-0's heavy footstep.

"If you stopped hovering and let us do our job, you'd get more sleep, don't you think?" the man asked. An odd click followed his words.

"And let you make a mess of things?" Jeza asked. "Not a chance."

They both chuckled, and their footsteps resumed, carrying them away from R-0's hiding spot.

Eren was wrong—King Hadrian still needed R-0. The palace security was stretched too thin. If R-0 had so easily evaded detection, more nefarious people could as well . . . like the intruder in King Hadrian's room earlier that evening.

But how could R-0 find the intruder?

They flickered through their memories, searching for anything that could help. The construct's scarf had covered their designation, but they had shown they were equipped with voice capabilities and adept at fighting. This matched the constructs assigned to guard duties within the palace, but their size was wrong. Even the smallest line of guards was larger than the construct R-0 had fought, and only royal constructs were capable of changing their size. The constructs' plates were too thin to belong to a royal construct.

None of the other palace constructs were trained in combat, which meant the intruder wasn't stationed here. If R-0 could find where they entered, perhaps they could discover more about who they were or where they came from.

They headed for the gardens, easily maneuvering around the patrols and avoiding more unplanned stops. There was only one guard they couldn't avoid—the guard stationed at the exit of the palace.

R-0 considered going back to King Hadrian's room and out the window. But if Eren was following protocol, his room and the surrounding hallways would be swarming with guards. And their chance of running into Eren was too high.

No, R-0 wouldn't bother with backtracking. They would walk through the doors, and if the guard asked, they would share their plan. It was an efficient use of time. The guard would have to understand.

R-0 silently rehearsed what they would say. The guard would greet them, and they would return the greeting. If asked, they'd explain they were investigating the intruder.

But as soon as the entrance came into view, their plan fell apart.

The guard didn't look up as R-0 approached. The young merfolk sat on the floor, knees pulled into her chest and head leaning back against the wall. Soft snores whistled with each rise and fall of her chest. Even as R-0's heavy steps thumped next to her, she didn't stir.

R-0 could easily pass her, and no one would ever know they had been here. Was this how the intruder had entered the palace—walking straight through the front gates? No, that wasn't possible. The guards outside King Hadrian's room would have seen them. The intruder had to have entered through the open window. Still, a sleeping guard was a security risk.

"You shouldn't be sleeping," R-0 said.

The guard didn't respond. R-0 repeated themself louder with the same result. It was common for noise to wake King Hadrian, but perhaps this guard was different. They searched their memories for other methods of waking organics up, settling on a memory of Jeza running her fingers through King Hadrian's hair.

R-0 gently reached out, starting at the crown of her head, then ran their fingers across her scales.

The guard's eyes snapped open, followed by a startled shriek.

"R-0!" She ducked away from their touch and jumped to her feet. Her hand flew to the sword at her side. "What are you doing?"

"You're not supposed to sleep while on guard," R-0 explained.

"I—uh—" She stepped back as she stumbled over her words. It wasn't unusual for organics to be disoriented when first waking up, but she was struggling more than most. She studied R-0, and slowly, her hand left her weapon. "You were just waking me up?"

R-0 nodded.

"Thank you?" Normally gratitude was a statement, but her voice rose at the end like a question. She bit at her bottom lip as she returned to her post. "Please don't tell Eren. This is my fourth day running doubles. I'm doing my best."

R-0 wasn't sure what to say. Sleeping posed a risk to the king's security, but now that she was awake, the issue was resolved. What would they report?

"What are you doing out here anyway?" she asked.

"There was an intruder," R-0 explained. They were prepared for this line of questioning. "Investigation is required."

"But that doesn't explain why you are here." The guard rubbed her eyes. "I thought all the constructs were staying in the storage rooms."

"They are."

"But you're not?"

"No." R-0 shook their head. "It's inefficient."

What if she thought the same as Eren? Could she tell just by looking at R-0 that they were broken? How could they ever prove they could fix things if they weren't given the chance?

This *was* their chance.

"Thank you for your time," R-0 said. They attempted to shift their plates into an approximation of a smile as they stepped through the door, quickening their pace to give the young merfolk less time to respond—less time to stop them or ask more questions. When they were a few paces away, they called back over their shoulder. "Enjoy your evening."

R-0 waited, expecting the guard to call out, to stop them. But only silence followed, and they walked freely into the gardens.

Outside the palace, ambient sounds filled the cold night. The managrid underfoot hummed, critters scurried about, waves rhythmically crashed in the distance, and the wind oscillated between loud gusts that shook the leaves from the trees and quiet whistles that weaved through R-0's exterior plates. R-0 didn't soften their steps, letting metal crunching against frost and concrete join in with the variety of sounds.

They walked the walls, then circled in, making detours when they needed to leave space between them and the patrols and stopping once they were close to Eren's investigation perimeter.

Nothing.

The two back entrances leading to the servant's quarters were locked and barricaded. R-0 didn't inspect the front gate. It would have been covered in the initial investigation. Instead, R-0 checked the walls for damage—three times, just in case the corruption had caused a distraction they were unaware of. Missing something once was a possibility. Missing it three times? Impossible. Just to be sure, they checked the walls a fourth time. After seeing how King Hadrian snuck out, they also looked for low-lying trees. But besides King Hadrian's tree, there was only one other possible route an intruder could have used to scale the walls: a rocky outcropping that, if someone were agile enough, would let them leap to the wall.

But they found no sign of footprints, and the other side led to a sheer cliff face. If the intruder had entered through here, they would have to be an extremely skilled climber. R-0 didn't know of any construct unit with that skillset.

Unless they went straight through. The palace structures were warded against magic, but what if the blackouts were affecting the wards or the construct had found a way to bypass them?

Magic was the only explanation for R-0's failed chase and the intruder's disappearance, so it had to be considered for their entry as well. But how could they check for magic? The stone in the hallway had returned to its original state with no evidence of disruption. Out here would be the same. Still, they checked the entire perimeter for footprints, just in case.

Nothing.

R-0 had ruled out a few possibilities but was no closer to locating the intruder. They had tried, but they couldn't fix anything. And no amount of wandering around the palace grounds would change that.

R-0 sat on the rocks of one of the raised garden beds. For a moment, they were lost in the colors of the flowers, the soft texture of the petals underneath their fingertips. An owl flew above, casting shadows across the foliage that left their vibrance muted. R-0 pressed too hard, and the petal tore in half. They held the torn petal in their palm. Another broken thing.

As beautiful as it still was, the realization that it couldn't last hit R-0. It was alone in their hand, nature surrounded by hard, lifeless metal. It had no soil to retrieve nutrients from. No water to sustain it. They had been careless in picking it, and it needed to be returned to its original state if it was going to survive.

R-0 held the petals as gently as they could between two fingers and tried to lay them on top of one another, but a gust of wind separated the pieces, leaving them to spiral to the ground. R-0 tried again but only tore the petals more and crumpled what remained attached to the stem.

R-0 sat in the center of the path, staring at the destroyed plant remnants in their hands. Perhaps the healers could put it back together. Or maybe King Hadrian would know what to do.

No. Eren was right. R-0 caused more problems than they fixed, and they couldn't fix this. They couldn't put the plant back together—they couldn't return things to how they were before.

The plant would die.

The tremble that had begun back in the storage room intensified into full-blown shakes. Their face plates spasmed, and a choked gurgle escaped their throat. They couldn't feel any heat from the fire in their chest.

The thoughts that had overwhelmed R-0 since the incident grew quiet, and a wordless, indistinguishable roar filled their mind. R-0 dropped the flower to the ground and clawed at the metal on their chest, shoving the end of their finger into the head of the screw to take it off. Had something happened to the flame? Was that the reason they felt this way? The screw fell to the ground as R-0 moved on to the next ones. Then, they removed their chest plate.

Inside, a golden flame still burned.

The roar in their mind quieted, creating space for thoughts that had been silenced to overwhelm R-0. What were they doing? What did any of this mean? Why did they feel . . . bad? They had no visible injuries or evidence of external malfunction, but still everything felt wrong. The air moving through their internal tubes didn't flow naturally, and R-0 had to force it to circulate. Their limbs still trembled. Their vision blurred around the edges, and their eyes couldn't stay focused. Even though the shining golden flame still burned in their chest, it was only an echo of the roaring blaze they had seen on the first night.

They were broken. Corrupted.

A cold breeze blew, and R-0 curled their knees into their chest to protect the flame from the wind. They should have reattached their chest plate, but the screws were strewn about the pathway, and they couldn't bring their hands to move. One rested on a crumpled flower petal, and another unexplainable wave of corruption washed over R-0. Their vision deteriorated until they could hardly see, and they closed their eyes, resting their head on their knees.

R-0 sat, listening to the ticking gears and drowning in the wordless roar, until the sound slowly became comforting. It was a certainty they could rely on, and they focused on the ticks. As they did, the noise grew steadier—stronger. After two hundred ticks, they opened their eyes, but continued sitting with their head resting on their knees. Their vision had returned to normal, and the flame in their chest was burning a little brighter, although still not as strong as it had been.

They lifted their head . . . and came face to face with one of the council members.

She sat in the center of the path, only a few feet away. Her hands relaxed on her knees as her legs crossed over each other, revealing simple pants under her long robes. She appeared around Eren's age, but worry didn't wrinkle her expressions the same way it did Eren's. Instead, her expression was serene, her green eyes as calm and steady as the night air. Like R-0, she had a sheath strapped to each leg. Each held a simple dagger, matching except for the base of the handles, where one had a sun engraved and the other had a moon. The symbols representing Eclipse on the cuffs of her sleeves were the only thing ornate about her outfit, and light from the managrid lamps caught on the golden thread embroidered into a sun that matched her hair. Tucked into her palm was a handful of stripped screws.

R-0's screws.

R-0 had been too distracted—they hadn't even noticed her approach, much less seen her retrieve their parts. How long had she been here? R-0 tried to search their memories for her name, but their mind was too loud. They couldn't remember.

But they remembered her words.

We first must answer what the constructs have become, and what responsibility we have not only to our people, but also our creations.

The memory rang out above the chaos of R-0's mind, as if they were back in the council chamber for the first time after the incident. She had spoken in favor of the constructs.

This was worse than being caught by guards. Now not only would Eren find out about their insubordination—the entire council would hear of it. They had been trying to make things better, but only made them worse.

R-0 clenched their fists, trying to stop their whirring gears.

Seeing R-0's movement, the councilwoman slowly held out her hand, offering R-0 their screws. "Here."

Her voice was as quiet as a whisper, but without the husky strain that normally accompanied the tone. She was Quiet. It was a fitting title, much easier than wracking their memories for her given name.

R-0 tried to form words, to express gratitude, but instead they were silent as they retrieved their screws. They closed their chest plate, and slowly began to twist the screws back into place.

"You're not supposed to be out here," Quiet said.

R-0 couldn't deny it. "Apologies ma'am."

"You don't need to apologize to me."

When R-0 finished securing the plate, the damage they had caused was hardly noticeable. The technomancers would likely notice when they performed maintenance, but not before.

"But I am curious," Quiet continued. "What happened?"

R-0 couldn't explain the corruption that had overwhelmed them or all of their thoughts and questions about death, storage rooms, and constructs abandoned by their king. Instead, they picked up a piece of the flower from the ground. "It cannot be fixed."

"May I?" Quiet stretched out her palm.

R-0 dropped the petal. Her fingers trailed across the membranes without disrupting them. She gathered the remaining pieces, R-0 carefully helping.

When all the pieces had been retrieved, Quiet cupped the flower petals in one hand and cleared a spot of dirt with the other. She dug her fingers into the soil until an indentation formed, then dropped the flower into the hole. She separated the petals to the side like a wreath, leaving a pile of pods in the center that she pressed down deeper.

Quiet drew one of her daggers—the one with the moon at its base—and her skin began to glow. Magic. Warmth radiated from the light, and she slid the blade across her palm with ease. Blood trickled from the wound.

"Are you okay?" R-0 reached for the dagger. Orders that had seemed so far away surged to the front of their mind. R-0 was supposed to protect. They could protect Quiet, even if the danger was herself.

Quiet sheathed the dagger before R-0 could grab it and pressed her bleeding palm into the ground. "Where there is death, where there is hurt, there is also life and growth."

RISE OF THE FORGEHEARTS

Her magic spread to the soil, and a speck of green wriggled out of the dirt. The stem was as thin as one of R-0's wires, but it reached up toward the other plants. As another droplet of Quiet's blood fell, it grew thicker and sturdier.

"Sometimes things do not need to be fixed." Quiet pulled her hand away. "Sometimes it takes being broken to find the space we need to grow into what we're meant to be."

The plant stopped growing, a tiny bud curling at the end of the stem.

That wasn't what R-0 had been told, but it made far more sense given what they had seen of the world. R-0 couldn't make themselves behave the way they were before. They had been mindless—following orders without thoughts or feelings. They'd been an empty husk, a tool to be used by the organics. Without orders, they didn't act. They couldn't be the same, but what did that mean for what they were now?

"Will it flower again?" R-0 didn't dare touch the delicate plant but leaned as close as they could to examine it.

"Only time will tell." Quiet curled her hand along the stem, leaving small bloodstains where it rubbed against her wound. She looked straight at R-0 and continued, "But tonight has me feeling optimistic."

R-0's chest warmed. The trembling in their fingers had stopped. Somehow the night air had become more inviting, and R-0 could enjoy the beauty of the new growth, as well as the flowers around it.

Quiet sat with them, rubbing at her palm occasionally. They were grateful for her presence—her help. Without her, they might have still sat collapsed on the ground, succumbing to the corruption. But . . . what was a council member doing out on palace grounds in the middle of the night? First King Hadrian, then Jeza, now Quiet. R-0 double-checked their memories. Organics *did* require sleep.

"Why are you out here?" R-0 asked.

"There's serenity in the twilight," Quiet said. "I try to get what I can done before sunrise." She looked off in the distance where the sun would eventually peek out from the earth and rise over the castle walls. The sky's colors had already started to shift. It was almost morning. More time had passed than R-0 realized, but that still didn't explain Quiet's actions.

"All council members are supposed to be accompanied by guards."

"Does Eren have a guard?"

"No." R-0 hadn't considered it. It wasn't uncommon for Eren to rotate between assignments or perform her duties alone. Eren was a council member, but as captain of the guard, she was also a guard. By a technicality, she could fulfill both roles at once.

"Then I won't either." Quiet smiled. "Eren learned to stop fighting that battle long ago. I advise you do the same."

Advice. Not an order.

"It is not required?"

"No."

R-0 waited for Quiet to offer further explanation, but she didn't, leaving R-0 to mull over her words. They didn't have to listen to her. But she had been kind to them, and they would accept her advice. Besides, if Eren had agreed to Quiet's lack of guard detail, then it was sanctioned. R-0 had no reason to argue.

As the first rays of the sun peeked over the castle walls, Quiet stood. The emblems on her robe seemed to shimmer, the sun and moon blurring together in between the shining thread.

"Are you returning to King Hadrian's service this morning?" Quiet asked.

"Yes ma'am." R-0 mimicked her movements, standing next to her.

"I have a few matters to attend to first, but I'll see you at the council meeting later." Quiet smiled and started to walk away.

The discomfort in R-0's flame returned, growing as Quiet moved farther away. With the morning sun lighting the palace grounds, R-0's presence would likely bring unwanted attention. Besides, they had already searched—and failed—to find the intruder.

They hadn't considered this part of their plan. If they had discovered something it would have been simple to report their findings to the king. But they had nothing to report. Eren had assigned different guards to King Hadrian. They were supposed to be in the storage room. There was no order, no predictability to their actions.

R-0 followed Quiet.

It was routine and familiar, and R-0 easily fell into the pattern of her steps. She was more graceful than the king, her feet gliding across the cobblestones as quiet as the wildlife that peeked out of the flower beds. She occasionally looked over her shoulder, but mostly faced forward as she headed back toward the palace.

When they neared the front door, she paused and turned to face R-0. "Are you following me?"

"Yes ma'am."

"You could have asked to accompany me." Her statement carried no accusation, and nothing indicated if she was upset with R-0's presence.

R-0 wasn't sure what to say. They tried to find the words to ask now, but their voice failed them. Instead of speech, a cloud of smoke exited their mouth as their flame huffed.

Quiet walked farther away, and R-0 waited, unsure if they should continue following. Before they could make a decision, she called over her shoulder. "Come on. We don't want to be late."

CHAPTER 17

R-0 and Quiet had completed half a day's worth of tasks before most organics in the palace had even started their day. They started at the library, where Quiet exchanged an unlabeled, worn leather journal for a new book—*Deconstructing the Basics of Magic.* R-0 had only managed to scan part of the back blurb before she slid it into her bag and hurried off to their next stop. Priests and priestesses from across Haiden had sent her letters, and she read them while grabbing breakfast from the kitchens. She dropped an extra serving off at the guard stations, since—according to her—Eren would collapse of starvation if Quiet wasn't around to remind her to eat.

Quiet didn't ask R-0 as many questions as King Hadrian did, and when R-0 asked questions, she didn't give as many answers. But they kept a quick pace as they shuffled between tasks, never giving R-0's mind too long to wander. The familiarity of the palace made it easier for them to focus, especially in the early morning when distractions were few and far between.

Along the way, R-0 remembered the woman's designation—Councilwoman Riley. She wasn't a clan leader like the other council members. She was a priestess of the goddess Eclipse, representing not only Eclipse's followers, but all the religious organizations throughout the country. She was the most recent addition to the council after her predecessor—a retired dragon-scaled paladin of Eclipse who'd sat on the council for decades—passed a few years prior. Still, Quiet felt more fitting than her formal designation, and R-0 continued to use the nickname in their mind.

Even with all of their errands, they were first to arrive at the council meeting. The others slowly trickled in, their gazes lingering on R-0 and Quiet far longer than normal. R-0 was accustomed to this treatment, and if it bothered Quiet, she didn't let it show.

When Eren entered, she took a seat next to Quiet. "R-0 was supposed to be in the storage rooms." She kept her voice to a whisper and glanced between the other council members.

Quiet smirked. She reached under the table, threading her fingers through Eren's. "I thought you'd be happy to see me with a guard."

"Will this continue?"

"Probably not."

"That's what I thought." Eren slumped in her chair. But at an eye roll from Gretta, she straightened back up. "I hate these meetings."

"You could leave," R-0 said.

"Not a bad idea." The beginnings of a laugh escaped Eren's lips before her face returned to a scowl. "If the king doesn't show up soon, I will."

King Hadrian was the only one missing from the council chamber, and it made R-0 uneasy. The rays of sunlight shining through the window crept across the floor, almost reaching the table. The meeting should have started long before now. King Hadrian had been fine when R-0 left him last night, and the guards had found him quickly. He should have been safe.

So where was he now?

"He specifically requested that all of us attend this morning," Quiet said. "Have patience."

"Do you think it's because of the construct?" Robin leaned close to Gretta. His whispers were pointless, since his voice was barely lower than when he spoke normally. And even if R-0 couldn't overhear, Robin did little to hide his gaze falling on them.

It wasn't R-0's fault King Hadrian was late, and it wasn't their duty to correct the council members. But that didn't stop the comments from slipping in between their plates. Their gears turned in slow, choppy movements, like they hadn't been oiled in too many maintenance cycles.

"He can't be bothered to show up, but he expects us to trust him and follow his lead?" Robin scowled.

Jeza leaned forward. "I'm sure King Hadrian has a very good reason to keep us waiting, and after the night he had, we can extend him a little grace."

"If he'd done something about the constructs, maybe he'd have had a more peaceful night."

"Or maybe the construct would have been an assassin instead." Jeza narrowed her eyes. "We still don't know whose orders the construct was operating under. You wouldn't have any information on that, would you, Councilman?"

"What are you implying? I cannot believe—"

"I will get an update." Quiet stood, her chair scraping against the floor and cutting off Robin's words. "R-0, would you accompany me?"

Everyone's eyes fell on R-0. They tried to speak, but instead just nodded and followed Quiet out. Checking on King Hadrian was much preferable to remaining among the bickering council members.

The two hurried through the twisting halls to the king's room. Two organic guards stood next to his door, bowing respectfully as Quiet and R-0 approached.

"Councilwoman Riley, how can we help you?"

"I'm here to see King Hadrian."

"He's still sleeping."

"You two are dismissed. Thank you." Quiet waited in front of them.

"The next shift change isn't until this afternoon." The guard ran his fingers through his hair. "We can't leave him unguarded."

"I wouldn't call 'under the protection of a royal construct' unguarded." Quiet's voice remained soft, but it carried a sense of authority that was impossible to ignore. "Would you?"

"Well, um, I'm not sure—"

"I am. Take a break, both of you."

Their hesitation was evident in the furrowed looks plastered across their faces and their fingertips dancing along the hem of their clothes. But they dipped their heads with mumbled agreement, then scurried off.

Quiet seemed sure of R-0's abilities, but that wasn't what Eren had said last night. Was Quiet aware Eren herself had changed the guard assignments?

"Eren assigned them to guard the king," R-0 said before Quiet could knock. "Not the constructs."

"Then she is a fool, wouldn't you agree?" Quiet smiled and knocked on the door.

Eren was many things—a skilled warrior and a competent leader to name a few. The guards obeyed her without question, and although King Hadrian often disagreed with her, he respected her opinion and called her for counsel on many occasions. She hardly seemed a fool. If anyone was the fool in this situation, it was R-0, thinking they knew better. What had they accomplished by ignoring Eren's orders? They'd discovered nothing new about the intruder and inconvenienced Quiet.

A few moments passed, and Quiet knocked again—two quick raps with enough force that the door shuddered.

There was no chance King Hadrian didn't hear it, which meant he didn't want to be interrupted.

"Perhaps he should be left alone," R-0 said.

But as Quiet continued waiting patiently, their earlier thoughts resurfaced. What if King Hadrian wasn't answering because something had happened? What if Jeza was right, and the next intruder was an assassin?

R-0 grabbed the doorknob, preparing to snap it off, but it twisted beneath their fingertips as King Hadrian swung the door open.

"Riley." His eyes softened as he saw Quiet. Then his expression tightened as he turned to R-0. "And R-0! You're okay?"

The spiral of what-ifs disappeared, and R-0 relaxed seeing their king. He was safe. R-0 hadn't failed in their directive by leaving him alone last night. "Yes sir."

"Planning on wearing that this morning?" Quiet gestured at his robe and slippers. "Or do you plan to make the council wait even longer?"

King Hadrian rubbed his eyes and looked over his shoulder at the window. "It's already that late?"

Quiet nodded, and King Hadrian cursed. "Delay them for me, if you would?"

"I have a riveting speech already planned."

King Hadrian's eyes flickered up, hiding his irises and revealing more of the white sclera. "I'm sure it'll be lovely." His lips turned down into a frown despite his positive words. R-0 wasn't sure why. They looked forward to Quiet's speech.

"Where are the guards?" King Hadrian looked down the hallway.

"I thought it best we speak in private," Quiet said. "Many on the council are unhappy with the direction you seem to be taking. When you had control of the constructs, you were sheltered from their wrath. Without that, you are vulnerable."

"What are you saying?"

"I'm saying if you do not prove you are still worthy of being their king, the council may move against you."

King Hadrian's face fell. "Do I still have your support?"

"Most of my clergy are ready to embrace the constructs, but not all of the churches share that sentiment. The Hunter's Inquisition ruled whatever happened is unrelated to Xefcvew, so there is no need for a hunt. But Shalloth's followers are split, and there are many who feel chaos such as this could only be a curse from Del'Star."

R-0 wasn't sure how Quiet kept up with it so easily. There were over a dozen gods mortals worshipped, each with their own demands, ethos, and conflict. Some dead, some alive. Some like Eclipse and Shalloth had multiple grand churches throughout Haiden, while others had nothing more than a few priests working from their homes. The gods themselves warred—like the Hunter aiming to eradicate Xefcvew and his followers—and even within each church, dissenting opinions were commonplace. The more R-0 learned about the gods, the more certain they were that the only unifying factor among them was that they were all trapped behind the barrier, unable to enter the mortal world. But Quiet simplified the pages and pages of letters she'd received with ease.

"For now," Quiet continued, "you can count on my support, but with what I've heard from the council, I fear it won't matter."

"I won't let it reach that point." King Hadrian shook his head. "Just because the constructs are not bound to me doesn't mean they are against us. Look at R-0."

R-0 straightened after the king's compliment, but despite his order, Quiet didn't even glance at R-0. "You have to convince the others, not me."

"How long until Councilman Uxius is back?"

"He wasn't due back for a month, but they've sent messages for him to return sooner. They haven't heard back yet."

"Then I still have time. They won't make a move without him." King Hadrian's voice cracked. "I won't abandon the constructs."

"I would advise you to keep R-0 close."

It was the opposite of what others were saying—to keep the constructs far away until what happened to them was understood and the resulting issues resolved.

King Hadrian nodded. "I will."

R-0's flame rose in their chest, filling the cavity and spreading through their interior tubing until their whole body felt warm. King Hadrian *did* want them around.

"Is there anything else?" King Hadrian asked.

She left with a silent shake of her head. Alone with the king, R-0's hands once more fidgeted at their side. They searched for words to fill the silence that was beginning to suffocate their flame.

It was King Hadrian who spoke first.

"I'm sorry, R-0." He ushered them into the room. "Things got a bit out of hand after the intruder last night. Eren was paranoid."

"There's no need to apologize."

King Hadrian's room had transformed overnight. A large map of the palace lay across his comforter, and papers were scattered along the edges. The ink was fresh, and two empty ink vials sat on the king's nightstand. His royal stamp was also wet, but whatever he had been working on had been sent already.

"I didn't realize they'd ordered you to the dungeon or the storage room. I assumed you were investigating the intruder with the others. Once I realized where you were, I went to get you, but you weren't there."

"You went to the storage rooms?" R-0 asked. Their flame flickered in their chest.

"I'm the one who should be surprised, not you. Where were you?"

"The intruder was investigated." R-0 wanted the king to know their time hadn't been wasted.

"What?"

"There is no evidence of entry along the palace walls. There were no disturbances in the gardens."

"You investigated it?" King Hadrian asked. "But Eren said she sent you to the storage rooms."

"Eren did not order the investigation."

"You did it on your own?"

R-0 nodded.

"By the gods . . ." King Hadrian clutched his hands into fists at his side. "What were you thinking?"

"Time spent there would be wasted, and it was more efficient to expedite the investigation."

"Did you discover anything? About the intruder or the other missing constructs?"

"No."

"The guards didn't either. We assumed the construct who broke in was one of the missing ones, and this is just the start of whatever they are planning."

"They were searching through the cabinets." The mess had been cleaned off the floor, but the papers had been shoved back into drawers, and some weren't fully closing. "Was anything taken?"

"Most of that is just my mother's old things I never could bring myself to get rid of or move into the archives." His gaze lingered on the cabinets for a tick, then he sighed. "But Eren doesn't think it was a thief. The crown, magic gemstones, even my gold was untouched. She's worried it was an assassination attempt."

"Then the investigation will continue until they are apprehended," R-0 said. If the construct was an assassin, the king wouldn't be safe until the intruder was caught. Just because they had failed once didn't mean they would stop trying. Perhaps they had missed something last night and a second look would reveal a clue.

"I'm still not sure it was an assassin," King Hadrian said. "Wouldn't they have left when I wasn't there? Or hidden while they waited for me to return? Something's off." He dropped the stack of papers back on the desk. King Hadrian stepped forward, looking into R-0's eyes with an intensity R-0 wasn't accustomed to. "But the guards will continue the investigation. I don't want you going off alone. Not until I have this figured out."

"Yes sir."

"Did anyone see you while you were alone?"

R-0 replayed the events of the night. "Councilwoman Riley."

"No one else?"

"One guard. At the front gates."

"Okay." King Hadrian's shoulder fell, and he seemed to relax a little. "I'll deal with them. I'm glad it was Riley who found you."

"She was kind."

The king traded his soft, cotton sleep robes for an elegant black suit jacket. He disappeared into the closet for a moment before returning with matching pants and a vibrant golden tie hanging over his shoulders. "She may be the only one on the council you could say that about."

"Not even Jeza?" R-0 asked. King Hadrian had seemed friendly with her last night, and she had defended King Hadrian against Robin's unkind words.

"Kind isn't the word I'd use. Driven. Accomplished. Smart. Her clan relies on the managrid more than most, so she's had to overcome a lot to earn their support despite her issues with the Flow. You don't become as successful as she is by being kind. But she'll use compassion when it's necessary."

Using compassion only when necessary didn't sound like a good thing. If Jeza had found R-0 instead of Quiet, what would she have done? Quiet's compassion wasn't necessary, but it had improved R-0's situation and eased their worries. Shouldn't a leader want to make things better?

"That sounds . . . problematic."

"The council isn't that bad. They're just looking for answers." He adjusted his tie in the mirror. It looked like it was done properly to R-0, but the king scowled, uncurled it, and began retying it once more. "As long as I'm the one with those answers, there's nothing to worry about."

But that wasn't true. Whenever R-0 attended a meeting, the council—especially Robin—reacted poorly. This morning had been the same. R-0 was the common factor.

"Would the council react more favorably if you assigned a different guard?" R-0 asked.

"Probably."

R-0 fidgeted. They didn't want to cause problems for King Hadrian, but they didn't want to be left behind either. They unhooked the king's cape from the coat rack and smoothed out any wrinkles in the velvet before handing it to him.

King Hadrian took the cape, securing it around his neck and twirling in place once, watching the hem of the fabric in the mirror over his shoulder. He reached for his comb next, combing his hair back out of his face and slicking it against his scalp. "But if I'm going to change their minds, then I need to commit to this. Fully commit to this. So I want you in there with me, to show them the constructs are not our enemy.

"Besides, you weren't the only one who was busy last night." He paused at the door, turning back to R-0. "And don't you want a front row seat at the reintegration?"

CHAPTER 18

"Finally," Robin whispered under his breath. His scowl transformed to a forced smile as he addressed King Hadrian louder. "My king, I'm glad you have arrived. We have much to discuss, and so little time to—"

"I have a different idea for today." All signs of sleeplessness had disappeared from King Hadrian's face, and his smile beamed. "Why don't you all come with me?"

The king didn't wait for the council's response and left the room before anyone could object. The council members murmured questions about what was going on but followed anyway. R-0 shared their curiosity but had different questions. How had the king gotten the council's support for the reintegration? Would the other constructs have the same opportunities as R-0 now? Memories of the constructs stuck in the storage rooms with nothing to do flashed through R-0's mind, and they hurried after the king, eager to replace those memories with a new reality.

King Hadrian waited for the rest of the council members to join him in the hallway before continuing through the palace. "First announcement. R-0 has proven that despite any changes, the constructs are still more than capable of performing their job duties."

R-0's gears sped. Even with the corruption, King Hadrian believed they had proven themself. Maybe Quiet was right—they didn't need fixing. They needed to grow into their new self.

"As of today," King Hadrian continued, "I am reinstating some of the constructs to their positions in the palace. Our staff is tired and overworked, a problem I wish to remedy immediately. All of you can check with your head staff. You each have five constructs back on your rotations."

Thirty constructs was a small percentage of the palace's staff, but it was a start. R-0's plates warmed, and they shifted their face plates to try and match the joyful expression that hadn't left King Hadrian's face.

The rest of the council didn't share their reaction. Robin's face grew red, his eyes narrowing and fists shaking. Jeza and Quiet were stoic—their expressions set and unchanging despite the king's proclamations. Gretta's face paled, and her frown exacerbated the wrinkles on her forehead. Eren reached for her sword, fiddling with the hilt instead of drawing it.

Robin was the first to speak. "But—"

"No. I know you have a million reasons this won't work, and I don't want to hear them. All I want to hear is how you, as one of the leaders of this country, are going to rise above the difficulties we are facing and make this work. I expect daily reports from each of you on the progress. Our goal is for these constructs to be functioning at full capacity with minimal supervision within a week, so we can begin reintegrating a second, larger batch."

"My king, no disrespect," Robin said. His face tightened, and he spat his words through clenched teeth. "But this should have been discussed in this morning's session."

He said he meant no disrespect, but wasn't questioning the king disrespectful?

"The morning session will still be held as planned, and you will have ample time to voice your concerns then." King Hadrian smiled. The group reached the front doors of the palace, and King Hadrian pushed them open, waltzing outside. "But allow me to finish my proposal first."

R-0's flame sank, crawling across the base of their chest compartment instead of blazing upward. If the council still disagreed, even after the king's proposal, what would King

Hadrian do? He had the authority to instate the policy anyway, but would he?

"There's more?" Gretta asked. She balled up her dress in her fist, raising it so the hem didn't drag across the cobblestone path outside.

"I've received reports from some of our citizens." King Hadrian conveniently omitted certain details, such as how he had received those reports. Although after the intruder last night, R-0 wondered if everyone already knew about the king's excursion. "Many of them are acclimating to the changes far better than we have in the palace and are living in harmony with their constructs."

R-0 heard a rumbling in the distance, like a storm on the horizon, but every window they passed showed nothing but glimmering rays of sunshine. It grew louder as they neared the palace gates. None of the council members reacted to it—maybe it was too quiet for organic hearing. R-0 tapped on their side, drawing their focus back to King Hadrian with every repetition.

"That does not invalidate the reports we have received stating the opposite," Jeza said. "Many are struggling, suffering, and scared."

"Exactly. Their concerns do not go unnoticed." At the front gates, King Hadrian motioned to the guard. "Open the gates."

"There was an intruder in the palace just last night. It's not safe to go out," Gretta said.

"We aren't going anywhere." King Hadrian's smile already seemed too large for his face, but somehow, it spread even wider. "I've asked them to come to us."

The gates swung open.

People and constructs lined the walkway and spilled into side streets. At the sight of the king, the crowd cheered, and the low rumbling became overwhelming as voices overlapped and metal clanged.

"It will take time to reintegrate the constructs into society, a task I am dedicated to and have already begun working on in the palace." King Hadrian raised his voice, and the crowd quieted. Even those in the back, who likely couldn't hear a single word, leaned forward, straining to listen. "It won't be easy. I recognize that all of you today have your own struggles and challenges, and the changes to the constructs can create undue burdens.

"For that reason, I propose we open the palace to anyone who would like a safe place for their construct to remain while these issues are investigated and overcome. You can leave them here today, and then, as soon as you are able or comfortable, retrieve them at your leisure. If you choose to permanently surrender them, the crown will offer a small sum for them to join my staff."

R-0 wasn't sure if it was the king's words or the energy from the excited crowd making their plates vibrate. It was a different feeling, one R-0 couldn't place as either positive or negative. There was worry, but also fear, apprehension, confusion, and . . . hope, all blended together. R-0 couldn't distinguish where one feeling ended and another began. Despite standing still, they felt as though their insides were sprinting into a future they couldn't even begin to imagine.

The crowd pushed forward, and the guards held them at bay. Some cheered, and all looked on, scared but hopeful for what came next. King Hadrian lowered his voice and turned to the rest of the council. "This is what our people want. What they *need*. Would anyone here like to suggest we turn them away?"

"This is . . . unexpected." Jeza spoke first. "But it looks like you found the support you needed after all. This discussion is still far from over, but I will not oppose something my people desire." Her rings glittered in the sunlight as she waved at the gathered crowds. She addressed the king in a low voice. "If you'd like, in addition to my personal staff, I will oversee the reintegration of the managrid staff."

Slowly, one by one, the rest of the council members agreed with King Hadrian, offering words of support or promises of future action to facilitate the reintegration. Quiet offered to establish drop off zones at some of the churches in Graywal for citizens who couldn't make it to the palace, and as a potential avenue to expand the reintegration throughout the rest of Haiden in the future. Although Gretta frowned while she spoke and still seemed hesitant, she offered Clan

Murdha's blacksmiths to train constructs in the palace forges. Eren immediately sent one of her guards to fetch the patrol schedules with promises that she would find a way to give each council member additional security and support from the guard while they reintegrated their constructs.

Only Robin refused to offer any support, instead whispering to his guard. R-0 strained to hear, but with the rumble of the crowd, his words were too quiet and jumbled to make out.

"It's decided then." King Hadrian clasped his hands together and addressed the crowd once more. "Welcome! Please form an orderly line, and we'll get everyone taken care of."

CHAPTER 19

Within a couple of hours, the process was running smoothly. The council had tried to delay things—urging King Hadrian to treat this as an announcement ceremony and begin the actual transitions once they had time to adjourn and create a more thorough plan. But King Hadrian was ready for every objection they had.

He had already recruited extra staff to oversee the lines, created paperwork to record each construct and their owner, and spread word of the new policy across the city. It was no surprise he'd overslept. With all the preparations he'd made, R-0 doubted he'd slept more than an hour—a pitiful amount compared to what organics usually operated on.

There were two lines—one to temporarily house constructs at the palace and a second to permanently turn over constructs. The organics in the latter line left carrying bags jingling with coin, while the former looked more worried.

R-0's gears spun into overdrive. There was too much happening, too many people, and too many things to observe. Despite the clearly marked and orderly attempts at lines, people zigzagged down the paths. Some who didn't have constructs with them lurked on the edges without a clear purpose, further crowding the area and adding to the cacophony of sounds.

R-0 tried to ignore the periphery—beyond the occasional scan to ensure there were no threats—and focus on their immediate surroundings. But wherever King Hadrian went, commotion followed.

People flocked to their king for guidance on which line to choose. Some focused on R-0—asking about the constructs and what was happening. R-0 didn't have the answers, and more than once King Hadrian swooped in to answer when R-0's words failed them.

Conversations with the king generally ended with people joining the line to temporarily surrender their constructs. Some abandoned the process entirely, bringing their constructs home to try to adjust to the new normal. Few who listened to King Hadrian's encouraging words chose to surrender their constructs permanently.

"How are you doing?" King Hadrian asked.

The man he'd been talking to walked away, two constructs trailing behind him as he made his way to the temporary line. R-0 repeated a quick scan of their surroundings to ensure they had the situation properly accessed. "There is nothing to report."

"I've got things out here under control. I want to know what's going on in here." He tapped the side of R-0's head. "Your thoughts. Feelings."

"It is . . ." R-0 looked around, searching for words.

Unlike when curious citizens asked questions, King Hadrian didn't offer suggestions for how R-0 could finish their sentence. He waited patiently, watching them.

What did they feel? What was this emotion?

R-0 was gaining confidence with a few emotions: curiosity, excitement, anger, uncertainty. Uncertainty was one of the few certainties of R-0's existence. But this wasn't any of those. It was loud, it was fast, and it was too many things at once, like the wind, slipping through their fingers. They knew it was there, but they couldn't grab onto it or make any sense of it.

"It's overwhelming," R-0 decided.

"You'll get used to it," King Hadrian said. "It seems different, but it's the same as it's always been."

But it wasn't the same. It was nothing like before. Everything was louder, brighter, and spurred so many extra thoughts. They couldn't help comparing every construct they came across with last night's intruder, wondering if they could be the same. Before, the children running amuck, laughing and knocking into people, would have been largely overlooked, only requiring a cursory glance to confirm they had no weapons that could threaten the king.

But now R-0 wondered where their parents were and if they were playing Slay the Kraken like Kaili and Kalani. Which made them wonder where Kaili, Kalani, Lykren, and Minna were. Were they safely at home, playing pretend under the supervision of JJ? Or was JJ here, in one of the lines, being left at the palace? JJ had seemed at peace with the dragon-scaled family. The kids treated them with the same warmth and familiarity they had shown their own mother.

Were any of these constructs the same as JJ, surrounded by organics they viewed as family? Would the palace be a better place for them to stay than the home they'd been in since before the incident?

They had too many questions, too few answers, and everywhere R-0 looked—everything they saw—raised even more questions. They could spend a century doing nothing but asking questions, and they still wouldn't have answers to all the thoughts that plagued them.

"Did you hear me?" King Hadrian asked.

R-0 snapped to attention. Had they missed something again? The last thing they remembered King Hadrian saying didn't match the expectant look on his face.

"No sir." R-0 focused on the king, trying to push away all the chaos and distractions. "Apologies."

"It's fine. I was just wondering—"

"King Hadrian!" A messenger squeezed in between two constructs on either side of the path with hurried steps.

"Duty calls." King Hadrian sighed under his breath. "Yes?"

"The storage rooms have run out of room," the messenger whispered. "Jeza is convening the council to make alternate arrangements."

"Tell them we'll be there soon."

"They, um." The messenger bit at his lip and swayed from foot to foot.

"Just say it, I don't bite."

"They specifically requested R-0 remain outside."
"Who said that?"
"Councilman Robin."

King Hadrian sighed. "Thank you for the message. Please let them know I'll be there as soon as I can get away." After the messenger scurried off, he turned to R-0. "I hate to ask you this, but do you think you'll be alright out here alone?"

R-0 would hardly be alone. Being out here alone would have been far easier than managing the gathered crowd. It was King Hadrian who would be alone. "You are vulnerable without a guard."

"This place is crawling with them." King Hadrian tilted his head to the palace, where triple the usual number of guards were stationed by the doors and more waited in the nearby gardens. "I'll bring a few with me."

"Yes sir." R-0 nodded, despite their hesitations.

"I'm sorry. But after the stunt I pulled this morning, I should probably try to cooperate with him a little."

"No apologies are required."

King Hadrian grinned. "Then later tonight, I'll show you my gratitude instead."

"Gratitude is also unnecessary."

"Come on, I feel bad. Let me do something for you."

Why would King Hadrian feel bad? But if it would make him feel better, R-0 would acquiesce to his request. "Yes sir."

"Great!" King Hadrian's face lit up. "Okay. Let's get you situated at one of the tables up front, then just keep doing what we've been doing. Answer questions, help people out, and don't get into trouble, okay?"

"Yes sir."

At the intake table, King Hadrian signaled for one of the staff. "Iza, this is R-0. I was hoping they could help you here for a bit while I attend to some affairs. Would that be possible?"

"Yes sir. Absolutely!" Unlike many of the organics in the palace, Iza didn't shy away from R-0's gaze. Her expression hardly shifted as she turned to them, a smile plastered in place. "If you'll follow me."

R-0 nodded, hesitantly following her. Their attention wandered from where they were going, focusing on the king who was walking the other way. Two organic guards fell into step with him, and R-0 relaxed some. They bumped into the edge of the table, and it jostled into the man in line.

"Watch it!" The man stepped back a few steps.

"Apologies." The tables were spaced so organics could easily pass between them, but R-0's bulky form couldn't. They had to turn sideways to shuffle through.

"Here." Iza moved the table slightly off-center so the walkway was large enough to accommodate R-0. Then she turned her attention to the man in line. "This is R-0. They are the first of the royal constructs designed to protect the king. They've continued their duties without any cause for concern, a fantastic example of what our king is hoping to accomplish with all the constructs through his reintegration efforts."

The man stared for a moment longer before pushing his construct forward. "Here. Is there any more paperwork?"

"I've got everything I need here." Iza checked over the paper before setting it to the side. "Once you're ready to take them home, please let us know."

The man grunted, hardly glancing at the construct before walking away.

Iza signaled for the next person in line to wait a moment. "R-0, would you mind escorting J-12 to the dining hall?"

"The dining hall?"

"A temporary measure, until we figure something else out." She quickly sped through the different holding areas. Constructs in need of repairs would go to the maintenance rooms, while the others were divided between the ballroom, the dining hall, and the hallways outside the storage rooms based on their previous occupations and current status.

"Yes ma'am." R-0 nodded and turned to J-12. "This way."

Like M-118, they had no voice capabilities, but they nodded in response to R-0's request and followed them without hesitation. The next construct asked questions—what would they be doing at the palace? How long until they received an assignment? Would they be working with King Hadrian directly? R-0 tried their best to answer but shared many of the same curiosities. The process continued with over a dozen constructs until they caught up to the intake staff, and there weren't any constructs ready to be escorted, leaving R-0 to stand behind the staff tables as intake continued.

R-0 stood entirely still—making no sounds and doing nothing that would draw attention to themself—but still the organics stared. They could hear the hushed whispers, but it was too chaotic to discern the words—just static as loud as the waves crashing underneath the pier. But there was no lull to this. It only grew louder and more difficult to ignore, grating on R-0.

Overwhelming was the perfect word to describe it, and R-0 decided they didn't like being overwhelmed.

Perhaps this was the true reason for the missing constructs. Nothing nefarious like the council feared—just constructs overwhelmed by reality stepping away for a moment. R-0 tried tapping on their side, but with nothing to focus on, the movement did little to drown out their surroundings.

R-0 walked along the palace wall until the noise subsided. They could still watch the staff tables to see when the next construct was ready for transport, and they were still in view of Iza and the other guards. They closed their eyes, trying to mimic the deep breaths organics often used to settle their emotions.

On their second inhale, a new noise broke through their relative peace—a sniffle.

There was someone else in the gardens.

CHAPTER 20

R-0's eyes snapped open. No one was supposed to be in this area.

The noise was coming from their right where there were rows of tall plants. Even if a new guard rotation had been issued or a staff member had decided to take this path, why would they hide?

R-0 followed the noise and found a small dwarven girl nestled between two rose bushes. Her too-big coat wrapped around her knees tucked into her chest, and dirt covered her hands. She looked up at R-0 with puffy eyes. Dirty handprints on her cheeks streaked a trail of mud through her tears.

R-0 briefly flickered through memories of the few children they had seen in the palace before, but she didn't match any of them. She was a stranger. "You are not supposed to be here."

"I-I'm sorry." She hiccupped as she tried to wipe her tears away, but only succeeded at spreading more dirt across her face.

She didn't seem like a threat. She seemed . . . sad.

"Are you okay?" R-0 asked.

"I'm looking for beans. Can you help me find them?"

Hunger. That explained her sadness and scrawny form. But this was a strange place to look for food. Perhaps she had thought the palace's flower gardens were vegetable gardens. Regardless, she was still unauthorized.

"You're not supposed—"

"Please?" she interrupted. "I tried to find them by myself, but I can't!" Tears quivered in the corner of her eyes, threatening to fall once more, and she averted her gaze to the ground. "Please help me."

R-0 shouldn't help her. They had a job to do—orders to follow. But . . . a quick glance at the intake tables showed they weren't needed again yet, and the kitchens were only a small detour.

"How did you get here?" R-0 asked.

"I came through the gates with my mommy, but then I got lost trying to find beans."

Sometimes citizens visited the palace requesting aid, and in the chaos of the reintegration, it would have been easy for her to be separated from her mother. R-0 flickered through their memories—a farmer who had lost their crop to rot had come begging for seeds, a father who had lost his oldest three children to the plague had asked for medicine for his only remaining child. And there had been countless others. Whenever possible, King Hadrian helped them. R-0 could do the same.

"After you find beans, will you leave?" R-0 asked.

She nodded vigorously, her braids bouncing up and down like fish leaping from the sea. "Does this mean you'll help me?" She was even more impatient than the organics in line. R-0 had hardly a tick of their gears to process what she said, and already she was on her feet knocking at their knee. "Please?"

R-0 wouldn't turn her away.

"This way." R-0 said.

"Really?" The tears glistening in her eyes were replaced with a sparkle and smile.

"Yes ma'am." R-0 led her through the garden, careful to stay on the paths and not harm any of the flowers.

"You don't have to call me ma'am." The child giggled. "That's for old people."

"What should you be called?"

"My name's Seraphine. What's yours?"

"R-0."

"That's a boring name." Seraphine tilted her head to the side and looked R-0 over before jumping in the air. "Can I call you Potato?"

"Potato?"

"Yeah. Like mashed potatoes. It's one of my favorites."

It wasn't uncommon for flesh beings to be named after things. King Hadrian was named after his grandfather, and R-0 had accidentally given Quiet a nickname based on her mannerisms. Usually there was a reason, a connection. R-0 tried to understand what connected them to mashed potatoes but couldn't find any similarity. Still, the tiny human seemed excited by the idea, and R-0 saw no reason to deny her excitement. "Yes ma—Seraphine."

She followed in R-0's footsteps, quite literally. Every time they took a step, she placed her feet in the same spots, hopping from tile to tile when her legs were too short to match their strides. She began to fall behind and paused to catch her breath.

R-0 slowed their pace and shortened their steps, making the game easier for the child. She grinned. When they arrived at the kitchen, R-0 knocked, and the door swung open from the impact.

Inside, a chef stood in front of a cutting board, his knife hammering down again and again. His focus was absolute, and he didn't react to R-0 and Seraphine entering.

"Potato, why are we in the kitchen?" Seraphine asked.

"This is where beans are kept."

"They're here?" Seraphine reached for the countertop, pulling herself on to her tiptoes to peer over. "I don't see them."

The chef stopped his cutting and looked down at Seraphine. "Whatd'ya need?"

"Beans," R-0 said.

"Beans?" The chef seemed surprised, then shrugged. "Second pantry, fourth shelf, third box."

"A box?" Seraphine's eyes widened. "Why are they in a box?"

Any sign of her previous giggles and excitement vanished. Her tears threatened to return, and her tiny hands wrapped around the ends of her braids, crossing them beneath her chin and tucking her chin into her chest.

"It's okay." R-0 frowned. Why would a box be so concerning? Perhaps it was a phobia. Most organics had nonsensical fears—fears of spiders, fears of falling, fears of bees. Perhaps Seraphine's fear was boxes. It was a simple problem with a simple solution. "They can be removed from the box."

"O-okay."

R-0 opened the pantry door, and Seraphine bolted forward. She turned in a circle, eyes wide as she surveyed the towering shelves of dried goods. Her awe quickly subsided, replaced by a frown.

"Where's beans?"

"Here." R-0 retrieved a container filled to the brim with dry beans from the fourth shelf and held it out to Seraphine.

"That's not beans." She crossed her arms over her chest.

R-0 frowned. They opened the container and examined one of the small objects within. It was the right shape, the right size, the right color, and exactly where the chef had said it would be.

"This is a bean." R-0 insisted, dropping the bean into Seraphine's open palm.

"Beans isn't a bean." Seraphine giggled. "You're funny."

"If beans are not beans . . . what are they?" Even as the words came out of their mouth, R-0 realized the statement made no sense.

But Seraphine was unfazed. "Beans is like you." She tossed the bean into the air and caught it with both hands before shoving it into her pocket. "Mommy brought beans here this morning."

Beans was a construct. What a silly name—no more fitting to a construct than Potato, which Seraphine had designated them. In hindsight, it was obvious she wasn't referencing the food. They should have asked her to specify.

"The constructs left in the palace's care will be safe," R-0 echoed one of King Hadrian's lines from earlier. "There will be a constant guard rotation in the storage rooms, and if there are any issues, you will be compensated for the loss of your construct."

"But I need to find them."

That wasn't one of the responses King Hadrian had dealt with earlier, and R-0 couldn't continue to echo his words. "Why?"

"They lost this." She held out her hand, revealing a screw nestled in her palm. "And they have to be okay. Because once I convince Mommy, Beans will get to come home."

R-0 pinched the screw between their fingers. It was old and slightly rusted—Beans was not as well-maintained as R-0. This screw should have been replaced many maintenance cycles ago. On the screwhead was a pink heart, painted with messy lines.

The screw was in disrepair. Even if Beans had it, the technomancers would replace it.

"The screw is unnecessary," R-0 said.

"No, it's not! Beans needs me." The tears that had so quickly sprung to the corners of her eyes spilled over again. "What if they fall apart?"

One rusty screw wouldn't stop that, but regular maintenance could. "The technomancers can repair them."

"I don't want the technomancers to repair them." Seraphine stumbled on the word technomancers but kept talking. "I need to give this back. Can you please take me to them?"

"Beans's location is unknown." Even if R-0 knew where Beans was, all the citizens participating in King Hadrian's reintegration program were supposed to stay in the gardens. "It's time for you to go."

From the other room, the kitchen door slammed open. R-0 listened closely as a man started talking to the chef, looking for a young girl that matched Seraphine's description. According to him, the girl's mother had stopped on her way home to count her coin, and when she'd finished, her child was nowhere to be seen.

Still crying, Seraphine didn't react to the man's words. "But Beans promised to be here when me and Mommy came back. I was supposed to give it to them this morning, but I forgot, and when I went back to the table, they were gone!"

RISE OF THE FORGEHEARTS

The door opened, and a guard burst through. "There you are. What are you doing in the pantry?" His eyes narrowed when he saw R-0. "What the hell are you doing with her?"

Before R-0 could respond, he grabbed Seraphine by the wrist and pulled her away from R-0. He knelt and wiped the tears from her cheeks. "Are you okay?"

"I'm okay, but—"

"Come on." The guard picked Seraphine up, balancing her on one hip. "We're getting you back to your ma."

The guard paused and stared at R-0, then wordlessly walked out of the room.

"Wait!" Seraphine's words rose to an indistinguishable cry as she struggled against the guard's grip. The chef paused his cutting long enough to peek over a rack of pots and pans before dipping back out of sight.

R-0 waited for the guard to leave the kitchen before exiting the pantry and hurrying toward the front gates. King Hadrian had forgiven them once for not being where they were supposed to, but R-0 wasn't going to make a pattern of it.

"Potato!"

R-0 turned around, and Seraphine ran down the hallway after them, her arms flailing with each step. The guard followed, the frown on his face replaced with a scowl as he yelled various directions, all of which Seraphine either didn't hear or ignored.

"Potato!" she yelled again as she got closer, tripping on her feet as she came to a stop in front of them.

R-0 held out their arm, and the young girl steadied herself with it.

"Thanks." She huffed out a long breath. She grabbed R-0's hand, pulling it close to her, then wiggled her fingers between theirs. R-0 let her force their palm open.

"Here."

Beans's screw.

"This belongs to Beans." R-0 held their hand open, offering the part back to Seraphine.

"This man says Mommy is looking for me, and I have to go home." She pointed at the guard who'd almost caught up to her again. "Can you give it to Beans for me?"

Before R-0 could answer, the guard was scooping Seraphine up once more. This time he didn't even look at R-0 as he began a lecture on the importance of obedience and the dangers of wandering off alone.

R-0 held up the screw. It wasn't anything special. To most people, it would be considered trash. But it was important to Seraphine. She'd risked punishment twice to make sure Beans received it.

It had a . . . sentimental value that couldn't be measured by weight or explained by its composition but was made clear by the actions of a young child. And who really was the judge of what was important and what wasn't? Who decided what mattered?

The longer R-0 considered it, the more convoluted everything became. There was no answer. No amount of math or logic could determine why this piece of trash didn't belong in the garbage.

It was up to R-0 to decide the screw's fate.

They turned the screw over in their hand, the tiny spirals leaving trails of rust along their palm. The head was stripped. The technomancers might not be able to reinstall it even if it was delivered. The tip was dulled with wear. It was worn, broken, and most people would dispose of it.

But not R-0.

R-0 would make sure it got back where it belonged.

CHAPTER 21

R-0 expected returning the screw to be nothing more than a short detour from their other assignments. It should have been a simple task. Check the records, locate Beans, and deliver the screw. But when they arrived at the gates, their extended absence had been noted, and the guard who found Seraphine had complained about their behavior.

The rest of the afternoon, R-0 was assigned to stay with Eren and ordered not to talk to anyone. They silently watched Eren, who first investigated R-0's encounter with Seraphine, then managed the crowd, adjusted the guard shifts, and handled complaints until the lines thinned and a majority of the citizens returned to their homes or work. A few stragglers remained, but most of the staff was dismissed. R-0 and Eren sat at one of the empty tables, waiting for the council meeting to end and King Hadrian to return with new orders.

No one knew how long the intake was supposed to last or what they were expected to do next. They had gathered all the constructs, but there wasn't enough space to house them, and resources were already spread thin. Some of the organics had been working since yesterday without sleep.

"Are there any additional tasks to complete?" R-0 asked.

Eren shook her head without looking up from the stone puzzle in her hands. There were seventeen pieces, each carved in a different shape and containing a pearl within. Eren had explained that the goal was to remove the pearl without breaking the stone. Her brother had broken more than one of the puzzles, sometimes on purpose from frustration, and sometimes by accident while trying to force together pieces that didn't fit. Once the pearl was freed, she would bury it in the earth for a year of good fortune.

"Should you head to the council meeting?" R-0 asked.

"Absolutely not."

Earlier, Eren's refusal had made sense—there were other tasks to complete. She was constantly busy, and whenever it looked like she might be finished, someone else appeared with a new request or problem for her to solve. But now she had nothing to do. All the other council members were in attendance. Why would she be the exception?

"Why—"

"Because if you could be quiet, I might get a moment of peace." Eren slid the pieces of the puzzle against each other, then yanked at the stone, but the pearl remained firmly lodged inside. "And opportunities for peace are in short supply right now."

She was moving the pieces wrong. R-0 had figured out how to solve it within minutes of watching the dwarf struggle but didn't want to steal the good fortune for themself. Instead, they silently watched Eren get it wrong again and again and again.

Eren had seven of the pieces clicked into place and was inches away from sliding the eighth to the side, freeing the next set. She wiggled a different piece unsuccessfully, then dropped the puzzle in her lap with a grumble, erasing the progress she had made. She sat for a few moments, clicking her tongue against the roof of her mouth and staring at the sky, then attempted the puzzle once more with a different approach that would lead to a different failure than before—but still a failure.

R-0's fingers fidgeted at their side. Eren didn't want their help, but that didn't stop them from wanting to reach out and solve it. There were so many things they could be doing. While they weren't supposed to interrupt King Hadrian's council meeting, they could locate Beans for Seraphine. Relieve the tired guards whose shifts had extended far longer than planned. Continue investigating the intruder that had entered King Hadrian's room. Search for the missing constructs. But instead, they were forced to stay here doing nothing. Worse than nothing. They had to watch Eren doing nothing but fail again and again and again.

R-0 tapped the bottom of their chair every time the urge to grab the puzzle rose. What started as just a few stray taps steadily increased to a constant patter, like raindrops on the roof.

"Shalloth be damned." Eren threw the puzzle on the table, and the stone clattered closer to R-0. "I've been an unlucky son of a bitch for how many years? What's one more?"

R-0 leaned over, peering closer at the stone. "Is it magic?"

Eren shook her head. "Just a regular old misery-inducing stone."

If it wasn't magic, perhaps they could trick the stone rings. R-0 could solve the puzzle, and Eren could still receive her year of luck. Everyone would win.

"How does it provide the luck?" R-0 asked.

"Do you ever run out of questions?"

R-0 frowned. Without knowing the rules, it would be difficult to predict, but perhaps they could just do the first sixteen steps. Then, Eren could free the pearl. R-0 wouldn't actually *do* the puzzle. Just . . . help.

They reached for the stones, but just as their fingers brushed against it, Eren swatted their hand away.

"What are you doing?"

"The puzzle is incomplete—"

"Of course it is. Because the thing is impossible." She swept the puzzle across the table, out of R-0's reach. "Don't touch my stuff."

"Apologies."

Multiple sets of footsteps echoed in the distance. One set was easily recognizable as King Hadrian's, and the longer R-0 listened, the more certain they were that the others belonged to the rest of the council members. Their meeting was over, and R-0 would no longer be haunted by the puzzle.

Eren shifted in her chair, leaning forward on the table, then quickly readjusted to lean back. "You mean it when you say that?"

"What?" R-0 asked.

"When you apologize, do you know what that means?"

"It is an admission of wrong-doing and conveys intent to do better."

"And you know what you did wrong?"

R-0 replayed the memory, double-checking before answering. "The puzzle is yours. You were upset, and that was not the intention. Your belongings will be left alone in the future to avoid that outcome."

King Hadrian and the council stepped out of the palace, but Eren didn't react to their approach. R-0 moved to stand, but the king shook his head and signaled at his side—at ease.

"So you apologized because I was upset?"

"Yes ma'am." R-0 nodded.

"And earlier—" Eren's fingers threaded through the puzzle. It didn't seem like she was actually trying to solve it anymore, just tugging aimlessly at the stone. "Why'd you let Seraphine into the palace?"

"She said she needed to find Beans. She seemed hungry."

"You wanted to help her," Eren said, "even without orders to do so."

"King Hadrian provides aid to citizens when he can."

She leaned back and grabbed a thin metal chain concealed beneath her armor. The Ainfen clan ring—a simple band forged of steel and blood by Haiden's founders—hung from the chain, and she twirled it between her fingers. "I mean Riley said y'all were something else now, but this . . . this is—"

"Incredible, right?" King Hadrian put a hand on Eren's shoulder. She jumped to her feet, jostling the table and causing the puzzle to slide off the edge.

On instinct, R-0 grabbed it before it hit the ground. They weren't sure how fragile it was, but if Jorgunn had broken several of them, it couldn't be too hardy. Instantly, they realized their mistake. Eren's eyes met theirs, and they both looked at the stones in R-0's hand. Just a few ticks earlier, they had declared their intent to do better—to *not* touch Eren's belongings.

"Apologies." R-0 dropped the puzzle, and it clattered to the ground. "Again."

King Hadrian and Eren both chuckled, and she scooped the puzzle up, muttering under her breath. "Maybe I'm the one who should be saying sorry."

"This is for you, for the reintegration." King Hadrian handed a sheet of paper to Eren. "Gave your brother a copy as well, but he figured you'd want to handle it yourself."

R-0 peered over the list. Dozens of constructs had done guard rotations before, but only five were listed. How long would the rest be forced to wait?

The thought sputtered through R-0's flame. They hadn't been able to convince themself to spend one night in the storage room. But the other constructs had been there for many cycles already and would likely remain there for weeks longer. R-0 had done their best to show that the constructs were capable and safe. And even though this was progress, it didn't feel like enough.

"I still don't agree with this, you know. My guards reported two more constructs missing today, and that's just from the palace." Eren pocketed the sheet of paper. "There's enough missing constructs to pose a serious threat to Graywal, especially if they're working with an established criminal like Ryder. One was even in your room! And we still don't have a lead on why they were there or what they wanted. What if they intended to kill you?"

"Then it's a good thing I have a royal construct to protect me, right?" King Hadrian put his hand on R-0's arm, and their plates warmed at his touch, combatting the chill from Eren's words. The intruder hadn't acted like they were there to kill the king—if they were, why weren't they hiding and waiting to strike? They'd been out in the open.

But what was their goal? And not just the intruder. Why had M-118 gone to the docks? When it came to the constructs, R-0 wasn't the only one with more questions than answers.

"Until we figure out what they're doing, we should focus our efforts on containment and security," Eren said. "We need to find the missing ones, not create more vulnerabilities."

"Just give them a chance," King Hadrian said. "And if anything goes wrong, come straight to me."

"I'll do it because you're the king and I must." Eren sighed. "But you need to know, even if I can see the humanity in the constructs, it doesn't make them less of a threat—especially the missing ones. My first priority will always be to keep the council and our people safe." Her hand went to her clan ring once more. "And until you can prove these concerns are unfounded, I can't support you on this."

"I'll prove it to you," King Hadrian said. His voice shook, his normal confidence wavering.

"I hope you do. Quickly." Eren raised her hand to her shoulder, bowing respectfully before heading back into the palace.

King Hadrian raised his voice to address the staff remaining in the courtyard. "Intake will continue for the rest of the week, but I expect the majority came today and attendance will be lower. You'll receive your schedules soon. But for now, take the night off. It's been a long day for everyone, and you all deserve it."

Murmurs of appreciation and confirmation spread through the staff as they packed what remained and made their way back into the palace. King Hadrian helped with the cleanup—no matter how many times he was told it wasn't necessary—and R-0 followed suit. No staff objected to R-0's help—especially when they lifted all four remaining tables at once and carried them inside.

"Thank you for all of your help today, R-0." Iza waited in the doorway as R-0 placed the tables in the supply closet.

"Your gratitude is unnecessary."

"That's for me to decide, not you." She smiled. "And for you to accept gracefully."

"Your gratitude is accepted."

"I'll see you around." She waved, then curtsied to King Hadrian. "Goodnight, King Hadrian."

King Hadrian waited for Iza to round the corner before turning to R-0. "Most people just say, 'You're welcome.'"

"Most people do not say what they mean."

"That's the truth." King Hadrian sighed. "Better you learn that sooner rather than later, I suppose."

"Sylas!"

Even from afar, R-0 recognized Robin's screechy voice. It was rare for him to yell like this outside of the council room, and even rarer for him to address King Hadrian by his first name.

"What now?" King Hadrian mumbled under his breath. He straightened his crown and adjusted his robes so they sat properly on his shoulders.

Robin strode around the corner, his face flushed red. The two organic guards at his side matched his pace with far more elegance, even in their heavy armor. He scowled at R-0, and his hands balled into fists.

"Sylas!" he yelled again.

"Councilman Robin, I wasn't expecting to see you again so soon." King Hadrian's face shifted slowly and unnaturally into a forced smile. Was that what R-0 looked like when they tried to shift their plates and mimic that facial expression?

"Then you're as shortsighted as you are stupid."

"Excuse me?"

"I've had these constructs for barely an evening and already they're rebelling!" He stopped in front of King Hadrian, and his guards followed suit, blocking the hallway. "Did you honestly expect anything else?"

Constructs rebelling? But why?

King Hadrian raised his eyebrows. "Report, immediately."

"I caught one going through my armoire." Robin held up his hand where the Conradh clan ring rested on his pinky. It was carved out of wood, and if Robin followed tradition, the wood originated from the most notable ship he'd helped build before joining the council. Carvings resembling waves wrapped around his finger in an endless loop. "It stole my ring!"

"Which construct?"

"E-4."

Silence fell over the hallway. King Hadrian took a deep breath but didn't respond.

"Well?" Robin asked. "What do you have to say about that?"

"I'm still waiting for your report on this supposed rebellion."

"I just told you—"

"You told me about a petty thief."

"Which is entirely unacceptable!"

King Hadrian looked past Robin to his two guards. "You're dismissed."

"You are *not* dismissed!" Robin screeched. But the two guards nodded to King Hadrian and retreated down the hall.

"Councilman Robin." King Hadrian's words were smooth, a stark contrast to Robin's complaints. But even so, the words didn't flow together. Each one was deliberate, its own beat demanding attention. "I entrusted five constructs to your care. The same number I entrusted to every other member of our esteemed council. And yet you seem to be the only one having any difficulty. Perhaps I overestimated you."

"Did you not hear me? It *stole* from me! A thief. What's next?"

"Are you not capable of handling a thief on your own?"

"Of course I am! It's in the dungeon."

The dungeon. R-0's flame sputtered. When they had been in the dungeon, they had known it was temporary. But what of this construct?

"Then include the information in your report, and we'll discuss it tomorrow."

"Even after this, you can't see that your plan won't work?"

"How many thieves do we have in our dungeon right now? Steel or bone, this is nothing new. It's sad to hear, of course, but it changes nothing. I intend to judge the constructs as individuals, based on their own actions, and I expect you to do the same."

King Hadrian was right. There were plenty of thieves in the dungeon, and R-0's thoughts rarely lingered on them. So why did their flame react every time they imagined E-4 standing in a cell? If they had committed a crime, then it was logical for them to be imprisoned.

But logic couldn't stop the surge of curiosity and unease. Why would E-4 steal from Councilman Robin? What benefit would a ring grant them? The intruder in King Hadrian's room had a ring too—was it stolen as well?

"This won't be the only problem." Robin shook his head. "The reintegration won't work."

"I'm sure I will hear about every screw out of place."

RISE OF THE FORGEHEARTS

"Is that so?" Robin scowled. "If you know everything there is to know about the constructs, then surely you can provide an update on the missing ones. I can call a meeting now."

"Not yet, but—"

"How can anyone trust you to have this under control when more constructs are going missing each day and you have no clue what's going on? If the ones here are committing crimes right in front of us, what worse things are they planning behind our backs? The managrid has had more outages since this started with the constructs than it has in the past decade. You're telling me this isn't sabotage? What happens if they shut it down completely?"

If only R-0 had caught the intruder in King Hadrian's room, or if their investigation at the docks to find M-118 had been successful. Maybe then R-0 could have eased Robin's concerns.

"I admit there's still much we don't know," King Hadrian said. "But we are learning more each day. I'm investigating the missing constructs and will update the council accordingly."

"We know more than enough already to make these decisions."

"And my decision has been made. Do not forget that I am your king."

"Don't forget who granted you the crown." Robin stepped forward, leaning close to King Hadrian and whispering, "And who can just as easily take it away."

CHAPTER 22

After Robin stalked away, King Hadrian headed to his room in silence. R-0 tried to continue their conversation—first asking what Robin had meant, then trying to share details about their day—but the king's responses were short and distant.

When they reached his room, King Hadrian kicked off his shoes, letting them hit the wall and fall to the ground. His robe quickly joined the untidy pile, and King Hadrian flopped back on his bed with a sigh, his legs dangling off the side though his eyes remained open. He didn't deactivate the managrid lamp on his nightstand, even as he tossed his crown beside it.

"I'm sorry, R-0. I know I said we would do something fun tonight, but I don't think I have it in me."

"The fun was supposed to be inside of you?" R-0 frowned. As far as they knew, organics were incapable of storing items within their form. They lacked the internal compartments that constructs had. Opening flesh would cause injuries that could take weeks to heal, and anything stored inside would be covered with blood and other fluids.

King Hadrian's cheeks grew red, then his frown returned. "Forget about it."

"Yes sir."

So much of R-0's existence had been spent in silence, and they were beginning to resent it. Silently following the king around, silently watching Eren work on her puzzle, silently standing in the storage rooms awaiting new orders. Since the falling star had found R-0, they had questions, and silence didn't provide answers.

"Are you going to sleep?" R-0 asked.

"I don't think I will be able to after that."

"Then what will you do?"

"Is wallowing in my problems an option?"

"It is." But it didn't seem like a productive or enjoyable activity. It also wasn't sensible. Why wallow in problems instead of solving them? "But it is not a good option."

"You're probably right." A yawn interrupted his words. "Might as well try to get something done."

R-0 didn't understand. King Hadrian was clearly tired—a necessary prerequisite for sleep. And he continued staring at the ceiling—which didn't seem like a productive way to work. Perhaps he needed assistance.

Papers and letters on the king's desk were stacked so high, R-0 worried a stray wind—or an angry scream from Robin—might have enough force to knock them over. R-0 grabbed the shortest pile and brought it to the bed.

King Hadrian rose, leaning back on his arms, and gave R-0 a questioning look.

"These are for you."

"This is a terrible gift, R-0."

R-0's grip involuntarily tightened, crinkling the papers. They hadn't intended it as a gift, but they had intended to be helpful. Not terrible.

It seemed like anything R-0 said to King Hadrian was the wrong thing. Terrible. The word lingered in the air between them. "Apologies sir."

"No, no." King Hadrian took the stack from R-0. "It was just a joke."

R-0 let go of the papers, but no one was laughing. "People laugh at jokes."

"People laugh at good jokes," he said. "I was just trying to lighten the mood. I'm not very good at it."

"Perhaps you need a different audience."

"You're too generous." King Hadrian set the papers in front of him, staring at the one on top far longer than it should have taken him to read it.

Back in the silence, the onslaught of questions returned. R-0's mind wandered to E-4. Thieves were lawless beings, with no respect for the order of the land or the people who inhabited it. They selfishly broke the rules. It was not the way of the constructs. So why had E-4 become a thief? Had someone ordered them to steal the ring?

R-0 tried to remember what became of thieves, but it was rare for the king to personally handle a relatively minor crime like theft, and R-0 had typically been stationed with King Hadrian.

"What will happen to E-4?"

King Hadrian looked up from his reading. "We'll go chat with them tomorrow and see what we can learn. But unless we convince Robin otherwise, they'll likely be decommissioned."

R-0 had heard of units being decommissioned—usually due to extensive physical damage. They'd seen one unit that had their chest blown into pieces, their arm barely still attached. R-0 had taken them to the scrapyard themself. It hadn't seemed as sad then as it did now. But they would remain there, unable to perform any functions.

Forever.

R-0 wasn't sure how long forever was. They had over a decade of memories stored, and already, it was overwhelming to remember everything they had seen and everywhere they had been. Lying in a scrapyard with junk sounded worse than watching Eren do puzzles, and forever seemed incomparably longer than a single evening.

Why would Robin want to do that to E-4? And could King Hadrian stop it?

"What are you thinking?" King Hadrian suddenly straightened. He asked so many more questions now, and R-0 often struggled to answer.

"There was a unit five hundred and eighty-two cycles ago that was decommissioned. Their parts were taken to the scrapyard."

King Hadrian waited. Expectantly. What else could R-0 say?

"It was sad." R-0 tested the words slowly. Was sadness what they were feeling? A hollow ache in their flame made their insides feel cold despite the burning fire. "Will that happen to E-4?"

And will it happen to me one day?

R-0 left the second part unspoken. They couldn't bring themself to say it out loud.

King Hadrian leaned forward and stared at R-0, setting the papers aside and patting the bed next to him. "Come sit with me."

R-0 plopped down, mimicking the king's position. Their head clacked against the wall as they relaxed their body. Nothing was softer or fluffier than the king's bed, and they pushed their fingers against the sheets, letting the metal slide against the satin. This was what flying must feel like—or falling.

Flying and falling weren't that different if R-0 thought about it long enough.

R-0 resisted the temptation to lie down. Distractions came in many forms, and if they could anticipate them, they could avoid them before they became detrimental. Like now—if R-0 did lie back, the cloudy bed would swallow them whole. It could be seconds, or hours, before they surfaced for air.

Somehow staring at the darkness with their eyes closed was the most distracting place they could be. If they let their eyes linger closed, all they could see was the view of the sky from the scrapyard, as if they were the ones lying in the junk instead of the unit from their memory.

R-0 stopped blinking. "What is being decommissioned like?"

"Now that—" King Hadrian shook his head and laughed. "That's the question everyone wants answered."

"Everyone?" R-0 asked. "You're not at risk of being decommissioned."

"We don't call it being decommissioned, but death comes for all of us."

"Death." The word felt strange and foreign as it left R-0's mouth.

"What do you know about death?"

"Nothing." Before the corruption, R-0 had never thought about death, much less how it might apply to them. In the past, their job had been a constant whirlwind of death, handing it out to any enemies of the king as needed. Those days, R-0 was also always on the brink of death themself—any of those enemies could have struck them down just as easily—they'd just never realized it.

"When I was younger, I used to always ask what came next. My mother would just laugh at me and tell me next was breakfast, or studies, or whatever she had planned on the schedule for us that day."

The more R-0 heard about the late queen, the more they liked her. R-0 had served under her occasionally, but that was before the stars when Queen Hadrian was nothing but an objective, not a person. It wasn't the same as hearing about her now. Every time King Hadrian mentioned her, she came with a bundle of plans and schedules. She seemed to have everything figured out.

"Eventually I wore her down. I wanted to know what happened to my father, and why he wasn't there. Where could he be that was better than being with us?" King Hadrian grabbed the crown from his nightstand and ran his fingers along the high golden points. "So she told me about the Watcher, the god of death, and his grand library hidden in the beyond."

"Death is a library?" R-0 asked.

King Hadrian laughed. "Death's library is what comes next. Death itself is still a mystery. It used to drive me crazy. She told me she couldn't give me all the answers—I had to figure some of it out on my own. I thought it was her way of saying she would tell me when I was older, but when I was older, I realized she was just as clueless as I was."

"It's a shame she's no longer here."

"Count your blessings. You wouldn't be sitting on my bed if she was still around."

"Is there something wrong with this arrangement?" Queen Hadrian had consistently assigned R-0 to be her son's guard. Why would she have a problem with it?

"My mother viewed constructs as tools to be used and discarded, nothing more. Which made sense given what you used to be, but . . . I don't think what's happening would have changed her mind. The constructs granted her power, and she wielded that power to accomplish her goals, cement her control over the council, and pave the way for me to become king."

Queen Hadrian had been in power for years before the constructs were created. R-0 flickered through memories. Although they had primarily been with the young King Hadrian, they had seen enough demonstrations of the queen's authority to know it was unquestionable. "She was queen. Did she not already have power over the council?"

"It's never that simple." King Hadrian sighed. "Clan Hadrian was founded by monster hunters. It was a worthwhile job when Haiden was nothing but a small village trying to survive. Hell, my ancestors are credited with founding this country. But as walls were built and more infrastructure was established, people didn't need monster hunters anymore. They needed food and craftsmen. Other clans increased in power, and our influence faded. When the council was first established, all clans held a seat. But as Haiden grew and changed, its needs changed. Clans fractured and new clans formed, but the council remained seven members and only the most influential clans keep their spots. My mother should have been the last leader our clan ever put on the throne, maybe even the last to sit on the council."

But if Queen Hadrian was meant to be the last... "You were never supposed to be king."

"Exactly. After my mother passed, Robin was expected to take the throne. And much like Riley speaks on behalf of the churches, the clans agreed that the underwater cities were prominent enough to be given a voice instead of a clan as small as mine. They planned to fill my mother's spot with an ambassador from the merfolk capital and begin politically uniting the land and the seas. If she hadn't tied our bloodline to the constructs, our clan would have slowly disappeared. And it still could. If I don't have control over the constructs, then Robin will try to reclaim the throne he thinks should be his. I have no recourse if the council turns on me. Clan Hadrian is smaller than the others on the council, and most of my clan is off in the Serenading Mountains fighting their own battles."

"That's why you listen to Councilman Robin even when you don't want to."

"Yes," King Hadrian said. "It's give and take. I took a stance he strongly disagreed with by starting reintegration with the constructs. We may have to work together for many more decades, so I'm trying to cooperate with him where I can."

"Like decommissioning E-4?"

"Yes." King Hadrian's words mixed with his sigh to the point R-0 almost didn't hear him. "I don't know why they stole from Robin, but it likely doesn't matter. The more I push against Robin, the more he'll push back, and the less likely the rest of the council is to support me. If I push too far, I risk losing everything I've ever worked for, everything my mother worked to make sure I would have."

"The ends justify the means," R-0 said. They'd heard that saying before, but never understood. The means were what led to the end. Should they not align? But hearing King Hadrian's predicament, it was beginning to make sense.

"Exactly. Sometimes I have to make decisions I don't agree with—or do things I don't want to do—in the name of progress."

Every time King Hadrian tried to do something for the constructs, the council pushed back. Memories of R-0's summons to the council chambers and their trial flickered through their mind. Their actions protecting the king and M-118 had upset many of the council members. The crimes R-0 was accused of—assaulting citizens and disobeying Eren's orders—were serious. But King Hadrian had protected them.

"Why . . ." R-0 wasn't even sure what they wondered. Why did King Hadrian choose to stand up for the constructs despite the conflict it caused with the council? And why . . . R-0? Why were they in the king's room when the other constructs involved in the reintegration were back in the storage rooms for the night? Why were they the first to be integrated?

And why did King Hadrian protect them from the council while E-4 was sitting in the dungeon?

King Hadrian waited while the whys swirled through R-0's thoughts. They were glad there were no threats to King Hadrian right now, because the buzz filling their mind made it

RISE OF THE FORGEHEARTS 187

impossible to focus. There were too many whys, too many questions, and too much they didn't understand.

"Why what?" King Hadrian prompted, after another few ticks of waiting.

"Why did you choose this guard rotation?"

"You mean, why did I choose you?"

"Yes sir."

King Hadrian's cheeks turned red, and R-0 listened as his pulse quickened. The roar of their thoughts quieted, replaced with the steady rhythm of King Hadrian's heartbeat as they regained focus. They scanned the room, but there were no changes to the environment. "Are you okay, sir?"

"The truth is . . ." King Hadrian stumbled over his words. "You . . . you've always been there for me, even before this most recent development. Everyone else in this world has ideas about who I should be, what I should do, and how they can get what they want from me. Every day is a game—when I was a child, I lost far more games than I won. But you always listened to me. And when my mother passed, and the council was ready to toss me aside, the constructs stopped them.

"After what happened with the stars, I was back in that same position—back at the council's mercy. I was terrified and just wanted things to be like they were before. I thought that was the end to my reign as king, the end of the constructs and everything my mother had worked for. But then . . . you protected me again. Even without any magic to bind you, you were there for me, like you always had been. How could I not give you a chance?"

R-0 flickered through memories. How often had King Hadrian sat before them and shared his problems? He had cried on his thirteenth birthday—his first after the late queen's passing—lamenting her loss. He had ranted about poor outcomes in council meetings and asked for advice on difficult scenarios. R-0 had never responded before, only listened silently.

Now, they interrupted the king's speech with responses and questions. R-0 acted less like the construct in their memories, and more like the organics King Hadrian usually interacted with. R-0 was different, and they weren't sure if that was a good thing.

"Things are . . . different now," R-0 said.

"They are. The more I see of the corruption, the better I understand it." King Hadrian paused. "The better I understand you. We may not have all of the answers, but I don't plan to let fear of the unknown squander an opportunity for my people."

Everything felt like an unknown for R-0 at this point—how their plates and gears inexplicably turned, the flame in their chest that shifted from a gentle warmth to a raging blaze in an instant, the way they felt when Robin looked at them in the hallway, so different than the feelings caused by the gentle look on King Hadrian's face.

R-0 stared, trying to understand. Even when Robin's expressions were similar to King Hadrian's, it didn't feel the same, and they couldn't identify why. King Hadrian caught R-0's gaze for a tick.

"Well." He straightened the papers in front of him, blocking their line of sight. "If I'm going to stay up, I guess I should actually get something done."

R-0 shifted slightly so they could more clearly watch King Hadrian work. After reading through a dozen papers, King Hadrian had four stacks surrounding him. Despite the repetition of the action, it was far more interesting than Eren's puzzle work. There was a purpose to it, and he was making progress.

R-0 wanted to help.

They weren't sure what to say or how to ask. It was outside of their orders, but they'd done many things outside of their orders recently, although the variations had been met with mixed results. Perhaps this aspect of the corruption could make R-0 more useful. They could protect King Hadrian *and* assist with paperwork. They sat up straight, staring at the letters.

"Is something wrong?" King Hadrian asked.

"No sir." R-0 opened their mouth to continue but couldn't find the words.

King Hadrian studied them for a few ticks of their gears. "Would you like to help?"

"Yes sir." The flame in R-0's chest sparked up, warming the edges of their chest. It was a . . . good feeling.

King Hadrian explained his organization system, and R-0 quickly set to work categorizing the papers. They moved far more quickly than the king, often sorting four or five letters to his one. As the moon inched across the sky, R-0 retrieved another stack of papers from the nightstand. When they set it down, King Hadrian didn't stir. His eyes were closed, and a small snore escaped him. Luckily, his descent into sleep hadn't disturbed the unsorted piles in front of him, but R-0 knew he was likely to toss and turn throughout the night. The papers didn't belong in bed with him.

They moved the papers to the table, but something still seemed wrong. R-0 examined the sleeping king. They gently lifted King Hadrian's head, slipping a pillow between his face and the mattress. Even though magic from the managrid kept the king's room warm, he never slept without a blanket. There was no way of moving his comforter without disturbing him, so R-0 retrieved an extra blanket from the closet and placed it over the king.

Content that King Hadrian could sleep soundly, R-0 continued working, quickly finishing the remaining letters. As R-0 returned them to the king's desk, they hesitated. All they had been doing was sorting, but . . . what if the answer to the missing constructs was hidden within these pages? King Hadrian had asked some of the staff to set aside the most important reports for his review, but what if something had been overlooked?

Anything that could explain where M-118 went or why the intruder infiltrated King Hadrian's room would help the investigation. It could also help with the reintegration efforts, allowing more of the constructs to return to work.

R-0 sat at the desk, hesitating when the chair creaked under their weight. When they were convinced it could hold them without breaking, they picked up the first in the stack of reports that mentioned the constructs. R-0 wasn't sure why the organics opted to sit instead of stand when concentrating, but they were willing to try it.

Hours passed as they read stories of constructs refusing to work or asking strange questions. While R-0 might have done the latter, they couldn't even consider doing the former. They had one job: protect the king. One look at him peacefully sleeping proved R-0 was good at their job. Why would they refuse to work?

Other letters gave more detailed accounts of constructs performing strange acts—attempting to eat food designed for organics, walking along the shoreline without a purpose, or sitting silently, unresponsive to external stimuli. One described a construct that had tried to forge a sword their own way instead of following the blacksmith's instructions. The result had been a mangled lump of iron. Still the construct insisted their method held promise, only lacking in execution due to their inexperience. The blacksmith signed the letter with urgency, asking the king to please send word soon on what he was doing to resolve this issue.

A mangled lump of iron wasn't useful, but R-0 wondered if there was any value to the construct's new method. It couldn't truly be as concerning as the blacksmith believed, could it?

There were a few reports on Ryder, although none related to the constructs other than the one sighting of him at the warehouse with M-118. It was strange to find any reports on him at all. Despite Ryder's long list of crimes, he historically stayed out of sight and away from the guards. What had changed recently?

Despite the variations, R-0 only found two missing constructs not on the lists compiled during King Hadrian's initial investigation—a fisherman who lived along the coast feared his construct had fallen into the sea and drowned, and a storage facility claimed after the chaos of the falling stars, they reclaimed all but one of the constructs under their care.

R-0 attempted to tiptoe across the room, but despite their efforts, their heavy steps still clanked. King Hadrian mumbled under his breath and turned in bed, but a snore followed. They had only intended to add the letters to his investigation, but there was plenty of time before dawn. Without waking the king, they gathered all the reports on the missing constructs.

There wasn't enough space on King Hadrian's desk, so instead R-0 sat on the floor, spreading the pages around them. They started by reading each one, then categorized them, looking for a pattern in any of the variables. Sorting by date received, incident time, construct model, and other details revealed nothing, but when R-0 sorted the papers by location, something was off.

The reports of missing constructs within the palace were varied. Some were quickly scribbled, untechnical notes by a random chef, others were the methodical and detailed notes of a technomancer, and a few were submitted by council members or other high-ranking staff.

In contrast, the reports of missing constructs that came from throughout the city were more uniform. On over half of them, despite different names being signed at the bottom, the handwriting was the same. They reported different circumstances in different places, but the word choice was repetitive.

It was as if the same person had written all of them.

But why would one person sign their letters under different names? And why would one person report so many constructs?

Unless they were fake. Organics lied. R-0 had seen that demonstrated repeatedly. It would also explain why JJ and the others interrogated during their visit to the city hadn't known about the missing constructs.

But why would someone fabricate these reports? They set the questionable reports to the side and repeated their original investigation, organizing the remaining reports by various attributes and searching for a pattern. This time when they sorted the papers by location, one pile towered above the others.

Whatever was happening with the missing constructs, the palace was at the center of it.

CHAPTER 23

As the sun rose higher in the sky, R-0 waited beside King Hadrian's bed for him to wake up. Sleep was a nuisance. R-0 understood it was necessary for organics to function, but it was slow, tedious, and useless, especially when they had a lead on the missing constructs to investigate. The investigation wasn't R-0's only task. They hadn't had the opportunity to return Beans's screw last night, but they wouldn't forget their promise to Seraphine.

The longer R-0 spent waiting and thinking, the more their thoughts wandered to the constructs stuck in the storage rooms with nothing to do, and the more guilty they felt. But doing something—even just planning the next step of the investigation—made R-0 feel better. They hadn't fixed the situation yet, but every time they proved their usefulness or learned more about the missing constructs, they moved closer to a resolution. The same couldn't be said while they stood motionless in King Hadrian's room, watching his still form and waiting for him to wake up.

If King Hadrian followed his normal routine, his eyes would flicker open any minute now, and R-0 could request additional records on the palace constructs. Perhaps they could even retrieve the files before breakfast, and R-0 could analyze them while King Hadrian ate. That would be an efficient use of time.

But the sun continued to rise higher, and King Hadrian still slept. R-0's fingers fidgeted at their side. Would it be rude to wake him up?

They raised a hand to his head, preparing to wake him, but stopped. He looked so peaceful. His face was relaxed, free of the creases that too frequently covered his brow. A soft smile made him look younger than the set, motionless expression he usually wore. Maybe he could use a little more sleep.

R-0 lowered their arm, and the metal clanked against their side. King Hadrian huffed in a short breath and rolled onto his back. His amber eyes slowly blinked open, and the peaceful look was quickly erased.

"R-0?" His voice was still groggy, and he rubbed at his eyes.

"Yes sir." R-0 straightened their posture. Their intentions hadn't mattered, and they'd managed to wake him anyway.

"Why"—he stifled a yawn—"are you watching me sleep?"

"It is morning."

"And?"

"It is time for you to wake up."

"That doesn't really explain . . ." He sighed and pulled the blanket to his chin. "What's this?"

"A blanket."

King Hadrian sat up, looking between the letters organized on his desk and the blanket. A smile returned to his face, larger than the one he'd worn while sleeping. "Thank you, R-0."

He dragged himself out of bed, his feet grazing the floor as he trudged to the bathroom adjoining his room. Magic sparked from his hands as he activated the managrid, causing water to fill the basin in the counter. He splashed it over his face. "Sorry. I didn't mean to fall asleep like that."

"All of the papers have been organized. Also, further investigation into the missing constructs was completed. Additional information is required."

"I thought you were sorting the letters I'd received?"

"Yes sir," R-0 said. Worry seeped in. Continuing the investigation hadn't been part of their orders. But the other constructs weren't as lucky as R-0—they didn't have an objective or the freedom to pursue it. Until the reintegration progressed, they would be stuck in storage rooms. "There was additional time after organizing the letters to review the investigation."

"You finished reading *all* of them?"

R-0 checked the room once more. They hadn't seen any other papers, but perhaps they had missed something. "They can be double-checked, if you would like."

"No, no, I trust you. I'm just surprised. It was a lot."

It was the second time King Hadrian had told R-0 he trusted them, but it surprised them just as much. He had said trust was not something easily given, and something that could be dangerous as well. But he gave it to R-0 freely.

And R-0 trusted him. R-0 searched for the words to tell the king, but despite their spinning gears, no words formed. Why was it so hard to say?

"So you said you need additional information." King Hadrian waltzed out of the bathroom, his sleepwear replaced with fine robes. "Like what? What did you figure out?"

R-0 recounted their discovery of the strange letters, then the disproportionate ratio of palace constructs missing after the fakes were removed.

"These are definitely forged." King Hadrian set down the pile of reports written in the same handwriting. "Which means someone wanted us to believe this was happening all over the city when it's really just concentrated here." King Hadrian bit at his lower lip as he paced the room.

R-0 hadn't stopped to consider the implication of their discovery. If the palace was the source of the disappearances, was King Hadrian in danger? If the constructs themselves were organizing and planning something, wouldn't it be happening across the city, not just here? And there were still a few disappearances that didn't connect to the palace.

"M-118 was not stationed here."

"That's true. And if the reports were right that Ryder was involved in their initial disappearance, he also shouldn't have any connections at the palace. If he showed his face around here, he'd be arrested in an instant."

The investigation was like Eren's puzzle. Every time they slid a new piece into place, the landscape changed. But there were details missing, pieces not quite fitting. People and their motivations were not as straightforward as stone, and it was much more difficult to decipher how they fit together.

"Come on." King Hadrian gently smoothed down his hair before placing the glittering crown on his head. He thumbed through the pile of papers R-0 had marked as most important. "Eren keeps the records in the guard stations. I have a few other matters to attend to first, but then we can head there and see if you can find any patterns in the full schedules. We can visit E-4 as well."

"There is one more task to be completed," R-0 said.

"What's that?"

King Hadrian watched, confusion framing his face as R-0 unscrewed the compartment on their arm. They retrieved Beans's screw and held it out to the king for examination. "This needs to be returned to Beans."

"A screw?"

"It is from Seraphine."

"Ah, your little encounter yesterday." King Hadrian nodded. "I heard about that. It shouldn't be a problem."

King Hadrian didn't finish reading the rest of the letters before heading out. R-0 struggled to stay silent as the king handled his daily tasks. They had a lead on the missing constructs—they needed to be investigating it. But King Hadrian reassured them that his tasks were equally important and the dungeon would have to wait.

After King Hadrian had taken care of far more than a few matters and had been served not only breakfast but lunch as well, they finally visited the dungeon. The guard on duty stood at attention upon seeing King Hadrian, then directed them to E-4's cell.

They walked past empty cells until they reached a fork. R-0 moved to follow King Hadrian to the right, but the sound of clanking metal from the left stopped them.

Down the left hallway, constructs filled the cells and lined the walkway, leaving a narrow strip through the middle unobstructed. As in the storage rooms, they had little space to move. Even the beds had multiple constructs crammed on them.

R-0 froze where they stood. Why were so many constructs imprisoned? What had they done?

"R-0, you coming?" King Hadrian looked back at them.

Yes sir. R-0 thought the words, but their face plates stayed frozen in place, their voice silent, and their legs unmoving.

They were supposed to be protecting King Hadrian, but they could barely take their eyes off the scene in front of them long enough to glance at him.

"Are you okay?" King Hadrian had come back and now stood at R-0's side. He placed his hand on R-0's arm, then quickly pulled back. "You're burning up."

R-0 had been so preoccupied with the constructs, they hadn't noticed their own flame raging in their chest or the heat transferring across their plates.

"Apologies sir." R-0 looked at his hand. "Are you injured?"

"No, it's okay." King Hadrian kept his focus on R-0, not even glancing at the rest of the constructs.

R-0 slowly began walking away, but each step was forced and heavier than normal. They could feel the weight of each and every one of their plates, and their body was reluctant to move.

"What are their crimes?" R-0 finally asked.

"A few are hiccups in the reintegration efforts, like Robin and E-4. But most we just didn't have space for in the other holding areas." King Hadrian shook his head. "Don't worry about them, R-0. We're working on something else."

Despite King Hadrian's comforting words, it was impossible to suppress their worry.

"I'd like you to take the lead in questioning E-4. They may respond better to a construct than to me."

"Yes sir." R-0 fought to keep their gaze on the king and not look back over their shoulder at the rest of the constructs. They had known there wasn't enough space in the storage rooms—they had escorted constructs to the halls and ballroom themself. The prisons shouldn't have been any different. It was just an alternate placement while arrangements were made, but . . . seeing the constructs staring at them from locked cells left an uncomfortable sensation coating their insides like smoke filling the air.

King Hadrian continued down the hallway and stopped in front of E-4's cell. "Here we are."

It was the same cell R-0 had been kept in, but the chain had been replaced with thicker and heavier metal. The tral prisoner they had spoken with was gone, and the cell across the hall was empty.

R-0 had been worried about E-4, but E-4's situation was much better than the other constructs. E-4 had a cell to themself, room to move around. They could stand, sit, lie down.

But their fates differed. The others would be reintegrated in time or return home when their owners retrieved them. Even among constructs facing sentences due to issues with the reintegration, few crimes would result in extended sentences or death. Or in the constructs' case, decommissioning.

But if King Hadrian's efforts to change Robin's mind failed, E-4 wouldn't be reintegrated. Visions of the scrapyard haunted R-0 once more. This time, it wasn't them lying among the scrap. They were standing above E-4, their metal cold and still.

R-0 stopped blinking.

"R-0! King Hadrian!" E-4 bowed their head in respect, then rushed toward the bars of the cell. "Are you here to release me?"

No. They weren't.

"R-0?" King Hadrian prompted, but R-0 remained silent. There was nothing they could say to E-4.

"What's going on?" E-4 asked.

"We aren't here to release you," King Hadrian said. "I'm working on it, but there are no guarantees."

E-4's posture slumped. Their gears slowed, and their head tilted down. "Then why are you here?"

"We wanted to ask you a few questions." King Hadrian put his hand on R-0's back, pushing them forward slightly.

"I already told the guards everything," E-4 said.

"We're just being thorough."

King Hadrian looked at R-0 expectantly, and R-0 searched for the right words. They had witnessed interrogations plenty of times, but never led one. Questions bounced around their mind like water sloshing to fill its container.

"Why did you steal?" R-0 asked. Perhaps if they better understood why the crime occurred, they could stop it from happening again during the reintegration efforts. Or maybe the information could help King Hadrian free E-4.

E-4 pushed at the bars, then let go. They walked back to their bed and plopped down. "I didn't steal. Councilman Robin had been complaining about a missing ring. While he was out, I conducted a search for it. I was trying to return it, but the councilman saw it first and wouldn't listen."

"No one ordered you to steal?"

"No."

King Hadrian grabbed onto the bars of the cell. "And you didn't receive orders from anyone other than Robin in that time period?"

"Correct," E-4 said.

"Then it's all a misunderstanding." R-0's flame sparked, but not with worry. Since E-4 was innocent, their stay in the dungeon would be the same as R-0's—temporary. They wouldn't be decommissioned for a crime they didn't commit.

"The guards didn't seem to care. Or they didn't believe me." E-4 slumped back on the bed. "Doesn't matter which. I'm still here."

"If you are innocent, then you should be released." R-0 reached for the lock and looked over at King Hadrian. The reinforced metal might be enough to keep a standard issue construct contained, but R-0 could break it just as easily as they had the original.

"Unfortunately, that's not something we can change right now." King Hadrian kept his voice soft. He gently pushed R-0's hand back to their side. "Do you know anything about the missing constructs? Has anyone asked you to leave the palace?"

"No to both questions." E-4 stood from their bed and stepped as close as they could to the bars. "You're the king. Can't you do something about this?" They gestured at the surrounding cell. "R-0 is right. I shouldn't be here."

R-0's fingers slid against one another, accelerating with each passing second. Occasionally R-0 applied too much pressure, and a shrill squeal accompanied scraping metal. E-4's circumstances were unjust. Why couldn't King Hadrian do something?

"Your report will be investigated and verified," King Hadrian said. "And I'll discuss the situation with Robin."

"Please." E-4 slid their hands around the bars, gripping tight.

"I'll do what I can." King Hadrian rested his hand on top of E-4's. "But for now, we have to take our leave."

E-4's expression fell. A barely visible puff of smoke escaped from some of their joints as they went back to sit on the bed.

"Do you believe them?" R-0 asked.

King Hadrian sighed. "To be honest, it doesn't matter what I believe. It matters what Robin believes."

"Even if they're innocent, it's still up to Robin?"

"Here we are." King Hadrian pushed open the door to the guard station and ushered R-0 inside, without answering their question. He quickly began a conversation with the guard on duty, detailing the records they would need and handing him a list of constructs.

R-0's flame gurgled, and unease filled them. Memories from their own time in the dungeon flashed before their eyes again and again. They didn't want to leave E-4 alone. But King Hadrian had made it clear that E-4 would remain here unless he could convince Robin to release them.

"Over here, R-0." King Hadrian's voice pulled them from their thoughts and back to reality.

The guard had already brought two tall stacks of records to the table, and he had a third stack in his arms. The cabinets behind him were still ajar, and as soon as he set the papers down, he returned for more. They couldn't help E-4 directly right now, but if they could figure out what the missing constructs were doing, perhaps it would help to convince Robin of E-4's innocence.

R-0 started with the reintegration paperwork from yesterday. Locating Beans would be a far quicker task than retrieving all the records on the missing constructs. It only took a few minutes to find an intake form that matched Beans. Their official designation had been shortened to L-6 in dark, bold ink across the top, but a shaky line crossed out their official designation and messy scribbles were added underneath. It was barely legible, and the letters didn't follow an orderly pattern, but R-0 deciphered them one by one.

B - E - A - N - S

The rest of the form detailed where they had been taken and gave information about the owner and the construct's history. R-0 frowned. The records were wrong.

Beans was listed as an abandoned construct.

R-0 scratched out the line indicating that they'd been abandoned and instead wrote in that they were eligible for pick up. In the field for owner name, they added Seraphine's name.

Now that they knew where Beans had been assigned, they just needed to figure out where in the dungeon they were stationed. They pulled out the check-in logs, searching for any entry of Beans or L-6. But even after checking every block twice, they couldn't find any records of Beans arriving in the dungeon.

"Please hold." R-0 left the room and walked back down the hallway.

R-0 scanned the rows of constructs once more, checking every spot, but none had a designation of L-6, and none were in a state of disrepair that matched the rusted and broken screw.

Beans was missing.

Seraphine had promised to come back for them, and Beans had promised to be here. So why would Beans leave? They had been mis-categorized as abandoned property, but that could have been resolved easily when their family came to pick them up.

"What's going on?" King Hadrian followed them into the hallway.

"Beans is missing."

"From intake yesterday?"

R-0 nodded, showing King Hadrian and the guard the discrepancy between Beans's intake form and the check-in form.

King Hadrian cursed. "I wonder how many more. In all the chaos . . . Who knows how many are unaccounted for."

R-0 frowned. "Beans was not supposed to leave."

"None of them were supposed to leave, but here we are." King Hadrian led the way back to the records room. "Do you see any more like Beans?"

Comparing intake forms and check-in logs was slow, but after around fifty forms, R-0 found another discrepancy. After twenty more, another. They set them to the side and continued their search, but King Hadrian stopped them.

"I'll assign one of the scribes to go through everything again, and we'll have them manually check the construct holding areas and confirm who is where. Yesterday was chaotic. This could just be a paperwork error." He shuffled the papers in front of him, then moved the stack of intake logs farther away from R-0. "In the meantime, let's keep looking into the ones we know are missing."

R-0 cross-referenced each schedule log with the list of missing constructs they had compiled from King Hadrian's notes last night. Separating out only the relevant files cut the paperwork into a more manageable stack.

R-0 had been right that the disappearances had a central area in common. They had thought it was the entire palace but were able to narrow it down even further.

"The largest concentration of disappearances is in the eastern sector."

"Get me Councilwoman Riley and Councilwoman Eren." King Hadrian motioned to the guard. "And arrange a guard detail for me as well."

R-0 frowned. King Hadrian had said R-0 could handle the position alone. Why had that changed? R-0 started to ask, but the guard's lingering gaze stopped them. They weren't supposed to question King Hadrian's orders. They especially shouldn't question them in front of others in the palace—it could jeopardize the reintegration efforts.

As soon as the guard left, King Hadrian placed a hand on R-0's shoulder. "Do you know how many entrance points the managrid has in the palace?"

"Nine," R-0 said.

"And how many of them are in the eastern sector?"

"Seven."

"Do you think that's a coincidence?"

R-0 considered it. If the missing constructs were focusing their efforts in an area where the managrid was easily accessible, it was possible they were using the tunnels to avoid detection . . . and it was plausible they could be responsible for the blackouts. "You believe the managrid is in danger?"

"I believe we can't be too cautious. We thought people were upset about the constructs and the temporary blackouts . . . but if the managrid goes down, the entire city will grind to a halt, and there'll be riots before morning." He sighed. "This has to be investigated immediately, and with as few people knowing as possible. You'll accompany Riley in the tunnels, and I'll have Eren set up additional guard routes around all the entrances until you've finished. You cannot tell anyone else, do you understand? This stays between us."

"You believe someone in the palace is involved?"

King Hadrian nodded. "If the constructs have been doing this right in front of us without us noticing, they likely have someone helping them. I don't know how else they'd cover up something like this."

"Who?"

"I have a few ideas—" The guard walked back into the room, interrupting whatever King Hadrian was going to say next. Instead, he turned to the guard. "Send word to Councilman Robin. I need to speak with him immediately."

CHAPTER 24

As they traveled through the palace, Quiet didn't make conversation. R-0 didn't either. They expected to resent the silence as they had with Eren and King Hadrian, but their flame burned steady. With others, silence was the lack of something, but with Quiet, it was an aura she exuded. Nothing was missing, things simply were.

Though the managrid ran under a majority of the city, there were limited access points, and no one was allowed below without authorization. To R-0's surprise, more guards than usual stood at the entrance. Quiet had arrived before Eren, so how had Eren already assigned additional guards?

Quiet greeted the guards. Lies rolled off her tongue smooth and quick, as she described flickering power at Eclipse's temple that a priest had asked her to look into. She didn't need to bother the technomancers with something she could do on her own—everyone was overworked as it was.

If R-0 hadn't known the truth, they would have believed every word. She didn't hesitate or give any indication she had made up the story.

As they followed Quiet, the conversation with the guards lingered in their mind. R-0 would have no way of knowing if Quiet was lying.

Torches lit the entrance at the base of the ladder, and deeper inside—where tunnels were lit only by the glow of the managrid's magic—unlit torches had been tossed haphazardly along the pathway. With the blackouts, it was wise to have an alternative light source, but R-0 hoped it wasn't necessary. There was something different about the world cloaked in a blue gleam. Their plates looked closer to Levian steel than normal dull gray steel. Quiet's appearance was also affected, her golden hair sparkling blue.

She led them down the tunnels, and R-0 tried to memorize every twist and turn. The tunnel repeatedly split into multiple passageways, some extending deeper into the ground, others turning back on themselves. Every tunnel looked the same—metal tracks glimmering with magical energy ran along the floor, and plain, smooth stone bordered its edges and the walls. Everything was too similar. How could they separate which memory came from which turn or opening?

R-0 paused. Even if they could remember, it was shaping up to be a time-consuming task. Quiet would need to sleep multiple times before they finished exploring.

"Is there a problem?" Quiet stopped and looked back at R-0.

"The managrid is expansive."

"It covers the entire country. Did you expect it to be small?"

"No, but it will take a long time to search."

"We're not going to search the whole thing." Quiet continued forward. "If there were issues in the grid—a broken part or missing piece—the effect would be localized to where that grid reached. Something of this scale has to go through one of the manacores."

"How many manacores are there?"

"Under the palace?" Quiet asked. "Only six."

That sounded like a far more reasonable area to cover with the time they had left in the day. King Hadrian had wasted most of the morning sleeping, and the rest of his tasks had taken the entire afternoon. Even if they only investigated six manacores, it would likely be dark before they finished.

"Haven't the manacores already been investigated?" R-0 asked. It seemed like a logical starting point to triage the blackouts.

"The technomancers have checked them, but if King Hadrian's suspicion that someone is helping the constructs is true, we'd better verify their reports for ourselves. We'll start with the lower quadrant. If I was sabotaging the grid, that's where I'd go."

"Why?"

"Less foot traffic, and until recently, it was primarily constructs working that sector. It's also an end point—it's easier to pull and push energy into it. Both of which could cause the blackouts we've been seeing."

"You believe the constructs have been sabotaging the grid?"

"They have motive and means. And with the timing and the missing . . . well, it makes sense."

Means R-0 understood. Many of the missing constructs had worked on the managrid. They would have the technical knowledge to maintain and repair it. But motive?

"What would be their motive?"

"I could write a list." Quiet chuckled.

After a few more steps, when it was clear she didn't intend to elaborate, R-0 asked, "What would be on your list?"

"The constructs are being treated unfairly. If they haven't already, it's only a matter of time before they organize and strike back."

Quiet's words named the feelings of discomfort that plagued R-0 whenever they thought of the constructs. It was unfair. Wrong.

"The constructs should not have to remain in the storage rooms," R-0 said.

"Exactly. It's cruel. But it's convenient, so I expect the constructs will take issue with it before the council finds its heart."

"You and King Hadrian both disagree with the council, but . . ." R-0 trailed off. Unlike when they talked with King Hadrian, Quiet didn't fill in their missing words. Their footsteps echoed through the empty tunnels while R-0 processed. "You *are* the council."

"Which is why sometimes we have to make plans of our own."

"Like what?" R-0 asked.

"Whatever the situation might call for." Quiet winked. "Come on, the first manacore is just past here."

After the next turn, the tunnel widened into a small room. A massive blue crystal floated in the center. A metal band hovered around it, not directly touching it. Sparks of bright, wild magic cackled at the stone's surface, coalescing into a familiar blue glow when it hit the metal. Curved rods traveled from the band into the floor, then extended out in every direction, forming the grid they had been walking on.

Quiet placed her hand inches from the stone, and the light arced to her, curling around her fingers.

R-0 mimicked the movement, and a rush of adrenaline washed over them. As the magic sparked against their plates, their vision shifted. The crystal shone brighter and more intensely, while the tunnels and walls blurred together. Although their flame remained static, heat flushed through their body as if they were walking into a furnace. A buzz filled the air, so loud that it masked even Quiet's breath beside them, and R-0 had to watch for the gentle rise and fall of her chest to ensure she was still breathing.

"Beautiful, isn't it?" Quiet asked.

R-0's words failed them, and they simply nodded.

While they investigated the first manacore, Quiet explained their function. The crystals were enchanted with complex, ongoing spells that siphoned magic from the air and earth around them. A portion of that energy was used to keep the spell functioning, perpetually gathering more mana and growing stronger, and the rest was channeled through the grid.

R-0 examined the physical aspects of the manacore and its surroundings while Quiet meditated, exploring the Flow and its connections to the manacore with her own magic to ensure the enchantments hadn't been modified. Everything was in perfect working order. Neither of them found evidence of any tampering apart from regular maintenance. The second and third were similar.

On the walk to the fourth manacore, one of the branching tunnels caught R-0's attention. It wasn't unusual for the tunnels to come to a sudden dead-end as they reached the edge of a structure on the surface. But usually, when the managrid ended, a stone border surrounded the end point.

Here, the managrid extended straight into the wall, continuing into rock.

R-0 turned down the passageway. "What's this?"

"It's been like that forever." Quiet hardly glanced over. "They'd originally planned to extend it farther, but when plans changed, the tunnel got filled in."

"You know a lot about the tunnels."

"I'm down here a lot."

It seemed odd. Quiet was on the council to represent the churches and the Goddess Eclipse. None of the council duties required spending time in the tunnels or around the managrid, and as far as R-0 knew, no religious duties were typically performed down here.

"Why?" R-0 asked.

"It's more peaceful down here," Quiet said. "And fewer guards to worry about."

"The guards are here to protect you. Why do they cause worry?"

"I value my freedom more than their protection, which is something they and some of the council members resent."

It explained a lot—not only Quiet's knowledge of the tunnels but also how she often seemed to come and go on her own while other council members were constantly attended to. Still, R-0 worried. How would R-0 know if her explanation was a lie or the truth? Quiet had already admitted that she would make plans without notifying the council. What would stop her from circumventing R-0 as well?

At the fifth undisturbed manacore, Quiet sighed. "If you were going to sabotage the palace, what would you do?"

"Sabotaging the palace would never occur."

"Pretend."

R-0 tried to copy what Kaili and Kalani had done. If they pretended the manacore was a boat, and they were a pirate . . . what would they do? But there was too much that didn't make sense. The ocean waters were far too dangerous for a construct's flame, R-0 could never be a pirate, and manacores were infinitely more complex than a boat.

"Or how about this," Quiet said, "if King Hadrian ordered you to sabotage the palace, where would you start?"

"With the guards," R-0 said. "Eliminating defenses would make future tasks more efficient."

Quiet tilted her head from side to side but didn't offer a rebuttal to R-0's plan. If that was what the missing constructs were attempting, they were doing a poor job. There were even more guards than normal, not less.

There was another possibility that Quiet was ignoring—one that R-0 couldn't help thinking about.

"What if the missing constructs aren't sabotaging anything?" R-0 asked.

"You don't think they are?"

"No ma'am."

"Why?"

"Because why would the constructs leave? And where would they go? How does this help them?" R-0 couldn't fathom an answer. Maybe some were like Quiet had described—unhappy with their circumstances and looking for something more. But most of the constructs R-0 had met were scared. They were looking for orders and guidance, not revenge.

And there was Beans, who was supposed to be waiting for Seraphine. Why would they have abandoned her?

"Beans wasn't supposed to leave," R-0 said. "They promised to wait for Seraphine."

"One of the missing constructs? You knew them?"

R-0 recounted the story—starting with Seraphine crying in the gardens and ending with their discovery that Beans was missing.

"R-0 . . ." Quiet's voice trailed off. "Beans's form wasn't a mistake."

"But Seraphine said—"

"Seraphine likely repeated what her mother told her. King Hadrian's policy left families divided, unsure. Seraphine may have had good intentions, but I doubt her family shared her views."

"It could have been a mistake." Organics made mistakes all the time, but memories flickered. The guard had said Seraphine had gotten lost when her mother stopped to count her coin. Had she gotten that coin from abandoning Beans?

"No one is coming back for Beans." Quiet rested her hand on R-0's shoulder. "And I wouldn't be surprised if Beans was smart enough to know that." She pulled away. "Which would give them a powerful motive to leave. Either to return to those they cared about or to oppose the system that put them in this position."

As much as R-0 wanted to reject Quiet's suggestion, they couldn't. R-0 themself was proof that constructs would act exactly like that. When they had been sent to the storage rooms, unneeded by King Hadrian, they had disobeyed Eren.

All their orders and intentions were becoming muddied. Nothing was the simple yes or no that it had been before the incident. When they'd agreed to return Beans's screw, they had meant it, but now, it was an impossible task unless the missing constructs were found. Perhaps if R-0 had insisted on returning the screw immediately, they could have found Beans. Instead, they were gone, and R-0 had failed Seraphine.

"What's wrong?" Quiet asked.

R-0 checked the branching tunnels twice, but they were empty. They quieted their flame, listening as far into the distance as they could, but they couldn't hear anything other than the distant static of the manacore.

"Nothing is wrong."

"No, with you," she said. "You seem . . . bothered."

Bothered. Was that how they felt about Beans being missing? They weren't sure if that was the word they would use. They had a responsibility, they had made a promise to Seraphine, and they had failed.

"Seraphine requested a delivery be made to Beans. It cannot be completed."

"What was the delivery?" Quiet asked.

R-0 slowly unscrewed the metal plate on their forearm, opening their arm compartment. They let the screw roll into their other hand and held it out to Quiet. "Beans lost this."

Quiet's eyes widened, and she reached out. "May I?"

R-0 dropped the screw in her palm. She ran her fingers along its spirals so gently no rust rubbed off onto her fingertips. It seemed R-0 wasn't the only one who didn't see it as trash—they had made the right decision. First Seraphine and now Quiet treated it like it was important.

"I'm glad you kept this." Quiet turned and began walking in the other direction—away from the rest of the tunnels that still needed to be checked.

"That area has already been explored."

"I know."

R-0 frowned. "Are you not going to check the final mana-core?"

"No."

R-0 quickened their pace to keep up with her and reattached the plate on their arm. They hadn't found anything to report, and already, Quiet was leaving. Was this why King Hadrian wanted R-0 to go with Quiet? To ensure the task was completed?

Or to see what Quiet would do instead?

King Hadrian's words about who to trust echoed through their mind. Could they trust Quiet? They wanted to. She was . . . kind. Not just to R-0, but to others as well.

"Where are you going?" R-0 asked. "The task is incomplete."

"We're supposed to be investigating the missing constructs, right?"

"Yes ma'am."

Quiet mumbled a few words to the guards as they resurfaced into the palace, then hurried down the halls to the far wing. Most of the council members had their chambers in this section, and Quiet was no exception. She unlocked her door with an ornate silver and gold key.

Unlike the other council members, Quiet's chambers were simple. The room was empty except for a bed pushed into one corner with a desk next to it. Quiet rummaged through the desk drawers, retrieving a few flowers from one, a small glass bottle filled with a murky liquid from another, and a silver bladed knife from a third.

She pulled a leather pouch from her pocket. Inside was a compass with a golden chain. Both sides were pure gold, dulled but clean, and each side had a different engraving—one of the sun and the other of the moon. She flipped it open.

A bright red stone sat in the housing with a needle pointing north.

She poured the murky liquid onto the desk, then one by one, placed the flowers in a circle. Finally, she laid the compass in the center with Beans's screw balanced on top.

For a moment, nothing happened. Then Quiet's hand began to glow in a muted silver, and the compass matched. As the light faded, Quiet opened her eyes and picked up the compass, tilting the face so R-0 could see it as well.

"Rezten," she whispered. The compass began to glow again, and the screw spun rapidly before coming to an abrupt halt. Quiet pointed at the tip, then outward in the same direction. "Let's go find Beans."

CHAPTER 25

R-0 held the compass gently, careful not to risk it slipping through the cracks between their fingers. Beans's screw remained balanced on top. In the same way the red needle twisted to mark north, the screw rotated in place, always pointing toward their destination: Beans. The compass was warm to the touch, and the closer they stood to Quiet, the stronger the heat became.

R-0 stayed right on her heels—as close as they could without bumping into her—reveling in the warmth. In the *magic*.

It was beautiful. The colors, the feeling, all of it. They hadn't been so enamored with something since they had lost themself in the falling stars the night of the incident. This couldn't be explained with logic or replicated with instructions. It was something more.

"R-0," Quiet said.

"Yes?"

"Has anyone ever explained to you the concept of personal space?"

"Yes ma'am." More than once. It was a strange concept.

"I would appreciate it if you would give me some."

R-0 paused, letting her pull ahead before following behind her once more, careful this time to leave space between them. They had modified into their condensed form, which made the task easier. The compass dropped in temperature ever so slightly but still retained its allure. They peeked between their fingers again, and the soft glow reflected off their steel.

R-0 had so many questions. They normally reserved their questions for King Hadrian, who had warned them that others might misinterpret their curiosity, which would cause unnecessary tension. But that wasn't the case with Quiet, right? She had always been . . . patient with them.

"How long will the magic remain?" R-0 asked.

"Until it reaches its target."

"Indefinitely?"

Quiet nodded. "It's been in the church for generations, a gift from our goddess." Something changed in her tone when she spoke of the goddess. "When my mentor left Lexica's Domain to come here, her mentor gave it to her so she could always find her way home without losing something if things in Haiden didn't pan out. I inherited it when she passed."

"It's . . ." R-0 searched for the words to describe it. "Beautiful. But why would going home cause her to lose something?"

"Most of Eclipse's casters are capable of tracking magic, but any spells we cast come at a cost. It's how our goddess seeks balance. Something found, something lost. Something hidden, something seen. Something learned, something forgotten."

"Back in the gardens with the flower . . ."

"Life given, life taken." Quiet held up her palm, where the cut was still healing. Other scars lined her skin, some old and some fresh. "What do you know of the goddess, Eclipse?"

"Eclipse is the goddess of duality," R-0 recited. "Light and dark. Sun and moon. Life and death."

"Technically true." Quiet smirked. "But it's not just about opposites."

R-0 frowned. "It's not?"

"When you look at the sun and moon, it's easy to see the differences. But there are far more similarities, and that is where we focus. The harmony between things that are different, opposite. The gray area in between." Quiet gestured to the skyline, where the sun had dipped out of sight, but its color still lingered. "Twilight."

The sun and moon both provided light. Both were in the sky. But those were the only similarities R-0 could think of. The sun was a constant, while the moon changed its shape.

One shone during the day, the other at night. What was the area in between?

They continued in silence, even as the managrid blacked out again. Although the outage was brief, a lasting tension hung over the people on the streets, as well as Quiet. They kept walking until the twilight dissipated into the darkness of night.

R-0 meticulously maintained the space between them, careful not to invade her personal space again. They did not want Quiet to view them as rude or inconsiderate. They wanted Quiet to consider them a friend.

The compass took them past the harpy district and deep into the dragon district, its light growing brighter. R-0 also felt more heat emanating from it as they approached their destination. Gone were the well-maintained streets close to the palace grounds. The few people still out on the streets pulled their coats tight around them and walked with hurried steps. Every few blocks, R-0 would peek at the screw to ensure they were still heading in the right direction.

A gust of wind blew from the coast, whistling between the buildings. Unsecured shutters banged against the windows, and even though R-0 knew the source of the sound, it didn't stop them from turning to verify. Peering out from the alley next to the building was a face with shining blue eyes that followed R-0 and Quiet's movements.

Ryder.

Although partially obscured in shadows, R-0 recognized him from the wanted posters around the castle. Most of his scales were blue, but some had been replaced with silver, creating an illusion of waves ripping across his cheek. His list of crimes was vast—from theft to murder. More importantly, he'd been seen heading into the warehouse with M-118 before R-0 found them.

R-0 tightened their grip on the compass. Quiet had said the tracking spell would last indefinitely, so as long as they had the compass in their possession, they'd be able to find Beans. Their opportunity to apprehend Ryder wouldn't last, however. He'd evaded capture numerous times already, and this was their chance to discover what he knew about the missing constructs.

If they were alone, it would be easy to sprint ahead and confront the criminal. But they couldn't endanger Quiet. R-0 paused at the next intersection, searching for a landmark that would help them determine where they were and where to find the closest guard station, but they only saw buildings, lampposts, and more turns than they could count in every direction.

"Did the compass shift?" Quiet stopped beside them.

"A detour is required." R-0 lowered their voice to the softest whisper they could manage and tucked the compass safely into their arm compartment. "Ryder is here. The guards must be alerted."

"Ryder?" Quiet's eyes widened. "You're sure?"

"Yes ma'am."

"This way. There's a guard station not too far."

At the next intersection, Quiet turned right, but R-0 stopped her. Farther down the street, a group of organics walked toward them, weapons far more sophisticated than the average person would carry for self-defense hanging from their waist. The dwarf in front met R-0's gaze, and their flame sputtered. R-0 had seen him before.

"Those are the organics who attacked M-118," R-0 whispered.

"Let's head the other way then."

The organics followed, obviously watching Quiet and R-0.

"Perhaps they need to go this way." R-0 didn't want to assume ill-intent, but as they looked along the street, they didn't see a single business open. Half the nearby shops were boarded up. The other half were beaten in, missing parts of their structure.

"I don't think we're quite that lucky."

R-0 didn't think luck had anything to do with the organics' motivations, but before they could argue, Quiet took off at a run. "Stay with me."

R-0 easily kept pace with her. Some of the organics accelerated to a run as well, but not all of them. There was no longer any question that they were following Quiet and

R-0. But something wasn't right. They could have run faster, but they didn't. They remained a consistent distance behind, always staying within sight.

They were waiting for something. But what?

"Do you know what they want?" R-0 asked.

Quiet took another turn. "I doubt it's anything good."

"You could ask."

"I'd rather not." Quiet smirked. "I'm not much of a people person."

R-0 didn't know there was any other type of person than a people person. Perhaps it was Quiet's way of distinguishing between organics and constructs. People-people and construct-people. But as far as R-0 could tell, Quiet was a person-person.

Around the next bend, another group of organics waited with their weapons drawn. A dwarf held a dagger in front of her, and two humans had bows ready, their sights set on Quiet. Ryder stood in front, sword unsheathed.

As they skidded to a stop, R-0 stepped between Quiet and the bowmen.

"It's a bit late to be out, don't you think?" Ryder paced the width of the alley.

His voice sounded familiar, but between the reintegration, their journey into town, and all of King Hadrian's meetings, R-0's memories were filled with hundreds of voices, and they couldn't place where they'd heard this one. He twirled his fingers, and the blade followed suit, dipping toward the ground between words and rising back toward the sky as he spoke.

The sword was unique. Seaweed clung to the blade, defying gravity as Ryder twisted it through the air. As if it were still alive, it pulsed and moved along the length of the sword. A string of pearls hung around the base, falling against Ryder's webbed fingers.

"Ryder." R-0 couldn't advance without leaving Quiet vulnerable to the archers, so they stayed where they were. "You are under arrest. Please return to the palace."

"Ha!" Ryder laughed. Like a signal being sent through the managrid, the organics behind him lit up, each echoing his laughter. "Well, I guess since you asked so nicely."

Ryder stepped forward. He kept his sword in his hand but extended both wrists. If only R-0 had thought to bring shackles ... but when they went to investigate the managrid, they hadn't expected this scenario. Still, they could adjust.

As R-0 reached for Ryder's wrists, the merfolk yanked them away and swept his blade in an upward arc. R-0 stepped back, bumping into Quiet. The blade whistled by their chest, so close R-0 could feel the air quiver.

Were all organics liars?

It wasn't a question they could answer now. Their flame flared, but it wasn't the out-of-control blaze or the inconsistent stuttering that normally accompanied their emotions. It was steady and strong. R-0 had spent their entire existence before the incident protecting organics. This is what they were made to do.

R-0 drew both their blades as the organics that had been following them—two more bowmen and a second merfolk wielding hand axes—closed in, blocking off their escape. R-0 gently guided Quiet to the side of the alleyway, maneuvering their body to remain between her and the bowmen with each step. With their back to the wall, they spread their arms to the side, shielding Quiet.

"Please lower your weapons." Even as R-0 made the request, they expected the resistance to continue.

"I would advise you to listen to R-0," Quiet said. "We aren't looking for any trouble."

"Somehow I doubt that." Ryder's tongue clicked against the roof of his mouth. "But unfortunately, your intentions don't matter. I've got orders to bring the two of you in."

"Orders from who?" R-0 asked.

"Enough questions." Ryder raised his hand, and the bowmen fired. Their arrows bounced harmlessly off R-0's chest plate. "Consider that your first and final warning. The next time we'll be aiming for the councilwoman."

R-0 wished they were bigger, but modifying their form would take too long and leave Quiet vulnerable while they changed. Their smaller form had made sense while investigating. Now, not as much.

"R-0, can you handle this?" Quiet whispered.

"Yes ma'am." They still weren't sure *how*, but this was their job. They would find a way.

"Thank you." She pressed her hands against R-0's back and began mumbling under her breath.

"Stop her!" Ryder yelled.

Arrows thudded into R-0's chest plate without injury. The metal was scuffed, but it was nothing that couldn't be resolved during routine maintenance.

As Ryder charged forward, a wave of warmth centered on Quiet's hands rushed into R-0's body, spreading through the metal faster than an echo through an empty hall. R-0 turned to see what had happened, but Quiet had disappeared. One tick she was beside R-0, and the next she was gone.

"Quiet!" R-0 yelled. Their flame fluttered. Where was she?

The warmth surrounding them escalated to a buzz. Magic danced across their plates, growing brighter until they were a beacon of light in the dark alleyway. They didn't feel any different, but every glance at their body proved that something was happening to them.

They had no time to look farther. Three organics were upon them—Ryder, the dwarf who'd attacked M-118, and a second merfolk wielding two hand axes. R-0 deflected most of the blows, but Ryder managed to slice into R-0's leg.

"Useless." As he struck, light sparked, and the seaweed crawled from his weapon onto R-0's plates.

"Corrupted." He attacked again, but this time R-0 was focused. They raised one of their swords to block his strike. They tried to counter, but their leg wouldn't move.

What was wrong with them?

R-0 tried again to advance, but their leg was entirely unresponsive. The front of their thigh plate was cleaved apart, remnants of seaweed wriggling along the surface. The seaweed ate away at the steel, widening the gash. Within, the gears that attached their leg to their hip were fractured, and the wires holding them together frayed.

How could seaweed cause this much damage? It was just a simple plant.

With their swords in their hands, they should have been at ease, but their flame gurgled uneasily. They were designed to protect others—it was one of the few things that the incident hadn't changed. But their body had never reacted this way.

And the person they were supposed to protect was gone.

A strike from the hand axes caught their leg in the same place, widening the split. R-0 tried to calm their flame. Now wasn't the time for curiosities or distractions. They needed to subdue the organics and find Quiet—in that order. They'd rather find Quiet first, but they doubted their attackers would wait.

Another volley of arrows hit R-0—this time aimed at R-0's injured leg. They couldn't lift their leg to dodge. They couldn't hop back. So they dropped their arm, catching the volley on the back of their reinforced plates instead of their inner mechanisms. R-0 took one deep inhale, then focused on the three assailants surrounding them.

The dwarf was the first to give R-0 an opening. His strikes were slow and sloppy. R-0 parried and immediately pushed back, the sudden shift in momentum knocking the weapon from the dwarf's hand. He stumbled back. The others took the opportunity to strike, but R-0 leaned back out of range. Even if their leg was grounded, they had other ways to dodge.

R-0 sliced with both of their blades in tandem, leaving two deep gashes across the dwarf's stomach. His tunic turned red as he fell to his knees, clutching at his sides.

Ryder snaked forward, targeting R-0's stationary leg. They tried to move it out of the way, but the blade cut through the metal like butter, creating a second gash on the outer plate. He danced outside of R-0's range, taking advantage of their limited mobility. A confident smile spread across his face. R-0 tried to use the brief respite to locate Quiet, but other than their attackers, the alleyway was empty.

Where could she have gone?

The bowmen fired again, and R-0's momentary distraction was punished. Without their plates to protect them, the arrow lodged in one of their internal gears, prohibiting it from spinning. It screeched as it jittered in place.

R-0 didn't know much about technomancy, but they knew that wasn't a good sound. In the past, their body had been injured. Once when an assassin had targeted the king with an explosion, R-0 had taken the brunt of the blow and their entire arm had been detached. They hadn't worried about it at the time, but now . . .

What would happen to the wound? What would happen to them if they couldn't stop the organics?

They'd never worried about the outcome of a fight before.

The bowmen fired another round of arrows, but R-0 deflected them with their blade. They needed to end this—even with Ryder staying out of their range—and the bowmen gave them the perfect idea.

R-0 waited for the next volley, then when the bowmen were busy nocking new arrows, raised their sword. They focused on Ryder's movements, waiting for him to take a step, then threw their sword.

It was far less graceful than the arrows sailing seamlessly through the air, but it was effective. Their sword spiraled forward, the light shifting on the blue blade sparkling like the ocean's surface reflecting the stars. Their aim was perfect, and the sword stabbed into Ryder's thigh, matching R-0's injury.

Ryder grabbed at the wound, his webbed fingers spreading to create a sort of bandage. But blood spilled across his hand. The remaining organics looked nervously between Ryder and R-0.

"Don't just stand there—get them!" Ryder gestured to R-0. Droplets of blood flung from his hand, dotting the ground around him. Then, he directed his attention to the bowmen. "Get reinforcements."

The merfolk with the hand axes tried to finish what the others had started, but even immobile, R-0 could easily dispatch him once he came into range. He was fast, but his attacks followed a pattern that R-0 could anticipate and match every time. He aimed for their injured leg, but they deflected the blows, waiting for their opening. The first time their attacker overextended, R-0 struck. Blood coated their blades as the organic fell motionless to the ground.

But while R-0 fought the merfolk, Ryder had limped away, and Quiet was still nowhere to be found.

Technically, they'd succeeded. All of their attackers had been defeated or fled. But their flame roared, unease and worry overwhelming them.

"Quiet?" R-0 asked. Their leg still wouldn't move. They were frozen in place. As logic caught up to their panic, R-0 realized that the councilwoman didn't even know that they referred to her as Quiet in their thoughts. They raised their voice and tried again. "Councilwoman Riley?"

The light buzzing across their skin faded, and as it did, Quiet stepped forward, materializing from nothing.

"Quiet?" she asked.

Relief that she was okay competed with the awkward grating of their gears as they tried to answer her question. "A nickname," they finally said.

Quiet's brow furrowed, but a smirk settled on her lips.

"Where were you?" R-0 asked.

"Magic," Quiet said, as if that explained everything.

If R-0 didn't have more pressing concerns, they would have had dozens of questions. Instead, they scanned the alleyway to confirm there were no remaining combatants before turning back to her. "Are you okay?"

"I am." She knelt on the ground next to one of the collapsed organics and began searching his pockets. "Are you?"

"Yes ma'am."

She raised her eyebrows. "Come here, then."

R-0 frowned. Their leg was still unresponsive. They used their hands to grab their leg and lift it. They set it down a step forward, then stepped normally with their uninjured leg. It was an awkward gait, but it got them moving. They repeated the process until they stopped in front of Quiet. "Yes ma'am."

Relief that Quiet was okay flooded through R-0, a cooling sensation that countered their burning flame. But as their situation calmed, their mind couldn't. Why was Ryder trying to capture them? Who was Ryder taking orders from? How had Ryder known they would be here? This wasn't random—they'd known Quiet was a council member.

Ryder could have answered all of their questions—maybe even those about the missing constructs—and R-0 had let him get away. He was gone. For how long, R-0 wasn't sure.

"Reinforcements may be coming," R-0 warned.

Quiet stood from rummaging through their attackers' pockets, a crumpled letter in her hands. "I think that's the least of our problems."

"What is the most of our problems?"

"Whatever Ryder was up to, his orders came from someone in the palace." Quiet flipped over the paper. On the back was a broken seal of red wax with the council's emblem. "Someone on the council."

CHAPTER 26

R-0 cycled through the council members in their mind.

King Sylas Hadrian, leader of Clan Hadrian, representing the monster hunter and adventurer's guild.

Councilwoman Jeza, leader of Clan Doblin, representing the crafting industry.

Councilman Robin, leader of Clan Conradh, representing the shipwrights.

Councilwoman Eren, captain of the guard and leader of Clan Ainfen, representing the military.

Councilwoman Gretta, leader of Clan Murdha, representing the blacksmiths.

Councilman Uxius, leader of Clan Rhain, representing the fishing industry.

And Quiet herself, Councilwoman Riley Eyla, priestess of the Goddess Eclipse, representing the churches and temples across Haiden.

Councilman Uxius was unlikely. No one had seen him since before the constructs changed, and he had yet to return from his voyage. R-0's memories of him were few and far between. He attended fewer meetings than any other council member—even Eren—usually because he was at sea. Even when he was there, he rarely participated. Although, King Hadrian had said that Uxius disagreed with anything he wanted on principle, so if the king supported the constructs, Uxius wouldn't just to spite him.

Another layer of politics R-0 didn't understand.

And Quiet . . . R-0 didn't want to believe it could be her. In the managrid tunnels, she had talked about motive and means to explain the missing constructs' behavior, and R-0 tried to apply the same logic here. Quiet had the means, but what motive would she have to attack herself?

R-0 watched her search the remaining organics. She started at their heads, running her hand across their eyes to close them. Even as she moved to their pockets, they didn't react. R-0 watched their chests for movement and listened for any signs of life, but there were none. No heartbeats. No breaths. They were dead.

R-0 had killed them.

It wasn't the first time R-0 had killed. When King Hadrian was a child and allies and enemies alike had tried to take advantage of his vulnerability, R-0 had killed to protect him. When criminals and other hostile organics had posed a threat to Haiden, R-0 had occasionally accompanied the guards to apprehend them. These situations often turned violent.

They'd never stopped to consider the implications before. But now . . . who were these people? What had their lives been like?

"We need to return to the palace and inform Sylas." Quiet stepped away from the last body. "Immediately."

R-0 hesitated. Once they walked away, their life would be entirely unchanged. It shouldn't matter to R-0 if these men had lived or died. But . . . the weight in R-0's chest grew heavier the longer they thought about it. There were infinite possibilities for what they could have been and what they could have done. What right did R-0 have to take a life and end it?

"R-0?" Quiet asked. "Can you walk?"

It was a valid question, and R-0 wasn't sure. But injuries weren't what kept them stuck in place.

"They're dead," R-0 said.

"And we're alive." Quiet returned to R-0's side. "If you had not acted, our positions could be reversed."

Imagining Quiet's body lying broken on the ground instead and themself discarded in the scrapyard filled R-0 with a heaviness that made their current circumstances feel lighter.

"Should their bodies be taken to the sea?" R-0 asked. Though different organics had different customs for their deceased, most throughout Haiden preferred to return to the sea after death.

"Leave them to their people. We need to get out of here before Ryder returns with reinforcements." Quiet knelt and reached for R-0's injured leg. "May I?"

Upon closer inspection, their interior wires and gears were as mangled and non-functional as the external plate. A few sections of metal were cracked, likely due to the increased load. Six gears were degraded, and most of the visible wiring was frayed or snapped.

R-0 struggled once more to move their leg, but the gears moving in their chassis weren't connected to anything. Their leg remained stationary. "Maintenance is required."

"Can you do it yourself?"

R-0 surveyed the damage once more. Routine maintenance was a possibility. They had memories of countless maintenance sessions, and the technomancers' movements could be replicated. But something like this? R-0 had never seen these types of repairs performed.

"No."

Quiet's hands gently searched the hole in their leg and retrieved some of the broken parts that had fallen into the cavity. She handed them to R-0, then began tying snapped wires together.

"Can you perform maintenance?" R-0 asked. They had never seen Quiet work with the technomancers before, but compared to King Hadrian's attempts at maintenance, her movements were decisive and steady.

"No, but I can try to help." With the wires secured, she placed her hands against the broken gears. Warmth emanated from her, and her skin glowed. But when she pulled away, there was no change. She frowned and closed her eyes once more, magic pulsing from her and the managrid, but R-0's body remained unresponsive. "The magic of his sword cut through you. Why won't my magic heal you?"

Magic. That explained the strange reaction R-0's plates had to Ryder's weapon, and the disproportionate damage the strike had caused.

"I'm sorry." Quiet sighed. "It was worth a try."

"The technomancers can assist." R-0 used their hands to lift their leg once more, then set it down, mimicking walking. Each step was methodical and forced, and their movements were much slower than normal, but they moved forward.

Quiet frowned but retrieved R-0's sword, then returned to walking beside them. She was even more attentive than the organic guards that sometimes watched the king. Her eyes darted down every alleyway, any opening where danger could lurk. She even checked the rooftops, and when her searches came up empty, she began the cycle again, never relaxing.

Hardly two streets later, she cursed the stars under her breath.

Ryder stood ahead of them, flanked by four organics on either side. They didn't approach. Quiet turned the other way, but more organics blocked that path. Behind them, the situation was the same.

"Would you like to fight?" R-0 asked. Their last encounter had ended in violence. Perhaps that was where this one would start. No one spoke or tried to exchange pleasantries.

"I'm afraid we wouldn't win."

There were more organics than before, and this time, R-0 was starting off injured. If Ryder had told everyone about their vulnerability, the organics could easily take advantage of it. Quiet was right—it was unlikely they could win in a direct fight.

R-0 considered other alternatives. Peaceful negotiations had failed, and with a malfunctioning leg, it would be impossible to match the organics' speed. But Quiet was fast, and her magic had already proven once it could hide her.

"There's an alleyway to the right," R-0 whispered. "If you run and turn invisible, they won't be able to find you. You can return to the palace and warn King Hadrian."

"What about you?"

Visions of the scrapyard flashed through R-0's mind. Would these organics take their body there? Or would they be decommissioned and discarded in the streets?

Their plates refused to move. R-0 couldn't speak the words. Instead, they focused on Quiet, protecting her. "You will be faster alone."

The organics slowly advanced, closing in on all sides. The archers stayed back, arrows trained on them. Quiet's window to escape was closing fast.

"You need to leave," R-0 said.

Quiet clasped her hands together and closed her eyes. She turned so she stood back-to-back with R-0, pressing her soft flesh against their metal. A cool wind whipped across R-0's plates and spiraled around Quiet.

"Fire!" Ryder yelled. A volley of arrows rained down. R-0 crossed their swords behind them, trying to shield Quiet. Arrows plinked against their body like raindrops on the rooftops.

One grazed Quiet's arm, and blood leaked onto her robe. She grimaced, but kept her focus, chanting under her breath. The ground beneath her feet brightened with the same blue glow of the managrid, then shot out around her in every direction. Lines of light, like the conduits embedded into the underground floor, branched out from Quiet, snaking their way to the lampposts on either side of the street.

"Hide." Quiet's eyes snapped open, and she pushed at R-0. "Now!"

R-0 grabbed their leg, trying to follow Quiet as she darted toward the alleyway. Her magic sparked at the first lamppost, and one by one the lights flickered out until the street was cloaked in darkness.

R-0 couldn't see a thing, but Quiet's hand wrapped around R-0's arm, guiding them forward.

"What did you do?" R-0 asked.

"The managrid is a give and take of power," Quiet said. "Take too much and . . ."

"You can do that?"

Quiet shushed them as footsteps sounded nearby, but under the cover of darkness, Quiet and R-0 remained undetected. The organics cursed and shouted at one another, Ryder's voice rising above the rest. "Light a torch!"

"We don't have much time. Here." She stopped suddenly, and R-0 had to drop their leg back in place to avoid running into her. She guided R-0 until their back pressed against the wall. "Goddess, hear my prayer."

Magic outlined Quiet's form, shedding light across R-0's plates, and as her magic strengthened, R-0's body began to fade. It started with their fingertips. What had been there seconds before was missing. R-0's flame roared. This was worse than a malfunction in their leg. They reached for their hands, and . . .

They were entirely normal. They could feel them. Their fingers could move and rub against each other. When they clicked together, it still made a noise.

"What—" The phenomena spread up their hands and arms, then to their chassis. R-0 reached for their chest, and it still felt warm. The flame raging within didn't quiet as the magic crept down their legs until there was nothing left of R-0.

"R-0, I need you to listen to me." Quiet's eyes shone, and her entire body matched. "They won't be able to see you. They'll only be able to see me. You need to stay completely still and quiet until they're gone. You understand me?"

"What about you?"

"I'll run," Quiet said. "I'll make it back to the palace and get help, then come back for you. Just don't let them find you, okay?"

Though she spoke hurried words, they retained their steady and sure tone. Was this what Seraphine's promise to Beans had sounded like?

"Are these your orders?" R-0 asked.

"No." Quiet softened her voice. "But I would appreciate it if you would listen to me all the same."

"Yes ma'am."

"I'll need one of your swords."

R-0 hesitated momentarily, unsure which sword to give her, before settling on their right sword. R-0 shifted their grip so they were holding the blade, then set the handle into Quiet's waiting hand. As they let go, the weapon became visible.

Quiet's arm sagged under the weight for a tick, but then she adjusted and held it steady. The golden glow of her magic danced along the blue metal.

"Thank you," she whispered. "I can track you with this. And R-0—"

"There she is!" Whatever Quiet was about to say was cut off. One of the organics pointed at Quiet, a blazing beacon in the dark landscape, and thundering footsteps responded to his call.

Quiet leaped—not toward the crates, or even deeper into the alley, but up the wall. It reminded R-0 of the night of the corruption. Quiet was like the stars, a shining light defying gravity and shooting upward. She grabbed the edge of a windowsill, climbing up. A second jump was all she needed to hoist herself onto the roof.

R-0 followed her orders, remaining still, even as the organics dashed into the alleyway, torches casting bright light all around them. They fought to keep their flame docile. The organics' hearing wasn't as good as the constructs, but how close would they need to get before they could hear its crackle? One was inches from R-0. A single step back would cause them to collide, but all eyes were on Quiet. They made plenty of noise on their own, whispering voices, clamoring footsteps, clanging weapons or armor.

And no one noticed R-0. It reminded R-0 of life before the stars. They were here, but no one reacted to them. People looked straight past them as if they weren't even there.

While most of the organics scrambled after Quiet even as her glowing form dimmed in the distance, a few remained. "Where's the construct?"

"It couldn't have gotten far. Spread out, search this area top to bottom. No one goes home until we find it."

"What happened to the lights?"

"Hell if I know. Ah, we're so screwed."

"We're only screwed if they get a chance to tell someone. Get eyes on every road leading back to the palace and the nearby guard posts. They can hide as long as they want. Just make sure they don't return to the palace."

Quiet's magic kept them from being seen, but would it keep them from being heard? R-0 didn't dare experiment until the organics deemed the surrounding alleyways and rooftops sufficiently searched and left down one of the main roads. They waited a few more minutes, making sure no one returned, before daring to move.

Their gears were stiff, and their body creaked as they took a tentative step forward. Any hope R-0 had that only they could hear themself vanished as a rat that had been chewing on the burnt remnants of a piece of bread startled and scurried away.

They half-walked half-dragged themself down the alleyway a few times, trying to mimic Quiet's movement. She glided across the pavement, silent even when her foot touched the stone. But no matter what R-0 tried, or how careful they were, their whirring gears echoed through the street and even their uninjured leg clanked with each step.

If the roads were being guarded, they wouldn't be able to get back to the palace. And the closer they got to the palace, the more likely they were to be caught by Ryder or the other organics. But where else could they go?

They only knew a few places in the city—the bakery and a couple other businesses King Hadrian had visited while lobbying for reintegration. But they didn't know how to get there. Even if they knew where the places were, they didn't know which would be a safe place to wait for Quiet. Assuming she even found her way back.

R-0 had assumed Quiet would outrun her pursuers. But what if she didn't? If she was captured, it would be R-0's responsibility to warn King Hadrian about the corruption within the council. Every moment they wasted, King Hadrian could be in danger.

But getting caught could be even worse, and Quiet had said she would return for them.

R-0 resigned themself to standing still—staying silent. Maybe if their leg wasn't malfunctioning, they could try something, but as it was, their options were limited. The organics had already searched here. They were unlikely to come back, and if they did, they still wouldn't find R-0. As long as Quiet's magic remained, they were safe.

R-0 repeated that thought, again and again, until an eerie cold crept across their plates. Their flame hunkered in the corner of their chest, and their gears creaked as they scanned the alleyway for the source of the feeling. As suddenly as it began, the feeling washed away.

And when R-0 looked down at themself, their body was fully visible.

CHAPTER 27

This was not ideal.

Quite far from ideal, actually. Ideal would have been back in the palace, King Hadrian and Quiet both safely in their sights, a fully functioning leg, and the support of the entire guard staff should any trouble arise from the few, well-documented threats that existed. In contrast, R-0 was alone. They had no idea if King Hadrian or Quiet were safe, their body was malfunctioning, they were being hunted by an unknown group, and they had no one to help them.

This was very, very not ideal.

They couldn't stay here. It was too close to where they had been discovered, and heading back toward the palace would lead them straight to Ryder and the other organics. They wouldn't go to any of the places King Hadrian had brought them—not while they were being hunted. King Hadrian had wanted to help those people, not bring trouble to their door, and R-0 would honor his intentions.

So where?

Decisions were impossible, R-0 decided. There were too many options, too many possibilities. And each had a myriad of factors that would determine their outcomes. They couldn't analyze every single one like they'd done with King Hadrian's papers. Where would they even start? Alphabetically? In the top left corner of the city?

It had been simpler to follow Quiet, and R-0 wished she was here to lead the way. But . . . she hadn't been leading, had she?

At least not entirely. They pulled out the compass from their arm compartment.

Quiet had just been following the magic. R-0 could do that. They held their palm out flat, and the screw spiraled in place before settling. Even if Ryder and the other organics were watching the roads to the palace, they couldn't be everywhere in the city at once, and the compass pointed away from the palace.

For a moment R-0 hesitated, a million what-ifs highlighting everything that could go wrong with this plan. What if they wandered too far and Quiet couldn't track them? What if they led trouble to Beans? What if whatever was waiting for them at Beans's location was more dangerous than Ryder and the other organics? What if Ryder wasn't the only one with orders to capture them?

But R-0 couldn't stand around and do nothing, waiting to be found by friend or foe. Once they would have, but not anymore.

R-0 double-checked the compass before trudging through the city. The streets were more ominous now. Every passing organic was a potential threat. R-0 examined them closely, looking for weapons or any indication they were hunting constructs. Hunting *them*. But no one carried more than basic knives or daggers, nothing like Ryder's magic sword.

R-0 had grown familiar with the looks on their faces. Fear. Apprehension. Confusion. Though no one said it, most were uncomfortable with a construct alone in the streets. Their state of disrepair was unlikely to provide reassurance. Still, R-0 tried to smile.

R-0 followed the compass until it took them in a circle. At four consecutive intersections they turned right in an attempt to stay on course, landing them back where they started. They lapped the block once more, this time staring at the compass the entire way until they narrowed down the location it pointed toward. It was . . . a hattery.

This was it. This was where Beans was.

The small building was smushed between what appeared to be apartments and a trash-filled alley. A large piece of wood nailed into the frame covered the door with CLOSED painted in bold letters. The lone window on the front of the building was boarded up, and the glass between the pieces of wood was too dark to see through.

It wasn't large enough to house all the missing constructs, and none of the missing construct reports had come from this area. For a brief moment, they wondered if Quiet's spell had failed—like the magic that had concealed their presence. Perhaps the tracking had faded when she got too far away. But Quiet had said the spell would last indefinitely, and when R-0 closed their fist around the compass, they still felt the magic. And... R-0 double-checked their surroundings. They weren't too far from the docks where they'd lost sight of M-118 and their companion. Had M-118 come here as well?

But why would either of them come here? If a hat was required, tailors in the castle could be commissioned. It would have required requisition orders, and many questions as to why they would need a hat... questions that R-0 considered now. Why would a construct need a hat? And why would Beans break their promise to Seraphine to obtain one?

Unless Beans hadn't left by choice.

Nothing in R-0's thoughts or memories could answer their questions. There was only one way to find out. They climbed the steps to the front door, surprised when the wood didn't creak under their weight. Despite its dilapidated appearance, the structure was sturdy.

At the top of the steps, they knocked.

But nothing happened.

R-0 waited a few moments then knocked again, louder this time. It was outside of normal operating hours for most businesses in Graywal, and for a moment, they considered waiting—morning was only a couple hours away. But the compass burned in their hand, still pointing toward the hattery. Regardless of the time, Beans was here, and they needed to be found.

It was impolite to enter without knocking, but they had knocked. Twice.

As they twisted the doorknob, it resisted. R-0 increased the pressure until something snapped, and the doorknob turned freely. The door swung inward a couple inches, then stopped.

RISE OF THE FORGEHEARTS

Six chains—four steel, one silver, and one Levian steel—bridged the wall and the door, holding it in place. R-0 frowned. This was not typical security for a hattery. The owner must have been quite concerned about safety. R-0 admired that about them.

They pushed against the door, slowly at first, watching the chains and waiting for them to snap. But the chains held. This was more than the simple obstacle they had expected. What was inside that required this level of security? Whatever it was, they wouldn't find out by waiting outside.

R-0 punched the door.

Wood splintered and caved, and R-0's fist easily passed through to the other side. They felt around for the latches that secured the chains, unhooking them one by one until the door swung open.

Inside, large swatches of fabric were scattered across a central table, tools lined the walls, and scrap metal was piled in the corner. Despite the raw materials, they didn't see a single hat. What kind of hattery didn't have hats? Perhaps R-0 had been mistaken about the shop's purpose or perhaps there was a secondary function, which was why Beans was here.

"What the—" A section of the floor flipped up, revealing a ladder and metallic fingers reaching through the opening. Tiny screws at the tips of their index fingers dug into the wooden floor, providing leverage as a construct pulled themself the rest of the way up. They looked past R-0 at the door, swinging freely from its hinges. "My door! What happened to my door?"

They scurried past R-0 to what remained of the door. It creaked as they pushed it closed and examined the damage. The hole was small enough that organics couldn't squeeze through, and the door could still mostly serve its purpose.

Still, the construct ran their fingers along it delicately, and smoke flared from between their plates. Even standing feet apart, R-0 could hear the roar of the flame within their chest.

"Apologies," R-0 said.

"Don't apologize to me!" The construct swiveled in place. Their ankle joints turned in unnatural ways, but their plates shifted to accommodate the movement. When they lifted their legs, their parts snapped back into their standard orientation as if nothing had happened. "Say sorry to the door!"

"To . . . the door?" R-0 asked.

"I'm not the one you damaged. Unless you plan to damage me next." They crossed their arms over their chest plate, dulling the sound of their flame.

They had a point. It was . . . unusual to apologize to inanimate objects. But it was also unusual for R-0 to break into a hattery. There was nothing mundane about the evening's events, and if R-0 could have entered without damaging the property, they would have. "Apologies, door."

"Good." The construct rubbed their hands together and looked R-0 over twice. "Wow, took quite a blow to that leg, didn't you?"

R-0 nodded. "An unfortunate encounter, but irrelevant to current circumstances. There is a missing construct. Their designation is Beans. Are they here?"

R-0 had learned their mistake with Seraphine and made sure to specify that Beans was not a small vegetable meant for organic consumption.

"Beans, huh?" The construct tapped their hands together several times. "Not sure. You'll need to talk to Jasper. You can head down and wait for him." They gestured toward the open panel in the floor and the ladder. R-0 couldn't see much of the basement—just a stone floor and a table with more miscellaneous tools.

R-0 opened their hand just enough to take a peek at the screw and compass. It was standing mostly on its tip now, though slightly slanted. This was still the direction they needed to go.

"Thank you," R-0 said. With a nod, they stored the compass in their arm compartment and descended the ladder deeper into the building.

"I'm Winter, by the way. What's your name?"

"R-0." It was hard to climb with a malfunctioning leg. They had to rely on one arm to hold them in place, while the other maneuvered their legs into the proper position.

"Well, I'm glad you found your way here." If Winter noticed their slow progress, they didn't show it. "It's good to see you again. Jasper will be excited. He's been talking about constructs like you, but we haven't been able to find any."

Again? R-0 had never seen Winter before, and what did they mean by constructs like them? R-0 opened their mouth to ask, but their injured leg slipped off the rung. The sudden weight yanked their other leg down as well, until they dangled from their arms.

R-0 should have paid more attention during their encounter with Ryder. If they had been more efficient, they wouldn't be dealing with such a troublesome limitation. How were they going to climb back up?

"You okay?" Winter asked.

"Yes." Although R-0 didn't consciously change their voice, their face plates hardly moved, and their voice came out in a low grumble. They didn't bother putting their legs back on the rungs of the ladder, relying instead on their arms to lower themself down. Perhaps they could climb back up the same way.

It was easier than walking. At the bottom, R-0 returned to their awkward shuffle, dragging their damaged leg behind them manually. Winter hopped off the ladder only halfway down, their metal legs clanging against the floor.

"Jasper!" Winter yelled. They waited, cocking their head to the side, but there was no response. "I guess I'll have to go get him. You wait here, alright?"

R-0 nodded and looked around at wherever here was.

The basement was much larger than the room above. It likely ran under at least three buildings on this street, although the ladder R-0 had climbed down appeared to be the only way back up. There were two doors—one that Winter left through, quickly closing it behind them, and one on the opposite wall.

Scattered across the tables were advanced tools R-0 had rarely seen—outside of some of the elite technomancers who had visited them in the past few weeks—as well as spare parts matching all manner of constructs. But there were no maintenance logs or notes on the tables and many tools R-0 had never seen before.

Despite the lack of notes on the tables, overlapping sheets of paper covered the walls. It was all in the same handwriting, but the language was inconsistent. Some sections R-0 could read, other parts were foreign, and some didn't look like words at all, just symbols and drawings with lines connecting them.

The back wall was covered by a large canvas depicting a royal construct in their extended form. It was life sized, and every detail matched R-0 perfectly, down to each internal screw and gear placement. Scrawling text as well as intricately drawn symbols surrounded the depiction of the royal construct.

R-0 wracked their memories. They'd seen script like this once before—when helping King Hadrian clean his mother's room after her passing. Piles of papers were written in the same handwriting with the same symbols. King Hadrian had looked at the pages in awe—it was magic. Written depictions of the pathways through the Flow that mages could use to change the fabric of reality.

Despite his awe, King Hadrian had filed them away. The information was too valuable to get rid of, but he had larger concerns at the time. And even with instructions, he couldn't cast magic on his own. He wasn't cut off from the Flow like Jeza, but neither was he an experienced mage like Quiet. Like most people throughout Haiden, he couldn't cast magic by himself and was only able to activate magic items with the help of the managrid.

R-0 ran their fingers along the wall, tracing the symbols and committing them to memory. Even if they didn't make sense to R-0 now, perhaps Quiet or King Hadrian could interpret them when R-0 returned to the palace. The legible notes were short and didn't provide much explanation either.

Test later — Replace M40 with M30. Check for range of motion.
Fear is a poison.
Manacore power supply?

Perhaps they would make more sense if the remaining text was translated. Whatever it was, it had something to do with the constructs—royal constructs like R-0.

They should have asked Winter more questions before they left. R-0 walked over to the door and quieted their internal gears, straining to hear anything beyond. When silence met them, they tried to open the door.

It was locked.

R-0 frowned. Why would Winter lock the door? R-0 checked where they'd entered, but the hatch into the hattery was also chained shut.

Something wasn't right.

R-0 looked at the parts scattered among the tools on the table. They had assumed these were spare parts, but . . . what if they weren't? What if they had belonged to other constructs?

What if they'd belonged to Beans?

R-0's chest tightened, the plates around their flame condensing and the fire struggling to expand beyond its compartment. Their face plates clenched together, and they paused their breathing. Winter had said Jasper was looking for a construct like R-0. What did he want with them? Their parts?

The possibility was . . . unpleasant. But the longer R-0 thought about it, the more it made sense.

Royal constructs were different than most of the other units. From the alloys used in their gears and screws to the strength of their plates, their parts were superior in almost every metric.

R-0 forced themself to loosen the restrictive formation their internal plates had taken. The fire in their chest expanded temporarily before reluctantly returning to its normal, slow burn. Even with their physical state returning to normal, the unpleasantness remained in R-0's chest, like a tangled ball of wires spinning in a circle, tightening and worsening with each rotation.

If R-0 let themself, they would end up with an endless list of questions. But more questions wouldn't help them right now. They had come here for answers, and they could still complete that function.

R-0 retrieved the compass from their arm compartment. The light from Quiet's magic shone, and the screw spun rapidly in place. It settled, pointing directly toward the other door in the room.

As R-0 approached, the compass grew warmer until it was so hot an organic likely wouldn't have been able to comfortably hold it. But the heat was comforting to R-0, and they tightened their grip around it. Like the door Winter had used, this door was locked.

R-0 leaned close and whispered, "Apologies, door."

They turned the doorknob until metal snapped, then pushed forward. Additional locks broke, but R-0 kept the pressure steady until the door broke from its hinges, then set it to the side.

R-0 froze.

Never had they seen so many decommissioned constructs. Even in the scrapyard there had never been more than one or two. Construct decommissioning was rare, and parts were quickly utilized for new projects. But here . . .

Constructs in various states of disrepair lined the walls, sprawled across tables, and lay discarded on the floor. R-0 had to step over a chest chassis, still attached to a construct's head but missing limbs. The hinges where their chest plate once protected their flame were mangled, and inside, only a thin layer of ash remained. The metal was cold, and their eyes lifeless. A few steps away, the remains of their arms and legs were nothing more than scrap.

"B-B—" R-0's voice stuttered, refusing to form the words in their mind. They tried again. "Beans?" R-0 asked, but their voice only echoed back to themself.

R-0 unclenched their fist, their joints creaking, and the screw oriented itself forward and slightly right. R-0 followed it, trying not to look at the graveyard of parts surrounding them. Trying not to think about each and every construct. Gone. Forever. But their efforts were worthless.

Who did this to them? What had happened? Why were they here?

Was this the fate of the missing constructs?

Would R-0 join them?

They had no way to get those answers, so instead, they focused on Beans. Where were they? It was a question they *would* answer, and the heat of the screw and compass kept them tethered to their task. If they could find Beans, that might shed light on R-0's other questions.

R-0 kept their eyes on the screw as they walked, ignoring everything else, until they reached the far side of the room, where the magic faded. The heat dissipated, leaving cold, rusted metal in R-0's palm.

In front of R-0 was the body of a construct. Their metal was worn and rusted in some places but mostly intact except for their chest, which was missing the plate and flame. Their arms were painted with bright, messy flowers, and green squiggles trailed down from their shoulder, connecting each flower. At their wrist, rust streaked through pale yellow petals where a screw was missing.

R-0 lifted the construct's hand. Decorating their palm was a depiction of a small dwarven girl with long braids standing next to a construct. Red lines traveled across their fingers above the two figures, and when R-0 pressed their fingers together, the lines came together to form a heart.

R-0 gently placed the screw into their wrist. It was a perfect fit.

Beans was dead.

"Oh, dear."

R-0 spun at the voice. Winter stood in the doorway, a human man beside them. His hair was uneven and short, soot staining his graying hair. Thick goggles covered his eyes, but as he stepped forward, he peeled them away from his face and let them rest on his hairline, revealing light gray eyes. An apron covered his clothing, and a tool belt swung at his waist.

"You shouldn't be in here."

CHAPTER 28

"What happened to Beans?" R-0 pushed all the other questions aside. They couldn't ask them all, and even if they could, it wouldn't help them to make sense of everything they'd seen.

"Beans?" The man stepped forward, and R-0 resisted the urge to shuffle back. Not that there was anywhere to go. The only thing behind them was Beans's corpse and a wall of dirt. The human and Winter blocked the sole exit.

If the unpleasantness in R-0's chest was a ball of wires, theirs was knotted so tight it could no longer move. All it could do was struggle until the wires snapped and gave way.

"Unit L-6." R-0 recited the official designation they'd seen on Beans's intake forms.

"Ah, I see." He rifled through the tools and grabbed a vial, humming under his breath. "I didn't expect anyone to come looking for them."

Beans's hand was still in R-0's, and the depiction of Beans and Seraphine's smiling faces stared up at them. They would never get to stand together like that again. Beans couldn't keep their promise to Seraphine.

R-0 had thought about being decommissioned a lot recently. The weight of that thought had nearly suffocated them. But they hadn't understood it, not like they did now, holding the hand of the dead.

"What happened to Beans?" R-0 repeated their question. Their voice didn't shake. It projected through the room, louder and stronger.

"To be entirely honest, I don't know."

"You . . . don't know?"

The man picked up a pair of pliers, tested them on a gear from their apron pocket, then set it down. He repeated the process with a different pair, this time pocketing the tool before moving to the next table. "They were like that when I found them. Flameless, lifeless, discarded. More intact than the rest." He gestured around the room. "But when they share the same fate, that's little solace. Some say the key to life's greatest mysteries are in the whispers of the dead, but the longer I live, the more confident I am it is only horrors, not wonder, that we would hear on their dying breath."

His words felt comfortable, familiar. R-0's flame sizzled as if King Hadrian were speaking, not some stranger. Still, R-0 remained skeptical. Organics lied.

"Where did you find them?" R-0 asked.

"Not so fast." He wagged his finger in the air and tsked. "I answered a question for you. Now you answer one for me. What is your purpose here?"

"Beans was missing and needed to be found."

"Are you here of your own volition, or did someone send you?"

"One question has already been answered," R-0 said. "It is your turn."

"Right you are." The man grinned. He slipped a vial of blue liquid into an apron pocket, then walked toward the door. "Come with me. We'll talk while I work."

R-0 hesitated. They'd planned to bring Beans back to the palace, but there was no point now. Beans couldn't reunite with Seraphine. They couldn't join the reintegration efforts or answer questions about the missing constructs. Their parts could be salvaged for scrap, and that was all. There was no more reason for R-0 to bring them back than for R-0 to gather all the tools and parts strewn across the table.

But it felt wrong to leave them behind.

"Are you coming?" Winter waited in the doorway. "Jasper's not very patient."

"Yes." R-0 draped Beans's corpse over their shoulder. "Beans is coming as well."

Winter's eyes widened, and smoke escaped through the joints connecting their neck to their shoulders. But their expression quickly returned to normal, and they shrugged. "Need any help?"

"No." R-0 balanced Beans with one hand and moved their leg forward with the other.

In the other room, a construct leaned back in a chair. One of their arms was detached and lying on the table. Their chest plate was missing, which left their flame—hardly larger than a match—exposed to the world.

"You asked where I found Beans." Jasper sat next to the construct and pulled the tools from their apron pocket, arranging them in a neat row next to the severed arm. "They were washed up on the shore near the forge ring. That's where we find most of them. We assume someone is dumping them. The currents lead there."

If Jasper was right, the constructs could have been decommissioned almost anywhere. There were miles of coast where the bodies could have been dropped, or anyone with enough funds could sail a boat out into the waters.

Jasper began removing the screws along the construct's shoulder where their arm was missing. "Your turn." He tapped the screwdriver against the table. "Did someone send you here?"

King Hadrian hadn't wanted anyone in the palace to know about his investigation into the missing constructs. Surely that extended to strange men in hattery basements.

"Yes. Someone did." R-0 spoke slowly, making sure their words both answered Jasper's question and maintained the king's privacy. "What are you doing to them?"

"Repairing them." Jasper set a piece of metal in the gaps between their shoulder plates. He measured the overlap, then cut and bent the edges to better fit the construct's form. "Someone thought it would be funny to throw our friend here overboard. Between the sailors, the sea, and the rocks, it's a surprise they're still with us."

R-0 had been right to be apprehensive of the ocean. "You're a technomancer?"

"It's not your turn." Jasper chuckled. "But I have just one more question for you. Do you intend to harm me or my companions?"

A simple question. "No."

"Then I hope you'll stay. I'd like to take a look at that leg of yours."

"Why?"

"Because you're right. I am a technomancer of sorts, and that's what I do." With a crystal rod, he mixed a vial of bubbling blue liquid and slowly poured it into the construct's chest. It circled around the flicker of fire, like a predator circling its prey.

The flame was barely burning. How could Jasper say he was repairing the construct, then try to harm them? R-0 reached forward.

"Wait." Winter grabbed their hand. "Watch."

The bubbling liquid hissed to a sizzle as it met the fire. Instead of being smothered, the flame consumed it, expanding in the process. The construct's gears slowed, but their movements were smoother and less erratic.

"You repaired them." R-0 watched in awe as the flame grew stronger and the construct sat up straighter. Their eyes seemed more focused and alert. R-0 had never seen anything like it.

"Gears and wires can fix the body, but a wounded flame is much more difficult to heal. Took a lot of experimentation to find a workable formula, but well worth it. We've been working night and day to get it right, and it still needs improving. But it's serviceable for now." Jasper shook the vial slightly, coaxing the last remnants of bubbling liquid to the edges. The construct's flame blazed, consuming every last drop. Jasper pushed his chair back, tiny wheels on the bottom letting him roll across the room like a wagon through the streets. "Winter, why don't you finish the repair while I chat with R-0?"

"Sure." They sat in front of the construct and began reattaching their arm.

Jasper moved to a different table and gestured R-0 over. "You can set your friend down wherever. I am deeply sorry for your loss."

"They were not a friend." R-0 placed them in a nearby chair, then sat next to Jasper.

"What were they to you?" Jasper asked.

"Nothing."

"Then why do you look so sad?"

R-0 didn't have an answer for that. Perhaps it was Seraphine, the hopefulness that overflowed from her, and the happiness she'd exuded when talking about them. Perhaps it was their own sense of responsibility—they were supposed to find Beans. Alive. A corpse was never part of the plan.

"Do you know who is doing this?" R-0 asked.

"Is that what you're investigating?"

"Yes sir."

"Perhaps this will help you." Jasper pulled a large wad of paper from his apron pocket, almost dropping one of his tools in the process. As he shuffled through the pages, R-0 could read snippets here and there—a list of quotes attributed to Winter, a sketch of a construct model R-0 had never seen before, and many pages of indecipherable spellwork. "Apologies for the mess. It's in here somewhere."

Winter spun a mangled gear on the tip of their finger, then flicked it at Jasper. "If you ever got rid of stuff, maybe you'd be able to find what you need."

Jasper snatched the scrap out of the air and pocketed it. "If I was the type to get rid of things, you'd still be in a scrapyard."

"Maybe the scrapyard would have been fun."

No matter how casually Winter and Jasper spoke, a chill still crept across R-0's plates as they considered the scrapyard. Was that where they should take Beans now? R-0 averted their gaze from Beans's body, as if not seeing them would change the reality of the situation.

"Why were you in a scrapyard?" R-0 asked.

"It was years ago, long before the Awakening," Winter said. "The technomancers tossed me out, but Jasper found me and got me working again."

What was the Awakening? And why had the technomancers disposed of them? Before R-0 could voice their questions, Jasper finally found the paper he was looking for.

"Aha! Here it is." He held it triumphantly in the air, then set it between them. "A list of the constructs we've recovered."

"Can a copy be made?"

"Of course." Jasper pulled out a crumpled blank page and a quill, offering both to R-0.

R-0 scanned the list of constructs as they copied the information. They paused at L-6. Their hand trembled as they scratched out L-6 on the original list, writing "Beans" in its place. They couldn't explain it, but they also couldn't help the sadness that overcame them.

They handed the pen back to Jasper and tucked the page of notes into their arm compartment. If their memories were accurate, every construct on Jasper's list had already been reported missing—and they'd all been stationed at the palace. None of the constructs mentioned in the forged letters were here.

The missing constructs weren't organizing something nefarious. They were being targeted. Taken. So why had a construct broken into King Hadrian's room? Had someone ordered them to? And why did M-118 leave?

"Do you know a construct designated M-118?"

Jasper's movements became choppy as he returned his papers to his apron. R-0 might have overlooked the stutter if it didn't correspond with Winter dropping their tool.

"I do," Jasper said slowly. "Why do you ask?"

R-0 wasn't sure how much information about their investigation they could reveal. But Jasper had helped them figure out the fate of over a dozen missing constructs. It was fair for R-0 to reciprocate.

"They were listed among the missing." R-0 spoke deliberately, careful not to implicate King Hadrian. "But their journey seemed different than what happened to Beans."

"They're safe, if that's what you're asking. I found them at the docks and took them somewhere safe."

R-0 hadn't been able to make out details in the darkness, but M-118's companion had been humanoid and matched Jasper's build. "You were at the docks? Where is M-118 now?"

"Safe, and that's all that matters." Jasper shuffled the papers as if trying to organize them, but before he was successful, shoved the mess back in his pocket. "My turn to ask some questions. What happened to your leg?"

If Jasper had been keeping track, it was long past his turn. "There was an attack."

"An attack?" Jasper raised his eyebrows and dragged a stool over for R-0 to rest their injured leg on. "I can take a look if you'd like."

The other damaged construct was looking better with every minute Winter worked on them. Their arm had been repaired, and Winter had started threading new wires into the connection point. If Jasper could do the same with R-0's leg, then they could safely return to the palace.

R-0 adjusted their leg on the stool and recounted the events of the night, careful to leave out any identifying details about Quiet or their mission, while sharing about Ryder and the seaweed sword.

"That's rather odd." Jasper ran his fingers along the edges of the wound. "You don't by any chance have his sword, do you?"

R-0 shook their head.

"Ah, what a shame. I would have loved to study it. Magical enhancements usually require very specific intention in the spellwork. What you're describing . . . I've never seen magic react to a construct's plates like that." He pulled his hands away. "Now, if it's alright with you—"

A loud thumping noise interrupted from above.

"Winter—"

"On it." Winter dropped the construct's arm in their lap. They snapped a few switches on the base of the chair, unlocking the wheels, then wheeled the construct toward the door.

"Follow Winter," Jasper said. "Lock up behind you."

"What's going on?"

"Whatever it is, I'll handle it. Best you stay out of sight though."

"Why—"

The trapdoor at the top of the ladder burst open, and Quiet peered down, followed by Eren and Jorgunn. Eren was the first to climb down but was followed quickly by the others.

R-0's sword was strapped across Quiet's back, coated in the same golden glow as the screw and compass.

"Do you know them?" Jasper asked.

"Yes sir."

"Not your attackers?"

"No." R-0 shook their head.

"That's a—" Jasper stopped speaking when King Hadrian looked through the trapdoor. His face was obscured with the same glamours he'd used when he visited the city, but R-0 recognized him immediately.

Over a dozen questions popped into R-0's mind, but none were as prominent as their relief to see that not only was Quiet okay, but King Hadrian was here. Together with Eren and Jorgunn's help, it would be easy to return to the palace without Ryder causing any more issues.

"R-0!" Despite the guards' protests, King Hadrian scrambled down the ladder. At the bottom, Eren and Jorgunn had already drawn their weapons, and Quiet stood behind them, magic circulating at her fingertips in dark wisps.

King Hadrian stared down Jasper. "The construct is leaving with us. It's up to you if this encounter is a peaceful one or not."

R-0 reached for their remaining sword. Why wouldn't the encounter be peaceful?

"Your weapons are unneeded." Jasper rose to his feet and extended a hand to R-0. "Even unarmed and injured, a royal construct would have no difficulty killing me."

R-0 stood and methodically dragged themselves toward King Hadrian and the others.

"That is, if their king ordered it." Jasper tapped one of his tools against the table, never taking his eyes from the king. "Welcome, King Hadrian. It's been far too long."

CHAPTER 29

"How do you know who I am?" King Hadrian asked.

"You barge into my lab looking for a royal construct. Who else could you be?" Jasper laughed. "Besides, if I look past your little glamour, you look the same as you did when you were a boy."

"Who are you?"

When Jasper hesitated, R-0 spoke up. "His name is Jasper."

"Jasper as in . . ." King Hadrian's mouth fell agape. "As in the father of the constructs?"

"Fa . . . ther?" R-0 asked. When the king talked about his father, he expressed a sense of familiarity, a sense of loss. He wanted a dead man's advice, approval . . . love. It was impossible, but it didn't stop King Hadrian from getting the same distant look whenever R-0 asked too many questions about him.

R-0 studied Jasper to see if the same feelings surfaced. But despite his proclamation, R-0 felt nothing toward the man.

"You know of me," Jasper said. "I'm surprised."

R-0 was as well. They'd never heard anyone mention him.

"Of course. My mother's journals spoke of you often. When the constructs changed, I thought if anyone had the answers, it would be you. I sent guards to search for you, but no one could find you."

"The Awakening." His lips crept into a slow grin.

Children could inherit behaviors or features from their parents. Although R-0 knew there was no way metal would

RISE OF THE FORGEHEARTS 251

resemble the soft curves of skin, perhaps their mannerisms could mimic his. They tried to move their plates in a similar movement, but the metal couldn't curl, and their plates remained straight.

"The Awakening?" King Hadrian asked. "Did you plan this?"

"I wish I could take credit. It is a gift from the gods, far beyond my capabilities." He looked over at the construct schematics on the wall. "Sentience, true sentience. The constructs have become far more than experiments in my lab."

Sentience. The ability to experience thoughts and feelings. R-0 had never considered that the term could apply to them. But . . . that was exactly what had changed. Before there had been nothing but their directive to protect the king. That was still there, but a new layer of thoughts and feelings wrapped around it. R-0 liked the sound of the word.

"Do you know why it happened?" R-0 asked.

"I don't know if anyone will ever be able to say for certain," Jasper said. "But I have enough theories to cover these walls and then some."

Although notes already sprawled across the walls, covering them fully would require thousands of words—close to a million potentially, depending on how large the handwriting was. It was more than most books R-0 had seen.

"You could write a book," R-0 said.

Jasper's grin grew. "I could waste my time and write dozens. Doesn't mean anyone would read them."

Given the time and opportunity, R-0 would read them. "Someone would."

"A theory to test on another day." Jasper held a hand toward R-0's leg. "May I?"

They had been willing to let Jasper work on them. It would improve their mobility and their odds of making it back to the palace with the answers about Beans. But now, with King Hadrian here, R-0 looked to him, deferring to his judgment.

"If you can help R-0, I would be grateful." King Hadrian waved his hand, and Eren and Jorgunn lowered their weapons. "Why don't you three wait upstairs?"

"Sir, is that safe?" Eren asked.

King Hadrian nodded, and the three of them returned upstairs.

"I appreciate the show of trust." Jasper set a hand on R-0's. "I need your permission, not his. Do I have it?"

"Yes sir."

"Thank you." Jasper wasn't nearly as gentle as some of the other technomancers as his fingers skimmed the plates, but at the joints, his pressure shifted. The wires hardly moved even as he pinched them.

"It'll be easier if I remove the leg."

"Remove it?" R-0's flame roared.

"Only temporarily, I assure you."

King Hadrian placed a hand on R-0's shoulder. "I won't let anything happen to you. Eren and Jorgunn are just a yell away, and we've got over a dozen guards outside."

R-0 reluctantly nodded. "Okay." R-0 expected their flame to grow uneasy as Jasper removed their leg. But it remained steady and strong.

"How did you end up here?" King Hadrian asked.

"Now that story could cover these walls three times over. I don't know if you have the time." Jasper counted out the screws from the table, splitting them into four equal groups. "I hear the king is a very busy man."

"Just the highlights then."

"Of course. Just tear out the heart of the story. Forget the past, so that the future will be as bleak as what we leave behind."

"That's not what I was trying—"

"I know." Jasper sighed. "For many years, your mother was my sponsor."

"I never saw you."

"Do you plan to listen or interrupt?"

King Hadrian fell silent.

Jasper set R-0's leg in his lap, methodically removing the damaged pieces. He disconnected the wires Quiet had tied together, replacing them with fresh wire. It was strange to watch. Their leg was a part of them. But everything Jasper did was distant, as if it was happening to someone else.

"Queen Hadrian kept me out of the palace. I assumed she was doing me a favor. I never liked the fanfare or red tape. Guards knowing your schedules. People—so many people—always around and always watching. It wasn't a place for creativity or progress."

R-0 looked around the basement. The palace wasn't a place for progress and creativity, but this place was? The notes and pictures seemed disorganized. Even the language didn't remain consistent between sections.

Jasper pulled a wad of tangled and fraying wires out of R-0's leg, then grabbed a fresh spool of wire to replace it. "But what she was really doing was keeping my research secret from the other council members."

Winter scoffed from the other table. "Oh, the council with their 'I'm so much better than you' attitudes and their seats made of gold."

Jasper sighed. "Apologies for them."

"Don't pretend like you don't agree." Winters gears chittered, and their voice replicated the sound. It was reminiscent of organics' laughter, and even their plates shifted a little higher in amusement. "You sometimes forget I spent years listening to what you had to say when you thought no one was listening."

"Because no one *was* listening," Jasper said. "Not then. It's incredible how much the constructs vary in their reactions to the Awakening. Some like Winter take to it like they've never known anything else. Others take longer to adjust. I've noted a correlation with how they were previously treated, but nothing definitive."

During the reintegration and their talks with E-4, JJ, and B-7, R-0 had seen something similar. Despite all of them experiencing the fallen stars—the Awakening—they had reacted differently. Within minutes, B-7 had left their post and run through the palace. JJ acted more like Winter, fitting naturally into their new life.

Jasper exchanged his tool for a different one. "But I'm sure you've seen enough of that yourself and that's not why you're here today."

"Why would my mother keep you a secret?" King Hadrian asked. "The constructs provided so many opportunities. The death count in the mines decreased. With the money Faylviln sent, we were able to extend the managrid across the country and even improve it in some areas. The constructs made our lives better."

"Faylviln doesn't think twice about continuing a war when they are only hauling away scraps of metal instead of mourning friends. But the Kingdom of the Holy Rose does not have the same luxury. Every day, more of their people die. Every day, the constructs kill more."

It was easy for R-0 to forget about the war on the other side of the continent—they had enough of their own problems and distractions. But now R-0 couldn't help but wonder what the constructs drafted in Faylviln's armies were doing. Did they feel the same way about the war they were fighting as R-0 did about the organics they'd left in the streets?

"The constructs aren't dangerous," King Hadrian said.

"I would disagree." Jasper twirled a wrench around one finger. "They are incredibly powerful with unimaginable potential. That was true before the Awakening, and it's even truer now. What is done with that power can create danger or opportunity. And too often, the constructs have been used as tools that separate us from our humanity and create openings for tragedies our hands would hesitate to commit."

Before, R-0 had killed without a thought. Now even being attacked, R-0 hesitated to use violence to stop their attackers. They had changed. They could no longer walk away and never think about the dead again. Their actions followed them, remaining in their thoughts long after the events were over. R-0 couldn't change the past, so why did it linger in their mind?

R-0's fingers fidgeted, and before they accelerated, R-0 spoke. "Before the corruption, there was no hesitation."

"The Awakening," Jasper corrected, but he nodded. "You just followed orders. There was no one to feel the guilt of your actions. Not you, not those who ordered you." Jasper fell into silence, focusing on the internal mechanisms of R-0's leg.

"What happened after my mother passed?" King Hadrian asked.

"My research died with her. Thanks to your mother's betrayal, the council didn't trust me. They took my lab, my research, everything I'd built. I didn't matter, and I was easily discarded." Jasper squeezed a tool R-0 didn't recognize, and magic sparked to life. The tool rotated something within R-0's leg until it clicked, then Jasper turned his attention to King Hadrian. "As long as they had you, they had control of the constructs, and I had nothing."

"I never knew," King Hadrian said. "That's . . ."

The injustice in Jasper's story brought heat to R-0's plates. He had worked his entire life toward a goal, only to have it taken from him.

"That is unfair," R-0 said.

Jasper chuckled. "I was angry about it for many years. But my anger wasn't going to make it right, and they'd already taken enough from me. I decided I wouldn't let them take any more of my time, so I let it go."

"You let it go?" R-0 asked.

"They're going to do whatever they want to do. I can't stop them—learned that lesson the hard way. I tried walking away from it all, but everything always brought me back here. The only thing I can do is live my life. Try again and do better. So that's what I've done. I set up shop here to continue my research in private and provide maintenance and repairs to families that couldn't afford real technomancers."

"I'm sorry," King Hadrian said. "R-0 is right. If I had known—"

"You were just a boy who'd lost his mother. The council had you wrapped around their finger. I'd be surprised if that's changed."

"I am not their puppet."

"Perhaps they've just grown more subtle."

King Hadrian clenched his hands into tight fists at his side. His jaw tightened, and his eyes narrowed, but he remained silent. R-0 didn't understand why Jasper thought King Hadrian was a puppet when he was clearly a man, but based on the king's reaction, it wasn't intended as a compliment.

R-0 tried to speak up in defense of their king, but what could they say? They exhaled a puff of smoke.

Jasper glanced over his shoulder at King Hadrian. "Don't bite your tongue, boy. Spit it out."

"Nothing."

"You may have your father's eyes, but they shine just like your mother's. I'd know that look anywhere."

King Hadrian's expression softened. "You two were close?"

"As close as the flowers in the gardens are to the sun." Despite Jasper's words about sunshine, his eyes were misty like a rainstorm. "She saw something in me when no one else did. And not just me. She gave life to this city where there could have been nothing."

Flowers were far from the sun—an unfathomable distance. But Jasper spoke with a familiarity that seemed much closer.

"How far away is the sun?" R-0 asked.

"Unreachable." Jasper snapped two new gears into place with a sharp click, then held out the old parts to R-0. "And right in the palm of our hands."

"That doesn't make sense."

"It does to him." Jasper tilted his head toward the king and winked.

R-0 squinted at King Hadrian, but if he understood Jasper, he didn't explain it.

"Come back to the palace with us," King Hadrian said. "Whatever you need, you'll have it."

"It's a kind offer, but I'm quite happy here."

"Here? No tools, no funding . . . Name your price, and I'll arrange it."

"You aren't the first to seek my services after the Awakening. What I need, you can't provide." Jasper gestured around at his lab. "This may not look like much, but it's ours. Not the council's. Not the crown's. We're ruled by our hearts, by our conscience."

"By our humanity," Winter added.

"Yes, and by our humanity." Jasper smiled warmly.

"But you could help so many more people. If you speak to the council—"

"Then the council could ignore me again, and I could repeat the failed cycle of my history?" Jasper shook his head. "My answer is no."

If Jasper was the father of the constructs, surely, he could do something to help those still held in the storage rooms and the dungeon. If nothing else, his knowledge of healing and repairs would be invaluable to the technomancers. He'd said no, but . . . organics frequently changed their minds.

"Is there anything that could make your answer yes?" R-0 asked.

"Perhaps, in time, I might be willing to consult." Jasper's rejection was softer when he spoke to R-0, but the result was the same. "But for now, I am needed here."

"But—"

"Let's get this back on, shall we?" Jasper interrupted the king, leaning R-0's repaired leg against the edge of their chair.

R-0 turned their attention to their leg, carefully examining all of Jasper's work as he replaced it. It fit into the socket perfectly, and the material seemed stronger than the original. Instead of soldering a patch to the plate, Jasper had entirely replaced the external plate, and as far as R-0 could tell, it was an upgrade.

R-0 slowly kicked out. After some initial stuttering, their leg responded. They stood unassisted and took a few tentative steps that quickly progressed to their normal gait.

"Thank you." Relief flooded through R-0, no longer hindered by their injury. But as they walked back to their seat, the damaged parts sitting next to Jasper's toolkit caught their eye.

R-0 couldn't look away from the pile of mangled gears. Those gears were theirs. A part of them. Left abandoned to be forgotten, replaced by something new and shiny.

It was not unlike Jasper, being discarded by the council.

"What will happen to the old parts?" R-0 asked.

"Some will be melted down and recast. Some are repairable. Either way, they will be used to repair other constructs or further our research."

The parts would be useful. They would help other constructs. But R-0 still couldn't look away. They searched for the words to explain, but they didn't know what questions to ask, much less how to describe what they were feeling.

They pinched one of the mangled gears and watched the light reflect on the smooth curves.

"You can keep them, if you'd like," Jasper said.

"Really?" R-0's hand instinctively wrapped around the piece, clutching it to their chest and trembling in anticipation as Jasper gathered the rest.

"I'll get a box to put them in."

R-0 jittered in place, struggling to stay still as they waited. They twisted the gear between their fingers. What would they do with the box full of metal?

The thought made them pause. It wouldn't have any use. The decorations in the palace sat untouched, only receiving attention when it was time to clean the gathering dust. The king kept a few baubles in his room—shiny rocks imported from across the world and pieces of art he enjoyed. But R-0 had no room. They had nothing that belonged to them, and no place to put it.

Except for their swords. They ran their fingers along both sheaths. Their blades were their only belonging, and storage was never an issue since they were attached to R-0. But the box couldn't be stored the same way.

It was impractical. It would get in the way. Despite that, R-0 ... wanted it.

"Here you go." Jasper returned from the other room and handed a box to R-0.

They peeked inside, taking a quick inventory. All their parts were there, down to the smallest stripped screw. It was what they'd wanted, but R-0 hesitated.

"What's wrong?" King Hadrian asked.

"Is it selfish to want these parts?"

"They're yours." He placed a reassuring hand on R-0's shoulder. "If you want them, take them."

Sitting in their condensed form, R-0 didn't tower over King Hadrian and could stare directly into his eyes. "That does not answer the question."

"You've got to find those answers for yourself," Jasper said.

"How?" R-0 asked.

"You get as much information as you can. You ask the people you trust for counsel. Then, you search your heart."

Gather information. Ask questions. R-0 could do that. But search their heart?

"Constructs do not have hearts."

Jasper took their hand and placed it on his chest, then placed his hand on R-0's chest. "Tell me, does your flame not burn as strong as my heart beats?"

"They are different metrics."

"Don't think." Jasper pressed harder against R-0's chest. "Feel."

Beneath their fingertips, Jasper's heartbeat was strong, rhythmic. Proof he was alive. R-0 closed their eyes, focusing on their own flame. A fire had always existed in their chest, warming them and giving them strength. But now the fire raged. It responded to Jasper's touch, to R-0's thoughts. It reached out, wanting more. More emotions. More connection. More knowledge. It wasn't as steady as Jasper's pulse, but it didn't matter.

It proved they were alive. Just like Jasper, the king, and all the organics that had come before them.

R-0 was alive.

The fate of the metal in the box seemed less significant now. Although their flame still called out for their lost pieces, R-0 knew it would be selfish to keep them. They had no use for them, and the parts could help other constructs.

"Here." R-0 handed the box back to Jasper. "Keep this."

"Are you sure?"

R-0 nodded. "Help the other constructs."

It wasn't all they wanted to say. Words churned in their mind, unable to take shape. So they kept them as a silent plea to themself.

Help my people.

CHAPTER 30

As the sun rose into the sky, R-0 carried Beans's body back to the palace.

They considered following the organics' custom and giving the body to the sea but given the unease that filled their flame whenever they stared at the churning waters, it didn't seem a fitting resting place. They asked King Hadrian about other customs for the deceased. There were plenty—underground burial, leaving the body where it died, burning the body and preparing a feast with the resulting fire—but none seemed practical or right for the construct. However, there was one common factor among every custom.

The deceased's loved ones led the events.

So R-0 requested King Hadrian to return Beans to Seraphine. She knew them. Loved them. If anyone should decide their final fate, it should be her.

Once they were back in King Hadrian's room, the king pulled R-0 close. His arms slid under R-0's, and he pressed tight against their chest plate. R-0 stood stiff and listened to the king's heartbeat vibrating through their plates.

A hug.

The gesture was surprising, but also . . . pleasant. It was nothing but pressure. In all practicality, there was no measurable difference between the current arrangement and leaning against the wall or sitting in a chair. But the more R-0 experienced feelings, the more they realized how many things couldn't be measured. Only felt.

And King Hadrian's presence felt comforting. Good.

R-0's flame strengthened, and warmth shot through their body. Maybe Jasper was right and the constructs' flames weren't that different from organics' hearts.

"You scared me." King Hadrian's pulse sped. He pulled away slightly and looked up at R-0. There was no sign of the bold and unapologetic man that had barged into Jasper's lab making demands. His gentle smile was overshadowed by his eyes, where tears pooled in the corners.

"Why?" R-0 asked. King Hadrian had nothing to fear.

"When Riley woke me in the middle of the night and said she left you out there injured . . . I was worried I wouldn't find you before something bad happened."

R-0 wrapped their arms around King Hadrian, mimicking his gesture. If he could comfort R-0, perhaps they could reciprocate.

"Maybe not so tight." King Hadrian's voice was strained.

"Apologies sir." R-0 took a step back, and his breathing normalized. Organics were so delicate. R-0 had tried to imitate the same pressure King Hadrian had used, only a fraction of their full strength, and it was still too much. R-0 filed the information away for later. They would have to be more careful next time.

King Hadrian stepped away. "You don't have to call me that when we're alone, you know."

"What?"

"Sir. You can call me Sylas."

"Sy . . . las." R-0 tested the word. It felt strange. "Sir is meant to be respectful and acknowledge positions of power."

"And first names are meant to be familiar and comfortable."

"A name used by friends."

"Friends, family, lovers . . . all manner of personal relationships."

"Is this a personal relationship?"

"We're friends, right?" King Hadrian chuckled.

"Yes." They didn't say sir, but it didn't make the words seem any less stiff. "Yes, Sylas."

That sounded worse.

But King Hadrian's face lit up. His eyes crinkled in the corners, and his cheeks puffed up.

"Does that make you happy?" R-0 asked.

"It does."

Despite the awkward way the syllables caught in their gears, R-0 would continue saying it if it made King Hadrian—Sylas—happy. "Okay, Sylas."

King Hadrian smiled, heat rising to his cheeks. Organic skin couldn't get nearly as hot as a construct's plates could, but the shift in color that accompanied the change in temperature made it more noticeable.

Before R-0 could ask about it, King Hadrian went to his closet and began opening drawers. He pulled out a few stacks of paper and moved them to the bed, where he quickly divided them into piles.

"These are all of Jasper's records that I have. Jeza gave them to me when I was young. I've been meaning to go through them since the Awakening, but I haven't had a chance." King Hadrian had adopted Jasper's name for the incident, and it warmed R-0's flame almost as much as the hug had.

The papers matched those on the walls of the hattery basement, and an unintelligible mix of foreign language, symbols, and nonsensical phrases were interspersed through legible text. Tabs poking out along the side designated various categories—spellwork, hypothesis, and daily reports, to name a few—as King Hadrian added to the stacks.

Curiosity overwhelmed R-0. This wasn't just research, it was the constructs' history. R-0's history. Even if it couldn't explain the Awakening, it would detail R-0's origin fourteen years ago. They reached for the top paper, then stopped themself. Jasper had been able to tell them valuable information about the missing constructs, but the rest of his research was nothing but a distraction from their investigation. And after what they'd learned from Ryder and Jasper, solving the mystery of the missing—no, taken—constructs was more important than ever. If someone on the council was targeting Quiet and R-0, were they also targeting the king?

"Is there something here that could help the investigation?" R-0 asked.

"I couldn't find anything, but we can get a copy made and return these to Jasper. If we want any chance of convincing him to return to the palace, a gesture of goodwill could go a long way."

It was a valuable task, but . . . R-0 couldn't focus on the papers in front of them. Even if they hadn't succeeded in making Jasper an ally, he wasn't a threat. But there was a threat to R-0, Quiet, the constructs, and maybe even the king. Now that R-0 was repaired and fully functional, they should be investigating Ryder and whoever he was working with on the council before they hurt anyone else.

"What about the threat on the council?"

"Riley is already investigating that."

"Is assistance required?"

"How are you at sneaking around and breaking into people's room?"

"Rooms can easily be broken." R-0 flexed their fingers. More than once they had broken doors when it apparently was *not* the right thing to do. But if an appropriate situation existed, R-0 would be an expert.

"And what about the sneaking part?"

As R-0 flexed their fingers again, their gears clicked and whirred. Not to mention the metallic clanks that followed every footstep they took.

"That's what I thought," King Hadrian said. "Leave it to Riley. She'll report back when she knows more."

"So we wait?"

King Hadrian nodded.

Since the Awakening, R-0 had often accepted the king's orders without question. Waiting was simple, and King Hadrian's logic made sense. But it felt . . . wrong. Constructs were being taken and decommissioned. Was the next Beans being killed as they stood here?

How were they supposed to do nothing while others were in danger? They might not be as sneaky as Quiet, but there had to be other ways to help.

"Perhaps other assistance could be provided," R-0 said.

"Like what?"

"The council members could be interrogated." They knew Ryder was receiving his orders from one of the council members. All of their suspects were already conveniently located nearby. If King Hadrian called a council meeting, they could all be apprehended at once. It would be simple and efficient.

"I can't order an interrogation on one of the council members without strong evidence. If I'm wrong, their clan might never forgive me."

"If all of the council members are interrogated, you will be right."

"Which would still require five wrongful accusations and a political nightmare." King Hadrian shook his head. "And that's the best-case scenario. More likely, the interrogation reveals nothing and lets them know we're on to them. It would give them time to cover their tracks and figure out an alibi."

"Perhaps—" R-0 paused as footsteps from outside the room grew louder. They focused on the sound, differentiating three separate people. Based on the sounds and timing, it was likely a noblewoman and two guards.

"What is it?" King Hadrian asked.

"Someone is coming this way." R-0 reached for their weapons, relieved that their second blade hadn't been compromised during Quiet's tracking spell.

"At ease, R-0." King Hadrian signaled the same with his hand.

Knowing their enemy was in the palace put R-0 on edge. How were they supposed to know if the king was in danger?

The footsteps stopped outside the door.

"Has King Hadrian returned?" Jeza asked.

"Yes ma'am," the guard stationed outside responded.

Relief that it was Jeza and not an unknown threat was short-lived. King Hadrian trusted Jeza, and she had supported him for years. But was that trust rightfully placed? The only thing R-0 knew for certain about their enemy was that they were on the council.

King Hadrian opened the door before the conversation outside could continue. In the hallway, Jeza stood poised to knock, two guards at her side. She took one look at R-0, then at King Hadrian. "Councilman Robin called an emergency council session."

"Now?" King Hadrian asked. "I just met with him a couple hours ago."

"Prepare yourself, Sylas." Jeza clasped her hands in front of her, her rings clicking together. "He's calling for a vote of no confidence. He plans to take your crown."

CHAPTER 31

"No, no, no," King Hadrian muttered. "Robin can't do this. Uxius isn't even back yet."

"Robin alone cannot, but the council most certainly can."

"Impossible." King Hadrian shook his head. "Whose support does he have?"

R-0 played out potential scenarios in their mind. Robin would be one vote for, King Hadrian one vote against. That little was certain. For a majority, Robin would need three votes in favor of dethroning King Hadrian out of Quiet, Eren, Gretta, Jeza, and Uxius.

"Whose loyalty are you so confident in?" Jeza asked. "Riley is the only council member who agrees with how you've handled the constructs, and even if she supports you, what of the churches she represents? Not only that, the council backed Robin as king after your mother's death. Are you so certain they wouldn't again?"

"What will you vote?" King Hadrian asked.

"I don't know whether to be proud or offended you feel the need to ask that." A smile crossed Jeza's face that was quickly replaced by concern. "You do not need to question my loyalty to your family, though Robin may be surprised to learn that."

"I need to speak with Eren. I need to make sure—"

"No. We need to get going. The rest of the council has already been summoned, and being late *again* is not the message you want to send right now."

"You're right." King Hadrian took a quick look in the mirror, adjusting his robes and crown before returning to the doorway. "Let's go."

R-0's gears whirred in anticipation, ready to leave, but Jeza stopped them at the threshold.

"Why don't you have R-0 wait here?" Jeza asked.

"King Hadrian requires protection," R-0 said. In a council meeting, he would be sitting with their enemy. What if they decided to strike?

"They deserve to be there as much as any other guard," King Hadrian said.

"Sylas." Jeza leaned close to him, so the organic guards couldn't hear what she said, although her words were clear to R-0. "There are others you can entrust with your safety. Do you really want to jeopardize your position as king? Don't throw away everything you've worked for. Everything your mother did to make sure you'd be standing in these halls with that crown on your head."

King Hadrian bit at his lip and looked at the ground. After a deep breath, he turned his attention to the organic guards at his door. "You two come with us. R-0, wait here and keep watch over my chambers."

No.

That's what R-0 wanted to say. Staying here wouldn't protect King Hadrian from the threat on the council, and it wouldn't bring them any closer to finding the taken constructs. Even listening to a council meeting would have been preferable to doing nothing in the king's room. At least there, they could prove that the reintegration efforts were worthwhile.

But R-0 couldn't argue—not under the watchful eyes of Jeza and her guards. All that would do was prove to one of their allies that the others were right to worry about the constructs' noncompliance.

R-0 stopped breathing, trying to subdue their flame by limiting its flow of oxygen. It worked—only partially—enough for them to nod. "Yes sir."

Even after the organics rounded the corner, disappearing from sight, R-0 could still hear their conversation. They hung on every word, imagining they were following the others instead of being left behind.

Jeza asked a few questions about R-0—how they had been managing, how the reintegration efforts had impacted them, and if King Hadrian had continued testing their flame for any signs they were still bound to the royal bloodline. King Hadrian's answers were . . . sufficient. Not entirely accurate, although R-0 couldn't tell if that was due to a lack of knowledge of R-0's internal thoughts, forgetfulness, or a purposeful attempt to mislead Jeza. It wasn't until the distant voices faded to silence that R-0 managed to convince their body to retreat into King Hadrian's room.

R-0 should have been content. They were following orders, and with numerous guards typically present at a council meeting, King Hadrian would be well protected.

But they weren't content. Doing nothing didn't help anyone and neither pacing nor fidgeting would change their situation. With every passing tick of their gears, it became harder and harder to stay put.

If curiosity had ailed R-0 immediately after the Awakening, their current ailment was nothingness—their inability to do what they felt needed to be done. For a moment, they missed how things were before, when following orders wasn't complicated by endless questions, thoughts, and feelings.

R-0 sat at King Hadrian's desk. It wasn't what they wanted to be doing, but they had discovered doing *something* was better than doing nothing, and they could learn a lot from Jasper's files.

The first tab for spellwork was mostly indecipherable. The only comprehensible words were headers that titled the spell, dates, and page numbers at the bottom. It more closely resembled a child's drawing than an official report. Shapes of various sizes and types were connected via dots and lines. Some of the earlier spells were simple designs—a few shapes connected with short, straight lines—while many of the later spells spanned multiple pages. There were only a dozen distinct spells, but they filled seventy-four pages.

The spells themselves didn't seem useful. Some names R-0 recognized from maintenance sessions with the technomancers. Others focused on shaping metal to create various components used to build the constructs. There was nothing like Quiet's tracking spell that could find the taken constructs or anything that could give the constructs sentience like the Awakening had.

The daily report section had hundreds of the same notes. *Experiment A1 conducted. Result: FAILURE. Next Steps: Repeat.* As Jasper repeated his experiments, the number ticked up until, at A98, the result read success, and the next step was to advance. The following day's report started with experiment B1. R-0 flipped through rapidly, scanning the text just long enough to make sure the pattern continued until it ended at N432. It was dated one week after Queen Hadrian's death, and it was the final report.

R-0 was more thorough in their examination of the council tab, where Jasper documented the requests he'd received. Jeza, Gretta, and Robin had already been council members when Queen Hadrian first recruited Jasper, while Eren took her seat over the course of his experiments. Quiet and Uxius's predecessors were mentioned, but they hadn't joined the council until after Jasper's notes ended.

Most of the requests weren't specific to Jasper's research and didn't mention him by name. Robin, in particular, always seemed to have a problem but never mentioned the constructs or Jasper. There were also no discernable patterns to his requests. His letters were addressed to Layla Hadrian with an added note on top.

J. Take a look. Thanks. —L

It matched what R-0 had seen of the late queen's writing, and it reminded R-0 of Eren handing out assignments. From the notes, It was unclear if the rest of the council knew Jasper existed.

Jeza and Queen Hadrian were the exceptions. Their letters were the only ones directed to Jasper. R-0 stopped at the last one.

Jeza stopped by today, asking about other applications of flow conduits. If it was possible to connect magic to metal, what else could we connect magic to? Likely another attempt to connect herself to the Flow. I referred her to a Keeper's journal in Dunwal's library and advised if she had a more specific query, perhaps I could be of more assistance.

Most of Jeza's queries included ideas about applying Jasper's research to projects other than the constructs, and many were successful, leading to improvements in the strength and efficiency of the managrid. Despite her inability to cast magic, Jeza's letters showed a mastery of the subject, sometimes even including sketches in the same style as Jasper's spellwork.

In contrast, Queen Hadrian constantly mentioned the constructs. She wanted to know the full extent of their abilities. After the initial experiments in which Jasper created a metal shell that moved, she immediately made requests for constructs with combat capabilities and additional measures to control the constructs.

The spellwork to control the constructs matched what King Hadrian had told R-0. Jasper had tied the constructs to her bloodline. R-0 ran their fingers across the page, tracing the lines and shapes. This spell was the reason that for fourteen years they'd spent every moment following the king's orders. It was the source of the directive that had surrounded their every thought, overpowering everything else.

Even now, when R-0 grew quiet, they could feel the echo of that directive.

Protect the king.

No longer bound by magic, R-0 continued to serve their original purpose.

R-0 moved on to the next request, and their flame stuttered. It was a letter from Queen Hadrian to Jasper discussing potential countermeasures should the constructs become a threat. She wrote in great length about the council's concerns, her concerns, and the constructs' strength as weapons of war, but the last line drew R-0's attention.

The constructs are too dangerous to be left unchecked. Please explore options for mass decommissioning.

The next page gave Jasper's report. He'd only experimented for a few weeks before reaching a conclusion.

Result: SUCCESS.

R-0's flame leaped, clawing at their chest plate as if it could escape. The longer it raged, the more R-0 believed Jasper when he compared flames to hearts. Like an organic's speeding pulse, their flame pounded as they flipped to the final section—Jasper's journal entries.

R-0 started with the queen's request to bind the constructs to her bloodline. Most of the pages were filled with random scribbles and notes that, without context, weren't helpful. An incomplete shopping list was written in the margins. Farther down the page, Jasper wrote about the queen wanting control of the constructs.

I told the queen her request was impossible, and if I were a lesser mage, I could also call myself honest. But I am not. Her request was nothing more than a challenge I have solved. So why do I hesitate to deliver what she will see as good news?

When our greatest accomplishment and our downfall share the same face, how are we to know which is which? How are we to tell if we are the hero or the villain in our story?

But without Layla, where would I be? Who would I be? As much as it pains me, I know the answers.

I would be nowhere. I would be no one.

So if this is what she asks, I know what I must do.

The next entries contained less specific descriptions of Jasper's everyday life. R-0 skimmed again until they found notes on the queen's second request: mass decommissioning.

I shouldn't be surprised that the queen has asked this. These days, Jeza has her ear more than I. She whispers to the queen about rebellion. If I was capable of magic to create the constructs, who is to say another mage could not break the queen's control?

I have tried to convince the queen that my spellwork is foolproof. She has seen it time and time again. Wards on the palace. Enhancements to the managrid. The constructs themselves. Where lesser mages balk at the impossible, I thrive. Still, she is insistent, and for her, no order is too grand.

It saddens me to think of a future where this spell would be used. Everything I have created could crumble in an instant. But machines can be rebuilt and research repeated, while we have only one chance at life. And this is what is required of mine.

The rest of the entry focused on the specifics of the spell. In addition to the typical magical components R-0 had seen referenced in other sections, three requirements were circled in red—royal construct, power source, and blood bound to the constructs. Farther down was a reference to where the spell was filed.

Header: Mass-Decomissioning. Page Fifty.

How could R-0 have missed a spell titled "Mass Decomissioning"? They hadn't looked at every indecipherable shape, but they knew they hadn't read anything like that. R-0 flipped back, searching the spellwork section. After page forty-nine, the pages skipped to sixty.

There were pages missing.

Right where the mass decommissioning spell was supposed to be.

CHAPTER 32

R-0 hadn't consciously made a decision before their body returned to the cabinets and drawers. Perhaps the spell was still here, just misfiled. The furniture was overflowing with papers, but R-0 took every sheet out, scanning it for any sign of Jasper's spellwork or mention of decommissioning.

Images flashed through their mind—potential futures. The storage rooms, devoid of flames. Constructs lined in their orderly rows completely still, each cold to the touch like Beans had been. JJ, unmoving in the backyard, the dragon-scaled children huddled around lifeless steel. The carnage of Jasper's basement spread everywhere.

If the mass decommissioning spell was used, those possibilities would become reality in an instant. And R-0 would be among the dead.

Soon papers were scattered throughout the room, covering the floor, the bed, the desk—any surface R-0 could find. They couldn't risk overlooking a single sheet. They had to know for certain if the spell was here or lost. After R-0 checked the last stack, they let the pages slip through their fingers and fall to the floor.

The mass decommissioning spell was gone.

Had it been removed before it was ever filed away? Or had someone taken it more recently?

R-0's mind was as messy as the room, their thoughts and roiling emotions scattered instead of papers. They couldn't recall when the files had originally been brought to the king's room, but the cabinet with Jasper's notes sat in the back corner. King Hadrian was rarely over there, and visitors never went in that section.

R-0 stopped. Someone *had* been there.

The construct that had broken into King Hadrian's room had been rummaging through his drawers. They weren't carrying anything, but something as small as paper could have easily hidden within their robes.

Had they taken it?

All the questions they'd asked when the intruder escaped resurfaced, accompanied by new ones. Who were they? How did they escape? Why did they want the spell? How did they know it was here? R-0 had spent years with King Hadrian and had no idea this spell existed. How did another construct know? Or who had given them their orders?

Footsteps interrupted R-0's thoughts—the heavy steps of multiple guards accompanied by King Hadrian's distinctive steps. R-0 grabbed the papers, trying to put them back where they belonged, but they'd barely managed to clear the bed before King Hadrian slammed the door open.

If the king noticed the mess, he didn't react. He stomped to the bed, trampling over papers as he went.

"Are you okay?" R-0 asked.

"No."

R-0 analyzed King Hadrian from head to toe. There were no visible injuries, but just to be certain, R-0 asked, "What's wrong?" When King Hadrian didn't respond, R-0 continued, "Should you be taken to the healers?"

"There's nothing you can do." His face shifted as he looked at the mess of papers sprawled across the floor. "R-0." He sighed as he spoke, closing his eyes. He took a deep breath before continuing. "What happened in here?"

R-0 tried to answer his question, but their voice betrayed them. They tried again. "Jasper had a spell to decommission all the constructs, and it's missing."

"What?" King Hadrian's eyes shot open, and he leaned forward. "What are you talking about?"

R-0 tiptoed around the papers littering the floor and grabbed Jasper's files. They spread them across the bed, pointing out the journal entries and the missing spell.

"You're sure it isn't here?" King Hadrian clutched Jasper's journal entry so tight the edge of the page tore.

R-0 nodded. "All of your files have been reviewed."

"Fuck." King Hadrian crumpled the sheet of paper in his hands and threw it to the ground. "Fuck!" He screamed louder and punched the wall. His knuckle buckled, and his skin turned red, but the wall remained unharmed. Still, King Hadrian pulled back his fist to punch again.

R-0 couldn't understand why the wall needed to be attacked, but they did know that if King Hadrian continued, he would harm himself more than the wooden planks.

"Here." R-0 grabbed his hand in one of theirs, as gently as they could while still restraining him. Then, with their other hand, they punched the wall. Wood splintered and caved in, leaving a gaping hole.

"R-0—" King Hadrian shook his head and huffed a sigh. "Nevermind."

King Hadrian didn't seem pleased. Perhaps he required additional damage. "Would you like the hole to be larger?"

"No. Please, please don't make it larger."

"You do not seem pleased with the result."

"If it would get us these notes, I'd let you punch this whole place to the ground." King Hadrian snatched a piece of paper off the bed just to let it fall to the floor. "Can anything else go wrong today?"

It was still early in the day—there were plenty of things that could go wrong. In fact, there were infinite possibilities of things that could go wrong. An assassin could breach the palace's security, sickness could plague the council, the managrid blackouts could escalate and Graywal's infrastructure could crumble, R-0 and the rest of the constructs could all be decommissioned . . .

"R-0, are you listening to me?" King Hadrian asked.

King Hadrian's voice was muffled and distant. R-0 hadn't been listening, but the king's words dragged them from their thoughts and back to the present.

"Apologies," R-0 said.

"Jeza was right. Robin is trying to take the crown for himself."

R-0 looked at the crown still on King Hadrian's head. "But he failed."

"Not quite." King Hadrian kicked at the papers on the floor. "He has half the council—himself, Gretta." His teeth clenched, and he took a deep breath. "Even Eren voted with him."

Which left Jeza and Quiet in support of King Hadrian, and one vote left. "There is a tie," R-0 said.

"And Uxius still has a vote. His messenger returned today. She was on a faster ship, but he won't be far behind. There's no chance he'll stand against Robin. His fishing operation relies too heavily on the shipwrights."

Which would mean a majority was in favor of replacing the king. Their list of problems kept growing—the taken constructs, a rogue council member, the mass decommissioning spell, and now King Hadrian losing his crown.

"What happens now?" R-0 asked.

"I don't know. That spell and the missing constructs need to be found. But . . ." King Hadrian's hand balled into a fist once more, and R-0 stepped forward to restrain him. His knuckles still bled from his first encounter with the wall. "I have to meet with Gretta and Eren. I knew Eren was worried about the constructs, but I never imagined she'd support Robin over me."

It was easy for R-0 to imagine—it was actively happening. Not only that, Eren had made it clear she would do whatever it took to keep King Hadrian and the council safe.

"If I don't change someone's mind before Uxius returns, my crown will be gone. That has to take priority. If I lose my crown, nothing else will matter." Before R-0 could speak, King Hadrian continued, "All I wanted was to do the right thing, and this is where it lands me. How are they so dense? So selfish? So . . ." The king threw his arms into the air. "So terrible!"

"Perhaps—"

"I've given up everything to be the best king I could. I've had mindless constructs following me around instead of friends, meetings with advisors and soul sucking council members instead of a childhood. I should be focusing on my people, my kingdom, *leading* us through this. Instead, I have to defend my right to lead? This is how they repay me? They're threatening to ruin everything I ever worked for. Everything I am. Without this crown . . . I'm nothing."

King Hadrian took the crown off every night, and he was still himself. He was more than a king. "That is not true."

"You're the only one in this whole place who thinks so. I don't even believe it myself." He stood and paced the length of the room, shuffling papers to the side with each step. "I could never do what Jasper did. I couldn't start over. This palace has always been my home, and the throne my responsibility. My mother set this up for me and for my children. With control over the constructs she all but guaranteed our clan's future. We were never supposed to go through this."

The Awakening gave R-0 so much, but now it might take everything from King Hadrian. If he still had control over the constructs, he wouldn't be in this position. No matter how R-0 thought about it, there was nothing they could do to change the council's votes or alleviate his situation. There were some things that R-0 couldn't protect King Hadrian from, and the politics of the council was one of them.

"Okay, okay, pull yourself together, Sylas," the king muttered so quiet an organic wouldn't be able to hear, then continued louder. "We can't waste any time. The sooner we deal with Robin, the sooner we can get back to the investigation. R-0, will you tell the guards to summon Eren? I'm more likely to change her mind than Gretta's."

King Hadrian was right. They had little time before Uxius returned, and if he wanted to save his crown, he needed to act now. But King Hadrian wasn't the only one in danger. R-0 thought back to Jasper's basement filled with construct corpses.

How much time did the taken constructs have? If the decommissioning spell was in the wrong hands, how much time did any of the constructs have?

None of the responsibilities of the crown seemed as important as the constructs' fate, but if that was King Hadrian's priority, R-0 trusted him. Still, they hesitated. Why did it have to be one or the other? King Hadrian wasn't the only one who could continue the investigation.

"While you meet with Gretta and Eren, the investigation could continue."

"I can't be in two places at once. There aren't enough hours in the day."

"Your presence is unnecessary."

"You'll do it on your own?" King Hadrian asked.

"Yes."

"No." King Hadrian shook his head. "It's too dangerous. Constructs aren't leaving on their own. They're being taken. Killed. What if that happens to you?"

"Is there another way for the investigation to continue?"

"I could assign someone else to it, but . . . who? I can't trust half my council—including my captain of the guard. We can't risk word of this spell spreading. I don't want anyone to know about it who doesn't already."

I could do it. R-0 tried to say the words, but they couldn't.

And they couldn't continue the investigation without the king's blessing. But they had seen countless others in this same scenario. The king's advisors, visiting executives, and ordinary people seeking an audience with the king all needed something—just like R-0 did now—and they found ways to convince him.

R-0 could do the same.

"Please, Sylas."

King Hadrian tripped, but R-0 caught and steadied him. His hand lingered on R-0's arm. "This is important to you, isn't it?"

"You're in danger," R-0 said. But that wasn't the only reason they wanted to resolve this. "The constructs are in danger."

"And you want to help."

"Yes."

King Hadrian sighed. "If anyone gives you any trouble, just leave them alone, and we'll handle it together once I have the time."

"Yes."

"If anyone asks you what you're doing, you're operating on orders from the king. Whatever you need to do, use the excuse that I told you to do it."

"Yes." R-0's plates heated, but there was no discomfort to accompany the feeling. Just their flame growing hungrier with the thought of finally being able to help. Despite the overwhelming urgency and the bleak future the constructs faced if they failed, R-0 was . . . excited.

The possibilities were endless—almost too open-ended. How would they know where to go? How would they know what to do? They'd traveled alone through the palace before, but almost always under specific orders. The only exception was their excursion to the gardens where Quiet had found them.

R-0 paused. They'd been so focused on what being alone would be like for them, they'd forgotten it also meant they wouldn't be able to protect the king.

"Will you be safe?" R-0 asked.

"Eren doubled the guard on my room, and Riley enhanced the wards. I'll be safe." King Hadrian smiled briefly, but the expression quickly faltered. "You're the one we should be worrying about."

"Why?"

"How to say this?" King Hadrian sat back on his bed. After a few moments of silence, he continued. "There are some things I can't protect you from, and that scares me. I worry about you."

R-0 understood that feeling. Like they couldn't protect King Hadrian from the council politics. But R-0 wasn't a politician, and they weren't the one in danger. "Worry is unnecessary."

"We don't need to feel anything, but that doesn't stop us, does it?"

R-0 frowned. King Hadrian was technically right. R-0 had functioned just fine for over a decade without a single feeling. But . . . they wouldn't want to go back to that. They had been empty, a shell of what they were now.

"It's important to feel, but . . ." R-0 didn't want to be the source of any negativity for the king. It was their job to worry about him, not the other way around.

"But sometimes feelings get in the way of what needs to be done. And I won't let my feelings get in the way. This is a good idea, R-0."

King Hadrian went to the door, commanding the guards to fetch Eren, then held it open for R-0. "Report back to me whatever you find."

R-0 hesitated at the threshold. Was this the right decision? What if something happened to King Hadrian while they were gone? What if they failed? R-0 knew they couldn't be helpful in swaying Eren or Gretta, but was doing something better than doing nothing if their actions resulted in nothing but leaving the king vulnerable?

R-0 took a deep breath even though their flame had plenty of air, then stepped into the hallway.

Alone.

CHAPTER 33

As the door closed behind R-0, they stopped.
What were they supposed to do?
King Hadrian always made it seem so simple. As soon as one task was complete, he'd move to the next task, then the next. Even the downtime between activities was filled with conversation, thoughts, questions.
Alone, there was nothing but infinite possibilities circling through R-0's mind, waiting to be chosen.
Waiting for R-0 to choose.
R-0 was acutely aware of the guards outside King Hadrian's room eyeing them. One had left to fetch Eren, but three remained, including Jorgunn. The longer R-0 stood, the more concerned their expressions became.
"Is there a problem, R-0?" Jorgunn asked.
"No sir."
R-0 couldn't just stand there, so they walked down the hallway. But how were they supposed to know what to do? How could they choose? Doing nothing was clearly not the correct solution, but there were countless somethings that could be done.
Gather as much information as you can.
When R-0 had asked Jasper how to find answers for themself, that was the first step he'd listed. R-0 sorted through the possibilities as they walked, focusing on tasks that would gather information. They had already reviewed the reports Eren had submitted for the king's intruder, as well as all the

information available on the taken constructs. They couldn't ask anyone about Jasper's spell—King Hadrian had made it clear that no one should learn about that.

But what about someone who already knew? Someone who was there?

In Jasper's notes, Jeza had encouraged Queen Hadrian to pursue a means of destroying the constructs if they got out of hand. The notes also indicated that both Jeza and the queen were pleased with Jasper's work. If Jeza was around when the spell was created, she might know who else knew of the spell as well as details that Jasper's notes hadn't mentioned.

Not only that, when King Hadrian had listed people he trusted, Jeza was at the top of the list, and she was one of the few council members still supporting him.

R-0 plotted their route through the castle. Their steps accelerated with newfound purpose and didn't stop until they'd reached Jeza's door. Two guards stood on either side, although R-0 didn't recognize either of them. Eren must have finally found the time to hire additional guards.

As R-0 approached, they stepped in front of the door, blocking their way.

"Is Jeza available?" R-0 asked.

"No."

When R-0 had visited the council members with King Hadrian, requests were always met with an immediate yes. Even when they were busy, council members rearranged their schedules to accommodate the king. It was going to be more difficult alone.

"Do you know when she will be available?" R-0 asked.

"No."

R-0's fingers fidgeted at their side. There was no telling how long this would take. But what other options did they have?

The guard shifted in place, his hand moving ever so slightly toward the sword at his waist. "If there's nothing else, please move along."

R-0 wasn't sure if the movement was intentional or not, but the message was clear.

"Is there a problem here?" The door creaked open, and Jeza peeked through.

"No ma'am." Both guards straightened at her appearance.

"R-0." Jeza opened the door the rest of the way and checked the hallway. "Is King Hadrian with you?"

"No ma'am."

"What a surprise." A smile curled across her face. "To what do I owe the pleasure?"

R-0 cast a nervous glance at the guards, but neither spoke. "Could you answer a few questions?"

"Well . . ." Her fingernails clacked against the doorframe. "I have a few minutes before I need to head out." She stepped back into her room and gestured for R-0 to come in.

Jeza's room was almost as large as the king's. The back of the room was decorated like a normal bedroom. A raised platform separated it from the rest of the space, which was set up as a meeting area. From the wood carvings on her bed posts to the embroidered pictures on each square of her quilt, every piece of furniture was unique, likely commissioned from the crafters in her clan. Clan Doblin's crafters were unmatched. Unlike the rest of the palace, there were no managrid lights—Jeza wouldn't be able to activate and deactivate them. Instead, sconces lined the walls.

Jeza quickly shuffled to the back of the room. She pulled a curtain along a track embedded in the ceiling until it obscured the raised bedroom area from view.

"Over here." Jeza led R-0 to a glass table with a chair on either side.

R-0 tried to be as gentle as possible with their movements. Even the floor looked breakable. Under their feet, sparkling blue thread wove through the dark blues, blacks, and silvers of an ornate rug. Despite the jewels embedded in the chair, it didn't creak even when R-0 let their full weight rest on it, and R-0 relaxed slightly. The last thing they wanted to do was break something. That was unlikely to make Jeza cooperative.

On the far wall was a closed rolltop desk with a large shelving unit above it. It reminded R-0 of the wine storage they'd seen in the kitchen, but instead of alcohol, each compartment held a tightly rolled scroll. Books, mostly old, unlabeled tomes, lined the shelves on either side of the desk.

"You said you had questions." Jeza sat across from R-0.

"Do you remember Jasper?"

"Now that's a name I haven't heard in a very, very long time," Jeza said. "I remember him vividly. He was one of the greats, and his research was inspirational."

"You were familiar with his research?"

"Familiar enough. Queen Hadrian was obsessed, understandably so after seeing the power he gave not only to her, but to Sylas. I was apprehensive about him. I just wanted to make sure there wasn't a dragon hiding within the gemstones."

Although Jasper's notes referenced multiple gemstones, R-0 hadn't seen a single mention of a dragon. Jeza's concerns were unfounded.

"Did the other council members share your concerns?"

"Not until it was too late," Jeza said. "Jasper was one of the queen's most closely guarded secrets. She was afraid others would see his potential and steal him away from her."

"But after it was too late?"

"Even before we knew the constructs were tied to her bloodline, it was obvious that the constructs were the start of a power shift. No one could deny their effectiveness, but everyone had questions. The queen couldn't keep him a secret anymore. Almost everyone was concerned."

"Almost?"

"Robin was the most vocal. He was opposed to the constructs from the start—then they became a constant reminder of the throne he was promised but never received. But others were upset as well. Gretta. Aldrunn."

If anyone on the council was going to decommission all the constructs, it would be Robin. Jeza's comments just cemented that. But if he had the spell, why hadn't he used it? Unless he was still trying to get the components. A power source, a royal construct, and King Hadrian's blood were all required. As a council member, he could acquire a royal construct with ease, but accessing the managrid would require King Hadrian's approval, and R-0 wouldn't allow anyone to get King Hadrian's blood.

If Robin's coup was successful though... Robin would have unrestricted access to the managrid, and without the crown, King Hadrian would lose some of his protection.

"Layla was deliberate in her actions, always one step ahead," Jeza continued. "Despite the enemies she made by bringing the constructs in, she ensured she had just as many allies. I supported Layla from the beginning, and—our personal relationship aside—support from within my clan was unanimous. They were hired to create the bodies of the constructs, which brought in money and prestige. Clan Rhain was initially interested in the constructs' potential—it wasn't until Layla's betrayal became public that their support shifted so vehemently away from the Hadrians in favor of Robin.

"For many of the minor clans, the constructs were an opportunity for them to gain more power and standing. Clan Gerghain started focusing on technomancy. Before the constructs, they were hardly a footnote, and now they have the potential to vie for a seat on the council the next time one opens. Many of the minor clans thought that could be them if they handled the change properly.

"And Eclipse is most well-known as the goddess of duality, but she also represents change. Given their ideologies, it would have been difficult for Eclipse's church to oppose the constructs—impossible after the queen had the royal constructs trained in dual blades in homage to their goddess. And while the churches' representative on the council was supposed to represent all religions, it was never that simple in practice. Eclipse's support all but guaranteed the rest would fall in line."

R-0 looked at their swords. They'd seen from Jasper's notes just how carefully designed every part of them was. It shouldn't have been a surprise that their fighting style was the same. But R-0 had hardly thought about the gods. Were they paying homage to Eclipse every time they drew their blades?

"It's easy to forget this is your history as well," Jeza said. "You're so different than you were then."

"Those memories feel like they belong to a stranger."

"They might as well." Jeza chuckled. "So much has changed. But I imagine you weren't coming here for a history lesson. Has Jasper been located?"

Eren, Quiet, and Jorgunn all already knew about Jasper, but if King Hadrian hadn't told Jeza, R-0 would respect that.

"No." R-0 lied. Their answer was as short and stilted as Jeza's guards.

"What a shame." Jeza twisted one of her rings around her finger. "I would have loved to see him again. You know—" She walked to her desk and pulled scrolls from the highest, dustiest shelves. She gave them a quick look before returning them to their places.

R-0 sighed in relief. They weren't sure if they would—or should—continue lying to Jeza, and any change in conversation was welcome.

"When Jasper left the palace, his research was left behind." Jeza checked the next scroll, storing it in her desk instead of returning it to the shelf. She checked a few more places, then turned back to R-0. "I must have put it with Layla's things and brought it to Sylas. If you'd like to learn more, I'd ask to see those. In fact, I may request a copy myself. Now that the constructs are changing, we need to know as much as possible about them."

"Did Robin know about Jasper's research?"

"What's your concern with Robin?" Jeza asked.

A lie had been easier before. Yes and no were R-0's only options, and saying yes would have gone against King Hadrian's orders. But now, there was no simple dichotomy between their possible answers.

"Robin is a threat to the king." It was a truth, but it didn't reveal the full extent of R-0's investigation.

"If only more within the palace were as devoted as you."

R-0 tried not to let their impatience show, but their fingers fidgeted, their joints closing and releasing rapidly to burn off the excess energy from their flame.

"To answer your question, I'm sure Robin found out eventually." Jeza rolled her eyes. "When Sylas was made king, Robin was a man possessed. He did everything in his power to find a loophole or reverse things."

"Did anyone else know about Jasper's research?"

"It's certainly possible, but if they did, they didn't talk to me about it."

R-0 already knew Robin had motive, and now they'd confirmed he was in the position to have the knowledge as well.

"Have any of the council members talked to you about doing anything to the constructs?"

"I'm surprised King Hadrian didn't tell you this already."

"The king wasn't asked."

"Very well. Robin did talk to me in-depth about his plans for the constructs, but they were shortsighted at best and dangerous at worst. If he's made king, the reintegration efforts will end. The constructs in the palace will be systematically decommissioned and their parts used for scrap." Jeza practically spat the words, her disdain clear. "Faylviln will be given the choice to choose whether their armies are returned and decommissioned or if they will take responsibility for them. Robin will order the citizens to turn their constructs in."

This was the future of the constructs if King Hadrian lost his crown.

"You disagree with those plans," R-0 said.

"Vehemently."

It was surprising, considering what Jasper had written about Queen Hadrian and Jeza, but it aligned with her recent actions. "That's why you support King Hadrian instead of Robin."

"That's a drastic oversimplification." Jeza laughed. "Yes, I disagree with Robin's construct policy, but more than that, Layla was like a sister to me, and Sylas is the closest thing I have to a child of my own. I made a promise to support him, and I—"

"Councilwoman!" a guard called from the hallway. A knock followed.

"Is it time already?" Jeza pulled a pocket watch from her waistband and sighed. "Unfortunately, I do have to get going now. There were already not enough hours in the day before Robin's little stunt."

"Understood." R-0 stood, careful to push their chair back to its original position. "Your help is appreciated."

"Of course." Jeza led R-0 to the door. "I'm happy to help. If you have any other questions, feel free to return. Although I'm liable to be gone the rest of the day."

Jeza's guards fell in line behind her as she stalked off, leaving R-0 alone to determine their next actions.

Robin was a threat to King Hadrian and the constructs. That much was obvious. But was he also behind the abducted constructs? If he planned to decommission them all by becoming king, why would he need to steal the decommissioning spell—and why would he use a construct to do it? Ordering Ryder to capture Quiet at least made sense. If she hadn't been there to support King Hadrian, Robin would have already had a majority to take the throne.

There was still too much information missing—and still no proof.

Where could they get more information?

It hadn't even been an hour. If history repeated itself, King Hadrian would have many more hours of wining and dining the other council members before he relented, and by then, he'd probably need to sleep. R-0 was on their own. They thought back through all of King Hadrian's notes. There were reports from guards, technomancers, palace staff, and even council members. But one source was missing.

In all the information that had been gathered, there were no reports from the constructs themselves.

CHAPTER 34

In the dungeon, the passageways were no longer being used as a holding area. Instead, constructs were locked and secured in the cells. Some of them watched as R-0 passed, but more remained still, their expressions almost as lifeless as they'd been before the Awakening.

What crimes had they committed? Had the Awakening turned so many constructs into criminals?

R-0 wanted to stop at each cell—listen to every story and learn everything they could. Maybe they could help one of them. But getting them out of prison wouldn't matter if they were decommissioned with the missing spell or if Robin took the crown and ordered the same. R-0 had to prioritize, and right now that meant finding E-4.

They found E-4 in the same cell, but two constructs now shared the cell across from them. There was still no sign of the tral. It was strange—it had sounded like he'd been in the dungeon for years. His disheveled appearance indicated the same. Why had he been released?

E-4 lay on their cot with their eyes closed, their head resting on bare wood. In most situations, it was polite to knock before entering someone's room. But there was no door, no real separation. Still, they did their best to adhere to proper etiquette and knocked on the stone separating E-4's cell from the next one over.

E-4 startled, quickly leaping to their feet and backing into the corner. Their gears creaked, and their movements were stiff and awkward—forced compared to their normal patterns. Seeing R-0, E-4 relaxed slightly and stepped forward. "What are you doing here?"

"Information is required on Councilman Robin." R-0 chose each word carefully to answer E-4's question without revealing extraneous details. "Can you be of assistance?"

"Here I thought you might be bringing good news." E-4 slowly returned to their cot and sat. "What do you need to know?"

R-0 began rattling off questions—where did Councilman Robin go while E-4 was assigned to him? Did he have contact with any constructs not assigned to his service? Did E-4 see anything that resembled Jasper's notes? Had E-4 observed any interactions that seemed out of the ordinary?

E-4 answered in-depth, but none of the new information implicated Robin in any crimes or provided a lead on location of the taken constructs.

What if it wasn't Robin? He was their most likely suspect, but all they knew for certain was that someone was taking and killing the constructs, and someone within the council had ordered Ryder to capture R-0 and Quiet.

There wasn't enough time to investigate everyone.

"What about the other council members?" R-0 asked. "Did Robin have any interactions with them?"

"Countless," E-4 said. "But none that stand out. He was angry a lot, but it was no different than his behavior before the incident."

"The Awakening," R-0 corrected. Incident was an accurate description, but . . . whenever the organics used the word, it felt like a curse. There was an implication that it wasn't just an event or occurrence—it was an unfortunate one. Jasper's term viewed it as a gift. It focused on the new possibilities that had awakened rather than the uncertainty surrounding the change.

"He was working on some trade routes, trying to figure out who actually supported the constructs, and who supported King Hadrian."

Nothing R-0 couldn't piece together from Robin's attempted coup. Jeza and King Hadrian had said multiple times not to enact a plan until they were sure it would succeed. With the vote of no confidence being split three to three, it was likely Robin had attempted to do just that.

"Did he ever meet with Ryder?" R-0 gave E-4 a description of the scarred merfolk and his magical seaweed sword.

"No," E-4 said. "Sorry I can't help more."

"I saw him." Down the hall, another construct pressed themself against the bars of their cell. They were closer to Seraphine's size than E-4's or the other standard issue constructs. Compared to R-0, it was hard to believe they were both constructs. Where R-0's thick plates had sharp overlapping edges that created their armored hide, this construct's plates were thin and rounded at the corners.

R-0 had seen constructs like this before—often used for maneuvering in tight corridors or tunnels in mines or the managrid. But rarely were they equipped with voice capabilities.

"Who are you?" R-0 asked.

"My designation is D-341 U-18, but everyone always called me Dara."

"Always?"

"My team thought Dara was cuter. Short for diagnostics and repair assistant."

At least that name was sensible—describing their function with an aesthetic that matched their form. Organics frequently described their tiny organic children as cute, and R-0 could say the same thing about Dara.

"It's a pleasure to meet you, Dara." R-0 extended their hand for a handshake.

Dara didn't accept, remaining entirely still and following R-0's movements with only their eyes. "You're asking about that merfolk, right? Blue scales, scarred face, talks like he's swimming with his mouth?"

R-0 nodded.

"I was in the managrid tunnels trying to track the blackouts. I heard him talking to someone—a woman. I liked her at first. She was trying to convince him the constructs didn't need to be destroyed."

None of those details matched Robin. But could he be working with someone else? "That sounds like a positive thing."

Dara shook their head. "That's what I thought too. But then she started talking about our flames. Said her experiments had succeeded, and she'd been able to extract and channel them so she could cast new magic. *Powerful* magic."

R-0's flame coiled back into the farthest corners of their chest. That's how they'd found Beans—decommissioned and flameless. Was this the answer to what had happened to them? Had their flame been extracted?

"How did you know it was Ryder? Who was the woman? Where was she going?" R-0's mouth could hardly keep up with their questions.

"Well, I had the same questions. Tried to peek around and see who was there, but it was just Ryder standing at a dead end."

"Did he see you?" R-0 asked.

"I don't think so—I hid around the bend before he could spot me, and he went running off real quick."

"And the woman?"

"Gone. I have no idea where she went."

Now it wasn't just the palace intruder who'd disappeared into a dead end. Dara's mystery woman had as well. The technomancers had insisted that the palace walls were warded. Magic shouldn't impact the walls, and whoever was there should have had to pass Dara to leave. But what if someone found a way around it? What secrets had been hiding right in front of them this whole time?

Or . . . R-0 didn't want to consider it, but what if there was another explanation that didn't require bypassing the palace wards? What if the intruder and the mystery woman hadn't left, they just hadn't been visible? It didn't explain the intruder's magic ring, or R-0 tripping during their chase, but R-0 couldn't ignore how easily Quiet had disappeared. Not only was she capable of that type of magic, she was on the council and knew the tunnels better than anyone.

"Do you know where Ryder went?" R-0 asked.

"No. Never got the chance to figure it out either. A guard found me on my own and brought me to Robin. Didn't take a minute for him to send me down here."

"Why?" R-0 frowned.

"What'd you say the guards said again?" Dara leaned out.

A construct in the cell across the hall clanged their hands against the bars. "Trespassing and destruction of property."

"But . . . you were helping diagnose the blackouts."

"Zikes tried to fight for me, but Robin wouldn't listen. He said I wasn't supposed to be there alone—which was true—and he couldn't know I hadn't damaged anything. Which is only true if his brains are full of seaweed. If he'd spent two seconds looking at it and seen it was broken before and working now, it'd be obvious I hadn't."

"Zikes?" R-0 asked.

"One of the technomancers. We were working together, but he forgot a tool and went back to grab it. That's when all this happened."

At least with E-4, R-0 could understand the source of the misunderstanding. They had been in possession of a missing object. There was reasonable suspicion for foul play, and Robin was not always easily swayed with logic. But for Dara? There was no evidence. No reason for suspicion.

R-0 turned to the construct across the hall. "Why are you here?"

"Disobedience."

"What'd you do?"

"There was dust left in the corners of the closet."

"Did you refuse to clean it?" R-0 asked.

"No."

"Then . . . why?"

"Let me spell it out for you." Dara paced the length of her cell and pointed to other constructs as she walked. "We're all here for the same crime. We're constructs."

"Being a construct is not a crime."

"On a technicality, maybe you're right. But they're in charge, we're not. So they make up whatever they want to get rid of us. E-4 was the first, but they won't be the last."

"This is unfair," R-0 said. "It cannot continue."

"Zikes said the same thing. Raised hell, but it didn't make a difference."

"When King Hadrian finds out—"

E-4 slammed their hands onto the bars of the cell, and the whole thing rattled. "He'll do what? Say sorry and leave all of them down here, just like he did to me? Just like you did to me? Who do you think Zikes complained to? And what good did it do for Dara?"

"He's trying to help," R-0 said. *I'm trying to help.* Instead of saying what they wanted, they walked back over to E-4's cell. "When the investigation is successful, you will be freed."

"I wouldn't count on it." E-4 pushed away from the edge of the cell and plopped face-first on the thin mattress, their heavy body sinking in and leaving an indentation.

"It will happen," R-0 said. They wouldn't stop until the mystery was solved, and King Hadrian could free the constructs.

"Tonight?" Dara asked.

They'd spent hours investigating, and their only clue was a disappearing woman working with Ryder in the tunnels. "Tonight is unlikely."

"Then E-4 isn't getting out of here," Dara said. "They're being decommissioned at dawn."

CHAPTER 35

R-0 double-checked the records. Then triple-checked them. And just to be sure, they checked them a fourth and fifth time.

This wasn't the theoretical what-if that surrounded the other taken constructs. It wasn't an out of reach spell that R-0 had no idea how to stop. It was E-4, standing in the dungeon, so close that R-0 could touch them, but still slated to be decommissioned for a crime they didn't commit.

R-0 considered relocating them. It would be easy to break the bars of their cell or remove the locks. But where would they go? It would only be a matter of time before E-4 was discovered once more, and then actual crimes would be tied to them.

To both of them.

R-0 had thought the reintegration effort was a way for the constructs to prove their worth and continue their lives. For R-0, working with King Hadrian, it had been. They'd learned and experienced more about the world than they could have ever fathomed.

But the experience hadn't been the same for the other constructs. They were judged, scrutinized. What difference did it make that the Awakening had given them sentience if they weren't able to use it?

E-4's only chance was for R-0 to not only prove to the council the constructs weren't at fault for the taken constructs and the managrid blackouts, but also to prove E-4 and the others innocent of their fabricated crimes.

Getting rid of Robin would have served that purpose well—but the more they learned, the more it seemed Robin's plans were the ones he'd made public. There was no reason to believe he was kidnapping constructs in secret. He hardly wanted to look at them—so why would he order one to break into King Hadrian's room? And if Robin was responsible, who was the mystery woman working with Ryder?

Before leaving the dungeon, R-0 checked on the reintegration efforts of the women on the council. It was possible Ryder was talking to an intermediary working for Robin, but it was also possible the woman he was talking to was the same council member he received his orders to capture Quiet and R-0 from.

Gretta's results were similar to Robin's, although not as extreme. Half of the constructs in her care had been arrested. If King Hadrian lost his seat on the council, the minor clans could aim for his spot instead of hers. Not to mention, the imprisoned constructs reported her and Robin meeting more frequently than the other council members. Could they be working together?

R-0 moved on to Eren's records. She'd sent one construct to a high security section of the dungeon that R-0 couldn't access without her permission. Which would be impossible. How could R-0 get permission without revealing the purpose of their investigation and that Eren was a suspect?

Jeza had sent neat, simple reports, listing each of her constructs with their current status. Green checks covered the page—none were having issues, and all were performing adequately.

But Quiet's scrawling notes were the most detailed. She'd even included a repair log. It mostly showed routine repairs, but a few lines showed more extensive maintenance. R-0 didn't recognize the codes listed in the description column, but the number of parts and types of tools used, as well as the time spent, far exceeded routine procedures.

Could any of those tools extract a construct's flame?

Logically, R-0 knew the answer. They definitely could, and the technomancers listed were some of the most experienced in the palace. They were more than capable of taking a construct apart.

Still, they couldn't stop their feelings from meddling in their thoughts. It felt . . . wrong. Why would Quiet do that? But the longer R-0 thought about it, the more they realized they didn't understand many of Quiet's actions. Why did she travel without guards? How did she make it back to the palace when the roads were blocked?

It was a dead end. But what else could they do?

Gather information. Seek counsel. Search your heart.

They had already searched everywhere, but there was no one else they could ask. King Hadrian had his own problems, and Quiet was a suspect. R-0 was supposed to be helping advance the investigation on their own, not waiting for instructions. That would leave them back where they started, doing nothing the entire evening while the king, the constructs, and potentially all of Haiden were in danger.

And at dawn, E-4 would be decommissioned.

R-0 tried to search their heart. They sat quietly, listening to the flame crackling. When that didn't work, they unscrewed their chest plate and stared, searching for an answer in the dancing golden wisps of heat.

But both attempts led to nothing. Their flame didn't have any more answers than they did. And maybe it never would. Perhaps Jasper was wrong to think a flame functioned like a heart.

R-0 circled back to the first step, racking their brain for anywhere else they could gather information. They'd researched everything they could on the council members, the intruder, and the taken constructs. But . . . what if they'd been approaching it the wrong way?

The intruder had disappeared somewhere within the palace, and the mystery woman had as well. If R-0 could discover where they'd gone, maybe they could find the taken constructs or the proof they needed.

R-0 stopped by the palace library. Compared to the many grand rooms in the palace, the library seemed small, but the space was used efficiently. The room was two stories tall, and its shelves spanned from floor to ceiling. The shelves were tucked against each other, leaving no aisles to walk between them or browse their contents. It was an unconventional arrangement, and there was no easy way to access anything. R-0 hardly had a chance to wonder how they were supposed to search before the librarian scurried over. R-0 had prepared answers for when she asked why they were here alone, but she never asked, focusing instead on what information R-0 needed and how she could help.

The librarian pressed her hands against a podium in front of the shelves, and the bright light of the managrid sparked beneath her palms. Blue veins crawled through the wood until the whole room was lit in an overwhelming glow. The shelves shifted, reminiscent to R-0's plates as they changed forms. The library seemed alive as the structures expanded outward, shelves moving from one unit to another and changing elevation.

The librarian kept her eyes closed in concentration until the room settled and the managrid's magic faded. Then, she scurried down the one available aisle, shoving book after book into R-0's arms until they held a towering stack on any and every subject they thought might be helpful. There was no chance R-0 could read them all in one night, but they were too in awe of the magic they'd witnessed to resist.

After R-0 spent far too many ticks confused about when the world exploded and how the books fit into the histories they knew, the librarian separated the books into fiction and non-fiction, then suggested they start with a few books about the constructs, one with details on Haiden's legislation, and a large map of the palace. The fiction books were nothing but lies that told of heroes who never existed slaying monsters that never threatened anyone. It was confusing. Who were they lying to? What was the purpose of their words? R-0 ignored the confusing stack of fiction and skimmed through the non-fiction books.

The laws didn't help them. Nothing prohibited what was happening to the constructs, and they didn't have enough evidence to convict Robin of any crimes.

They moved on to the books that mentioned the constructs. Jasper was only mentioned once. Everywhere it was written that the constructs were "Clan Hadrian's greatest invention," the "prized creation of the royal family," a "revolutionary success from Graywal's finest." Jasper's name was a blip in footnotes, hand-written and added later. It had been just over a decade and was already so faded R-0 could barely read it. Even the books would forget about Jasper.

Like R-0 had.

Could Jasper's lab be what R-0 was looking for? Based on his notes, the lab had to be located somewhere in the palace. Queen Hadrian had visited daily, sometimes multiple times a day, and he mentioned she wanted to keep him close. Despite that, few council members had known of him until after his experiments had succeeded.

None of the maps showed a lab. R-0 double-checked for unlabeled sections or anything that didn't match its surroundings, but the only rooms large enough to house all of Jasper's equipment were the council chambers, the ballroom, and the dining hall—and R-0 had seen those rooms. The librarian helped them pull the original palace blueprints, but the results were the same. There was no place for Jasper's lab. If it was here—and R-0 was confident it was—it was hidden. And if anyone could tell R-0 where it was, it was Jasper.

It didn't take long for R-0 to identify the vibration in their flame: excitement. Visiting Jasper could serve several purposes. He could provide counsel, not only regarding his lab, but also on the mass decommissioning spell and the council members.

R-0 had never left the palace on their own before, but waiting until after the king's meetings would waste too much time—time the constructs might not have.

They flashed through memories of their conversation with the king, focusing on every single word. If anyone asked, they were instructed to say they were following the king's orders.

R-0 was anyone.

"Who ordered the investigation to continue outside the palace?" R-0 asked themself. They paused, waiting a moment, then just as the king had commanded, they responded. "The king ordered it."

When R-0 had met Jasper, he'd done more than give them counsel. He'd repaired them. And R-0 wasn't the only construct Jasper had helped. He and Winter were repairing another construct, and he'd mentioned M-118. Jasper hadn't told R-0 all the details but had said they were safe.

Thinking of all the constructs in the prison cells, at risk of being decommissioned, and the constructs working in the reintegration efforts that were one bad decision away from the same fate, being safe was a luxury for most of the constructs. How many of them would do anything to swap places with M-118, knowing nothing other than they were safe?

E-4 would. Anything was better than the future they were guaranteed in the dungeon.

R-0 paused. Why couldn't R-0 bring E-4 to Jasper?

Why couldn't Jasper keep E-4 safe as well?

King Hadrian had said time and time again there was nothing *he* could do to help E-4. But those same constraints didn't apply to R-0. They had just lacked the means. Tonight . . . they were alone. Unsupervised. If E-4 was being decommissioned, they'd first be moved into a solitary holding cell. R-0 had the guard rotations and patterns committed to memory.

They could do something.

They could help.

Despite the what-ifs circling through their mind and all the things that could go wrong buzzing as constant as their ticking gears, those two thoughts kept the others at bay. The risk didn't matter—only the outcome. They quickly cleaned up their library table, taking the time to return the books to the librarian and thank her before leaving.

R-0 could save E-4.

CHAPTER 36

"Are you sure this is a good idea?" E-4 asked.

"No."

E-4's face fell, and their gears chittered in a nervous whir.

R-0 could tell it wasn't the answer they'd been hoping for, but it was the truth. Since the Awakening, they no longer lived in a world of black and white where instructions were simple and orders were followed without a thought. "Little is certain in this very uncertain world."

That seemed to comfort E-4 some, and their nervous chittering subsided.

R-0 stopped E-4 before they could take another step, pulling them into a side room while a pair of guards walked past. Eventually someone would notice the empty cell where E-4 should have been, but so far, R-0 had evaded detection. Perhaps R-0 should speak with Eren about upgrading her guard rotations. The current set-up was too easy to bypass if someone had the routes and schedules memorized. Although given the current corruption within the council, perhaps Eren was the wrong person to speak with regarding the king's safety.

"Maybe we should go back," E-4 said.

"You would like to return to your cell?"

"N-no. I don't think so."

"Then you should continue walking." R-0 ushered E-4 forward. They couldn't leave through the main entrance without encountering the guards. While R-0 could simply claim to be following the king's orders, they didn't want E-4's disappearance to cause him any trouble.

But there were other ways out of the palace. King Hadrian had taught R-0 that. They had requisitioned rope from one of the storage rooms, so any window on the upper floor would suffice.

"But . . . what's going to happen to me?"

"That is not known."

"Will I be safe?"

"That is also unknown. But if you remain in the dungeon, you are guaranteed to be decommissioned."

"I've never left the palace," E-4 said. "What will I do out there?"

R-0 couldn't answer that question. What would they do without the king—without their duty to protect him? They'd hardly managed a single night without his orders.

"Come on." R-0 led them into an empty guest chamber and opened a window. After they repelled down, R-0 threw the rope back into the room. They wouldn't leave that vulnerability unsecured twice and could retrieve the rope when they returned. Alone, they could return through the front gates. R-0 took the same path King Hadrian had, but this time they were leading instead of following.

"Will you get into trouble?" E-4 asked.

R-0 hesitated. Aiding and abetting a prisoner could result in a death sentence—or in their case, being decommissioned in E-4's place. Countless constructs had been imprisoned for far less. They tried not to think about that possibility. If they claimed to be following the king's orders, the king would be the one to suffer instead, so they couldn't use that as a defense.

They had been so focused on resolving E-4's predicament, they hadn't considered what this might mean for them.

"Perhaps," R-0 said. They tapped at their side, each impact a reminder to focus on their escape—*not* on what might happen if they were caught.

"What if they decommission you instead?"

They had almost eliminated the thought from their mind, but E-4's words brought it back. Their gears slowed, and their plates chilled. R-0 still didn't entirely understand decommissioning. They only barely understood living, and death was an enigma even among organics who'd had a lifetime to consider it.

But the thought of doing nothing, of returning to the king's room and awaiting orders while E-4 suffered and they could do something to stop it . . . that felt worse.

"If no one is aware of a crime, then there will not be a punishment."

"You'll keep it a secret?"

"Yes. Only King Hadrian will know."

"What if he decommissions you?"

Smoke blew from R-0's mouth, and their joints grated in quick chiming spurts as amusement spread from their flame to their gears. They had . . . laughed. It was instinctual, and R-0 wasn't sure if they could replicate it. "Constructs do not usually tell jokes."

"I'm not joking." E-4 frowned. "I'm worried about you."

R-0 ducked behind the rock at the edge of the wall. Once the next patrol traveled through, they could scale the wall. "King Hadrian would never hurt the constructs."

"He left me to be decommissioned. And I'm not the only one in the dungeon. And what about the others left in storage? They're treated worse than prisoners, and he does nothing. Does that not hurt us?"

"He's trying to help."

"Is he? He could free us all right now. One order from him and the guards would have no choice. But why would he?" E-4's voice rose as they spoke.

If only it were that simple. But more than anyone else R-0 had encountered, King Hadrian lived in a world full of gray situations where a binary, black-and-white view failed. There were too many moving parts, and some choices were out of reach.

"I've heard what people around the palace say about us. We were more valuable to them before. Our obedience was worth more than our sentience. And there are even rumors that Faylviln has demanded that the constructs be reverted to how we were before. So why would the king do anything other than try to control us and get things back to the status quo?"

A patrol came into view around the corner, facing R-0 and E-4's hiding spot. The distance was great enough that it was unlikely the guards could hear them, but R-0 didn't want to risk it. Besides, they didn't have an answer for E-4.

"Silence, please."

"Apologies," E-4 whispered.

R-0 ducked behind the wall, counting silently in their head. After the guards had ample time to pass, R-0 counted to twenty once more just to be safe, then slowly peeked their head out.

"All clear."

The walk through the city continued in silence until R-0 stopped outside of the hattery. "Here we are."

"A hattery?"

"There are no hats," R-0 said. "It's a deception."

"And you're sure the people here will help? Jasper, you said his name was?"

"He's helped others." R-0 walked up the steps and knocked on the recently repaired door. "Hopefully, he'll do the same for you."

"R-0! You came back!" Winter opened the door, cheerfully ushering them inside. Their greeting was dramatically more welcoming when the exchange didn't begin with destruction of property. "And you brought a friend."

R-0 tilted their head at E-4. Perhaps they had not truly learned the meaning of friendship. They would have considered E-4 an acquaintance, but E-4 nodded at Winter's words.

"Their designation is E-4," R-0 explained, then turned to E-4. "And theirs is Winter."

"Winter?" E-4 frowned. "What does it stand for?"

Winter carefully engaged each lock on the door, returning the chains to the proper positions. Since R-0's last visit, a large metal sheet had been added to reinforce the wood. "Just Winter."

"That's a strange designation," E-4 said.

"My original designation was W-4." Winter opened the trapdoor and waited for the two of them to climb down before following. "But that wasn't me, you know?"

At the bottom, E-4 whispered to R-0, "Do you know what they mean?"

R-0 shook their head. "No."

"I can hear you." Winter's words slid effortlessly into a laugh as their gears clicked together. "W-4 was the designation the technomancers gave to a suit of metal they created. But that's not me anymore. I'm someone different, and I changed my name to match that."

R-0 had met other constructs that didn't go by their designations—JJ, Beans, Dara. But they were given names by the organics who cared for them. More specifically, the first two were given by children, who frequently ignored the rules of language and called things whatever they wanted to. Crates were boats, constructs had nicknames, and logic was abandoned for giggles. None of the constructs had named themselves.

"Jasper's not in his lab right now, so it'll be a bit of a walk," Winter said. "Normally he'd be sleeping at this time, but we've had a bit of a hectic day, night, existence lately." They shrugged and opened the door on the far side of the room—not the one that led to the room full of corpses. "Follow me."

Through the door, a dirt tunnel extended into the dark. Winter lit a torch, creating an aura of light that danced out from them. Even with the light, R-0 couldn't see an end to the pathway. "Where does it lead?"

"Nowhere you would know." Winter set a quick pace. "The lab quickly got too crowded, so Jasper had to expand."

"Crowded how?" E-4 asked.

Winter smiled. "You're not the first construct who has come to us for safety."

"There's more of us?" E-4 stopped in the middle of the tunnel.

"You'll make seventeen."

"And they aren't prisoners?"

"No."

"Who gives them orders?"

"No one." Winter took E-4's hand and pulled them forward. "If you stay with us, you make your own orders."

"How does it work? What do you do? Why—"

"Patience, patience." Winter laughed again, interrupting E-4. "It'll be easier to show you."

The three returned to silence, the only noise caused by their heavy footsteps stirring up tiny clouds of dust.

Winter had . . . named themself? As much as it had initially surprised R-0, the more they considered it, the more sensible it seemed. R-0 had designated Councilwoman Riley as Quiet within their own mind. Why couldn't they do the same with their own designation?

R-0.

They weren't like Councilwoman Riley, with a given name that was nonsensical in the context of who she was. R-0's name was fitting. R stood for their class—a royal construct, designed for service to the king himself. Zero stood for their position within the unit—they were the first. R-0 was the most accurate designation they could have. Even if they were different after the Awakening, they were still R-0.

What else could they be called?

"Why did you choose Winter as your new designation?" R-0 asked.

"Because I love it."

"The name?"

"The season." Winter smiled. "The quiet on the streets. People coming together to gather around the hearth." Their eyes closed, and they held their hands up, twirling down the hallway. "Little droplets of cold falling from the skies and spiraling around us—you can't tell me that isn't magic."

As Winter talked, the entire tunnel grew warmer from the heat of their flame. R-0 could see it, illuminating their insides and peeking out from the cracks. Their words were easy and effortless, and their enthusiasm infectious. R-0's own flame strengthened as the warmth reached it, warming R-0 from head to toe.

Was there anything R-0 loved that much?

R-0 flickered through their memories, from before and after the Awakening, searching for anything that matched Winter's reaction. They loved their job—protecting the king. But not just him . . . protecting E-4 and Quiet was similar. Even helping the staff after a long day made their flame grow hot. But still, how they felt reflecting on those memories was nothing like Winter's explanation of winter.

Even if they enjoyed it, it wasn't who they were.

They were R-0.

"How do you rename yourself?" E-4 asked.

"Just do it. You introduce yourself. You decide what you're called. It's that simple."

"What if I choose wrong?"

"Then change it again. Maybe when spring comes I'll realize winter is overrated." Winter shrugged. "Jasper says we're all still learning who we are, and if we're like the organics, we always will be."

At the end of the hallway, another door came into view, identical to the one they'd entered in the basement. Winter knocked, alternating quick raps with momentary pauses in a long, complicated pattern.

"I'm not sure I understand," E-4 said.

A slit in the door opened, and two metallic eyes stared through. As quickly as it opened, it closed again. Then, metal slid against metal, and chains jingled before the door clicked.

"I don't understand it entirely either." Winter placed their hand on the doorknob. "But the way I see it, right, wrong, it doesn't matter. What matters is it's mine." They pushed the door open. "Welcome to Zealot."

CHAPTER 37

R-0 stepped into a large cavern with towering walls and a high ceiling. In front of them, a pathway traveled straight for a short distance then split into perpendicular paths. Lines had been drawn in the dirt, separating the area into sections. Some of those lines were accompanied by swatches of fabric hanging from the ceiling like walls, obscuring the area from view.

Winter stepped through first. The entrance was reminiscent of the palace guard posts. A construct stood well-armed and alert by a chair and a small desk. Their eyes matched the metallic eyes that had stared at them through the slit.

"Welcome home, Winter."

"Thanks, T-5. You know where Jasper is?"

"Sector 4."

Winter nodded and turned right. "We're not sure if we're going to stay here or not, so for now, we just use these"—they dragged their foot along the side of the path to emphasize a deep line in the dirt—"to keep things organized. We've been talking about putting up walls and making real rooms, but it doesn't make sense if we have to leave tomorrow."

"Why would you have to leave?" R-0 asked.

"Well, to start with, there were four of us in the beginning. If we keep growing at this pace, there's not enough space."

"And to end with?"

"This is definitely illegal. King Hadrian seems content to let us continue for now, but there's no guarantee that will last."

According to the book R-0 had just read, at least four different laws were currently in contention.

E-4 nudged R-0's side. "I'm not the only one worried about him."

"King Hadrian won't hurt the constructs."

"But would he ask us to join the reintegration efforts in the castle?" Winter asked. "Would he request we return to our original owners?"

Both courses of action seemed . . . logical. It would be a perfectly reasonable request for King Hadrian to make, and one that any citizen would be expected to follow. But the way Winter spoke about it made it seem like it wasn't a favorable thing. "Perhaps."

"Then we can't count on him. Free will isn't something that we can compromise on. We can't meet in the middle. Jasper said they'd call us zealots with that sort of attitude."

"That's what you called this place," R-0 said. "Zealot."

"If they're going to call us that no matter what, we might as well help them be accurate." Winter chuckled. "But Jasper is optimistic, says Sylas has his mother's heart. From everything I've heard, I figured she was heartless, but Jasper says it like it's a good thing."

"She wasn't heartless." It was impossible for organics to survive without their hearts.

"I guess we'll see." Winter shrugged, stopping in front of a section where Jasper worked on a construct's chest. He sat between two tables, tools scattered around him. His hair was as much of a mess as his workspace, graying flyaways sticking out from under his goggles at all angles. Despite the late hour, he was alert, no signs of restlessness marring his concentration. "Jasper!"

"Ah, Winter can you—" Jasper looked over his shoulder, and his smile grew as wide as his eyes. "R-0, what a surprise! If you know what a spinner is, grab me one from that table if you don't mind."

R-0 searched the table and brought the tool over. Jasper held a construct's chassis in place with one hand, his other balancing an arm attached by only a few fraying wires. The construct's leg kicked out periodically, and Jasper steadied a wooden board between them with his feet. "Thank you. Now if you could tighten those bolts into the floor. Just pull the trigger after you latch on."

R-0 knelt, placing the tool over the bolts along the edge of the piece of wood. They pulled the trigger and magic jolted through the tool and their hands as the bolt spiraled into the floor.

"Thank you." Some of the strain disappeared from Jasper's face. With the second bolt secured in place, he pulled his legs away and relaxed his lower body. "Much better."

"Apologies," the construct said.

"It's not your fault." Jasper looked between them and R-0. "Gear is caught in their leg, causing the spasms. Figured I'd take a look once I got them put back together, but it was driving me mad."

"You're already mad," Winter said.

"The difference between madness and genius is a matter of perspective. I thought you would see the genius."

Winter stepped between Jasper and the construct. "Doesn't mean I'm blind to the madness." They snatched the screwdriver from Jasper's hand and snapped a pair of goggles against their face plates. "I can handle this."

"Thank you, Winter." Jasper stepped into the path. "It's good to see you again, R-0. To what do we owe the pleasure?"

R-0 wasn't sure what to expect next. Bringing E-4 here was step one, but . . . what would happen now? "Assistance is required."

E-4 scuffed their foot against the ground, and Jasper immediately turned his attention to them. "Forgive my rudeness, we didn't get the chance to introduce ourselves yet, did we? I'm Jasper." He extended his hand to E-4.

"I'm . . ." E-4 paused.

"It's okay," R-0 said. "It is safe to talk to him."

"I'm . . . Clay."

R-0 frowned. That wasn't E-4's designation. Like Winter, they had renamed themself. Did they love the clay surrounding them down here that much?

"Clay is from the palace." The name caught awkwardly in their gears at first, but it was still more natural than calling

King Hadrian by his first name. R-0 quickly adjusted. "Clay was sentenced to be decommissioned for a crime they didn't commit, so they needed somewhere safe to stay."

"Is that so?" Jasper tilted his head to the side. "Clay, is this true? Are you innocent?"

"Yes sir. I can explain—"

"No." Jasper held up his hand. "That won't be necessary. If you tell me you're innocent, I'll trust you unless you give me a reason not to. I'll get you settled in temporarily, and then we can work on getting you a more permanent arrangement. Come on."

Jasper led them toward an empty section in the back. It mimicked an organic's room, with an earthen mound shaped like a bed in the corner and a small desk and chair beside it.

"We weren't expecting you, so unfortunately it isn't much, but on our next trip to the surface, we can get you some more items." Jasper pointed to a marking on the wall. "This is Sector 25. We label each room this way. Hopefully, it can help you find your way around quickly enough."

"This is . . . for me?" Clay tentatively stepped into the space.

"At least, for now," Jasper said. "Everything is changing so rapidly, it's impossible to know what tomorrow holds. But we'll do our best to keep this sector just for you."

Clay paced along the edges of the lines, reaching their hand through the empty air into the pathway and neighboring spaces. It was easily twice the size of their dungeon cell, and nothing caged them in.

"And I'm allowed to leave?"

"Of course." Jasper nodded. "There's not much to see down here, but there's a section set up for cards and games, and then some practical areas as well, like the technomancy sector you found me in. I'll have T-5 come get you for a tour in just a bit. I'd do it myself, but I'm sure R-0 needs to be getting back to the palace."

R-0 nodded. "As soon as possible."

Jasper rubbed his hands together. "Then regretfully, we are in a bit of a hurry. Are there any other questions you have for me, Clay?"

"What will be required of me to earn all of this?" Clay asked.

"We'll figure that out after you get settled," Jasper said. "I'm sure you have some skills you could use to help around here."

"What if I don't?"

"Your position here is not reliant on your ability to produce or what you can do. You are here, you are you, and that is enough. The rest is all just silly little details that can be worked out."

Clay slowly and cautiously sat on their makeshift bed. "I don't know what to say."

"That's okay." Jasper chuckled. "We all feel that way sometimes. I'll come back to check on you later, alright?"

Clay nodded and lay back on the bed, staring at the dirt ceiling.

As Jasper led R-0 back through the winding maze of sections, R-0 stared at the clay walls. No matter how long they looked, or what angle they looked at the walls, it was just dirt. Their flame didn't stir, and their thoughts remained steady. There was nothing to see, nothing to love.

But Clay had seen something in these walls that R-0 didn't.

"You did a good thing bringing Clay here." Jasper stopped in front of Sector 6, an area with a table in the center and a few chairs gathered around it.

"Their situation was unfair."

"As many things in this world are." Jasper pulled out a chair for R-0 before sitting in one across the table. "Now, what did you want to talk about?"

"To find answers, you said to ask the people you trust for counsel."

"That's true."

"Your counsel is required to proceed."

"I believe I also said to search your heart."

"You said the heart would give answers, but flames do not speak."

"Does it not speak, or are you not listening?"

R-0 quieted, straining to hear once more but only heard the same low crackle.

"Why did you bring Clay here?" Jasper asked.

"Leaving them felt wrong."

"And that"—Jasper excitedly pointed at R-0's chest—"that was your flame speaking."

R-0 frowned. They hadn't heard their flame say a single word, and they had been listening carefully for any noises. The walk here had led them through quiet, late-night streets. How could they have missed it?

"But I know you didn't come here for my lectures or sentiments. Tell me what brings you here, and I will do my best to provide the counsel you need."

R-0 started at the beginning, explaining their investigation with King Hadrian and progressing into their discovery that a council member was involved with Ryder.

When R-0 reached the part about the mass decommissioning spell, Jasper chuckled. "Took Sylas long enough to notice it was gone. Looks like I made the right decision taking it."

"You stole it?"

"By a technicality, no. It was Winter who broke into King Hadrian's room. But what matters is that the spell is safe. You don't have to worry about it."

"Winter?" R-0 frowned. They hadn't even considered them a suspect. But . . . the details aligned. They were the right size, and Winter showed prowess in a variety of skills that most standard constructs wouldn't have.

"I'd have gone myself, but Winter wouldn't accept no for an answer. In hindsight, I'm glad. It sounds like you were close to apprehending them, and this might have all gone very differently. I'm sure I couldn't have pulled off the escape they did."

"It is good that they escaped."

"I'm glad we agree."

R-0 had been hoping Jasper could give them a lead, but this was even better. If the spell was still with him, R-0 could return it to King Hadrian. "Where is the spell now?"

"It's safe, and that's all anyone needs to know. The fewer people who are aware of it, the better. I recommend you tell King Hadrian the same. Outside of anyone he's told or who've seen my notes, the only people still alive who know of that spell are myself, Winter, and Jeza."

"King Hadrian wanted the spell returned."

"Then perhaps he should visit himself and request it." Jasper smiled, but his movements were slow and rigid. "We don't want to transport something like that without taking the proper precautions. For now, it's safe. That's what matters, right?"

R-0 nodded. King Hadrian had been worried it would fall into the wrong hands, but it would be safe with Jasper. Once they made a better plan, they knew where to find it.

"One mystery solved." R-0 listened to their flame, but it kept its same whir. Perhaps the final step was unnecessary when their problem was already resolved.

R-0 continued their story, ending with what Dara had seen and overheard in the managrid tunnels. "Whatever is happening, it seems to be hidden within the palace itself," R-0 said. "How did Winter escape?"

Jasper pulled a ring from his apron pocket that perfectly matched the one the intruder—Winter—had worn. The amethyst sparkled under the torchlight as he turned the silver band over in his fingers. "One of the earliest magic items I crafted. You are correct about my lab. It is in the palace, and this is how I accessed it."

R-0's excitement rose. They had been right. Jasper's lab was hidden. And for the first time since they started investigating, they felt like they were close to finding the answers they—and all of the constructs—needed. "Where is your lab? How do you access it?"

"There's a few entry points, but the easiest one is in the managrid tunnels." Jasper gave more detailed directions, and the entrance aligned with the tunnel Dara had told them about. He held up the ring. "This ring draws on the user's intent to manipulate stone and dirt. If used in the right place, it'll reveal the lab's entrance."

"But the technomancers said the palace walls were warded against magic."

"Who do you think made those wards?" Jasper laughed.

"You?"

Jasper nodded.

"If you could bypass the wards, couldn't others do the same?"

"It's unlikely. Some of the best and brightest minds in the world have been trying for over a decade to recreate the spellwork I used to create the constructs without success. And a lot more resources are being put toward that than analyzing the palace wards."

R-0 frowned. If no one else could bypass the wards, then how could Ryder's mystery companion leave the tunnel without Dara seeing her? If she hadn't escaped through the dead-end wall as Winter had, then . . . had she turned invisible? What other explanation was there for what Dara saw?

"Has Winter visited the palace since they stole the spell?"

"No, and if Winter had met Ryder, I highly doubt the situation would have ended peacefully." Jasper's face fell. "But this ring is not one of a kind."

"Where are the others?"

"Layla had one. If Sylas doesn't have it, there's no telling who does."

"Investigating the lab could reveal the culprit," R-0 said. "Is there another way to access it?"

"Take this." Jasper pressed his ring into R-0's palm. "If you're right, then King Hadrian needs to be made aware of what's going on. And if he won't do anything about it, return to me and we will."

"What can you do that King Hadrian can't?"

"There's little I could do that he can't." Jasper stood from his seat. "But there's a lot I am willing to do that he won't."

R-0 understood that—it was the reason they'd brought Clay here.

R-0 unscrewed their arm and dropped the ring inside their internal compartment. It was far too small to fit over any of their fingers, but it would be safe inside them. It also meant that no one would see it and have a reason to question R-0 before they could consult with the king. "Thank you, Jasper."

"If you can put a stop to this, then I'll be the one thanking you." Jasper rested their hand on R-0's arm, and a spark of warmth traveled through them. "Every day we find more and more discarded bodies. Whatever they're doing, it's escalating."

Jasper's words brought back memories of Beans and the graveyard of constructs and parts surrounding them. Somehow, the wrongfully imprisoned constructs weren't even in the worst position. Any warmth from Jasper's touch dissipated to a chill.

R-0 wanted to tell Jasper that they'd do it—they'd find a way to stop whoever it was and save both the taken and imprisoned constructs. But as they stood, the only sounds they made were from the ticking of gears and the wooden chair scraping against the dirt floor.

"If you're investigating the council, I should let you know that Riley visited me after you were last here. Alone. She asked many questions about the constructs, and I obliged her with answers."

"What did she want to know?"

"Everything I could tell her and more I could not. Anything to help understand what was going on. She was disappointed to learn that I didn't have all the answers."

"Why?"

"Mysteries require solving. Answers are actionable."

"What action did she want to take?"

"The right one." Jasper winked. "I gave her information, but no one except her will know what answers she found in her heart."

Quiet's heart was more talkative than R-0's flame. How could she hear the answers inside her chest when R-0 couldn't? Were they doing something wrong?

"Why are you sharing this?"

"Because you asked me to help the constructs, and I will, but I am one man, and the city is large. You and your people need allies."

"She is a friend."

"And she has the potential to be far more than that."

R-0 hadn't thought about what Quiet could do for the constructs, but Jasper's words were heavy, worming their way through R-0's head like a loose gear clicking out of sync.

What could Quiet do for the constructs? They remembered her words from the first council meeting after the Awakening.

"When we asked, they answered," R-0 said. "When they ask, what shall we do?"

"What do you mean?" Jasper asked.

"It's something Councilwoman Riley said to the other council members." At the time, R-0 had been overwhelmed by all their new thoughts and feelings and distracted by Robin and the potential threat he posed to King Hadrian. R-0 hadn't had a chance to reflect on what she said, but the words echoed in their mind now.

"And what did they say?"

"They did not react well."

"I can't imagine they did."

R-0 waited for Jasper to say more, but silence filled the space between them. If there was nothing else R-0 could learn here, they needed to return to the palace.

"Your assistance is appreciated," R-0 said

"Be careful out there," Jasper said. "It's not safe on the street for constructs."

R-0 thought about King Hadrian needing their protection. Constructs going missing. Jasper, hiding in a hattery basement. "Is it safe for anyone?"

R-0 barely made it out of the sector before Jasper called out to them.

"R-0?"

They paused. "Yes?"

"Don't forget Riley's words or the response from the council. And the next time they ask something of you, remember what they would say if you asked something of them."

R-0 would not forget. "Then what?"

"Then tread carefully. If they would turn against their own king, what do you think they would do to you?"

CHAPTER 38

Before R-0 left Zealot, they returned to Sector 25 to say goodbye to Clay. They sat at the desk, their back to the walkway. As they heard R-0's approach, they swiveled in their chair. This time, they didn't startle or frown.

Instead, Clay waved. "Can you believe this is all mine?"

"Yes." There was no reason not to believe it, and Jasper had already confirmed it.

"When you told me there was a place I would be safe, it sounded too good to be true. I still don't understand how it's possible."

"Jasper wants to help the constructs. What was happening at the palace was unfair."

"Stay with me then." Clay grabbed R-0's hands in theirs. "I'm sorry I overstepped earlier, but you can't deny it's dangerous there. Even more dangerous now that you helped me."

"It's . . . complicated."

"Is it?" Clay asked. "I don't know what you've seen, but you know what I've seen. Where I've been."

"What about the other constructs?" R-0 asked. Clay was the only one who'd been scheduled for decommissioning, but if things continued, the others would quickly follow.

"You're a criminal now. What's stopping you from being next?" Clay asked. "It's safer here. Why not stay?"

"King Hadrian must be protected."

"But who's going to protect you, R-0?" Clay shook their head. "King Hadrian will be fine. He has a barracks full of guards. It doesn't have to be you. Stay here. Protect yourself."

R-0 tried to imagine it, but they couldn't fathom what even tomorrow would look like if they didn't return to the palace. There were few certain things in this world, but protecting King Hadrian was one of them. Even without the magic running through their body, forcing the directive to echo through them and control their actions, it felt right.

When they were protecting the king, their flame was at peace, and the world seemed just a little bit simpler.

There was nothing they would rather do. There was nowhere they would rather be. But words were too shallow to help Clay understand the feeling inside of them, and they couldn't force Clay to feel it as well.

So they lifted their hand in a small wave, mirroring Clay's earlier gesture. "It's time to go. Goodbye, Clay."

"Goodbye, R-0," Clay said. "I hope I'll see you again."

Their walk back to the palace was uneventful, and they arrived at King Hadrian's room just as the sun peeked through the window at the end of the hall. Its morning rays reflected off R-0, warming their plates. Maybe this was why stray cats would sometimes stop, close their eyes, and lie down where the sun hit the ground. Something about the warmth made R-0 want to curl up right where they stood.

But the urgency of their missions and King Hadrian's warnings about not drawing attention to themself made them hesitate. They'd never seen a construct bask in the sun before. The guards stationed at King Hadrian's door likely hadn't either. It would definitely draw unwanted attention.

The guards focused on R-0. They were growing used to the additional scrutiny their presence received. Whether walking the streets of the city or here in the palace, it was the same judgmental silence.

"King Hadrian was asking for you." The older guard gestured to the door. "Would you like me to let him know you're here?"

"Yes sir." R-0 nodded, then added, "Thank you."

The more they rehearsed their expected lines, the easier the pleasantries became. There was no reason to thank the guard. He had a job to perform. He was performing it. Gratitude was strange and did nothing but complicate the otherwise simple interaction. But it was an easy adjustment for R-0 to add it to their dialogue, and the guard seemed pleased with their words. His face relaxed into a smile as he knocked on King Hadrian's door.

"King Hadrian, R-0 has returned."

The lock on the door clicked. "Send them in!"

King Hadrian was a mess. His hair was unkempt, and the covers were thrown off his bed and wadded in the corner. The desk had been cleared, its usual contents scattered on the floor next to him. On the desk lay a single letter, a bright red envelope crumpled into a ball beside it, and gold wax shavings littering the desk beneath it. R-0 could just make out the corner of Faylviln's crest—the godking framed by trees. King Hadrian's breakfast remained untouched on its tray.

"Where have you been?" King Hadrian asked. "I had guards searching for you, but no one could find you."

"Jasper's hattery."

"You left the palace?" King Hadrian's eyes widened. He dropped the letter on his desk and stood up. He stepped closer to R-0, his head level with their chest. "Are you okay?"

"Yes, Sylas." Even after saying it a few times, R-0 couldn't stop their gears from gritting against the king's name as they spoke.

"I received news E-4 was missing. Someone broke the lock off their holding cell, and four other constructs from the storage rooms were gone as well. When I couldn't find you . . ." King Hadrian trailed off, and R-0 waited for him to continue. "I was worried they'd got you too."

R-0's worries had changed drastically over the course of the evening, but never once had they considered that they might become one of the taken. They added the concern to their list of worries to consider more later. Right now, they needed to report their findings to King Hadrian.

"Clay is not missing."

"Clay?"

"They chose a different name."

King Hadrian's brow furrowed for a brief moment, but his worried expression quickly returned. "Regardless, I'm sorry. I know you cared for them."

"They aren't—"

"I had the guards check the palace from top to bottom. Councilman Robin is officially being investigated as part of their disappearance as well, since it was clear he was unhappy with them."

As soon as King Hadrian stopped for a breath, R-0 said, "Clay is with Jasper."

"What?" King Hadrian asked. "How?"

"It wasn't safe for them in the dungeon. They were going to be decommissioned, so they were relocated to a safer place."

King Hadrian sat on his bed, sinking into the mattress. "R-0, I'm afraid to ask this, but I need to know. Did you break Clay out of prison?"

"Yes."

"What about the other four constructs?"

"Only Clay left," R-0 said. "The others were likely taken."

"Did anyone see you?"

"No."

"Are you sure?"

"Yes."

"What were you thinking, R-0?" King Hadrian sighed and leaned his face into his hands. "You know that's a crime, right? If anyone had caught you, I wouldn't be able to protect you from the council's wrath."

"Correct. That is why there were no witnesses."

"I don't know if I should be furious or impressed."

"This is what you wanted, right?" R-0 frowned. Why would King Hadrian be furious? "You expressed regret that you were unable to help Clay yourself, but it was simple to resolve their situation without your involvement."

"There's nothing simple about it. But I never"—his hands balled into fists at his side—"*never* wanted you to put yourself in danger."

"The intention was not to anger you. And danger was avoided."

"What did you find out? Tell me everything and spare no details."

R-0 recounted the events of the previous night, starting with their failed interrogation of Jeza and ending with their conversation with Jasper. When R-0 described breaking Clay out of prison, King Hadrian shushed them and forced them to speak in a whisper, despite the heavy wooden door and thick walls stopping sound from traveling beyond his room.

"It's official," King Hadrian said. "I'm never letting you out of my sight again."

"Is something wrong?"

"Everything."

It was likely an exaggeration but given how things had been at the palace lately, R-0 couldn't be sure. "Could you be more specific?"

"Let's skip past the fact that I spent the entire morning thinking you had been kidnapped. I just received word that Uxius's ship has been spotted off the coast. He'll be back before the day is over. And I'm not sure Eren or Gretta were swayed by our conversations. I've asked Jeza to talk to Gretta and Riley to work on Eren, but I'm worried there isn't enough time."

With Uxius returning, today was their last chance to resolve the matter of the rogue council member and overturn the vote of no confidence, or King Hadrian would lose his crown.

R-0 pulled Jasper's ring out of the compartment in their arm. "Jasper's lab could have the answers we need."

"We have no idea who will be waiting for us."

R-0 had learned something during their investigation. It didn't matter if there was a chance of things going wrong—that would always be a possibility. But standing by and doing nothing was worse than facing the consequences of trying to do the right thing.

"Regardless of the culprit, this could be where the missing constructs are. They need to be located before they all end up like Beans." R-0 gently lifted King Hadrian's hand and placed the ring in his palm.

King Hadrian's hand closed around the ring. "And if this can prove the constructs' innocence, it might be enough to sway

Eren or Gretta." He went to the closet, and when he returned, a golden sword hung at his waist. On the hilt was an engraving of Graywal's palace set against the ocean waves. "Let's go see Jasper's lab."

"Should Eren be notified?" R-0 asked. This was exactly the type of thing Eren would want to know about, and she could assign additional guards to accompany them.

"If she's the one behind this, we can't risk her knowing we're on to her."

R-0 hesitated. This was what they wanted—to find answers and help the constructs. But King Hadrian was right. They didn't know who was waiting down there, or what lengths they would go to in order to keep their activities secret.

"Perhaps you should wait here."

"Why?" King Hadrian asked.

"It could be dangerous."

"As long as you're around, I have nothing to worry about."

That was the one thing R-0 could do better than anyone else: protect the king. Even without their directive echoing through them, it felt right. It made their flame rage, their plates warm, and their thoughts focus.

I will always protect you.

R-0 tried to say the words out loud, but their gears failed them and nothing but a puff of smoke escaped their plates. It seemed so easy for King Hadrian to say the words—*I* or *we*. Everything he said took on a sense of involvement and ownership. It was *his* choices, *his* responsibility. But R-0 couldn't muster themself to mimic it.

"You will be protected."

CHAPTER 39

R-0 and King Hadrian headed into the managrid tunnels, searching for the passageway where Dara had overheard Ryder and the mystery woman. If R-0's guess was right and she had entered Jasper's lab, then the ring would allow them to use the same entrance.

King Hadrian's sword swung at his waist, knocking into his leg with every step, unlike R-0's blades that—secured into sheaths screwed into their legs—never moved, and certainly didn't disrupt their walk like his did.

"Are you experienced with a sword?" R-0 asked.

Red rose in King Hadrian's cheeks. "I've had some lessons."

R-0 tried to recall if they'd ever seen King Hadrian use a sword before but couldn't. In fact, they had no memories of the king wielding any type of weapon. Perhaps it was before their creation or while they were in storage.

"Okay, maybe I don't," King Hadrian said. "But I feel better having it."

"Are you worried something is going to happen?"

"Aren't you?"

"No."

R-0 had been apprehensive at first about King Hadrian accompanying them, but it was as if their nerves had been left in the king's chambers. They felt more certain with every step they took. After spending so much time not doing things and not helping, freeing Clay had changed them. If there was danger, so be it. Danger was what they were designed for.

"I could use some of that confidence right about now."

"It's not transferable," R-0 said. "You will have to find your own."

"Thanks for the encouragement." King Hadrian stopped at the dead end. "Is this the right spot?"

The pathway ended at a stone wall. The managrid, however, continued beneath the dead end, its coils flowing into the wall instead of ending in rounded edges. R-0 double-checked their memories from their conversations with Jasper and Dara, then nodded. This was definitely the right spot.

They pulled out Jasper's ring and tried to slide it onto their finger, but it only came halfway down their pinky before catching on their plate. It was far too small. The metal glimmered as they pinched it between their fingers.

"How is it activated?"

"Here." King Hadrian slipped it on. "If it works like the other magic items my mother had . . ." He closed his eyes and extended his hand toward the wall.

Magic sparked across his skin. The wall rippled like the ocean when a fish was thrown back in. Stone shifted, receding into the wall on either side and revealing a descending passageway lit by the blue glow of the managrid. The opening expanded, pushing the stone to the edges until there was enough space to pass through. On the other side was a tunnel, the rails of the managrid running along the floor.

The magic wasn't warm. R-0 wasn't drawn to it in the same way they had been drawn to Quiet's spells, but they still couldn't help watching the stone crawl away as if it were alive in amazement.

King Hadrian stepped through, and R-0 followed, ducking to avoid the low ceiling. As soon as they were in the tunnel, the wall silently rematerialized behind them. R-0 closed their eyes, focusing on their hearing receptors. But besides King Hadrian's footsteps and the hum of the managrid, silence surrounded them. They hurried to keep pace with him.

"Advance cautiously," R-0 said. Just because R-0 wasn't aware of a threat didn't mean there wasn't one.

King Hadrian slowed. "Why don't you go first?"

R-0 hesitated. What was at the end of the tunnel? Maybe this was why King Hadrian was always stressed—making decisions and leading others was harder than doing things alone. They tapped their side. With each tap, they took another step. After the first dozen steps, the taps were no longer required to keep a steady pace, and they walked more naturally, more confidently.

The air cooled as they descended, chilling R-0's plates. After a minute of walking, R-0 heard something in the distance—ticking gears. Not just one set, but several, all out of sync and at various volumes.

"There are multiple constructs ahead." R-0's flame gurgled. Flashes of Jasper's scrap room filled their vision. If they were right, they had found the missing constructs. But... what state would they be in?

"Anything else?" King Hadrian asked.

"Unclear."

"Draw your weapons."

R-0 slid their swords from their sheaths.

The ticking of gears grew louder until they reached the end of the passageway and found a large cavern-like room. The walls were rounded, extending farther to each side than some streets were long. They sloped to a point, where a crystal resembling a larger manacore floated close to the ceiling, surrounded by the same metal pieces that framed the manacores and hung suspended by magic alone.

Along the far wall were the constructs.

Most were shackled, but not with the basic restraints Eren had used to restrain R-0. Reinforced steel encircled their wrists, tethered to the floor by a heavy chain. A tiny floating stone hovered just above the surface of each one, slowly oscillating along the shackle. They barely glanced at King Hadrian and R-0 before bowing their heads and averting their eyes.

R-0 stepped toward the constructs, ready to snap the chains and free them. But before they could, King Hadrian grabbed their arm. "Wait. Look."

A second crystal sat in a metal frame at the center of the room. It matched the crystal on the ceiling, and the space between the two was filled with magic so thick it settled in the air like mist. Managrid rails in the floor traveled away from it, creating a grid-like pattern that emanated magic and connected to smaller manacores at various workstations. Some were nothing more than simple desks with tools scattered across them, not unlike the tables in the basement of the hattery. Others were more complex with tubes and wiring connecting to metal gadgets that clicked and whirred in the same patterns as the constructs' bodies, but R-0 couldn't determine their purpose.

At one workstation, the tubes connected to small vials and filled them with a bubbling golden substance. The liquid didn't settle at the bottom of the container. It crawled up the sides of the vial, swirling like smoke but far more substantial, then bounced off itself as more dripped in. R-0 followed the tubes back to the source.

A construct.

They lay on a wooden table, their chest plate removed and various tubes and wires hooked into their chest. Their flame flickered like a dying candle as it neared the base of its wick. There was no movement, no signs of life from the construct.

"What is happening to them?" R-0 asked.

King Hadrian was silent as R-0 moved closer to the workstation, and their flame roared in their chest. Another construct lay on the floor. Like the construct in Jasper's lab, their chest plate was missing, and there was no flame in their chest. The dead and discarded constructs . . . this was what had happened to them.

"We need to leave." King Hadrian turned back to the passageway. "Return with reinforcements."

R-0 stepped forward. The construct's flame was barely burning. R-0 didn't know how fast the machines worked, but—watching the quick drip of their golden flame into the vial—it couldn't be long before it was entirely gone. "They need our help."

"R-0, *now*."

R-0 tried to step back, tried to follow the king, but their feet remained stationary, their body refused to move, and they couldn't pull their eyes away from the construct lying still on the table.

"We can come back, but right now, we need to get out of here. This is—"

Stone shifted.

As when King Hadrian had activated Jasper's ring, grating stone echoed through the cavern, but his ring was dormant. It wasn't his magic. On the far side of the room, the cavern wall shimmered, creating a new opening.

Jeza stepped out. "Leaving so soon?"

CHAPTER 40

Jeza wasn't alone.

Two organics followed on either side of her—to her left, the tral from the dungeon, and to her right, Ryder. The seaweed sword hung from his waist, and a chill ran through R-0. Most weapons bounced off their thick plates harmlessly. But not that sword. R-0's leg still ached thinking about the damage it had caused.

Another mystery solved. Jeza was the woman working with Ryder in the tunnels. Which meant she was the one who ordered Quiet and R-0 to be captured, who kidnapped the constructs, and who was . . . R-0 still wasn't entirely sure what she was doing to them.

But why? She had supported the constructs. She'd helped King Hadrian. Why would she do this?

"Jeza." There was a stutter to King Hadrian's words, and his hands trembled. "What's going on here?"

Jeza's shoes clacked against the floor, and her robes swished with each step. As she moved closer, R-0 stepped between her and King Hadrian.

"This isn't how I planned to tell you, Sylas, but it was only a matter of time." Jeza turned to the tral. "Prepare a demonstration for our king, would you?"

Even under the blue glow of the manacores, the tral's eyes shone with an eerie yellow. His bare feet slapped against the floor as he approached the restrained constructs. R-0 tensed. They had seen enough—they didn't need to see these activities in action. They stepped forward, preparing to intercept the tral, but King Hadrian grabbed their arm.

"Wait," he whispered. "We need to understand what's going on."

R-0 trembled but remained in place, their eyes never leaving the tral. His focus shifted from the captured constructs to one of the discarded corpses beside them. As relieved as R-0 was to see he wasn't hurting the prisoners, it raised more questions. Without a flame, the construct was nothing but metal. What was the tral planning to demonstrate to the king?

"Haiden has always been a beacon of progress." Jeza stalked up to a workstation, Ryder at her heels. "First, the managrid. Second, the constructs. We've been responsible for feats of magic even the greatest mages in Benuoir envy."

"I'm well aware of our history," King Hadrian said.

"Allow me to show you our future." She picked up a stone from the table, then held out her other hand, palm up. The manacore in the center of the room sparked, and an orb of fire appeared inches above her skin. Her fingers wriggled, and the fire followed her movements. "Magic we only dreamed possible within our reach."

Jeza was cut off from the Flow—it should have been impossible for her to cast any magic, even with the help of magic items.

King Hadrian's face mirrored R-0's surprise. His jaw fell ajar, and his eyes widened. "How?"

"It's a miracle, isn't it?" Jeza placed the stone back on the table. "The constructs' flames are a pathway to the Flow, a connection to magic far greater than the managrid or anything we've ever been able to create. With this, I can do more than access the managrid. I can access the Flow directly." She reached for another stone on the table, and sparks jittered toward her. "Magic in anyone's hands."

"But at what cost?" King Hadrian motioned to the construct lying open, their flame hooked into the workstation.

"Every opportunity has a cost. For something like this . . . anything is worth paying."

How could the constructs' flame be a worthwhile sacrifice?

"No." R-0's grip tightened on their swords. "It's not."

"R-0's right," King Hadrian said.

"I was worried you might say that. You and half this country take magic for granted. Even if you can't wield it on your own, you've never known a world without the managrid connecting you to it. But those of us without that . . . we know the value of what we lack. A lesson I expected you to learn when you lost control of the constructs. This isn't just for me, Sylas. It'll help you as well."

The tral tapped his foot against a lever, and wheels sprang from the bottom of each table leg. He rolled the table over to Jeza, the decommissioned construct lying dormant on its surface. Jeza ran her fingers along the edges of their empty chest cavity, where their flame would have been.

The construct was already dead. There was nothing R-0 could do. But it didn't stop their fingers from fidgeting against their side. They looked to King Hadrian, hoping he could order this to end, but he only watched with wide eyes.

"How is any of this for me?" King Hadrian asked. "I've been chasing myself in circles trying to figure out what the constructs were plotting. Robin used it against me and almost stole my crown. It made me look weak. It—"

"You *are* weak." Jeza's voice retained its sharp, measured tone. She took a stone covered in runes from the table and set it in the construct's chest. "That hasn't changed in the years since your mother died, and it wasn't going to change in a few days. The constructs were your only strength. And they could be once more. When the flames are removed, their bodies remain unharmed. With Jasper's spellwork, they could be reanimated."

"Jasper would never."

"When Jasper left, he took his knowledge and magic with him. No matter what we did, we couldn't replicate the intricacies he created. But with the power from the constructs' flames . . . anything is possible. And replicating Jasper's spells is only the beginning." Jeza retrieved a scroll from another table. It unfurled, revealing the same symbols that had covered Jasper's research and the books in Jeza's study. She handed the scroll to the tral. "If you would do the honors."

"Of course." The tral dipped his head respectfully. He held his hands above the construct's chest, and the runed stone within began to glow. He read from the scroll, chanting the same phrases again and again, occasionally with slight variations.

Magic arced between the stone and the tral, then spread across the construct's body. It started at the edges of their chest, cloaking their metal in a warm glow that almost made R-0 believe their flame was returning. But there was no crackling fire, no light in the construct's eyes, no sign that their life force had returned. Instead, magic spread until every plate, every gear, every wire shone with the same pale glow.

"Sir . . ." R-0 couldn't find the words they wanted to say. They wanted to do *something*, anything. The construct was already dead, but . . . R-0 didn't want anything else to happen to them. Even if there was no one left inside to feel the damage to their body. Even if there was no one left to protect.

"Patience." King Hadrian didn't take his eyes off the tral and the construct, but if his words weren't clear, the signal that flashed across his fingers was.

Wait.

The tral's chanting stopped. He pulled a vial from his waistband. The golden substance within it swirled, its consistency somewhere between smoke and water. It sloshed at the edges of the container before folding back on itself and curling toward the cork. The tral opened it above the construct just long enough for a single golden drop to fall onto the runed stone.

For a moment, the glow encompassing the construct brightened. King Hadrian raised his hand to shield his eyes, and both Jeza and the tral averted their gaze. But R-0's eyes weren't as sensitive, and they didn't look away.

They couldn't.

Because the construct was moving.

Without assistance, the construct's gears slowly began to turn. Their wires glowed blue. As it had before the Awakening, energy from the managrid flowed to the construct, and their gears strengthened until they moved at a normal pace. A fire flickered in their chest, but it wasn't the golden flame that the stars left behind. It was a mundane orange fire, no different than a torch.

Somehow, the construct had become operational again. R-0 should have been relieved, but the empty look on the construct's face left their flame uneasy and their body chilled.

The tral took the runed stone from inside their chest and returned it to the research bench. Slowly the construct rose to their feet, then stood at attention. Despite the impossible circumstances, the construct didn't react. They didn't fidget.

"The power of their flames is a miracle." Jeza rested her hand on the construct. Her nails clacked against their shoulder plate, but the construct didn't stir. "We can make the constructs what they were before. You can regain your army, your control." Jeza left the construct behind and approached the king.

For a moment, R-0 hesitated. Their body didn't want to move a single step closer to the tral and his experiments, or Ryder and his magic sword, or Jeza with her cold, calculating gaze.

How many constructs had they already killed?

Would R-0 join them?

But another worry tugged at their flame. Jeza had lied to the king. Both Ryder and the tral had shown utter disregard not only for the lives of constructs, but of organics. Everyone in this room—R-0, the constructs, and King Hadrian—was in danger.

King Hadrian had said fear was a poison, leaving inaction where bravery had once fought. But as far as R-0 could tell, there was enough room in their plates for bravery and fear to coexist.

R-0 stepped between Jeza and the king, their grip on their swords tightening.

"We wouldn't have to do it to all the constructs." Jeza stopped in front of R-0, and for barely a tick of their gears, she shifted her focus from their chest to their eyes before turning to the king. "Just enough to give me the power I need and to help you protect your crown. For now, we could return Eren's guard force and the Faylviln armies to their obedient states. We could remove Robin from the council. Once things settle down and we know more about what the flames can do, we can reevaluate."

"They're just like before?" King Hadrian asked. He stepped around R-0 and Jeza, approaching the construct.

R-0 followed at his heels, careful to keep close.

"Like the incident never happened," Jeza said.

King Hadrian stopped in front of the construct. "Hello," he whispered, so low R-0 could barely hear. "Q-6?"

The construct didn't move. Didn't speak.

King Hadrian raised his hand toward the construct. "Sit."

Magic sparked at his palm, and the construct sat.

"Stand."

"Turn."

"Sit."

With every command, the magic activated, and the construct obeyed. They didn't question King Hadrian's pointless commands. R-0 looked into the construct's eyes, but they were empty.

R-0 had seen this before. All the constructs had been like this before the Awakening. R-0 had been like this. Jasper's spell and King Hadrian's bloodline had controlled R-0's actions for years, and they'd watched the same thing happen to all the constructs.

But seeing it now . . . it didn't feel the same as in their memories.

R-0 tried to find a word for the feeling roiling in their chest, but there was nothing that accurately described the flame-wrenching unease that fluttered between fear, worry, and rage. The construct's body may have been operational, but they weren't alive.

They were a moving corpse without a soul.

Whoever the construct had become after the Awakening was gone, and now their body was a puppet, fueled by the managrid and controlled by magic. Watching the corpse move, R-0 better understood organic burial rites—they wanted nothing more than to bury the construct's body deep in the earth where it could lie undisturbed. Even succumbing to rust beneath the ocean waves seemed a more peaceful fate than this.

"Only a fraction of their flame is needed for the reanimation." Jeza lifted a vial, and the golden liquid within slowly shifted. "From one flame, we have enough energy to reanimate dozens, possibly even hundreds. We've barely scratched the surface on other uses for the flames. It's magnificent, isn't it?"

Unjust. Cruel. Horrendous. R-0 could think of dozens of words that described what they were seeing, and magnificent wasn't one of them. There was nothing beautiful—nothing good—about any of this. They tried to say the words out loud, but not even smoke escaped their plates.

R-0 stiffened as Jeza grabbed King Hadrian's hands in hers. Their orders were to wait, but they weren't like the lifeless metal standing before them. Not anymore. How were they supposed to stand by and do nothing? Their gears accelerated, and their grip moved to their blades, tightening around the metal as much as they dared without bending them out of shape.

"This isn't just my power, Sylas." Jeza squeezed the king's hands. "It's yours too."

King Hadrian didn't pull away. His hands lingered in Jeza's.

"Think of what your mother would say," Jeza continued. "She built the constructs so that you could have your crown, and for years they've helped you secure your position. This is what they're meant to do."

"The Awakening does not stop the constructs from protecting King Hadrian," R-0 said.

The Awakening had changed them for the better as R-0 had proven day after day. How could any of them return to being an empty shell after they'd experienced so much?

"Jeza," King Hadrian's voice cracked. "Look at R-0. How could I . . ."

"There is a price to power," Jeza said. "Is this not a small sacrifice to keep your crown?"

"There's another way." King Hadrian pulled his hands away. His voice shook at first but grew steadier with every word. "Eren was already wavering. When I tell her the truth about the missing constructs, she'll see that they aren't a threat. I can keep my crown without doing this to the constructs."

"Are you trying to convince me or yourself?"

King Hadrian stepped back from the construct, leaving them dormant on the table. R-0 stayed right behind him, their unease fading with their inaction. Why would King Hadrian need convincing? He had seen more clearly than anyone how much good the constructs were capable of—why he needed R-0 and the others.

Despite this, he didn't answer Jeza's questions, returning instead to the lab's entrance. "This won't continue," he said. "I won't let it."

"If you won't . . ." Jeza lifted a vial, and the golden liquid within slowly shifted. "Perhaps Robin will."

"Jeza . . ." King Hadrian began.

"I can't stop you from sabotaging yourself, but I won't let you take this from me."

At her signal, Ryder approached and drew his sword. The tral quickly gathered his equipment. He swept an armful of glowing vials into a bag and then retreated to a different research station.

R-0 readjusted, stationing themself between King Hadrian and the threats as they slowly backed toward the tunnel. They couldn't protect King Hadrian from the council's politics, but when it came to danger like this, there was no one better equipped.

If they could remain in the choke point, they could protect King Hadrian. But if someone slipped past them, or if their movement was restricted like it had been after their last encounter with Ryder's sword, then he would be vulnerable. R-0 needed to get him to safety.

"What are your orders?" R-0 asked.

King Hadrian ignored R-0. "Don't do this. My mother asked you to take care of me, to watch over me. Is any of this what she would have wanted?"

"Your mother wanted to be *great*, and she was." Jeza's laughter rang through the cavern. "Nothing stood in her path—not the council, not your pitiful excuse for a father, and definitely not delusions of doing what is *right*. There's no such thing. There is only what we must do. Your mother understood that. She made every sacrifice necessary to forge her path to the throne. She would be ashamed you're unwilling to do the same."

Jeza pulled two crystals from her pocket and threw them into the air around the manacore. Then a beam of magical energy shot out, heading straight for R-0 and the king.

CHAPTER 41

R-0 pushed the king behind them and raised their swords. Before the magic reached them, stone rose from the ground. The blast smashed into it, spiraling bits of rocks and debris that harmlessly clinked off R-0's plates.

Magic faded from the amethyst ring on King Hadrian's hand.

"You need to leave. Now," R-0 said. It was impolite to not thank him, but with Ryder closing in, R-0 didn't have time for niceties. Right now, their priority was getting the king out of here alive.

King Hadrian retreated into the passageway they'd entered from and motioned for R-0 to follow. It would have been easy to retreat, but . . . R-0 looked at the rest of the constructs. There was no question of their fate if they remained here with Jeza and the others. Their flames would be extracted, their bodies experimented on.

R-0 couldn't leave them.

"Get to safety," R-0 said. They raised their swords.

"Not without you."

"The constructs need help."

R-0 waited, ready for King Hadrian to argue, but he nodded. He activated Jasper's ring and disappeared behind a wall of stone and dirt as the passageway sealed.

It took a moment for R-0 to identify the feeling coursing through them—relief. King Hadrian would be safe. Hardly a tick of their gears passed before Ryder reached them. He swung, the seaweed on his sword dripping with water that formed tiny puddles on the cavern floor. This time, R-0 was prepared. They deflected his blade with one of their own before countering, and Ryder dodged out of reach.

R-0's sword was fine. The seaweed didn't creep along its edges, tearing the metal apart like it had with their leg.

Abandoning their choke point, R-0 dashed forward. Ryder tried to dodge again, but R-0's strikes were relentless. When one parried, the other struck. When he dodged, they readjusted their second strike to hit his new location. He tried to fight back, but without the magic to interfere with R-0's movements and his companions to divide R-0's attention, they easily dispatched him.

He fell to the floor, blood leaking across his scales from a deep gash in his stomach. His chest heaved with struggling breaths, but he didn't get up. As long as he was tended to by the healers soon, he would survive. The justice in that made R-0 smile.

When the constructs were released from the dungeon, he could be put in one of their cells.

R-0 didn't have time to savor their victory. Ryder was only one of the threats. The tral had returned, but he didn't advance toward R-0. Instead, he stood by Jeza, strapping a large container to her back. It connected to two oversized gauntlets attached to her forearms. Plates not unlike the constructs' covered her arm from elbow to wrist. Her hands were exposed, spider-like rods forming a cage around them.

R-0 had never seen anything like it, but with or without magic, Jeza had to be apprehended.

"You're under arrest." Even as R-0 said the words, it didn't feel right. They'd spent time in the dungeon—as had countless other constructs—for fabricated crimes that paled in comparison to the atrocities Jeza had authorized in her lab.

"I'm not sure you have that authority." She flexed her fingers, and the rods expanded. No longer caging her hands, they had become long, spindly metallic digits that mimicked her movements. The managrid underfoot buzzed to life, lights on the wall flickering as energy channeled into a sparking orb between the rods.

"Under codes 13.4, 12.1, and—"

Magic blasted from Jeza's gauntlet. R-0 tried to dodge, but it caught their arm, snapping one of the gears holding it in place. Their shoulder tilted back at an awkward angle as their body flew backward.

They hit the ground with a heavy thud, their impact leaving an R-0-shaped indentation on the floor. A dust cloud plumed around them, the resulting grit settling into their plates. Before they could stand, Jeza fired another blast. It wasn't a direct hit but still sent them rolling into the wall.

Most of their plates were now dented, and their shoulder had been pulled even farther out of place. They'd managed to keep hold of their weapons, but the connections leading to their left hand were damaged. They couldn't release their grip or maneuver their arm anymore. Ryder's sword wasn't the only weapon that could damage them here.

Jeza and the others had been fighting and capturing constructs for weeks. She was prepared, and R-0 wasn't. They didn't have the slightest clue what she could do. All they knew was that every spark of magic Jeza created came from the death of the other constructs. The light at her fingertips came from constructs' flames burning out, and if R-0 didn't stop her, their flame would join the others—trapped in a vial, waiting to be used.

Magic arced from Jeza's gauntlet, but she missed, giving R-0 time to regain their footing and analyze the situation. The gauntlets reacted to her movements, not unlike the magic items R-0 had seen King Hadrian use. Although, based on the inaccuracy of the previous attack and the sweat beading on her forehead, it wasn't as effortless.

If R-0 could close the gap between them, she wouldn't be able to use magic—not without risking herself being caught in the blast as well.

It was easier said than done. As R-0 tried to dash forward, more blasts targeted them. It should have terrified them every bit as much as watching the reanimated construct had, but it didn't. Even when the magic reverberated through their body or their plates hit the floor, denting and scratching the metal, R-0's flame remained steady, burning strong.

All the time spent wandering, wondering, and doing nothing, they'd been afraid and uneasy. But here, even as they faced danger from Jeza, they found serenity in the violence around them.

This is what they were meant to do.

Serve King Hadrian and Haiden. Protect those who couldn't protect themselves. Help others.

The walls rumbled as stone shifted, but R-0 couldn't identify the source. Another blast spiraled toward them. They dove behind a workstation, only to be hit by the table itself as Jeza's magic knocked it backward. It cracked in half against R-0's plates, glass shattering and scattering across the floor. R-0 stumbled back and fell on the remnants of the workstation, pulverizing the glass into tiny shards that gritted against their plates.

Lying on the floor next to them was another construct. Although their head turned to face R-0, there was no light in their eyes. Their chest was empty. A tube led from the base of their chest plate to the floor, and the golden liquid dribbled out.

R-0's flame, which had remained so calm, now faltered, as if their own fire was spreading across the floor. They tried to scoop it into their hand, but it had no form. They couldn't hold on to it, and they couldn't put it back in.

The construct was dead. Killed by Jeza's machine.

R-0 understood now why organics cried. Because there was nothing else they could do. No thoughts could comfort the roar in their mind. No actions could change the reality of their situation. Nothing. They wished they could take this feeling, bottle it into tiny tears and release them. But they couldn't. It was theirs to keep and hold on to.

Theirs to remember.

R-0 forced themself to their feet, leaving the construct's body behind. They were gone, but dozens of other constructs would meet the same fate if Jeza wasn't stopped.

R-0 hid behind the manacore. Like those in the managrid tunnels, it was warm and sparked at their presence. As another blast shot nearby—where R-0 would have been if they had kept moving—the manacore buzzed to life. The managrid was fueling Jeza's invention. No wonder the city was experiencing blackouts. The magic that should have fueled the streetlights and items throughout the city was being funneled here instead. Another mystery solved.

The flames granted Jeza access to the Flow, but . . . R-0 risked a glance around the manacore, catching sight of Jeza long enough to see the familiar blue glow of the managrid buzzing between the grid on the floor and her gauntlets. The managrid was as much a part of this as the constructs' flames.

And the managrid could be shut down—sabotaged. But how?

Stone rumbled again. This time, R-0 had cover and could pause to find the source. On the other side of the cavern, King Hadrian emerged from the stone wall joined by some of the constructs Jeza had held captive. R-0 recognized the one in front.

Q-6. Jeza's experiment. Under King Hadrian's command and wielding his golden blade, they marched forward, cutting through the shackles of the still-restrained constructs. The constructs retreated into the stone alcove as Jeza fired another blast, this time toward the king. Before it hit, King Hadrian sealed the tunnel once more.

King Hadrian hadn't run.

R-0 expected to feel their worry compounding—one more thing in a long list of concerns that seemed ever-growing. But at the sight of their king, relief flooded through R-0's body, like a cool breeze fanning a fire. Not only was King Hadrian safe, he was helping the constructs. He'd already freed over a dozen, although dozens still remained shackled to the floor around the lab.

"Come out, R-0." Jeza fired again, but this time her attack landed nowhere near them. It hit the still-shackled constructs bound across the room. "Or would you like me to continue my demonstrations on your friends over there?"

R-0's flame blazed in their chest. The other constructs weren't their friends, but they doubted Jeza would care about the correction. And it didn't matter who they were—R-0 wouldn't allow innocent constructs to stand in their place against Jeza. They were defenseless.

RISE OF THE FORGEHEARTS

R-0 stepped out from behind the manacore. With their functioning hand, they dropped their sword. Their other arm dangled from their shoulder, unusable but locked in position, holding onto their second blade.

"Stop," R-0 said.

"That was easier than I'd expected." Jeza angled her gauntlet at R-0. The rods and her fingers both wriggled in anticipation.

One of the wires on the contraption on her back didn't connect to the gauntlets. It spiraled toward the ground and snaked across the floor. It almost blended with the conduits for the managrid, ending in the same destination.

Without the gauntlets, Jeza could be easily subdued. And if R-0 was right that the managrid was the power source, her magic wouldn't work if the connection was broken. They just had to reach the wire. But how?

"Stay where you are," Jeza commanded.

R-0 took one step forward, and Jeza fired a blast at their feet.

"Stay," Jeza repeated. "Is that too difficult to understand?"

R-0 froze. If they dove back to their cover, they could avoid Jeza long enough to reach the wire. But what of the other constructs? Shackled to the floor, they didn't have the same luxury. How many would die before R-0 could stop her?

"It won't be long before the king returns," Jeza said to the tral. "Get all the flames and the constructs relocated immediately. And as much of the research as you can."

"There's too much—"

"Do what you can."

Through their conversation, Jeza never took her eyes off R-0. Never gave them an opportunity to move.

"Jeza." Stone rumbled again, this time behind Jeza. King Hadrian stood in the opening, and Jeza's eyes flickered to him.

It was a small opportunity, the briefest lapse in her concentration, but that was all R-0 needed.

They dove toward the manacore, grabbing at the wire.

Jeza's focus snapped back to them. She screamed, and a blast of energy shot from the gauntlets. Her magic hit its mark, but it was too late. R-0 yanked the wire away as the blast hit not only them, but the manacore as well.

The metal supporting the crystal cracked, and the stone fell to the ground, shattering into pieces. Its counterpart in the ceiling followed suit, and crystalline shards fell around them like rain. Stronger than anything Jeza had channeled, magic exploded from the crystal and the damaged managrid, crashing into R-0. Their chest plate crumpled inward, and their arm was knocked completely from their body.

R-0 felt it. Slowly at first, then increasing with intensity every second. Their flame burned. It raged. But their plates were fragmented and out of position, crumpling in. Their flame struggled to reach open air, burning through R-0's internal mechanisms. Wires snapped and gears melted out of shape without giving any relief.

They tried to focus. They grabbed at their chest plate thinking maybe they could free their flame. But with every movement, the magic of the manacore exploded in a chain reaction that only seemed to grow stronger. It chipped at their plates and snapped parts out of place until everywhere around them was blue and bright and too thick with magic for them to move.

R-0!

King Hadrian was yelling, somehow simultaneously next to them and far away. They heard his voice behind their plates, close but muffled. R-0 tried to reach for their king, but their body no longer moved. Their vision blurred and faded until R-0 couldn't see. They couldn't feel their body. They could only trust that it was still there.

But was that trust misplaced?

They'd asked the question many times—what did death feel like? Perhaps this was how they found out. Not through questions, not through thought. Through actions.

Somewhere in the distance, King Hadrian continued to yell. Although R-0 heard the sounds, they were meaningless. But even if they couldn't understand it, Sylas's voice echoing around them was comforting.

The echo turned into the quiet ticking of gears. Their thoughts grew dimmer and dimmer.

Until there was nothing.

CHAPTER 42

R-0 had watched King Hadrian try to wipe the groggy look off his face many times before. It didn't make sense. Friction couldn't supply energy to his body. But R-0 found themself wanting to mimic the movement as their vision slowly shifted from endless darkness to the blurry edges of a room. Like the moon reflecting off the ocean, there were glimpses and glimmers of clarity, but more often than not, waves disrupted R-0's vision.

As the blurriness softened, the familiar pale green walls of King Hadrian's room came into focus, and they recognized the soft cloth surrounding them. They had been right to think the king's bed could swallow them whole, as if it really was made of clouds. The covers poofed up around them as they sunk deep into the mattress.

Two blurry figures solidified into recognizable forms. King Hadrian and . . . Winter? R-0 blinked a few times, but nothing changed. They stood by the desk, their back to R-0 as they stared out the window. Why was Winter there?

King Hadrian reclined in a chair, his eyes closed and his body still. R-0 listened for his pulse. There, as consistent as the ticking of gears, the king's heartbeat was strong and steady. His face was bruised, and there were cuts along his arm and shoulder, but otherwise, he appeared intact.

"Are you okay?" R-0 asked.

"R-0!" King Hadrian's eyes flickered open. "I should be asking you that."

R-0 frowned and looked over themself. They had been . . . R-0 didn't have a word for the time lapse they had experienced. They had seen it before in organics. Unconsciousness. It was unlike anything that had ever happened to them before.

Were they okay?

The last time they had seen their chest plate, the metal had been crumpled and caved in, but now it was flawless and polished. R-0 tentatively moved every gear, testing each section of their body methodically to ensure everything functioned as expected. Their analysis revealed nothing amiss.

"There is no damage," R-0 said.

"No damage *anymore*." Winter crossed the room, pulling a screwdriver out of an apron at their waist and immediately beginning to unscrew R-0's chest plate.

"What are you doing?" R-0 tried to move backward. Even though they hadn't noticed any damage, their movements were sluggish and uncoordinated.

"Fixing you up." Winter easily held them in place, continuing to unscrew the plate. "Some gratitude would be nice. Your little stunt almost cost you your life. Would have if Crownie here hadn't been smart enough to send for Jasper."

Winter's hands moved with a buzz, and quickly, their chest plate was detached. R-0 looked inside themself. Like their external parts, everything was in place. The only difference was their flame. The normally large golden fire was smaller than King Hadrian's fist.

King Hadrian leaned forward. "It's growing back."

Had it been even smaller before? Was that why they had become unresponsive—their flame had almost gone out?

Winter winked as they began screwing R-0's plate back on. "Told you it would."

"The technomancers said—"

"Your technomancers know more about taking constructs apart than putting them back together." Winter scoffed. "Not sure why you'd listen to them instead of me."

"Thank you, Winter." King Hadrian stood, then tucked his fist across his shoulder and bowed his head toward them. "Truly, thank you for coming here and for everything you did for R-0."

"Whatever." Winter rolled their eyes, mimicking the organic movement perfectly before turning to R-0, their voice softening. "Are you okay? Really? Not just your body. Mind, body, flame. All of it." They gestured to their head and chest as they spoke.

R-0 nodded, but before they could find the words to answer Winter's question, King Hadrian scurried to the closet and returned with a large box. "I saved these for you." He set the box on the foot of the bed and pulled out a mangled piece of scrap metal.

What was R-0 supposed to do with that? "The gift is . . . appreciated. Although, confusing."

"It's your chest plate," King Hadrian explained. "Well, your old one."

That was R-0's chest plate? They searched for the hinges or holes in the corners for the screws but found nothing. While the shape was somewhat accurate, it was unrecognizable.

"What happened?"

"You stopped Jeza." King Hadrian smiled. "Riley is reporting everything to the council now."

"Not you?"

"I wanted to be here when you woke up."

"There is no more threat?"

King Hadrian shook his head. "We were able to trace it all back to Jeza—with a few exceptions like our intruder here." He looked at Winter and chuckled. "The managrid blackouts, the missing constructs, Ryder. It was all for her experiments."

"Where is Jeza now?"

"Dead."

"How?" R-0 asked. Had they killed her?

"You weren't the only construct in that room loyal to me." King Hadrian's tear ducts quivered, but he quickly closed his eyes, and his face regained its composure. His lips slowly curled upward in the approximation of a smile. "Her own experiment was her downfall."

R-0 had been around King Hadrian long enough to learn when his smile was forced. "Is that not a good thing?"

"I just . . . still can't believe she did this. I can't believe she's gone."

R-0 flickered through their memories. After Queen Hadrian's passing, it was Jeza who had taken over many of her tasks—bringing King Hadrian presents on holidays, overseeing his lessons, giving him a shoulder to cry on as he grieved. Time and time again, Jeza's actions had seemed caring and genuine. How could King Hadrian have expected this?

"People are always capable of worse than you'd imagine." Winter shrugged.

"Not always." King Hadrian rested his hand on R-0's arm. "Some are capable of far greater things than we could have ever hoped."

R-0's flame stirred, and they waited for heat to flush through their body. Instead, only their chest cavity warmed. They shifted their plates into a smile at King Hadrian's compliment.

A knock sounded at the door, followed by Quiet's voice, strained and louder than normal. "King Hadrian, your presence is needed."

Winter tensed. "What's going on?"

"I'll go see." King Hadrian opened the door. Quiet wasn't the only one standing on the other side. Robin and Eren also stood in the doorway, flanked by guards.

"What a surprise to see all of you." King Hadrian smiled, but the expression was even more forced than when he was talking about Jeza's downfall. "I expect Councilwoman Riley has updated you on yesterday's events?"

Yesterday? R-0 had been unconscious for a whole day without realizing it?

"That she has." Robin signaled the guards to enter the room. "We're here to arrest the constructs, W-4 and R-0."

"What?" King Hadrian's voice rose. "Why?"

"Trespassing in the palace is a criminal offense." Robin's gaze settled first on Winter, then R-0. "As is assassinating one of the council members."

The guards tried to advance, but King Hadrian threw out his arms, blocking their way. "Absolutely not. R-0 was just following my orders and—"

"Sylas Hadrian, your part in this has not gone unnoticed. You're under arrest for the assassination of Councilwoman Jeza Doblin."

"Under whose authority? What—?"

Councilman Uxius walked down the hallway toward them. The councilman looked unkempt and unprepared for a council meeting. He usually wore elegant silks and kept his hair neatly combed back. Today, his grease-coated hair, more white than black, hung down his back in a braid that matched his beard and almost reached his waist. The notches were rough, with frizzy flyaways and swatches of seaweed peeking out. Grime coated his clothes, which were far more practical than his formal wear. At his waist hung an array of pockets and dangling tools, all filled with fishing gear. The only thing familiar was the Rhain clan ring on his finger—a stormy blue gemstone set in a thick band.

"Imagine my surprise when I return to find my country in chaos," Uxius said. "I apologize to everyone that my trip has caused undue delays in making this possible."

"We're down a council member," King Hadrian said. "Jeza—"

Robin cut him off. "In Jeza's absence, her clan's representative agreed to vote in her stead. It's done, Hadrian."

"Why are you doing this?" King Hadrian shook his head. "Did you not hear what Riley had to say? What Jeza was doing?"

"I did, and it was terrible. Truly." If Robin felt bad, his face didn't show it. "But it doesn't change the fact that you hid all of this from the council. We have no idea what else you or your little creations might be hiding, and—as evidenced by your intruder here—you have no control over them. You are unfit to be king."

"I am your king! I have—"

"We have tolerated you for far too long because of the control you inherited over the constructs. We won't tolerate it any longer."

Gretta nodded in agreement. "I'm so very sorry, Sylas. We do appreciate everything you have done. But you're soft for the constructs, and we're past due for a change."

"Take the constructs to the dungeon." Robin signaled the guards.

Eren stepped forward, Ryder's seaweed sword clanging at her side.

Winter grabbed for one of R-0's swords where it leaned against the wall. R-0 started to protest, but it would take time for R-0 to retrieve them—time they knew Eren wouldn't squander.

Their weakened flame coiled in their chest. What would happen if they were injured further? Could their flame continue to sustain them?

They were weak. Vulnerable.

R-0's joints creaked, and their wires stretched as they lifted themself first into a sitting position, then shakily stood. Their movements had always been easy, instinctual. Now every ticking gear, every extension of their wires felt forced and awkward. R-0 could feel their inner mechanisms struggling to keep up with their demands.

"Stop." King Hadrian's jaw quivered. "Is this how you want to start your reign as king?"

R-0 tried to cross the room to retrieve their other sword, but every movement was followed by the guards' eyes. They wouldn't reach their weapons before the guards closed the distance, so R-0 stopped.

"Is this how you want to end yours?" Robin asked.

Winter stepped into the center of the room, the Levian steel blade glistening in their hand. The council members scrambled back, while the guards held their ground, hesitation showing in their trembling hands and unsure expressions.

"I'm not a part of your games," Winter said. "I came here to repair R-0, and now they're better. I'm going home." They held the blade in front of them as they approached the door, but the guards blocked the way. "Move aside."

"Arrest them," Robin ordered.

"Stop them!" King Hadrian yelled.

R-0 couldn't reach their sword in time, but there were other options for a weapon. King Hadrian's bed had four columns, one in each corner supporting the canopy above. Even injured, R-0 easily snapped one out of place. They swung the column in a wide arc, catching one of the guard's sides. The dwarf tumbled over, hitting the floor with a thud. The impact slowed R-0's swing long enough for the rest to dodge out of the way.

"Get out of here!" Eren shoved the council members back as Winter danced forward. Gretta was hysterical, her cries mixing with the clash of steel, and she let herself be shepherded out. Only Quiet seemed to hesitate, but Eren grabbed her by her shoulders and forced her out of the room.

Winter's strikes were precise, even with the too-big sword. They knocked the guard in their way off balance, pushing past him to the doorway. Eren was waiting for them, Ryder's magical sword drawn and ready.

"Watch out!" R-0 yelled. "That sword—"

A guard struck at R-0, his blade scraping against R-0's plates. Maybe if they'd been at full strength, they could have helped Winter, but not like this. R-0 tried to knock the guard away with the bed column, but he dodged.

R-0 could hear Robin yelling for reinforcements, and footsteps—too close—stomping in response. Robin had been ready for resistance, and the guards in the room were just the beginning.

The next time the guard struck, R-0 let the hit land. He sliced at R-0's chest plate, leaving a shallow cut, and R-0 grabbed his weapon before he could pull it back. An organic's hands would have been sliced to pieces if they tried something like this, but R-0's plates remained unrelenting as they tightened their grip. The blade bent under the pressure, and they yanked it out of the guard's hands and jammed the hilt back into his gut. He clutched his stomach, doubling over, and R-0 slammed the hilt on the back of his neck, leaving him to crumple to the ground.

"We have to run," King Hadrian said. He held R-0's remaining sword in his hands, the tip dragging against the ground as he walked forward. He handed it to R-0.

"There are reinforcements in the hallway."

"What other choice do we have?"

Robin had a palace full of guards at his command. R-0 had managed to fend off this group, but they couldn't maintain this forever. Already they felt weaker, the sword at their side heavier than usual.

Exhaustion. It was a foreign feeling, and R-0 had no idea what to expect.

"Are you just going to stand there or what?" Winter stood in the doorway. Eren was nowhere to be seen.

King Hadrian and R-0 followed Winter. Guards waited in the hallway, but they were far enough away that they still had a chance to escape. But where would they go? R-0 knew the protocols. All the exits would be guarded. Maybe if they reached one quickly they could fight their way through, but Eren would expect that. R-0 had seen her handle situations like these before. She would be prepared.

Which brought up another concern—where was Eren? She wasn't among the organic bodies on the floor, and she wasn't waiting with the other guards in the hallway. She wasn't the type to flee or retreat. She had a plan. But what?

"Where's Eren?" R-0 didn't let their speed slow as they spoke. They still couldn't move at full capacity, but keeping pace with King Hadrian meant they didn't need to run as fast as they could.

"No idea," Winter said. "Spooked like a seagull, I guess. Do you have Jasper's ring?"

R-0 glanced at King Hadrian's hand, but it was bare.

He shook his head. "I turned it over to Eren as evidence. She has both of them."

"Well that complicates things." Winter's words were as easy as if they were in Zealot, sitting at a table and repairing a construct, not running for their life. Unlike King Hadrian. After a few flights of stairs and even more hallways, his breaths were ragged, and he gasped for air as his legs started to slow.

"I can't—" He took a deep breath. "Keep running."

"You have to." Winter pushed his back, moving him forward even as his feet tripped beneath him.

R-0 steadied him before he could hit the ground. Both of them were right. Organic bodies couldn't be forced forward in the same way the constructs could, but if they stopped . . . The echoing footsteps behind them weren't far off. They gained a little time at every twist and turn since the guards had to slow down to figure out which way they'd gone, but it wouldn't be long before they caught up, or before another group of guards circled in front of them, blocking their escape route.

"Here." R-0 scooped King Hadrian up into their arms.

King Hadrian let out a squeal as his feet were lifted into the air, but R-0 held him tight to their chest.

"What—"

"This is more efficient."

Winter pulled ahead, and R-0 increased their speed to follow. Around the next corner, Eren was waiting, her weapon sheathed.

"Can you fight and carry him?" Winter asked. They stopped before they reached striking distance of Eren.

"No," R-0 said. Not only were their movements awkward with King Hadrian in their arms, but if they tried to fight, every second would endanger the king's life.

"Then leave him behind."

"That is not an option," R-0 said.

"If it was up to me, I would have brought you back to Zealot—to *safety*. It's his fault we're in this situation," Winter said. "And it's not like they'll kill him. There'd be riots in the streets if their precious little king was sentenced. We don't have that same luxury. We're too dangerous. They'd decommission us before we even got assigned a cell."

"He will not be left behind." They would stay behind themself before they'd abandon their king.

"Thank you, R-0." King Hadrian's fingers slid into the crease between R-0's lower and upper arm plates, clinging to the edge of their plate.

"If you're done with the dramatics—" Eren advanced, but rather than drawing her weapon, she stepped to the side of the hallway and opened the closest door. R-0 immediately recognized where the door led. Eren's room. They'd never been inside, but they'd come here for assignments plenty of times in the past. "This way."

"You are supposed to be arresting us," R-0 said.

"Can't you just be happy I'm not?" Eren held out her hand, where Jasper's ring was nestled in her palm. She tossed it to King Hadrian. "You'll need this to get out of here."

Escaping was the opposite of being captured—the opposite of the guards' objective and Robin's orders.

"Why?" R-0 asked.

"Listen, I was wrong about the constructs, okay? I was so afraid of things changing, so caught up in my own problems, I didn't see y'all for what you were becoming, only as what I'd lost." She fiddled with the Ainfen clan ring hanging on the chain around her neck. "I have a duty to protect my people, and—flesh or metal be damned—that should have included you. I failed you and the rest of the constructs. I can't change that, but this is me trying to do better."

"Can we trust her?" Winter asked.

Trust.

It was back to trust again. King Hadrian had trusted Jeza, and they'd all seen how that turned out. Eren had been against R-0 from day one. But . . . even then, Eren had never hid her intentions. She'd never lied. When she had a problem with R-0, she confronted it head on.

"What are your choices?" Eren tossed her sword to the ground with a clatter, then braced herself in front of them. "Make it believable. Punch me."

"Wha—?"

R-0 couldn't finish their question before Winter reared back and punched Eren. Bones crunched beneath metal, and Eren swore.

"Shalloth's grace, you don't hold back, do you?" Despite the blood leaking from her nose and her pained expression, she managed a grin as she grabbed Winter's arm, yanking them toward the open doorway. "Now go!"

R-0 didn't wait for King Hadrian's response. They rushed into Eren's room and slammed the door closed as soon as Winter joined them.

CHAPTER 43

Inside, Quiet was waiting.

"Riley? What—"

Quiet clamped her hand over King Hadrian's mouth, muffling whatever he was about to say. With her other hand, she motioned for R-0 and the others to be silent. She reached past R-0 to lock the door, then helped King Hadrian out of R-0's arms and onto his feet.

"They went this way," Eren's voice was loud and commanding, easily discernable even with the thick door between them. Had that been Eren's plan all along? Convince them to detour into her room just to be trapped at a dead end?

"They got the best of you, aye?" R-0 recognized Jorgunn's voice. "Are you okay?"

"I'll be better once you get your ass moving and catch them!"

The footsteps didn't stop. They kept going farther and farther down the hallway.

Once they were beyond the range of organics' hearing, Quiet sighed. "I was worried that wouldn't work."

"I have to get out of here. Now." Winter tossed R-0's blade onto the bed, then began opening Eren's window.

"If you—" Quiet tried to speak, but Winter interrupted.

"Listen." They banged their fist on the windowsill. "Thanks for the help! Thanks for not killing me! Whatever pleasantries you want, you can have them. But after that, save your breath. I never should have come here. I have to warn Jasper and the others before Robin or the guards find them." The longer they spoke, the faster the words came. Their gears matched their pace, accelerating into a loud whir.

"I was just going to say that with Jasper's ring, you should be able to slip into the managrid tunnels here." Quiet gestured to the closet. Most of the space was filled with plain underclothes to wear under armor, but there were a few pieces of formal wear, including a set of robes far too long for a dwarf like Eren. Quiet pushed the clothes to the sides, revealing a stone wall. "The walls and gates will be well-guarded, but they can't cover all the tunnels."

Winter left the window. "Why are you helping me?"

"Do you want to waste time on the whys?" Quiet asked.

"Fair." Winter turned to King Hadrian. "Give me the ring."

King Hadrian had already slid it on his finger, and he held his hand out. With a jolt of magic, the stone shifted, revealing a staircase. Despite Winter's expectant, outstretched hand, he didn't give them the ring.

"The guards are stationed at the top of the stairwell," Quiet said. "You'll already be past them."

Winter hesitated, looking like they might say something more, then headed through the opening without a goodbye.

"I need to know the whys." King Hadrian sat on Eren's bed. He'd mostly caught his breath while traveling in R-0's arms, but his heart still beat faster than normal.

"Robin was ready," Quiet said. "Uxius was back, and he summoned Jeza's second to represent Clan Doblin and vote on their behalf. Until we put someone new on the council, that's her clan's seat. They have the right to vote."

"And I was the one responsible for Jeza's death."

Quiet nodded. "You convinced Eren. But losing Jeza's vote put you back to where you started."

King Hadrian swore under his breath.

"I can't stay," Quiet said. "The rest of the council will begin asking questions if I'm gone too long. Wait here, and I'll return once the council convenes."

She slipped out the door, locking it behind her and leaving R-0 and King Hadrian alone with only silence.

Solving the mystery of the missing constructs—proving they weren't a threat and that King Hadrian had everything under control—was supposed to fix all of this. It should have stopped the vote against King Hadrian and helped him keep his crown. And then King Hadrian would have freed all the constructs. They weren't supposed to be in danger of being decommissioned anymore.

All of their worst-case scenarios had become reality. Not only were King Hadrian and R-0 still in danger, with Robin in charge, more than just the constructs in the dungeon would be decommissioned. Robin's plan had been to decommission as many constructs as possible. And if he'd heard about Jeza's experiments, he could recreate them.

"What are we supposed to do now?" King Hadrian asked.

"The constructs could be freed from the dungeon," R-0 said.

It wasn't much, but like Clay, they could be relocated. They wouldn't be safe, but they would be safer than they were now, caged and waiting for their sentence.

"It wouldn't change anything." King Hadrian sighed. "I'd still lose the crown, and where would they go? Robin would find them. It would only be a matter of time."

"Then what can be done?" R-0 asked.

"I don't know." King Hadrian dropped his head into his hands. "I gave my whole life to them. Everything. Now it's just . . . over."

Once R-0 recuperated, they could take on the guard. With the stone shifting ring, King Hadrian could create an optimal battleground for R-0 and minimize the council's numerical advantage. But what would it change? They couldn't be everywhere at once, and they couldn't force anyone to listen to King Hadrian. Maybe if they brought in the rest of the constructs, but . . . they couldn't organize enough people in a single day. There was nothing in the law book they'd read—no technicality they could leverage.

R-0 couldn't help King Hadrian keep his crown.

But they could still protect him.

"You could leave," R-0 said.

"What?" King Hadrian asked.

"Like Jasper did when he was banished from the council. He built a new life."

King Hadrian shook his head. "I'm not like Jasper. The constructs, his inventions—that was his purpose. What is my purpose if not to be king?"

R-0 didn't know how to respond. They had spent so much of their time since the Awakening searching for a purpose, and there wasn't an easy answer. R-0 still wasn't sure if they knew their own purpose, so how could they answer for someone else?

"And leaving doesn't solve anything," King Hadrian said. "The constructs—my clan's legacy—would be destroyed by Robin. How does leaving help?"

"You would survive."

"I'd rather die."

R-0 wouldn't let that happen—they couldn't. Their flame boiled at the thought. "What other option do you have?"

"I don't know." He took the crown from his head and ran his fingers along its golden edges. His hands trembled and tears ran down his face. "I was supposed to be someone great, to do something great. Ever since I was a boy, my mother told me this was my destiny. To lead my people, to love them. I was going to expand the managrid, rid the seas of Del'Star's cultists." His voice cracked, and he took a deep breath. "It wasn't just about my reign either. This is my mother's legacy—my clan's future. I was going to have a child and pass this honor to them. It was just . . . it was never supposed to end. Not like this."

His grip on the crown tightened until the edges dug into his skin and tiny pricks of blood trickled down his hand. R-0 reached to take the crown, but before they could, the king placed it back on his head.

"I won't let Robin do this," King Hadrian said. "I have to take back my throne—whatever the cost."

R-0 recognized the sparkle in his eyes, even through his tears. It was the same look he'd worn before announcing the reintegration and before they'd snuck out of the palace together.

"Do you have a plan?" R-0 asked.

King Hadrian didn't answer. He wiped his tears on his sleeve and rubbed away the specks of blood on his palm. After a few moments of silence, he nodded.

It seemed impossible. He'd been trying for days without success to secure his position as king. Now that Robin had officially dethroned him, what more could he do? But if King Hadrian believed he could do it, if he had an idea, R-0 would support him.

"Do you need assistance?"

King Hadrian frowned. "Every time I think I know what needs to be done, you have to say something like that."

"Like what?" R-0 asked.

"What did I do to deserve your loyalty?"

His response didn't answer R-0's question. But King Hadrian's question was easy to answer.

"You are the king," R-0 said.

King Hadrian's gaze shifted out the window. "Not anymore."

R-0 hadn't considered that. Their directive had always been the same. Protect the king. But that king had always been King Hadrian. Even before he was granted the crown, the late queen had called him the future king and given R-0 those orders.

Were they required to protect Robin now? When R-0 thought of him, they didn't feel a thing. If anything, they felt anger, not compassion, for the dwarf that had betrayed their king and wanted the constructs decommissioned.

No, it wasn't the crown that R-0 was bound to protect. It was the man standing before them. Even when the Awakening had changed R-0's circumstances, he'd still been there for them. R-0 would be there for him now. The council could take away his title, but they couldn't change R-0's directive.

"You will always be protected," R-0 said. "The crown is irrelevant."

"I'm sorry, R-0."

"You are not required to apologize."

"No one is ever required to, but that doesn't mean you don't deserve it. I just . . ." King Hadrian glanced down then back to R-0. "I feel like I know what needs to be done. For my people who rely on me. For my clan's legacy that my mother entrusted to me. For the future I've been working toward. But every time I think of the constructs, I don't see any of that. All I can think of is you, and I'm just . . . I'm so sorry."

King Hadrian's words didn't make sense. What was he apologizing for?

King Hadrian stood. He twirled Jasper's ring around his finger. "R-0, I have no right to ask this of you. I'm not the king. But I need your help. I need you." He took R-0's sword from the bed where Winter had left it and offered it to R-0. "Will you go on one last mission with me?"

You are still my king.

Even if they couldn't say it out loud, they found comfort in the thought. For everything they still didn't understand, everything that felt wrong or was confusing, this wasn't. This was right. The council's decisions didn't matter. Robin didn't matter.

What mattered was right here. Right now. If R-0 could help King Hadrian, then they would.

R-0 took the blade from King Hadrian. "Yes sir."

CHAPTER 44

Before they left, R-0 stopped by Eren's nightstand. The dwarven puzzle was there, still unsolved. R-0 wasn't supposed to touch her things, but . . .

They grabbed it anyway, the pearl clinking against the sides as it rolled around.

"Does the luck come from the pearl or from solving the puzzle?" R-0 asked.

"If you believe the stories, then it's the pearl."

Eren had helped them. Without her, R-0 wasn't sure they would have gotten King Hadrian and Winter safely out of the palace. Not only that . . . her actions had endangered herself. Robin held the crown. Acting against him was treason, and if he discovered Eren's role in their escape, she'd be labeled a traitor.

It was a kindness that R-0 wanted to reciprocate.

They dug their fingers between two grooves in the stone, sliding a ring out of place. They twisted and shifted the stone through a dozen more stages. The movement loosened the upper section of the stone and the top section split. A chunk fell onto the nightstand.

King Hadrian eyed the puzzle, his eyebrows furrowing. "What are you doing?"

"An expression of gratitude." R-0 completed the last few steps, and the pearl gently slid free into their palm. They looked at the gem for a moment, then placed it next to the remnants of solved stone.

This made far more sense than the insincere platitudes the organics generally performed. This was tangible, actionable. If R-0 could, they'd give Eren a decade of good luck for the assistance she provided. But one year would have to do. And they would respect the organics' preference for spoken gratitude as well.

"Thank you, Eren," R-0 whispered.

"Come on." King Hadrian moved to the closet and reopened the stone. "We don't have time for this."

R-0 stepped past him, leading the way into the dark.

"What is the plan?" R-0 asked. They only had one option for now—down the staircase. But eventually, the path would branch, and R-0 had no idea where they were going.

"Just keep walking."

It was strange for the king to keep it a secret—especially when R-0 was guaranteed to find out. But as they continued to walk, King Hadrian remained silent. Perhaps he was worried about being overheard. Usually, the palace was his domain, but now . . . the guards that had once protected him were his enemies, and they had no idea what threats could lie behind every twist and turn of the tunnel.

At the bottom of the staircase, the managrid tunnels stretched out in multiple directions. King Hadrian stopped. "Do you know how to get to the city from here?"

R-0 didn't recognize any of their surroundings yet, but they knew approximately where they were positioned, and the managrid tunnels held plenty of possibilities. As long as they kept moving in the right direction, they'd eventually get there.

"This way." R-0 led them to a couple of dead ends, and more than once they had to backtrack or detour to hide from maintenance workers or patrolling guards. But King Hadrian's silence proved beneficial. R-0 always heard anyone before they could hear R-0 or the king, so they avoided any confrontation.

When they reached a ladder leading into the city, R-0 paused. Every entrance or exit to the managrid, even those outside of the palace, was guarded. It was unavoidable.

"There are two guards above," R-0 said.

"Be prepared for anything." King Hadrian stepped onto the lowest rung and hoisted himself up. "But let me try to talk our way through this."

Cold air greeted them at the top, and King Hadrian climbed out confidently, his head raised high. He wasn't the silent man skulking through the tunnels—he was the bold king that R-0 was accustomed to seeing.

"S-sir," the guard stuttered. "We weren't expecting to see you here."

"There are matters in the city I need to attend to. I'd appreciate your discretion."

"O-of course."

King Hadrian kept walking, and neither guard moved to stop him or R-0. Once they were out of earshot, he whispered, "Robin won't want word of this to get out until he has the situation under control. The farther we are from the palace, the less likely it is that anyone will know what's going on."

"You are safer out here."

"Exactly." For the briefest moment, a smile crossed his face. But as his eyes met R-0, his smile fell into a deep frown. He shivered and looked away from R-0, continuing down the street.

"Where are you going?" Maybe out here, away from the dangers of the palace, King Hadrian could be more forthcoming.

Silence.

R-0 tried to subdue their frustrations. It would be more efficient for R-0 to know. Maybe they could be more helpful. But even if they couldn't . . . King Hadrian couldn't hide it forever.

And as King Hadrian took familiar turns, R-0 quickly recognized the route.

"This is the way to Jasper's," R-0 said. "Is that your destination?"

"Yes."

"Why?"

For a moment, R-0 thought this question was also going to be met with silence. But after a few more steps and a heavy sigh, King Hadrian responded. "I'm doing what has to be done."

"What is that?"

"Do you trust me?" King Hadrian asked.

"Yes."

"Then all you need to do is follow my orders." King Hadrian's voice broke as he spoke. He kept his gaze on the ground and quickened his pace. "Let's hurry."

R-0 had mindlessly followed the king's orders for years. It wasn't something they regretted, but now . . . they had questions. They were curious, and King Hadrian normally acknowledged that. There were no time constraints to explain his strange behavior. It would have been easy to discuss while walking. So why was King Hadrian not telling R-0? Did he not trust them anymore?

R-0's flame grew uneasy and sparked in their chest. It had only been hours, but it already felt larger than it had during Winter's checkup. And its uneasiness was impossible to ignore. Still, R-0 tried. They tapped their leg every time their foot impacted the ground. But their finger accelerated, a nervous reaction that sped far past the pace they walked.

When they arrived at the hattery, King Hadrian knocked. And he didn't stop—pounding on the door continuously, despite no sounds being heard from within. He tried the doorknob, but the door didn't budge.

"Open it."

"Winter said—"

"It's just a door, R-0." King Hadrian kicked the door with his foot. It shook but didn't give. "If you won't help me open it, I'll do it myself. I need to know you will follow my orders."

"Yes sir. Apologies." R-0 wasn't sure if the apology was to King Hadrian for their hesitance or the door for what they were about to do. Perhaps it was for both. R-0 punched through the door—and the metal sheet Winter had added—then reached through the hole to unlock the various locks and latches.

The basement was empty.

Not just of people and constructs, but of any sign that Jasper had ever been there. The posters and text had been removed from the wall, and the tables were bare. Only the dust in the corners of the ceiling and a single scratched gear in the center of the floor remained. In the storage closet, the scenario was similar. All of the lifeless constructs Jasper had stored there had vanished.

R-0 picked up the gear. "They left."

"Winter didn't waste any time," King Hadrian said. "Let's hurry."

"Yes sir." R-0 headed down the long passageway that led to Zealot. The whir of gears and clanking of metal was obvious long before they reached the entrance. The door at the end of the hallway was slightly ajar, and the mess of noise separated into identifiable voices.

"We don't need that."

"We still have time."

"But what if we don't?"

"But what if we need it?"

"When are we ever going to need *that*?" R-0 recognized that voice—Winter. And the one that followed it.

"Calm down," Jasper said. "What we don't have time for is panic. If you have the space, pack it. I can make trips later on my own."

King Hadrian paused outside the door, his eyes closed. His breathing was exaggerated and evenly paced, despite his racing heart.

"Do you need assistance knocking?" R-0 asked.

"No." King Hadrian pushed the door open.

Upon seeing the two of them, many of the constructs startled. Most scurried away from the door, but a few stepped forward—Clay, Winter, and Jasper among them.

"King Hadrian," Jasper said. "Or is it Sylas now?"

"King Hadrian."

"I wasn't expecting to see you so soon." His words were slow, and as he spoke, the constructs behind him continued gathering their things. Some even left—walking down a tunnel R-0 hadn't noticed the last time they were there.

"I don't think any of us were expecting this after yesterday's events."

"I'm glad to see R-0 doing well."

"Thank you," R-0 said.

King Hadrian tensed. "I had hoped you would come tend to them yourself."

"They were left in capable hands," Jasper said.

Neither adhered to their normal speech patterns. Both followed the same slow, measured cadence, allowing little emotion into their words. It reminded R-0 more of the metallic speech of the constructs than the normal oscillating and varying sounds the organics made.

"Where are you going?" King Hadrian asked.

"I'm sure you'll understand if I don't share that with you."

"I do." King Hadrian nodded. "As I'm sure you'll understand that I'd like to get my belongings that Winter stole before you leave."

Winter had only stolen one thing—the spell to decommission all the constructs.

"No." Winter stepped in now. "Absolutely no way. Why would you ever need that?"

"I don't have time for your questions." King Hadrian's voice rose. "I need it. *Now*."

Jasper smiled. "Unfortunately, it has already been destroyed."

"Then you'll have no problem with R-0 doing a little search to ensure you're being honest."

"Do you think I'd lie to you?"

"I didn't before I came here." King Hadrian signaled at his side—*Be ready*. "But now I'm doubting that."

"Get everyone out," Jasper whispered to Winter. "Now."

"What'd he say?" King Hadrian signaled again, this time for R-0 to draw weapons.

R-0 slowly slid their swords from their sheaths. "He asked Winter to get everyone out now."

"No one move," King Hadrian ordered.

All the constructs stopped what they were doing, and all eyes turned to Jasper.

"What's going on, Sylas?"

King Hadrian shook his head. "Just give me the spell, and we'll be gone."

"You know I can't do that."

"You know you don't have a choice." King Hadrian tilted their head at R-0.

Was he implying that R-0 would . . . force Jasper to give it over? They looked at the swords in their hands. King Hadrian had ordered they draw them, but R-0 didn't intend to use them. Not against Jasper.

But . . . King Hadrian was right. Winter had stolen it. It rightfully belonged to the king.

Still, why would King Hadrian need it? With what was happening at the palace, it was probably safer with Jasper. Unlike when they'd thought it was an enemy who'd had it, there was no reason to be worried. It was Jasper's spell. With the time and resources, he could recreate it.

"I'd rather do this peacefully," King Hadrian said. "Please."

"What part of your planned genocide is peaceful, exactly?" Jasper gestured at the surrounding constructs. "It's not enough that your successor may outlaw their existence? You want to make sure he gets the job done? You think that will get you back in his good graces?"

"No—"

"Then what? What use is the spell if you don't plan to cast it? Why not the two of us end it here? Do what I should have done as soon as Winter retrieved it, burn it together right now, and make sure no one can ever use it against the constructs?"

"That is a sensible plan," R-0 said.

King Hadrian balled his hands into fists, and his entire body trembled. "R-0, apprehend Jasper."

"What?" R-0 asked.

"Those are my orders."

R-0 hesitated. Jasper's plan made far more sense. "The spell should be destroyed. It's safer that way."

"R-0!" King Hadrian yelled, then took a deep breath and lowered his voice. "You said you trusted me. I need you to prove that now. Get the spell from Jasper."

R-0 took a shaky step forward. None of this made any sense. But there was a lot in this world that didn't make sense, and King Hadrian had always protected them from it. His actions showed that he cared for R-0. Even as their flame raged in their chest, they stepped forward.

R-0 trusted King Hadrian.

So why was it suddenly so hard to carry out his orders?

"Get out of here." Winter intercepted R-0 before they reached Jasper. They placed their hand on R-0's chest, pushing back. "Leave, and never come back."

"Winter, it's time for you to leave," Jasper said.

"To hell with that." Their neck rotated around, farther than organics or constructs were generally capable of, while their hand remained on R-0's chest. "T-5, you heard Jasper. Get everyone out of here."

"Of course." T-5 grabbed the bags at their feet and distributed them to the surrounding constructs.

"Everyone stop!" King Hadrian screamed again. This time, no one listened. "R-0, get the spell."

R-0 took a tentative step toward Jasper. Was this really the best option? There was a reason Jasper refused to meet King Hadrian's demands—couldn't the king see that? Even as R-0 stepped forward once more, they turned back to look at King Hadrian, searching for some explanation.

While they were looking away, something hit their leg where the joints connected, and their parts buckled. Before they could react, another impact landed on their shoulder, forcing them to the ground.

R-0 caught themselves on one knee. Winter stood above them, a blade in their hand and fire shining in their eyes.

"Gotta be quicker than that." They were true to their words, quickly striking out again. R-0's flame quieted. Their blades collided, and R-0 pushed Winter backward as they rose to their feet.

R-0 didn't want to fight—but Winter didn't share those reservations. R-0 lifted their blades to defend themself.

In a battle of swords, they were closely matched. What Winter lacked in strength and skill, they more than made up for in speed. Constructs scurried out of the way, still being shepherded out by T-5, as R-0 pushed Winter back. King Hadrian stood by the door, and R-0 kept an eye on him—just in case.

On their next strike, R-0 knocked Winter's blade from their hand. They tried to retaliate with a punch, but R-0 dropped one of their own blades and grabbed Winter by the wrist.

"Why are you doing this for him?" Winter's plates were burning hot to the touch, and the heat transferred to R-0. "Why are you doing this to us?"

"Fighting is unnecessary," R-0 said. "Step aside, and it will not continue."

"Step aside so he can kill us all?" Winter swung around with a fist. "No thanks."

The spell was rightfully King Hadrian's—it wasn't wrong for him to demand it. It didn't mean he was going to use it, and it certainly didn't mean he was going to decommission all the constructs. But why else would he need the spell? What was his plan?

With one hand restrained, Winter couldn't use their dexterity to their advantage, and R-0 caught their strike, restraining both their hands.

"Let them go," Jasper said.

"Don't," King Hadrian said.

R-0 wanted to listen to Jasper.

There were no good options. They couldn't disobey King Hadrian. And they didn't want to fight Winter—they didn't want to fight anyone. Why did there have to be conflict?

"Please," R-0 said. "Step aside."

R-0 loosened their grip slightly. If Winter would only step aside, everyone would be satisfied. But Winter pressed down onto their wrist, and a blade sprung out of their forearm into R-0's palm. The pressure knocked their hand away, freeing Winter.

Winter ducked to the ground, grabbing their blade and stabbing up at R-0. The blade caught R-0's chest plate, scraping against it with a squeal. R-0 reached out again, this time grabbing Winter's chest plate instead of their wrist. Their fingers pierced into the metal, making small handholds to maintain their grip.

Now that they were unable to dodge, R-0 lifted Winter from the ground, just to be safe.

"Stop." Jasper placed a hand on R-0's shoulder. From his apron, he pulled out a faded parchment.

"That's the spell?" King Hadrian asked.

Jasper nodded.

"Prove it."

"Don't." Winter struggled against R-0's grip. They dug their fingers between two of R-0's plates and tried to pry them apart.

"Winter, this isn't a fight you can win." Jasper slowly unfurled the paper and held it out where King Hadrian could see it. "Let the others go, and then we can talk."

"Deal," King Hadrian said.

"Are you crazy?" Winter asked.

Jasper shook his head. "Desperate."

King Hadrian slowly nodded and signaled at ease. R-0 gently lowered Winter to the ground. Winter grabbed for their blade, but Jasper stopped them.

"I won't watch you die for me," Jasper said. "Go with T-5."

Jasper thought R-0 was going to . . . kill Winter? They had fought Winter—unwillingly—but conflict didn't have to end in death.

Memories flashed through R-0's mind. How many times had they killed for King Hadrian before the incident? They hadn't even hesitated. They'd simply followed orders.

And since the Awakening, they'd also killed. They'd killed the organics working with Ryder in the street. And while they hadn't held the blade that ended Jeza, they couldn't deny their involvement.

"What are you going to do?" Winter asked.

"Everything I can." Jasper gently pushed Winter back. "Please."

Winter took a hesitant step back. "Will I see you again?"

"I'm not sure." Jasper's lips quivered, but he maintained a smile. He placed a hand on their chest. "No matter what happens, remember, you are the hearth in the cold."

"Never give in to the storm," Winter whispered in response, placing their hand over Jasper's.

"I'm proud of you, Winter."

Both of their hands trembled as they separated, and Winter turned to the rest of the constructs. "Let's move out."

Despite the king's racing heart, Jasper's pulse remained steady as the constructs filed out of the room. When Winter paused in the doorway and waved goodbye, Jasper's heart stuttered. He waved to them with a smile on his face, but as soon as they turned down the tunnel, his eyes glistened with tears that didn't fall.

"I hope you would at least do me the courtesy of telling me why." Jasper fiddled with the edge of the page.

"There's no saving the constructs," King Hadrian said. "But I can still save my throne. If your decommissioning spell works, the constructs' bodies will be unharmed. And with the flames Jeza already extracted, the technomancers can recreate your original spellwork, so it'll be like before. The constructs will be bound to me once more, and I can reclaim my throne. If Robin is left in charge, the constructs will be decommissioned and dismantled. Haiden will be weak. Not only will the constructs suffer, so will all our citizens."

R-0 tried to wrap their thoughts around it but couldn't. King Hadrian wouldn't decommission all the constructs, would he? He was their king, their ally, their friend.

R-0 trusted King Hadrian.

They replayed his words in their mind, again and again searching for what they must have misinterpreted. Organics were confusing. But no matter how many times R-0 thought it through, King Hadrian's words were direct. Straightforward.

"Is that the lie you tell yourself, Sylas?" Jasper asked. "That this is for your people, and not for your power?" Jasper shook his head. "Those spells can't recreate the Awakening. Whatever happened . . . it was a miracle. I could never recreate it. My spell can bring back the constructs' bodies, but it won't bring back their souls."

R-0 looked to their king, their flame feeling as desperate as Jasper's words. This was King Hadrian's chance to explain how his plan could save not only his crown, but the constructs as well.

But King Hadrian averted his eyes from R-0's expectant gaze. "You asked, and I answered."

R-0 froze. There was no misunderstanding.

King Hadrian was going to decommission the constructs.

"Please, reconsider," Jasper said. "Robin taking the crown will make things difficult, but it doesn't guarantee genocide. There are people who will fight to protect their constructs. Entire units in Faylviln and everyone you saw here today would be safe from Robin and his guard. The constructs *can* be saved."

"R-0, take the spell from Jasper."

King Hadrian had saved R-0 from the council's wrath, taught them . . . cared for them.

"Sir—" R-0 began.

"We can discuss this later. Right now, I need your help."

This was R-0's purpose. Their directive. Protect the king.

"King Hadrian cannot be swayed, but perhaps you can." Jasper addressed R-0. "Please, reconsider. You brought Clay to us here because you wanted them to be safe. You didn't want them to be unjustly decommissioned. What do you think will happen to them and countless others if you take this?"

Everything Jasper said was true. R-0 wanted to protect the constructs. They'd done everything they could to keep them safe, but . . . they'd always done it *with* King Hadrian. Even when they'd saved Clay, they might have been working alone, but they hadn't been going against the king's orders.

They'd never disobeyed King Hadrian.

"Now, R-0," King Hadrian said.

They didn't want to, but . . . what else could they do? R-0 reached a hand toward Jasper. "The spell, please."

Rather than hand over the parchment, Jasper picked up Winter's blade from the ground. R-0 readied for him to strike, but he didn't move toward R-0.

"I'm going to teach you a lesson today," Jasper said. "Whether you learn it from my life or from my death is your choice." Jasper placed the sword handle in R-0's hand. "If you want the spell, you'll have to kill me."

"Jasper—"

"This no longer concerns you, *king*," Jasper said the word king with the same disgust many used when speaking of the constructs. "I sacrificed my morals for that crown once already. I'll die before I make that mistake a second time."

"Death is permanent," R-0 said. They weren't just thinking about Jasper and his potential death, but the end of all the constructs if the spell was used.

Jasper nodded.

"You're not afraid?"

"I'm terrified." Even as he said it, he didn't look the tiniest bit scared. A sad smile settled on his face, and his movements were calm and controlled. "But not of death. I'm terrified of living in a world where my worst fears come true, and I lay awake every night knowing that I could have stopped it. I'm terrified of the person I would see in the mirror if I prioritize my life over the lives of thousands. Death is not nearly as terrifying as living." Jasper's voice cracked, and the tears he'd blinked away returned, falling down his cheeks. "I'd rather die as the man I want to be than live in the shadow of my potential."

King Hadrian placed a hand on R-0's shoulder, his grip tightening until his entire hand shook. "Then you'll die the same as you've lived—a fool. You had your chance."

King Hadrian flashed a signal at his side. R-0's orders were clear.

It was a simple task. Jasper had made it even simpler by placing a blade in their hand. All that was required of them was to push their hand forward. Organics were fragile. The slightest pressure would break his skin.

But R-0's hand shook worse than King Hadrian's. The calm that normally fell over them when they held a weapon was absent, and their flame raged almost as loud as their thoughts.

"This is the only option," King Hadrian said. "The only way to keep me safe."

Protect the king. For a decade, that had been their only thought, their only purpose. What were they supposed to do when King Hadrian's orders conflicted with what they believed? What they thought? Jasper didn't deserve to die. Neither did the constructs.

But what if they were wrong?

Only one thing had remained consistent through R-0's existence, before and after the Awakening. Protect the king. It was the only thing they knew for certain.

R-0 pushed the blade into Jasper's chest.

CHAPTER 45

Although R-0's body followed King Hadrian back to the palace, their mind remained deep underground, lost in the memory of Jasper slowly bleeding out on their blade. They didn't want to remember, but every detail was seared into their mind. His weight sagging on the sword as more and more of his life drained out of him. His hoarse whispers, indecipherable pleas fading into quiet moans, and then, finally . . . silence.

Their flame that before had refused to answer no matter how many questions they asked now raged in a wordless blaze that left their feet fidgeting and their mind racing. R-0 tapped at their side, the soft metallic ring mixing with King Hadrian's heavy breathing in a dissonant whisper. They tapped faster and faster until the motions matched the speed of their racing thoughts.

What was R-0 supposed to do? How should they respond when King Hadrian's orders went against what they believed was right? They had done what King Hadrian had asked, but . . .

The tapping at their side brought them back to the present, and they slowed their movements into a rhythmic pulse, limiting themself to one question per tap.

Why did they want to disobey King Hadrian? *Tap.*

Was this what the organics feared from the constructs' Awakening? *Tap.*

Why couldn't they stop seeing Jasper's face? Hearing his last breath? Feeling his heartbeat slow to a stop?

Their fingers curled into a fist.

They followed King Hadrian's order. It was simple. Despite the thoughts and feelings coursing through them, they had executed their function perfectly. And for now, their king was safe.

So why did it feel so wrong?

"I'm only doing what I must. You understand that, don't you? I have to do this." King Hadrian shook his head. "We have to do this."

I don't understand.

R-0 couldn't find the words. Perhaps this was why. Even when he was unsure, King Hadrian didn't shy away from the ownership of his actions.

I. We. Whether he was taking accountability of the constructs, addressing the council, or just talking to R-0 as they walked down the palace halls, his actions were his own.

But R-0's weren't.

There had been moments since the Awakening where they thought they had free will—they thought they were making their own choices. Searching for the intruder, investigating the missing constructs, saving Clay from the dungeon. But even on their own, R-0 had been working under King Hadrian's instructions. R-0 had always worked toward his goals—his directive.

Until now, they had thought they understood. They had thought protecting the king was the right thing to do. It was their directive. Their purpose. Everything they had ever known.

"No," R-0 said.

"What?"

"It doesn't make sense."

"Do you remember asking me about good and evil?" King Hadrian asked. "Why someone would choose evil when they could choose good?"

"Yes," R-0 said.

"You try and you try and you try to be good. You try to be better, but then . . . you end up worse than when you started, and you look around and there's no good left. So you do the best you can."

This situation was . . . far from excellent. R-0 couldn't find anything desirable about it. How could it be the best when there was nothing good about it?

R-0 followed King Hadrian in a daze. When they reached the palace, their body seemed to move on its own, while R-0's thoughts, their feelings, their *soul*—as Jasper had called it—hid unmoving in the shadow of their flame. They checked each passageway to ensure it was safe before letting King Hadrian lead them to the dungeon.

King Hadrian stopped at the tral's cell and ordered R-0 to release him, so R-0 bent the bars out of shape until he could escape. They should have asked questions. They should have been curious about King Hadrian and the tral's whispered schemes. They should have wondered countless things.

But the only thing they could feel was the last thread of Jasper's pulse dying out beneath their plates, his last attempts at words an indecipherable murmur echoing through R-0's mind.

What had they done? And what were they doing now?

Jasper would be only one of many deaths on R-0's hands if King Hadrian completed the spell.

As they left the dungeon with the tral, none of the guards hesitated to follow King Hadrian's orders. Perhaps, like the guards in the city, they hadn't been informed of Robin's declaration. Or perhaps one look at the blood covering R-0's plates left them reconsidering resistance.

R-0 was vaguely aware of King Hadrian and the tral talking. What they would need and where they would go. Jasper's lab hadn't been cleared yet. Everything the tral needed to perform the spell was there. R-0 was a ghost of themself. Like the constructs before the Awakening, their body was an empty shell following the organics.

At the bottom of the tunnel, Jasper's lab was in shambles. None of the workstations were still standing, and shattered shards of crystal coated the floor. Every step crunched as stones shifted underfoot.

"This is the spell I need you to do." King Hadrian handed the parchment to the tral. His hands trembled and his voice cracked.

The tral studied it for a moment, shaking his head as his finger trailed across the magical runes and glyphs. "This is . . . complicated. Insanely complicated."

"Can you do it?"

"Yes. But it'll need—"

"A royal construct and royal blood."

"And you know—"

"I know what I am asking." King Hadrian glanced at R-0. The moment their eyes met, tears spilled down his cheeks, and he averted his gaze.

The tral righted a table and carefully laid the parchment across it. Then he rearranged the room, using crystalline shards to mimic the symbols on the page.

R-0 didn't understand the magic or the spell, but they didn't have to. They knew what it would do.

This was their death.

R-0 had never been able to think of death with anything other than fear and confusion. What was waiting for them? What did it mean? As King Hadrian had asked his mother—what was next?

To fulfill their directive, to protect King Hadrian, they had given everything, time and time again. R-0 hadn't just killed for the king, they had lived for him. And now, they would die for him.

R-0 expected their flame to rebel, like the flicker of a candle against the ocean winds. But it didn't. There were so many things R-0 didn't understand that they just had to accept, and this was one of them. If it meant King Hadrian would be safe, R-0 could accept their death. They didn't want to, and it terrified them, but if that's what was required of them, they would do it.

But what about the other constructs?

"Ready." The tral called out. "I need both of you here."

Where the manacore used to be and the rails from the managrid still fed into the room, the crystals had already been cleared away. A thick ring of shards surrounded it, leaving a small circle that both R-0 and King Hadrian could stand in.

"We'll need access to the construct's flame." The tral used a screwdriver to open R-0's chest plate.

"And you'll be able to reanimate them afterward, right?"

"I can recreate Jasper's original spell, but that's all."

"You'll be okay, R-0." King Hadrian's voice shook as he turned to them. He echoed the words, his voice nothing but a hoarse whisper. "We'll be okay." Despite his reassuring words, tears streamed freely down his face. He rested his hand on their shoulder. "I'll have my crown, and we'll still be together. It'll be just like before."

R-0 flickered through their memories of before—the memories of a stranger. A stranger who faithfully stood by King Hadrian's side. Who killed for him, without hesitation. Who protected him, without fail. Who obeyed him, without question. Without fear. Without thought.

Without love.

It wasn't R-0.

"Your blood," the tral said.

King Hadrian pulled a dagger from his waist and dragged it across his palm. As a pool of blood formed, he cupped his hand to keep it from dripping off. With his other hand, he reached into R-0's chest, his palm lingering next to R-0's flame even as his skin grew red.

Who was R-0, if not the stranger in their memories? It was the question they had been asked, first by King Hadrian, then by Jasper, and now, by themself.

Who were they?

Who would they choose to be?

"I never imagined having to say goodbye to you."

"Then don't say goodbye." R-0 gently raised a hand to King Hadrian's face, wiping away the tears that wet his cheeks. "Don't do this."

R-0 wasn't a killer, though the blood of many was on their hands. Even as the thought crossed their mind, they realized it was a lie. R-0 *was* a killer. They'd killed Jasper. The reality crashed down on R-0 more violently than the ocean waves during a storm. All the constructs that had relied on Jasper,

RISE OF THE FORGEHEARTS

all the good he'd brought into the world, the people he had helped . . . all of that potential, gone because of what R-0 had done.

King Hadrian had given the order, but R-0's hand had held the dagger. R-0's plates were stained with blood. R-0's flame cracked and crumbled.

It had been R-0's choice to follow those orders.

But it wasn't who they wanted to be. They wanted to be a protector.

They had failed Beans. They had failed Jasper. And if King Hadrian's spell succeeded . . . they would fail all the constructs. Winter, M-118, Clay, everyone Jasper had tried to save in Zealot. Dara and the others wrongfully imprisoned in the dungeon. JJ and the constructs living peacefully with their families all across Haiden.

King Hadrian raised his bleeding hand toward R-0's flame.

"Please." R-0 grabbed his wrist. "Please reconsider."

This was what they should have done when King Hadrian had ordered them to kill Jasper. They should have fought, they should have argued. They never should have obeyed.

"There's no other choice," King Hadrian said. "No other choice," he whispered.

He was wrong.

As much as R-0 didn't want to believe it, their flame strengthened at the realization.

King Hadrian did have a choice. R-0 had a choice. Everyone, every day, had the ability to control their own actions and shape the world around them. King Hadrian was choosing his crown, his power, and his life over the lives of all the constructs. He had done it when he left Clay in the dungeon and when he'd prioritized meeting with the council over finding who was kidnapping and killing the constructs. He'd done it again when he'd confronted Jasper for the spell.

King Hadrian was choosing wrong.

But R-0 didn't have to.

"The constructs have spent years without a choice. Today, you have a choice." R-0 paused. Their gears slowed, and their flame sputtered. Slowly, they shifted their plates open and forced out the words that had evaded them for so long. "*I* have a choice."

King Hadrian struggled against R-0's grip, but they didn't budge. R-0 wouldn't let him do this.

"I don't want to do this without you." King Hadrian wiped his eyes on his sleeve, and his expression shifted. He closed his eyes, taking a deep breath. When he reopened them, the warm familiarity was gone, replaced by the confident mask he wore when addressing the council. "But I can. You aren't the only royal construct."

King Hadrian was right. If R-0 wouldn't do it, one of the others could, or they could be forced into it. Jeza had already proven that constructs' flames could be extracted. It wouldn't be hard for King Hadrian to replace R-0.

As long as King Hadrian was alive, he could complete the ritual. The constructs would be at risk of being decommissioned. Even destroying the spell wouldn't help—King Hadrian and the tral had seen enough to recreate it without Jasper's notes.

"Please, Sylas." R-0 wasn't above begging. "It doesn't have to be this way. You don't have to fear Robin or the council. You can leave." Smoke poured out of R-0's mouth, but it didn't stop their desperate pleas. "I will protect you."

"You don't understand." His hands trailed the golden filigree at the base of his head. "I have to do this. It's the only way to keep my crown. My kingdom. My legacy."

If King Hadrian considered R-0's request, it didn't show. His response was immediate. Just like when Jasper had tried to sway him, the king didn't budge.

"What about me?" R-0 asked.

King Hadrian's tears fell down once more. His breathing hitched, and he turned away. He refused to meet R-0's gaze and turned to the tral. "Do the spell."

R-0's flame sputtered. Their gears shook. When it came down to R-0 or the crown, the king would choose his crown. He would always choose his crown. It was why R-0 had been created—it shouldn't have surprised them. But they had become more than what they were made to be. King Hadrian had become more to them than just a directive, and they thought they had meant more to him too. More than a simple guard. More than a construct bound to serve him.

For a moment, they wished the Awakening had never happened. For every good thing their newfound sentience had brought them, for every moment of joy and curiosity and hope, it had also brought them here. Had it just been their own life, R-0 would have done everything in their power to protect King Hadrian, even if he wouldn't do the same for them. But it wasn't just their life in the balance.

"Apologies." R-0 shook their head. That wasn't right. "No. I am sorry."

Still, the words didn't match the emotions churning inside them.

No words ever could.

R-0 didn't reach for the king's dagger. They placed their hand on King Hadrian's chest, feeling his beating heart and looking into his eyes.

"I am sorry." They pushed against his skin, and he stumbled backward, out of the ring of crystals, away from the managrid's power source.

As long as King Hadrian's bloodline persisted—as long as the spell was possible—the constructs would be in danger. King Hadrian could get another royal construct, but no one could get more royal blood.

"R-0, stop!" King Hadrian tried to push them away, but R-0 held tight. He yelled at the tral. "Do something! Stop them."

The tral reached toward R-0's open flame, but R-0 grabbed him by the back of his neck and tossed him to the floor. His spine snapped as his body bounced in the broken glass, dotting the ground with blood.

"Please, R-0." King Hadrian reached for R-0's hand, but instead of trying to push it away, he clung to it. "Don't do this. You're supposed to protect me."

Every inch of R-0's body was on fire, but they couldn't feel the warmth. They could feel their gears accelerating so fast one of them snapped, even though their body remained stationary. They saw King Hadrian's lips moving and knew the pleas that were spilling from them, but all they could hear was his heartbeat.

R-0 made their choice.

They held King Hadrian in place and pushed their hand inside his chest. Bones cracked and his skin split apart, and R-0 grabbed his heart. Instantly, his eyes glazed over. Blood poured from the wound and down R-0's plates, saturating the ground at their feet.

For a few moments, the heart in their hand beat, frantically pumping blood and trying to survive. But then, even it stilled.

R-0 collapsed to the ground, their body unwilling, unable to move. King Hadrian, their king, their best friend, and for most of their existence, the man who had been their entire world was gone. Pain wracked their chest, worse than anything they had ever experienced. Even when their body was crumpled beyond recognition, they'd felt some ounce of peace.

But now, there was only pain and emptiness.

R-0 pulled King Hadrian's body close to them, cradling him in their arms. They gently placed his heart back into his chest cavity. The crown fell from his head, clattering to the ground. Light reflected off its golden band and sparkled across the crystals like a rainbow after a storm.

"Goodbye, Sylas."

CHAPTER 46

R-0 stayed on the floor, holding King Hadrian close to them. There was nowhere for them to go. Nothing for them to do. It was over.

Time passed.

R-0 supposed time was the same as it always was. But it didn't feel that way. Every tick of their gears simultaneously felt like a lifetime passing around them while they were still living in King Hadrian's last breath. Thoughts danced at the edge of their consciousness. What had they done? Was this the right choice? What happened next?

But they couldn't think it through. They let the thoughts pass by, holding on to the only thing they knew.

"R-0?" Quiet's voice broke the endless cycle.

Fear danced in her eyes. It was the same fear that R-0 had seen often in the organics in the days following the Awakening, but they'd never seen it on Quiet's face. She kept her distance, and both Eren and Jorgunn stood protectively next to her, blades drawn and ready.

R-0 was everything the organics had feared the constructs would become after the Awakening.

"I—" Smoke coated their throat, spewing out of their mouth. "I'm sorry."

Their gears scraped against each other in a discordant screech, and they tightened their grip on the king's body as much as they dared without breaking him, searching for some modicum of comfort. If he were here, he'd know what to say to Quiet. He could have found the words that R-0 couldn't.

But if he were still here, R-0 wouldn't be. None of the constructs would.

Quiet's face softened. She stepped forward, even as Eren tried to hold her back, and crouched next to R-0. The blue lights from the managrid illuminated her, but R-0 couldn't meet her gaze. They looked at the ground where blood pooled on the floor, staining her shoes.

Blood R-0 had spilled.

King Hadrian's blood.

"R-0," Quiet repeated. She tilted their head up, so that their eyes met. "Are you okay?"

"No." Not a single thing was okay, least of all R-0.

"What happened?"

"He's dead," R-0 said. "I killed him."

"R-0, report." Eren's voice wasn't as gentle as Quiet's. It was a demand.

Even though R-0 could never again be the loyal, order-bound construct they once were, the familiar instructions allowed their words to come a little more easily as they explained King Hadrian's intention to activate the decommissioning spell.

R-0 waited for Eren to arrest them—it would be well-deserved after assassinating the king. Then Robin would order R-0's decommissioning. They'd committed a crime, and that was the expected punishment. R-0 had done what they had to do. At least this way, R-0 could visit the Watcher's library and face the mysteries of death knowing that they'd done what they could to save their people.

But Eren didn't move forward. Instead, she bit her lip until it bled, then turned her back to R-0. Jorgunn reached out to put his hand on her shoulder, but she pushed him away. R-0 couldn't see her expression, but her chest shook, and her breathing hitched. Quiet leaned forward and wrapped her arms around R-0 in a tight hug.

"You have to leave." Tears streamed down her face as she pulled away.

"What?" R-0 asked.

She tore off her sleeve and used it to cover the gaping hole in the king's chest, then gently closed his eyes. "No one can know what happened here."

"People will make assumptions." Eren turned back around, the corners of her eyes glistening. She put her hand on Quiet's shoulder.

"People will believe what they're told," Quiet said. "They will believe a story of a royal construct, who stayed with their king until the end and did everything they could to save him."

"But I—"

Quiet shook her head. She pulled out her dagger and stabbed it into King Hadrian's corpse. "And of the assassin who killed them both."

"That is a lie," R-0 said.

"With two witnesses and a confession, who will refute it?" Quiet looked over her shoulder at Eren and Jorgunn.

"Who knew Riley would ever do something like this." Jorgunn reluctantly shook his head. "If only we'd gotten here faster, we could have saved King Hadrian."

"But you didn't kill the king," R-0 said. "I—"

Quiet dipped her hand in the blood pooling on the floor until the bloodstains on her hand matched R-0's plates. "If you were to face trial for assassinating the king, it wouldn't just be you who was found guilty. It would be all the constructs."

Fear still governed the organics when it came to the constructs, and R-0 had proven just how dangerous they could be. Quiet was right. R-0's actions had been necessary to save the constructs, but even inexperienced with politics, R-0 could imagine the backlash that the constructs would face if the organics knew what R-0 had done.

They wouldn't care about why R-0 had done it or the constructs they'd saved. They wouldn't care about the pain that wracked R-0's flame, bringing them an understanding of what organics meant when they referred to a broken heart. They wouldn't care that when the king lost his life, R-0 lost everything they'd ever known. Everything they'd ever loved. All they'd care about is that constructs were capable of the same atrocities as organics were—and ignore how that proved they were also capable of the same greatness.

"You'll be imprisoned," R-0 said.

"I will."

"She won't be the only one." Eren stepped forward. "You were working with Robin to kill him, right?"

Another lie. But Quiet just nodded. "It could work."

"But it's not true," R-0 said.

"When it comes to the games the council plays, the truth is irrelevant," Quiet said. "The churches support me, and King Hadrian was beloved by the people of Haiden. If I testify that Robin was involved in his death, he won't be able to take the crown."

A new emotion wriggled its way through the dark chill in R-0's chest. With Quiet and Eren's help . . . the constructs could still have a future. Knowledge of the decommissioning spell had died with the king and the tral. They'd be safe—at least temporarily—from Robin. Was this what hope felt like? If R-0 kept their gaze locked on Quiet, they could almost forget about the skin against their plates growing colder with each passing second.

Almost.

"How did you know to come here?" R-0 asked.

"Winter found me."

"Jasper," R-0 said, "I—"

"I know." She offered her hand out to R-0—an impractical gesture. It was unlikely she could support R-0's weight. "And I can't imagine what you're feeling right now, but you have to get moving. You'll have time to feel all of this later."

She wanted to help them, and R-0 wanted to let her. But why? Why after what R-0 had done would anyone help them?

R-0 couldn't move. They couldn't leave King Hadrian behind. After everything . . . how were they supposed to just walk away? Where could they go? What could they do? They'd spent time wondering what happened after their own death, but they'd never considered a life after King Hadrian's demise.

"What happens next?" R-0 asked.

"This is the beginning of your own path, your own journey." Quiet slipped Jasper's ring from King Hadrian's hand and placed it in R-0's. "This will help you. If you leave through the managrid tunnels, you should be able to get away from the palace before the alarm is raised. You're free now."

"Free." The word felt strange, but there was something comforting about it.

R-0 gently laid King Hadrian's body on the ground in front of them. There was nothing left of the man they'd cared for, just a hollow corpse. Like the flowers in the garden, he couldn't be made whole again. He would never come back. But his death left space for the constructs to grow into something new, something more.

There were no words to change what they had done, and even if there were, R-0 wouldn't have said them.

R-0 had made a choice.

Now, they had to live with it.

They stepped back from King Hadrian's body and turned to Eren. "There's something that must be done before I leave."

CHAPTER 47

It was strange to have a place of their own.

A desk. A drawer. A bed.

The bed was impractical. It wasn't soft like King Hadrian's had been, and R-0 didn't need to sleep. But . . . it was theirs.

In the two weeks since R-0 reached Zealot, R-0 spent hours and hours and hours lying in their own bed, in their own room, reflecting on what they had done and what they would choose to do now. For days, R-0 had done nothing but sit and stare, reliving both Jasper and King Hadrian's final moments. Winter had screamed at them. They struck at R-0 with their blade, and R-0 couldn't manage to defend themself. They couldn't remember Winter's words, only that after a while they'd given up, throwing their weapon at the wall and leaving R-0 alone.

Alone. Where R-0 had returned to the prison of their thoughts. Their flame never rested. They couldn't move. They couldn't think. Even sitting doing nothing, their world continued to crumble around them.

After a week, Winter finally dragged them to one of the technomancy sections and scrubbed away the dried blood that covered their plates. They shared stories about Jasper—moments they'd laughed together, things he'd taught them about life, and advice he had given. It wasn't forgiveness, but the beginnings of an uneasy peace.

When R-0 returned to their room, they felt a little more whole. They hadn't required maintenance, but talking to Winter, they felt less like an empty shell. They'd needed the reminder that even though King Hadrian was dead, they were alive, and they could still make something of their life.

With Winter's help, they'd created a new living space for the rogue constructs—including the wrongfully imprisoned constructs from the dungeons who had followed R-0 to Zealot. But the work was never done. Yesterday they had expanded because T-5 wanted to paint a mural. The day before that, Winter had wanted a sparring area to train the rest of the constructs in combat. R-0 wasn't sure why the request had been so urgent when Winter still hadn't set up any lessons. Instead, the two of them had used it to spar—again and again. Every time Winter insisted they wouldn't lose to R-0 again, but they always did.

"Hey, you've got a message." Winter stood in the hallway, just over the line in the dirt that marked Sector 74. R-0 had insisted on their room being last, after making sure every construct from the palace dungeon was given a place of their own. They'd been in their cells for far too long and deserved better.

That was what R-0 had chosen—to be a protector. Releasing the wrongfully imprisoned constructs from the dungeon was just the beginning.

"Zoning out again?" Winter asked.

"Apologies."

"Don't apologize, just get your gears spinning. No more lying around." Winter knocked on the wall. "We have work to do."

"What task requires attention?" R-0 asked.

"An escape route. Saw some guards nosing around the entrance. I don't think they noticed anything, but just in case . . ."

"Understood." They couldn't be too careful. Even if the beds and furniture made this place look like any other home in Graywal, it wasn't.

R-0 slowly got out of bed, then carefully pulled the sheets back. They had seen some of the staff at the palace make the beds before, and Clay had been more than willing to teach them the proper way. They set the pillow on top, then readjusted it until it sat perfectly centered.

"Here." Winter pressed a sheet of paper into R-0's hand. The letter was sealed in wax with the council's emblem.

It was signed from the interim queen, Eren Ainfen, and addressed to Rob—a man who didn't exist. Although Winter would always say they imagined Rob as a rich, young dwarf with a cape made of gold and so many gemstones that he would throw them on the ground behind him as he walked. It was a nonsensical proposal. If that was who Eren was writing, there would be sufficient security to make sure it was delivered.

Instead, every message Eren sent to Rob ended up in R-0's hands. Most had confirmed actions R-0 and Winter had expected the council to take—like sentencing Robin to life in the dungeon and continuing the reintegration efforts—but some, like this one, held a surprise.

"I should also let you know—there's been an incident in the palace dungeon. One of the prisoners, Riley Eyla has escaped. We are spending the appropriate resources to make sure she is found and brought to justice."

Quiet was free.

She had assured them that she would be safe, but it hadn't stopped R-0 from lamenting her prison sentence. Especially when they heard she'd been sentenced to death. It was R-0's crime. They should have faced the punishment, not her.

"Good news?" Winter asked.

"Quiet has escaped." R-0 neatly and repeatedly folded the letter in half until the wax was flaking off and it was as small as possible, then dropped it in their drawer. They could read it again when they returned to their room later.

Winter led R-0 through Zealot. In just two weeks, it had changed dramatically. The wrongfully accused constructs stuck in the dungeon had all been happy to follow R-0 here in hope of a better life—in hope of any chance at life. Even though they had the space to spread out now, few constructs were alone. Some combined their sectors, which created entirely illogical numbering as they arbitrarily chose which sector number to keep, while others left their areas and spent their time in sectors designated for recreation.

"Did you ever imagine you'd see a group of constructs gathered like this?" Winter asked.

Constructs had gathered before—in the storage rooms, in the mines. Anywhere the organics had summoned them, they'd dutifully obeyed. But this was different. Everyone was here by their own choice, their own decision. No one was ordered to congregate.

Some were talking among themselves—not just talking, but laughing, smiling, trading stories. Dara had their head down, their fingers flying across a metal contraption that sparked and buzzed at every touch. Clay and M-118 were helping a newly recruited construct get set up in their new room, even clearing the lines between the two sectors to share some of Clay's space.

This would have been impossible for the constructs before the Awakening.

When R-0 had seen the falling stars, they had known something was different. It had just taken a little longer for them to realize how drastically their life had been altered. Everything had changed—a fact that deserved to be recognized. It was a beautiful, magical unknown that would shape Haiden for decades to come, and R-0 and everyone surrounding them would be at the forefront of it.

But not as constructs. They were something entirely different, something no one could have ever imagined.

"Constructs are what we were," R-0 said. "Creations in their image, their constructions. The technomancers forged our bodies, but it's up to us to forge our hearts. We are more than what they made us to be."

"That's what we should be called." Winter knocked on their chest plate a few times. "Forgehearts."

"Forgehearts," R-0 whispered the word to themself, and the flame within their chest burned just a little brighter, a little warmer. They forged their future as they forged their hearts. "It's perfect."

In such little time, they had come so far, but they had so much farther to go. With Robin, Jeza, King Hadrian, and Quiet all being replaced, the council was hesitant to do anything to upset the people further—and King Hadrian's reintegration plan was beloved by the people it helped. But that didn't mean they were allies yet. Jeza had proven how dangerous and powerful their flames could be, and just because the council wasn't their immediate enemy, it didn't make them allies.

But R-0 couldn't bring themself to worry about the future. Not in a room filled with celebrations. No matter where they were going, it was better than where they had come from, and it would be their future to make. Hope filled the air.

This was only the beginning for the Forgehearts.

Thank you so much for reading!

I hope you loved reading it as much as I loved writing it, and I'm so excited to share the rest of the series with you. To stay up to date on new releases, get your FREE copy of *Shattered Sacrifice,* and more sign up for my newsletter using the QR code below or visit my website at emilyhuffmanbooks.com!

Or view all my books below —

Check out more books in the Krajina universe!

Blaine thought being a hero meant saving lives–not being hunted by a monster.
The Shard will kill anything in its path, and after confronting its summoner, Blaine and his friends become its prey. Their only hope to save the world from the Shard's wrath is to unravel the secrets of its summoning and their connection to the creature.
But the secrets of the Shard are entangled in the gods, and to become the hero he wants to be, Blaine will have to face worse than monsters.

Shattered Souls is the action-packed introduction to an epic fantasy trilogy featuring tropes such as the chosen ones, found family, hidden truths, and unique magical creatures. The series is complete with three novels in the trilogy and two companion novellas.

Rocco has his future figured out. One magical tournament is all that stands between him and admission to the Academy--the most prestigious school for magic in the world and the place where he will finally belong. But when a mysterious stranger shows up with an offer from the God of Magic himself, Rocco is left with a choice: swear fealty to the god or follow his own path. Fueled by the desire to realize his dreams, Rocco plunges forward.

But the God of Magic cannot be ignored, and Rocco soon learns there is more to lose than just the tournament...

Glisenia Tideborn knew two things:

One - She wasn't dead anymore.

Two - She wouldn't let anyone hurt her ever again.

After being sacrificed to the Kraken by her family, Glisenia Tideborn never expected to have a future. Given an unexpected second chance, she wants to run far away from the people who sentenced her to death. But the Kraken still demands its sacrifice, and a dark whisper in her mind has different plans for her.

Will Glisenia do what the voice asks of her, or is she destined to die again?

Made in United States
Orlando, FL
24 May 2024